GRANDPA GETS A TATTOO

AND OTHER STORIES

Grandpa Gets a Tattoo
and Other Stories

by Michael Massee

Bachsez Press
Waterford Works, NJ

This is a work of fiction. Names, characters, businesses, places, events, locales, and incidents are either the products of the author's imagination or used in a fictitious manner. Any resemblance to actual persons, living or dead, or actual events is purely coincidental.

ISBN (paperback): 979-8-9938278-0-3

ISBN (e-book): 979-8-9938278-1-0

Cover art by Michael Massee

Bachsez Press
Waterford Works, NJ

masseeman05@gmail.com • masseeart.com

Contents

To "Rosie," my soul mate

About the Author

Born in Corvallis, Oregon, Michael Massee grew up on the West Coast. After majoring in Theatre Arts at Portland State University, he moved to New York City, where he worked as a scenic painter, a stage manager and a "sometime" actor, as well as a set and costume designer. He worked off-Broadway and on Broadway, and eventually went back to school to get his MFA in theatre at Rutgers' Mason Gross School of the Arts.

From 1989 to 2003, he headed the Scenic Design Program at Fordham University at Lincoln Center. Upon retiring, he began devoting himself to developing his skill as a painter. Among the venues where his work has been exhibited are the Montclair (N.J.) Museum of Art, Gallery 125 in Trenton, the Cosmopolitan Club in Philadelphia, and the Cherry Hill (N.J.) Library Gallery.

He now lives in the pines of Waterford Works, New Jersey, with his wife Carol Rosenfeld, an actress/teacher extraordinaire, with whom he proudly shares the responsibility for a wonderful son and three outstanding grandchildren. He is also sharing his studio with a family of foxes who have burrowed under the building. "So far we're all getting along just fine."

Author's Note

The following stories are the result of the lockdown caused by the pandemic of 2020. With so much time on my hands and the inability of the various art suppliers to furnish me with the framed canvases I favor, I turned to writing to avoid going bonkers. I'm a great fan of the short story, so what you will be reading are my attempts to paint pictures with words instead of pigments.

*

I wish to thank David Shih for his amazing work on my website, where these stories first appeared; and Nancy Trotic for her encouragement and support and for her excellent editing skills.

Thoughtful

Looking back, I realize this all started when I was a teenager. In the small town in New Jersey where I grew up, there was one barbershop, with one chair and one barber, Mr. DeRosa. Now this was way back before hippies and long hair arrived and before they almost put him out of business. Short hair on men was the required look, and I was sent to the barbershop for a trim at least every two weeks. "Not too short, Mr. DeRosa," I would reply to his "How do you want it cut?" "and please leave the sideburns." Sideburns were very important to me, a lonely, skinny kid wanting to fit in, and the group I wanted to fit in with were the Greasers. These were the tough guys in school who wore low-slung Levi's and white tee shirts with their Lucky Strike cigarette packs tucked in the fold of their short sleeves. And their hair—slicked back with Brylcreem into a DA (duck's ass) and often greased up into a pompadour in front—was their signature. But for me it was the sideburns, those masculine emblems of macho maturity, for which I longed.

While I envied the dagger-shaped line of hair that travelled down the side of the ear and ended at the tip of the lobe, I realized that I could never get my sideburns to reach that far. This was because my facial hair was still pretty wimpy and because my parents would have grounded me if I started looking like one of "those hoodlums!" So, all I wanted from Mr. DeRosa was to leave me about an inch of sideburn. That would have to do. At least I wouldn't look like a ten-year-old kid.

You'd think that not shaving off that skimpy inch would be the easiest thing in the world for Mr. DeRosa to do, but this was not so. Every frigging time I'd ask, he'd nod and then, zip, there went the sideburn. It was as though we were in a power struggle, and since he held the only weapon, I was doomed to lose every time. The final result always looked like a modified bowl cut, no sideburns at all.

It got to the point where I wanted to just let my hair grow. So what if I looked like a yeti. Big deal! But of course the family prevailed, and my visits to the barbershop continued. With each trip to the "Demon Barber of Main Street," my frustration, resentment and anger grew larger. Conversely, Mr. DeRosa seemed to be growing smaller. He was a large man, not tall but solidly built, and now he seemed to be shrinking. His clothes began to hang on his body. When he would lean in to buzz the hairs on my neck, I could feel how bony he had become.

I'll never forget the last time I walked over to the barbershop and discovered that it was closed. There was a sign on the door that read, "We are sorry to announce the passing of Anthony DeRosa, beloved son, brother, husband and father. The viewing is at Marinella's funeral home. His service will be this Friday at St. Joseph's. The shop will be closed until further notice."

It was a strange mixture of relief and remorse that washed over me. That I would not be getting any more shaved sideburns was wonderful, but at the same time, I was sorry I had thought so unkindly of this poor man who was dying. Here he had been wasting away, and yet every day he showed up to work.

*

Six years later, I'm riding up in the employee elevator at Manheim's department store in New York City. It's just my luck that I'm standing next to the head of personnel, Miss Sternberger, and we are the only two persons heading up to the eighth-floor administrative offices.

"What would you say if I said that that goatee has to go?" Miss Sternberger says, smiling a smile that would freeze iron.

"I'll shave it off when you shave the peach fuzz off your upper lip!" is what I wanted to say, but I didn't. Instead, I politely agreed with her, and the next morning I punched into work with a bare chin. I had been hired as a stock boy, which means I was the guy working back in the storeroom who was never seen by the public. However, I still had to wear a jacket and a tie, and as Miss Sternberger so graciously pointed out, my facial hair was not acceptable. No tattoos, no jewelry, nothing that would offend the customer. Ah, the good old days!

I had already been working at the store for three months and yet this was my first encounter with Miss Sternberger, also known by some of the employees as Miss Turdburger. It was not my last. Every once in a while I would be called up to the "Burger's" office for a lecture on initiative or deportment, and it seemed to me that I was the only employee subjected to these self-improvement seminars.

At the time, I thought of myself as being a rather compassionate individual, but the "Burger" woman really rubbed me the wrong way. I was good at my job, I was never late, I got along with everyone—except for Miss Sternberger. I was still living at home, and every so often I would let it slip how much I disliked the "Burger."

"There are times, Mom, when I swear I wanted to push her under a truck!"

"Oh, Danny, that's a terrible thing to say!"

"I know, I know. I'm just speaking metaphorically. It's only because she treats me so rotten. It makes me very angry."

"I understand, darling. But things will improve. It'll get better."

But things didn't get better. It got to the point that I was even planning to quit my job. And then, one afternoon when I returned to work after going out to get some lunch, I found several of my working friends huddled together at the employee entrance.

"What's up, guys?" I asked, noticing the long faces and Janice, from Lingerie, wiping her eyes.

"It's the 'Burger.' She was in an accident."

"She's dead," mumbled Ricky from Bed Linens.

I was stunned. At first I thought it was a joke, a very bad joke. "You're kidding! What happened?"

"She left to go to lunch and she was crossing Fifth Avenue when a garbage truck hit her. At least that's what we heard the police say happened to her."

"She wasn't the most fun person to be with," said Charlie from Men's Shoes, "but she sure didn't deserve to be run over by a truck."

*

I continued to work at Manheim's for the next eight years, eventually moving out of the stock room and onto the floor as a salesman in the Luggage Department. I then interviewed for a position over at Gimbels and became the youngest manager of the China and Flatware Department in the history of the store. As a celebration, I shared a bottle of champagne with my friend Charlie and started growing back my goatee.

*

It was this next episode that sort of opened my eyes. Once again it revolved around my facial hair, my cursed goatee. I had moved into a tiny studio apartment in Hell's Kitchen in Manhattan and was living the life of the confirmed bachelor. I had some lady friends, but nothing serious. I'll share a secret with you: Gimbels managers don't make a lot of money. At least I didn't way back then, so my entertaining was limited.

There was a little bodega on the corner of my street and Ninth Avenue, run by a Spanish family headed by a big lump of a man named Luis. I stopped by there at least twice a week for a Cuban coffee or a sandwich, and if Luis was manning the fort, I was always greeted the same way.

"Oh, is mi amigo, señor cunt face!"

After this endearing greeting, he would laugh like a crazed hyena and then ask the same question he always asked.

"How can you walk around with that chumino on your chin? Aren't you afraid some hombre will want to stick his pinga inside?" and then his whole blubbery body would shake with obscene laughter.

I tried to avoid the bodega on the days I knew Luis would be working, but often he would be in the back of the store and his daughter Tina would be at the front counter, and suddenly I'd hear his insane laugh and see him come barreling out of the storeroom and heading my way. There was no way to escape, and I would have to endure a repeat of his obscene monologue.

After about two months of this humiliation, I finally had had enough and made myself walk an extra three blocks to a little Korean market for my coffee and sandwich, and I stayed away from Luis. After a month or so, I found that I was still unhappy over my experience in Luis's bodega. That I had let this go on for so long made me feel ashamed and very angry at myself, as well as at Luis. I decided to confront him and demand an apology. Yes, I had in the past joked back at him in the hope he would get the hint and stop, but that was stupidly ineffectual.

When I entered the little store, I was immediately hit with the delicious perfume of strong coffee, and I realized how much I missed the place—not Luis necessarily, but certainly his place. Tina was busy at the checkout counter, so I wandered toward the back storage room, nervously searching for my nemesis. He didn't seem to be around. Disappointed, but also sort of relieved, I returned to the counter and Tina.

"Hi, Tina, is your dad around?" When she began to cry, I knew what she was going to reply before she said it. I felt the hairs on the back of my neck rise up like miniature antennae, and my whole body suddenly seemed to weigh a ton.

"He died last week. He was so sick. He—he was crying all the time."

"I'm so sorry. What was wrong? What was his sickness?"

"It was cancer of something to do with his man parts."

"You mean his prostate?"

"I guess that's what it was. Something that started with a P. They told us it was stage four, that he had waited too long."

"I'm so sorry," I repeated, and this time I really meant it, because deep down, I knew I was responsible. In some mysterious way, it was my anger that had killed Luis Alvaro Perez.

*

"That's nuts, Danny. People don't die because someone hates them or is angry with them." That was my friend Charlie's response when I told him what had happened to Luis. "The only way I know of killing someone you hate is with a gun or a knife or maybe poison."

"But this has happened before to people I've known, people I disliked. Take Miss Sternberger, for instance."

"That was an accident, you know that. And she was disliked by a lot of other people besides you."

"But there was this incident when I was a kid." And I proceeded to tell him about Mr. DeRosa. He was not impressed.

"Coincidences. For god's sake, Danny, get over it! When you're a little kid you think you're responsible for all kinds of things, your folks divorcing or your dad drinking or a stranger touching you where he shouldn't, but when you get older you realize it's not you, it's just the way things are."

"But this is different, Charlie. I can almost tell if it's going to happen. I mean, with Luis I had this recurring fantasy of him lying in a coffin and—"

"Man, you have got some ego. You actually believe you've got the power to kill people by simply willing them dead? Danny, you are not God. You are not even some avenging angel."

I knew what he was saying was right, but I still had this tornado of doubt twisting around in my gut. I told him that I was frightened it might happen again.

"Jesus H. Christ! What will it take to convince you that you are not Dangerous Dan, the killing man? There must be something we can do to prove this was all just a coincidence. Let me think on it and we'll talk later. Okay? Enough drama. Pour me a drink."

*

About a week later I got a call from Charlie. He was his usual upbeat self, and he sounded excited.

"So I got this idea last night while I was sitting on the john. Some of my best ideas come while I'm taking a dump. Anyway, I've been figuring that the only way you'll believe that you don't have the power to think someone to death is if you try to do it consciously."

"Are you kidding? I'm not doing that. I'm not about to take the chance of killing some innocent person!"

"First of all, I can guarantee you won't be able to kill anyone. You don't have any magical powers, my friend, sorry to disappoint you. Secondly, you wouldn't be attempting this on an innocent stranger; far from it."

"What do you mean?"

"What if I told you I have a person in mind deserving of a special place in Hell? A true monster that should have been blasted off this earth years ago."

"I thought Hitler was dead already."

"Ha ha, very funny. I'm serious here, buddy. This man, this monster, has ruined many lives, including my older brother's. And if I'm wrong and you've really got this superpower, then there'll be one less son-of-a-bitch around to make so many more people suffer."

"You said he ruined your brother's life. That's a serious accusation. Who is this guy?"

"He would have hurt me as well, but I fought back. He was the priest at my church when my brother Tommy was an altar boy. Gennaro Jesselli. He raped my brother and because my stupid brother trusted him and believed in his bullshit, Tommy kept silent. Then I come along, and of course old Jesselli tried his funny business with me, but I resisted. In fact,

I walked out of that church and I haven't been back since. So now I'm more than a lapsed Catholic. I'm a non-Catholic."

"What about your brother?"

"Well, I confronted him about what happened to me. You want to talk about angry! I was so furious! He had let me step into a trap, right into the arms of a monster. No warning, no brotherly advice. He started crying and saying he was sorry and what could he do to make it up to me. I told him he had to tell the authorities what Jesselli had done to him, that that disgusting pig needed to go to jail. Tommy was so scared, and he is so damaged. He's never been able to hold down a job or sustain a relationship. Anyway, to make a long story short, a complaint was sent to the diocese and, what a surprise, Jesselli was finally gone."

"That must have been a relief."

"Yeah, I suppose so. A little late for Tommy and me, but better for the other boys. However, here's the kicker: a few years later Tommy writes to me from the mental hospital, where he's been struggling so hard to get better, and says, guess who's the visiting chaplain here? You got it—Jesselli. Turns out the church just kept moving him from parish to parish. After he'd decimate one group of boys, he'd be sent to another church, where he would damage more young lives."

"But surely the church must have stopped him by now."

"You'd think so, right? That's where you come in, if you're up for it. Father Gennaro Jesselli is currently pastor at St. Peregrine's up in Yonkers. Still up to his old tricks. I thought you and I could take a little train ride north and scope him out."

"Charlie, you are out of your mind. You want me to try and kill someone I don't know, have never met, have never been angry at or have any reason to want dead. I mean, I understand your anger. You and your brother—"

"Listen, as they say on the radio, 'this is only a test,' and I fully expect you to fail it. In fact, since I know you won't be able to kill off the bastard, maybe I'll do it myself."

"Charlie!"

"Relax, just kidding. So meet me at the clock in Grand Central this Saturday around one and we'll go visit my dear old friend Father Jesselli. Just like old times. I'll get the train tickets. See ya."

"Charlie!" I exclaimed, but he had hung up.

*

St. Peregrine's was a small gray stone church on Roosevelt Street in Yonkers. It was hard to believe that this quiet town was actually the fourth largest city in New York State. After the hustle and bustle of Manhattan, I felt we were hundreds of miles away when actually, we were just over the city line.

On the train trip, Charlie had explained how we were going to confront Father Jesselli.

"I don't think he'll recognize me; it was a long time ago. I'll ask him to listen to my confession and then, when we are both settled comfortably in the confessional, I'll remind him about his previous sins. Hopefully, he will deny my accusations and stick around long enough for me to fill him in about you."

"What do you mean, 'fill him in'?"

"I'm going to tell him about this strange guy who is going to pay him a visit, a man who is going to lay a curse on him."

"A curse? What kind of curse? This is so ridiculous! It's like something out of an old Bela Lugosi movie."

"Right. If I could play the church organ, I'd run over to the keyboard and accompany you when you say your lines, give you some creepy background music."

"Lines? What lines?"

"Here, I wrote them out for you. Read them and then memorize them. It's easy. There are only two sentences."

*

We stood across the street from St. Peregrine's and waited until the priest appeared. He stepped out of a doorway located on the side of the church. I figured it was the entrance to the basement and it probably was where the various church activities took place. He was accompanied by two young boys, I guess about nine or ten years old, and he had his hand on the shoulder of one of them. I could hear Charlie's pattern of breathing change and see him clench and unclench his fists.

I watched Father Jesselli talking to the boys and then, after patting them on the head, he sent them on their way. To anyone else looking upon the scene, it would appear to be a beautiful Kodak moment: a sweet, kindly old priest blessing two innocent children and watching them head off for home. I found it hard to believe that this man, with the saintliest of smiles, was a pedophile and a sexual abuser of young boys. But I saw how disturbed Charlie was, and I believed what he said about his brother and the other victims.

Father Jesselli turned and climbed the front steps up to the two large oak doors and, pulling one open, entered and disappeared into the church.

"Come on," Charlie hissed as he grabbed my arm and started dragging me across the street. "I'll go in first, and when you see the two of us head for the confessional, you can come all the way in."

"I don't know, Charlie, this is so nuts—"

"Just sit in the pew closest to the entrance, and when he comes your way, stand up and say your lines."

By this time Charlie and I were through the doors and he was on his way toward the priest. I waited as they greeted each other, and Father Jesselli, smiling, indicated the curtained booths tucked away between the arches. They both walked in that direction and I seated myself in the closest pew.

I'd like to say that I came to my senses and, facing the fact that I had let myself be manipulated, got up and left the church and Charlie and his crazy scheme. But I didn't. I sat there and sweated and repeated my "lines" over and over. I just wanted to be done with this silly charade and back on the train to Manhattan.

After what seemed like an hour, I first heard and then saw Charlie running up the aisle like he was in a marathon race. He was out the door before I could say anything, and then—I was on. It was time for me to perform my part in this morality play. Father Jesselli suddenly appeared in the aisle, and I could see he was irate. No sweet old man, no saintly smile. Instead there stood an ugly troll with a twisted sneer on his face and his body shaking with rage.

I rose slowly from my position in the pew and took a step sideways into the aisle. I opened my mouth in preparation to speak when, instead of heading my way, Father Jesselli turned and started moving down the aisle toward the sanctuary. "What the hell do I do now?" I thought, and I heard Charlie's voice in my head: "Say your lines, doofus! Hurry up! Just say your fucking lines!"

"Father Jesselli!" My voice echoed off the stone walls. The priest stopped in his tracks.

"I have a message for you, from God!" He turned slowly and faced me.

"You will die within a week." I then circled around and exited the church. As I descended the steps, I had a sudden feeling of foreboding. The look on the priest's face as I had turned to leave was a mixture of terror and resignation. He believed what I had said.

*

After all these years, I look back and kind of wish it had all gone in a different direction. I mean, what would my world have been like if, instead of that phone call from Charlie, my life had continued rambling along on its typical middle-class journey: Gimbels China Department, marriage, suburban tract house, two cars, two kids, one dog, one mortgage and an acre of crab grass. But that call did happen.

"Hi Danny! Oh, man! My humblest apologies!"

"Hey, Charlie. What's up? What are you apologizing for?"

"For ever doubting you!"

"What are you talking about?"

"About you, Dangerous Dan, the killing man! You did it!"

"Shit, Charlie, are you talking about the priest?"

"You better believe it. He's dead." I stopped breathing. I felt like I was slipping through the floorboards. I was melting and flowing down into the basement.

"Dead?"

"As the proverbial doornail. Evidently he tripped going down the stairs into the basement of the church, cracked open his skull and bled to death before anyone found him. My aunt read about it in the *Yonkers Tribune*. You did it, man."

I did it. Later that night, lying on my bed in a cold sweat, those three words kept repeating: I did it, I did it, I did it! By early morning, I had determined that I never wanted it to happen again. It was bad enough that people I knew died because I unconsciously wished that they would. Almost everyone has done that at least once in their life, wished someone dead, but of course the intended person never died, except in my case. But now I had ended the life of a stranger, a person who meant nothing to me, who hadn't harmed me or insulted me or angered me, a stranger with whom I had spent all of about two minutes. I had simply looked at him, said those stupid lines, thought of him being dead, and—

*

"You realize that all you have to do," Charlie informed me as he sat on the futon in my little studio apartment drinking a Heineken, "is will a guy dead and he's a goner. Boy, I sure don't want to get on the wrong side of you."

"I didn't will the priest to die, Charlie. It didn't happen that way. I just sort of saw him dead, you know, visualized him no longer alive."

"Well, however you do it, it's amazing."

"It's horrific! It's not amazing or wonderful or something I'd proudly put down on a resume. It's the murder of another human being. I'm going to figure out a way to control myself and to never let it happen again."

*

Famous last words. Of course it happened again. It's easy for me to blame it all on Charlie, but, truth be told, there was something very seductive about having access to this power, this ability to determine whether an individual lived or died.

Charlie dropped by the China Department one day and found me at work displaying a set of Spode dinner plates.

"You got time for lunch, buddy of mine? I've got something I need to run by you."

"Sure. Just let me finish this," I replied, setting a decorative turkey platter down next to a gravy boat. I grabbed my jacket and we headed out of Gimbels and over to Keens Steakhouse. After ordering a couple of sirloins and a pitcher of beer, Charlie filled me in on what he'd been up to.

"I had a visit with an old friend of mine, Anthony Rossi. We went to high school together. Really nice guy. So, he's got this sister and evidently she's married to a real piece of work, this guy who knocks her around and beats up their little kids. He keeps her on a tight leash and won't even let her see her own family."

"Why doesn't she leave him?"

"Well, Tony says she's terrified of him and afraid he'll harm her or the kids."

"Sounds to me like he's doing plenty of harm already."

"Yeah, well, I think she's really afraid if she tries to leave him, he'll kill all of them."

"Is divorce out of the picture?"

"You're talking good Catholics, unlike yours truly, so not really an option, but even if it was, it's kind of like 'if I can't have her, I'll see to it that no one else can have her.'"

"Sounds like a really awful situation."

"Yeah, so that's why I offered Tony our services."

"Our services? What services?" I didn't like where this was going.

"You know, your special talent, your gift."

"Charlie, I hope you really didn't do that. You're kidding, right?"

"Danny, my boy, I can't explain it. I'm sitting there in Farrell's Tavern out in Ronkonkoma with Tony and we're drinking and talking old times and then he hits me with this story about his poor sister, and it's like an epiphany. I mean, I realize I have the solution to his problem—you!"

"Charlie—"

"There is a reason you have been blessed—"

"Cursed! It's a fucking curse."

"Danny, listen to me. You've got it all wrong. When I said you were no avenging angel, I made a big mistake. You are that and more. You are like one of those superheroes in the comics, you've got this power—"

"Stop it, Charlie! Just tell me what you told this friend of yours."

"Don't worry. I didn't say anything about you. I just said that I could take care of his problem and it would be done quietly and with nothing to trace back to him."

"Oh, my god! You sound like some two-bit gangster! What did he say to your proposal?"

"He asked how much."

"Oh, dear lord in heaven! This is bad, really bad. You didn't answer him, please tell me you didn't!"

"Listen, this guy is rolling in dough. He has a house in the Hamptons and a duplex on the Upper East Side. I think he's even got one of those chalets in Switzerland or Belgium or one of those countries. Maybe it's Monaco, I don't know—"

"Charlie!"

"Okay, okay. I asked for twenty thousand."

"Dollars????"

"No, pizzas. Of course dollars! Ten thousand as a down payment and the rest when the job is done."

"I'm going to be sick. Do you realize what you've done? You are going to be in such trouble—"

"Danny, calm down. Listen, listen to me. This is important. You have been put on this earth for a reason. It is your mission to eliminate toxic individuals; it's as simple as that. And I've been chosen to be your facilitator—your agent, if you will—and, as such, I will take care of all the details. All you have to do is—do whatever it is that you do."

"No fucking way! I'm not going to become some kind of amateur hit man! If this Tony of yours is so rich—and by the way, what does he do to make so much money?"

"I don't know—investments, import, export. Shit, I don't know."

"Well, it sounds to me like he might have other avenues he can follow, and if that's so, he can hire some professional—"

"He says he thought about that, but that that would be too close to home, too many people would put two and two together."

"Charlie, I'm ending this conversation. You call up Mr. Tony what's-his-name and tell him the deal is off—now!"

"Aw, come on, Danny. Give me a break. I can't do that. We shook on it."

"I don't care if you kissed his ass! Tell him it's off!" And that was when Charlie reached into his jacket pocket and pulled out an envelope and handed it to me. I opened the flap and took a peek. Tucked inside were ten crisp, new thousand-dollar bills.

*

It was easy, actually. That's what makes it so appealing. There's no violence, no confrontation, no physical contact. I look at the person, I imagine them dead, and then I walk away. Anthony Rossi's brother-in-law ran Esposito's Refrigerator Installation and Repair shop in Long Island City. I just walked up to the large window in front of his place of work, spied him repairing what looked like a refrigerator and, after double-checking the photo of him Charlie had given me, I rapped on the window. He looked up and frowned. Unpleasant fellow. I smiled, waved my hand, then turned and walked away. Done, finis, over, and so was Mr. Peter Esposito.

The freaky accident made the front page of the *Daily News*. "MAN DIES LOCKED IN FREEZER." What the police figured out was that Esposito had entered the walk-in meat-storage unit to check on one of the pipes, and when he finished and tried to exit, the safety release, which was supposed to prevent a person from getting locked in, jammed. It was a Saturday and no one was around, so he began to run out of oxygen. They found him early on Monday morning, curled up in a fetal position and frozen as hard as one of the sides of beef hanging from the ceiling of the freezer. Charlie collected the rest of the cash, and my career as a hired assassin had begun.

*

In the beginning, Charlie took a 20 percent cut of the fee, like any regular agent, but as this bizarre experiment grew into a million-dollar business, we agreed the money should be split down the middle, fifty-fifty. After all, Charlie did most of the work, the research, the planning, the setting of the price for my services, the collection of the fee, etc. I just completed the project, often in less than ten minutes.

I never knew how he found clients and their targets, nor did I want to. I imagine a lot of it was by word of mouth. Murder for hire is not something you advertise on TV or in your local newspaper. And it *was* murder; I never deluded myself about that. It wasn't always some altruistic act of mercy on my part, ridding the world of bad guys who preyed on good guys. Yes, it's true I requested that the target not be chosen just because he was in somebody's way or that he had ticked someone off. And I insisted that the target (I never used the word "victim") had to be a seriously dangerous threat. But what did I really know? I had to depend on Charlie telling me the truth about a client and why a target needed to be eliminated. However, it would have been very easy for him to add to the list a person unjustly targeted, and I would never know it. To be completely honest, I'm pretty sure he probably did that more than once. With Charlie, it was always about the money.

And if I'm going to be truly honest, the money was important to me as well. I could finally give my mother the things she never had. She could live in a large, bright, comfortable apartment, I could afford a decent car, I was able to buy my clothes at Brooks Brothers and eat at Le Bernardin, although I preferred to cook my own meals. But I wasn't into being ostentatious. I didn't want to stand out in a crowd. I valued my anonymity.

Any serious relationship with a woman was just not possible. Marriage was certainly not an option. I felt I could not involve someone I loved in something so dangerous and immoral. "Bye, honey. I'm off to work. Got to stare murderously at someone so they die. Love ya!"

I kept my job at Gimbels for two reasons: it kept the IRS off my back, and I actually liked working there. Charlie called it my Clark Kent disguise—mild-mannered department manager by day and avenging superhero by night. The money I earned "moonlighting" was never put in the bank. I had a large safe installed in my walk-in closet, and that was where the cash was stored. I made no major investments, didn't play the stock market, had no offshore accounts. To the state and federal government, I was a hard-working citizen earning a moderate salary, paying my taxes, owning only one credit card and maintaining a modest savings account at my neighborhood bank.

Charlie established an actual consulting firm to use as a front for his "real" business. It was manned by a legitimate staff of qualified consultants and was successful on its own. He was the CEO, and if he had wanted to, he could have quit the gun-for-hire business and just run this corporation. But I realized he really got off on being a god, because that was exactly what it was. He was the one making the monumental decision of who was going to "buy the farm." I was merely his instrument of death. It didn't make me any the less guilty, but he really enjoyed his role in this macabre drama, while I simply accepted the fact that this was a way to direct my "talent" away from accidentally killing an innocent person.

We both lived with the possibility of being found out, of maybe being caught up in a sting operation. In our case, however, the nasty truth is that authorities don't really care too much about the victims; it's the money that bothers them. All that money that never gets taxed makes them very angry. That's how they got Al Capone—not for murder, drugs or bootlegging, but for tax evasion. Anyway, as Charlie had pointed out several times, they would never believe or understand what I do, and so far, all the deaths had been declared natural or accidental. We just had to keep hoping that we wouldn't step into a trap and get caught accepting payment for our dubious services. So far, so good.

*

I mentioned the gangster Al Capone. Charlie sent me a file on another "Goodfella," whose name I can't reveal at this time. Included with several photographs was a list of his crimes, which covered everything from kidnapping and rape to torture and murder. This was one bad hombre. Reading the description of what he did to his victims edged out any feelings of sympathy I might have had and ramped up my anger. When I saw him standing in front of the local Brothers of Italy meeting hall, all proud and arrogant, it was easy to give him "the stare." He glanced up and saw me gazing at him. "What da fuck you staring at, skinny?" I just smiled and continued walking on down the sidewalk. Two days later, he suffered a massive heart attack while playing poker in the meeting hall. He fell out of his chair onto the floor and turned blue as his heart exploded. Too many cigars, too much alcohol, too much red meat and too many acts of violence.

*

Over the years, all of my targets were men, with one exception. When Charlie told me that my next target was a woman, I was a little shook up. I guess I naively thought women weren't capable of being truly evil. Sure, there were women who killed, but it was usually because they were provoked into doing so by abusive husbands, or they were stuck in circumstances that were intolerable and murder seemed the only way out. Shows you how sexist I was.

Brenda Felton was the widow of Bruce Felton, the famous real estate developer who reportedly owned half of Manhattan. If you looked at the New York City skyline from either New Jersey or Brooklyn and Queens and saw skyscrapers with their towers topped in gold leaf, you were looking at property owned by Felton. When her husband died (under mysterious circumstances), she took over the business and ran it like a military installation. She became known by the staff as General Felton, a nickname she enthusiastically adopted; and it was grudgingly admitted that she was better at the business than her recently deceased husband. She ran a series of glamorous commercials (starring herself, of course) inviting the public to enjoy living the high life by leasing an apartment, an office or a retail space in one of her fabulous buildings.

What the public, watching these sexy videos of posh condos and sleek corporate headquarters, didn't know was that she was also a member of that group of self-serving toads known as slumlords. When you are traveling through the Bronx on a commuter train and you see block after block of brick tenements, it probably never crosses your mind that someone owns those. General Felton owned hundreds of them, and she made a tidy profit off the income they provided. However, because she couldn't charge the kind of rent she got off of her gilded towers in Manhattan (although the tenement rents were high enough), she had to make cuts in the services.

She benefited from the New York City heating law that said she only had to provide heat from October 1 to May 31. God forbid there was a cold snap in September. She was under no obligation to have the heat turned on. And while the temperature in every apartment was to be at least 68 degrees during the day and 62 degrees at night, this was not always the story. The furnace would break down: "We'll get that taken care of right away!" The oil delivery was delayed: "We'll get that taken care of right away!" No hot water: "We'll get that taken care of right away!" Don't hold your breath.

It is also a city law that every building has to be clean and vermin-free. This means that there should be a manager living in each tenement who is hired to maintain the building. Felton cut back on that expense by employing one supervisor for every five buildings. In exchange for free rent and a small salary, the poor super was on call 24/7, and he or she spent hundreds of hours running back and forth between tenements, unplugging toilets, sweeping halls, replacing fuses, setting rat traps and spraying for cockroaches. Of course, it was impossible to keep this up for any length of time, so none of Felton's holdings were ever really clean and vermin-free.

Repairs and upkeep, such as window replacement, painting, and restoration of woodwork, all cost money too, so unless the building was a potential site for a lawsuit, Felton never wasted any cash on what she considered non-essential beautification. Therefore, her tenants lived in ugly, dirty, cold and damp apartments while they struggled to pay the rent. If and when they complained to city officials, the authorities would hand General Felton a fine, which she promptly paid, and the problem would never be addressed. It was far cheaper to pay the fine than replace the boiler or install better electrical wiring.

There were many other ways to avoid paying for what Felton considered unnecessary upgrades, and she wasn't alone in this. While many landlords took pride in their properties, a large majority neglected theirs and, like the General, provided little for the rent they collected. Felton, conversely, was very generous with city officials, and as the old saying goes, "money talks."

After reading through most of her file and admittedly being disgusted with the way she treated her less wealthy residents, I still found I didn't believe she deserved to be terminated—maybe exposed and punished, but not executed. And then I lifted the last page and found the reason why someone wanted her dead.

Some landlords don't want to wait around forever to evict a tenant. It means spending a lot of time and money, so they reach into their bag of dirty tricks and they start turning off the electricity or the water, dumping garbage in the hall, sending goons around to beat on doors in the middle of the night, leaving anonymous threatening letters, scrawling pornographic graffiti on the walls, and so on.

Felton took it a step further. Often, a mysterious fire would destroy the floor of one of her tenements. The cause would be determined to be a careless tossing of a cigarette or the spontaneous igniting of a pile of oil-soaked rags. This unhappy accident would put a tenant out on the street, and after a shoddy restoration of the apartment, the General would lease it again—with a sizable increase in rent.

Unfortunately, there was one time when one of these "accidental" fires spread to the other floors and the entire building was destroyed. Felton wasn't too upset, because she could collect on the insurance policy, and it was one less building she had to deal with. But there was one little problem. Usually, these "accidental" fires happened during a weekday afternoon when most of the residents were either at work or at school. But on this one occasion, it just happened that a grandmother was living on the top floor, where she was babysitting her two little granddaughters. The fire moved too fast and the smoke was too thick for the three of them to escape, and so they perished.

There were several newspaper articles in the file about the tragic fire and its aftermath. Felton Properties was sued for major fire violations and several other breaches of safety, and General Felton herself was eventually arrested and charged with arson and manslaughter. The trial made fascinating reading, with witnesses testifying that Felton had hired them to harass inhabitants and the General denying any wrongdoing. "I'm a good landlord and fond of my renters. This tragic accident has saddened me deeply. Mrs. Garcia was a fine woman, and I'm so sorry about what happened to her and her grandkids. But it was not my fault." Three weeks later, after a lot of money spent on the best lawyers and no solid evidence presented to prove her guilt, the jury agreed that indeed it was not her fault.

The Garcia family eventually slammed Felton with a civil suit, but it ended the same as the criminal trial. However, General Felton, being the generous, compassionate human being that she believed herself to be, handed the family a personal check for five thousand dollars. Mr. Juan Garcia, the deceased's son, tore up the check and threw it in her face.

*

I made an appointment to meet General Felton at her office. When I arrived, I was kept waiting for an hour in an opulent white and silver lobby, and then I was ushered into the General's inner sanctum. A tall, thin beauty, dressed in a Christopher Kane suit, rose from her glass and stainless-steel desk, stepped around it and came toward me, extending her right hand. I did not take it.

"Ms. Felton. You're going to die soon." I turned away from her and exited. I heard her call out my name (I had used an alias) and then a "What the hell!" But by that time, I was entering the stainless-steel elevator and beginning my descent.

Two weeks later, I was in my apartment making my lunch when I glanced over at the TV and saw a banner scroll across the screen: "Famous real estate mogul Brenda Felton killed in freak accident." I turned up the sound and listened as the Ken Doll of a commentator ominously revealed the gory details.

"Brenda Felton, prominent and influential real estate magnate, was killed early this morning while on an inspection tour of a new office tower under construction. It's reported that her jacket got caught on the corner edge of a descending service elevator and that she was dragged down several stories before the wire cage could be stopped. What her injuries were have not been revealed as of yet."

*

I've been doing this now for many years. Charlie said our life stories would make a good book or movie. It certainly hasn't been boring. I've been to many cities in the States, even Hawaii. I've been to South America,

Central America and Canada. I've handled cases in the U.K. (a plastic surgeon with sloppy hygiene), France (a gymnastics coach with a yen for nubile young girls), Italy (an up-and-coming young don), Kenya (a farmer big on torture). The list is endless.

One day, Charlie met with me and handed me a file the size of an old-fashioned telephone book.

"This is a biggie, Danny. The largest fee I've ever been offered. I'm talking six fucking zeros! We're going to have to go slowly and plan very carefully. You spend a couple of days reading this, think about it, and we'll talk next week."

I put the file on my desk to be looked at later. Instead, I perused the mail I had just picked up downstairs in the lobby. Bills, flyers and three invitations to upcoming charity events.

*

Over time, I found I had amassed a very large nest egg. I never was a big spender—no yacht, no second home, no second car, no private jet, etc. I therefore decided to start giving donations to various charities. Perhaps it was a semi-conscious attempt to atone for my many sins, but all I know is that it felt good to start emptying my safe of some of those ill-gotten gains.

I stayed away from political contributions and stuck to those charities that seemed to serve those who really needed help. As the years went by, my reputation as a major donor, one who didn't use a credit card or a check but an envelope of cash for my contribution, became known by most of the heads of these philanthropies. I received invitations weekly to dinners, auctions, masked balls, museum tours, concerts—you name it—and I was invited to it as an honored guest. However, I rarely attended any of these events and instead would just send, by messenger, several thousand dollars in a sealed envelope.

*

When Charlie and I finally got together, I had read the dossier of our next target. It was impressive, to say the least. It covered almost his entire history from teen years to his middle age, and it was eye-opening. This individual had committed so many illegalities, ruined so many lives, physically abused so many persons, and hid it all behind a façade of respectability. He was a true sociopath, a borderline psychopath and a monster of the first degree.

"So I've been trying to figure out," Charlie explained, "how to get you close enough for you to be able to zap him. This is a tough one."

"Charlie, I have a surprise for you. This is the one time when I have the plan."

"Oh, yeah? Moving in on my territory, are you?" he jokingly replied.

"You bet. You're not the only mastermind in this corporation."

"So, what have you got, genius?"

"I've written it all down," I said, handing him a couple of printed pages. "Check it out."

He sat back and began reading what I wrote. By the time he got to the second page, he was smiling. "Danny, this is great! Very clever. I think it'll work. How much time do we have to prepare?"

"The event is in two weeks. Plenty of time."

"Right. This is going to be amazing."

Easy for him to feel amazed. Me, I was just going to feel depressed, because once more I was going to violate the number-one rule that "thou shalt not kill."

*

This fund-raising dinner was taking place at the Plaza Hotel. It was one of those two-thousand-dollars-a-plate meals of prime rib with a large helping of boring speeches. I arrived wearing my Tom Ford tuxedo and joined the crowd buzzing around the bar, numbing themselves for the evening ahead. I asked for a tonic and lime, as I never want to be fuzzy when I'm working. I had only had one or two sips when Barbara Dunleavy, co-chair of the event, spotted me and came rushing over.

"Oh, darling Daniel! I'm so glad you could make it!" she gushed, all aflutter in a turquoise silk chiffon gown. "And thank you, thank you, thank you for your very generous pledge!"

(Money you'll never see if everything works out, I thought to myself.)

"I know how shy you are," she continued, "about all the good things you do."

(If you only knew.)

Barbara started to lead me into the ballroom, where the tables were set up for the evening's festivities, when a hubbub around the entrance indicated the guest of honor had arrived.

"Oh, he's here! Let's see if we can get over there," she said, pushing her way through the crowd like the prow of an ocean liner and dragging me behind her.

As we got closer, I saw this tall blond gentleman shaking hands and posing for selfies with middle-aged men and women who were acting like teenagers at a rock concert. His smile was very wide and very white, and his tan only made it appear whiter. The crowd around him was at least six rows deep, but Barbara wedged her way through to the first row and whispered something to one of the men standing next to the guest of honor. He in turn whispered into the tall man's ear, and the guest of honor spun around to face Barbara. His smile widened, if that was possible, and he indicated he wanted her to join him.

"Get over here," he shouted. "Bring that gorgeous body of yours over here, now!" And with the giggle of a sixteen-year-old, she stepped over to him, with me still in tow.

"My god, woman, you are getting more beautiful every time I see you!"

"Oh, hush, you silly man. Now, I want to introduce you to one of your fans—"

(When Hell freezes over.)

"And he's the donor who has made the highest pledge so far." She pulled me to her side and I found myself facing the man of the evening.

"It's my pleasure to introduce you to the man who is going to help you get reelected. This is Mr. Daniel Amateau."

I stared at the former President of the United States and smiled.

Grandpa Gets a Tattoo

Chester O'Connor made the announcement at the annual Thanksgiving family dinner. The main reaction to his declaration was a lot of hearty laughter. However, one person at the table was not amused.

"You most certainly will not!" was the reply that came from the lips of Maureen, Chester's only daughter. "No tattoos, no earrings, no nose rings, no lip rings or studs or whatever nonsense is the current fashion! You are not a juvenile delinquent!"

"You're a senior delinquent!" chimed in Patrick, the eldest of the O'Connor boys, creating another wave of beer-induced laughter. The irony of this attempt at humor was that no one was a more honest and law-abiding citizen than Chester Liam O'Connor.

A second-generation Irish American, he was somber, not big on conversation, and kept pretty much to himself. He had worked hard as a plumber in Trenton, New Jersey, to support his family: his now-deceased wife Patricia, daughter Maureen, and five sons, Patrick, Michael, Timothy, Sean and Liam. Now, as a widowed retiree, he kept himself busy by making improvements on his 1920s bungalow and by volunteering at the local food bank. His only form of relaxation was reading mysteries and watching soccer on the TV.

He had been a Democrat for years but had eventually turned to the Liberal Party when he noticed that the donkey party was acting more like an ass and wasn't getting anything done. And unlike the rest of the family, he was a lapsed Catholic. This was due to his learning of the rampant pederasty being practiced by priests all around the world, but most of all to the untimely death of his beloved baby sister, Alice.

"What kind of loving God takes the life of an innocent, sweet kindergarten teacher and then allows his priests to take the innocence of hundreds of children? And don't give me that malarkey about 'how mysterious are his ways' and 'we are not meant to understand.'" (These observations were being shared solely with Max, his faithful Labrador, as they sat on the back porch steps watching the sun go down behind the garage.) Chester very rarely opened up to anyone except his dog. He believed talking in public about your feelings to be a form of effeminate whining, very unmanly.

This was why the repeat of his pronouncement "I'm going to get a tattoo" became less of a joke and more of a shock. Grandpa Chester never joked about serious things. In fact, he rarely joked about anything.

"So why do you want to get a tattoo, Pops?" asked Michael as he served himself a second piece of pumpkin pie.

"That's my business."

"What is it going to be?" inquired Patrick. "A mermaid? A heart?"

"It's going to be nothing," interrupted Maureen, "and that's the end of this conversation. The man is obviously losing it."

"Ah, chill out, Sis," suggested Sean, the youngest of the O'Connor boys. "I've got a tattoo, right here on my bicep," he said proudly as he pushed up his shirt sleeve.

"I know," she replied, "and it's the ugliest bluebird, if that's what it's supposed to be, that I have ever seen. And tell me if I'm wrong, but didn't you break up with Debbie two years ago? And yet there's her name on your bicep for the rest of your life! Brilliant! You can make a fool out of yourself if you want to, but Dad is not getting a tattoo, period!"

Maureen had taken over the role of Chester's caretaker when Patricia, his bride of forty-six years, had died of congestive heart failure. Maureen loved her dad very much and worried about him to an extreme. While there were times when Chester wished Maureen would back off a bit, he appreciated the little things she did for him, like scheduling his doctor's appointments and picking up his medications. But, as he once explained when she was ready to step in and help him shop for new work boots, "I'm not eight, Maureen, I'm eighty."

*

It was around ten in the evening when most of the family had packed up their portion of the Thanksgiving leftovers and sleepily headed off to home. Maureen was cleaning up in Chester's kitchen and putting his leftovers in plastic containers, labeling them with a magic marker and stowing them away in the freezer. Sean and his seventeen-year-old son, Arlin, were storing folding chairs in the hall closet and removing the wooden leaves used to expand Chester's dining room table.

"If your cousin Sheila has twins," grunted Sean, "there'll be no more room at the table. How many of us were there here today, by the way?"

"I think nineteen," Arlin replied, "but there would have been twenty-one if the twins had been here." The twins were the sons of Maureen and her husband Carl who were off serving in the military, Beau in the Navy and Dean in the Marines.

"I don't want to have to sit at the little kids' table anymore, Dad," Arlin declared as he folded up the card table. "I mean, none of us are kids anymore."

"I know. It's just temporary. Maybe we'll all go out to a restaurant next year."

"Over my dead body!" announced Maureen as she charged out of the kitchen and headed into the living room to get her coat. She was toting a large shopping bag with her share of the leftover feast. "Mom and Dad have had Thanksgiving here every year, with all of us, since we were little kids. It was Mom's favorite holiday, so we're keeping up the tradition."

At that moment Chester came in from the front porch, brushing himself off.

"You better hurry up, Maureen. It's snowing. Carl is waiting for you in the car."

"Okay, okay. Just let me get my coat on," she snapped as she wrestled with both the coat and the shopping bag.

"Sean, help your sister," said Chester admonishingly, and he stepped aside to let the siblings argue their way out the front door.

"Stop holding it that way, dummy, you'll spill the cranberry relish!"

"It'll be fine, Sis. Don't go and get your knickers in a knot! Geesh!"

After the door closed and it was quiet, Arlin slid the folded card table into the back of the closet and turned around to face his grandfather.

"Do you ever wonder about those two, Grandpa? Aunt Maureen and my dad are at it all the time."

"I gave up long ago trying to figure out anyone, even myself. Waste of time," Chester responded as he slipped into his welcoming recliner and reached for the remote. Max lay down at his feet, glad that the crowd had left.

"Well, I better get going," Arlin said, putting on his jacket. "But before I leave, I have an early Christmas gift for you."

"What?"

"You said you were getting a tattoo."

"Yes—?"

"Were you serious?"

"I guess so . . . Yeah, a tattoo."

"Do you know where to go to get one?"

"Not yet . . . no."

"Well, I do."

The Secret Plan

Most of the snow had melted by the time Arlin picked up Chester and they began driving southeast on Route 206. It was the Monday after Thanksgiving and he had skipped school to accomplish what he called "Mission: Body Art." He had told his dad that his class was going on a field trip to the Pine Barrens "to study the wildlife in New Jersey."

"Well, that's a whopper and a half," Grandpa Chester replied, "and I don't know if I approve of you lying like that to your father."

"Oh, it's okay. He's used to it. And he'll be happy when he knows what we really did."

"And what is it, exactly, that we're doing?"

"Oh, come on, you know! We're getting you your tattoo."

"No—I thought we were just doing a little reconnaissance—checking out the possibilities."

"Whatever! We're heading to Big T's Tattoos on the boardwalk."

"Atlantic City? I thought we were going into Philly."

"Oh, come on, Grandpa. Why would we now be driving south on 206? I know you have a better sense of direction than that. We'll connect up with the Atlantic City Expressway in forty-five minutes or so, and then it's a straight shot to the shore."

Several miles passed in silence before Chester finally spoke up.

"I haven't been to Atlantic City in years. Gambling was never my thing. Waste of time and money," he grumbled. "I do remember liking the saltwater taffy, though."

Arrival

It was around noon when Arlin pulled into the Caesars Hotel parking facility. He and Chester got out of the car, stretched their legs to get the blood flowing again, and then headed down the block or so to the ocean and the boardwalk. The water and the sky shared the same gray color, so it was hard to tell where the horizon was. Chester was surprised to see that there were a few people, all bundled up, strolling along the boardwalk on this cold November day. While many of the storefronts were boarded up for the season, a few shops were still open, hawking souvenirs, hot dogs and, of course, saltwater taffy.

"When I was a kid," reminisced Chester, "I thought they made the taffy out of salt water. Later, my dad explained to me that it was called that because it was made at the seashore. I was very disappointed."

They passed the exterior of Caesars Casino, with its towering columns topped with five heroic Roman statues and its chariot fountain in front with four marble horses splashing in the water.

Further on, the giant façade of the Bally's Resort came into view like a yawning maw, threatening to suck them inside in order to help them empty their pockets. Behind the hungry mouth of the casino rose the twenty-four floors of the 1,200-room Bally's Hotel.

"All this fancy nonsense," muttered Chester, "just to give gamblers a choice of where they want to lose their money."

"Yeah, but it's changed a lot with the advent of legalized online gambling," replied Arlin. "That has really cut into the casino business. And all those casinos popping up all over the country. A lot of the hotels here have closed. All of Atlantic City has been struggling. And then when Covid-19 hit, it just about wiped out the whole place. The tattoo parlors were shut down, needles and blood being a big no-no, and they only reopened last year. And speaking of tattoo parlors, look up ahead."

About a block away, there was a giant marquee jutting out over the boardwalk. It floated like a crown over the façade of what appeared to be a theater. The marquee was all lit up and spelled out BIG T'S TATTOO PALACE. What was once the theater's original grand entrance had been converted into display windows with BIG T sweatshirts, baseball caps and large posters of incredibly complex tattoos, all of them fighting for attention.

"I was told that this was once one of those huge movie palaces," explained Arlin.

"Very impressive. But where's the real entrance?"

"It's over there, around the corner on the left side. Ready to go in?" asked Arlin.

"I guess so. How come you know about this place?" Chester inquired as he followed Arlin to a pair of double doors situated beneath a bright blue awning.

"Well, I could uphold my reputation as a liar and say that this is where Dad got his bluebird tattoo, but that wouldn't be true."

"Where did he get it?"

"Somewhere in Edison," Arlin replied as he opened one of the doors to let his grandfather enter. "Some freaky establishment rated the number one tattoo parlor in New Jersey. Nothing but the best for my dad."

"So how did you know about this place?" Chester asked again, as he stopped and stood staring at the giant photographs of dragons and skulls and naked ladies hanging on the sky-blue walls of the space.

"'Cuz I got a tattoo here."

"Jesus, Mary and Joseph!" Chester exclaimed, shocked but a little impressed. "You're a regular gangster! When did this happen?"

"I got it on my sixteenth birthday," Arlin answered in a low voice, as a very attractive young woman approached them. "Used a fake ID," he whispered.

"You did, did you?! Well, we'll talk more about that later," Chester whispered back.

"Good afternoon, gentlemen. My name is Audrey. How may I help you?"

Her dark hair was pulled back in a long ponytail, exposing a neck circled in yellow butterflies. She wore a blue sleeveless tee shirt, with a Big T logo on the front, that allowed her arms the freedom to display their "sleeves" of red tattooed roses, intertwined with black spiders and maroon scorpions.

"Let me guess," smiled Chester. "You're a Scorpio?"

"Very good, Pops," she replied. "And you are a Capricorn, right?"

Chester felt a little jolt of electricity.

"How did you know that?"

"You have 'no nonsense' written all over you," Audrey continued. "You're practical, super-organized, you count all your pennies and you're here to see that your son doesn't get rooked by some wicked old tattoo artist."

"Oh, no, Miss Audrey," Arlin started to explain. "This is my granddad, and he's the one getting the tattoo."

"I'm not getting a tattoo *yet*," corrected Chester. "Contrary to my grandson's enthusiasm, I'm just sort of window-shopping."

"Well, you're welcome to look around, and I'm here to answer any of your questions."

"Thank you. Actually, I do have one to start."

"Okay," Audrey replied, stepping behind a counter filled with silver rings, chains and other appliances used to fill recent body piercings. "What do you want to know?"

"In keeping with your analysis of me being a penny-pincher—"

"Oh, I'm sorry if you felt that I—"

"No, no. You were right. I am very careful with my money, so what I need to know is, how much does a small tattoo cost?"

"Well, depending on how elaborate the design is, it can run you between fifty and a hundred bucks."

"So the big ones you see covering a large area, like your sleeves, must cost somewhere in the neighborhood of a thousand dollars?"

"Yeah, but these," Audrey said, pointing to the rose gardens growing up her arms, "were done at a large discount, by Brian—"

"It gave me," interrupted a large, middle-aged man coming down the stairs from the second floor, "a chance to practice my floral talent." His voice was as big as his torso, and it filled the room. He had a mullet of bleached-blond hair and was dressed in jeans and a hooded sweatshirt with the now-familiar Big T emblazoned on the back. A tattoo of some kind of snake climbed up the side of his neck and rested its head on his cheek. His week-old beard made the reptile look like it was lurking in a patch of grass.

"Hey, kid," the big guy barked, turning toward Arlin. "How's your tat holding up?"

"Ah, hi Brian," Arlin replied, looking like he was caught cheating in class. "Brian did my tattoo last year. Ah, Brian, this is my granddad."

"It's a pair of lips, you know, like a lipstick kiss, on the left cheek—" Brian explained as he shook Chester's hand, "—of his ass." When he saw Chester's reaction, he began to stammer. "Oh, shit! I'm—I'm—damn me and my big mouth—I'm sorry—I thought the kid might of told—I thought you knew."

"Believe it or not, Brian knows the rules," stated Audrey. "We are not allowed to publicly reveal the design of a tattoo chosen by a client. It's all about privacy, but in his enthusiasm he sometimes forgets."

"Sorry, kid. So you come by for another tat? Maybe something for—you know, like they say, 'turn the other cheek?'"

"Brian! For god's sake!" exclaimed Audrey.

Arlin hurriedly explained, "No—no, it's not for me. My grandpa is getting one this time."

"Hold on, Arlin," Chester protested. "I'm still doing my research. And I'm getting hungry. We haven't had any lunch. You must be starving. Can you folks recommend a place where we can grab a bite?"

"Well, many of the fast-food joints are closed for the winter," Audrey said.

"But I'm sure the Philly Steak place is still open, and it's close by," Brian added, taking the time to give them directions. "But we'll see ya later, okay?"

The Discussion

There weren't many other people in the restaurant enjoying the hero sandwich known as a Philly Steak, but Arlin and Chester were really into it.

"I'd forgotten how good this is," mumbled Chester, his mouth stuffed with shredded beef, green peppers, onions and cheese, "when it's made correctly!"

Arlin simply nodded.

When the meal was done and they were left sucking the last of their Diet Cokes through paper straws that were getting soggy, Chester spoke up.

"Okay, Arlin. We need to get a few things straight."

"Uh-oh. Sounds serious. I don't like it when the conversation gets serious."

"I'm sure you don't, but as your grandfather, I have a responsibility to see that you are not getting into trouble. When I agreed to your offer to help me, I was pleased that you wanted to spend time with me. It's been years since you've been able to squeeze in a visit with your old granddad. And I realize how busy you are with school and friends—"

"Pretty busy, but you're right. It's been too long."

"And you've changed. Of course you've changed. You're growing up, and I realize you've got to do your teenage rebellion thing, but this deal with a fake ID and being underage and getting a tattoo on your—posterior, this troubles me."

"It's no big deal—"

"It is to me. Now, I know it's over and it's a done deal, but—"

"Are you going to tell Dad?"

"No, of course not. That's in the past, and what good would it do to bring it up now? But I *am* concerned about the future. Are there any other things I don't know about my favorite grandson? Any surprises down the road? Alcohol?"

"Nope. I don't drink, 'cause I don't like the taste and the hangovers are no fun."

"Drugs?"

"Oh, come on, Grandpa! Do I look like a junkie?"

"Okay, all right. I'm sorry. It's just that it's such a crazy world these days. I mean, pot is legal now—not for you, yet. You're still underage, but—" Chester took a couple of dollars out of his wallet and put them on the table as a tip—"you never know."

"Thanks for lunch, Gramps. It was really good," Arlin said, hoping to change the subject. "You ready to go back?" he asked as he rose from his seat.

"Yeah. Okay, but why don't we check out the beach? We could walk back to the tattoo parlor that way."

"It's kinda cold, Grandpa, don't ya think?"

"Are we wimps?!"

"Well, no—"

"So let's go."

The Walk

There was a cold wind blowing off the ocean, but both of the O'Connor men were too proud to give in to it. They marched on over the uneven sand, rocking side to side like boats on a stormy sea. It was hard going, and finally Chester had had enough.

"Let's go over there," he wheezed, pointing to a set of wooden stairs leading up to the boardwalk. "I got to catch my breath."

As they reached the wide stair unit, Chester promptly sat down on the second step as if it were a bench.

"Don't you want to go on up," Arlin asked, "and get out of this shitty weather?"

"I just want to rest here for a minute."

Arlin began to get concerned. "Are you okay, Gramps?"

"Yeah, sure. Just a little winded, that's all."

Arlin joined Chester on the step and put his arm around the shoulder of his grandfather, who had earlier been his usual robust self. Now Chester seemed diminished, as if the wind had blown some part of him away.

"What's going on, Granddad?" Arlin asked softly. "You really need to get out of this cold."

"I know."

"Then let's go," Arlin said, starting to help Chester get up.

"Wait—wait! Just let me sit here a little longer."

"Now you are really scaring me. What's wrong, Grandpa? Tell me," pleaded Arlin, getting ready to call 911.

"Nothing's wrong. I just don't want to rush—"

"Wait a minute!" Arlin exclaimed, beginning to understand. "I get it. You're backing out. Am I right? You're not going to get the tattoo!"

"No. I—I just need to think about it for a minute. It's a big step, and—"

"Grandpa, what's bothering you? You scared of the pain of the needles?"

"No, of course not. When you get to be my age, you have to have a high tolerance for pain."

"Then what's the problem?"

After a short pause, Chester let out a deep sigh. He sat up straight and rubbed his hands together to warm them up. When he finally spoke, there was a sad edge to his voice.

"I've wanted to get this tattoo for years, but you have to understand that I grew up at a time when the only men who got tattooed were sailors, gypsies, ex-cons or Hell's Angels. The only woman I knew that had a tat was the Tattooed Lady in the circus. Of course, in reality, a lot of ordinary people had tattoos, but when I was a kid, if someone sported a tattoo, it meant to me that they were a bad person."

"But that's crazy!" Arlin interrupted. "It's not like that now."

"I know. I look around and everybody has a tattoo—movie stars, ministers, politicians, fashion models, doctors—even a certain teenager I know. It seems like these days you're a nobody if you don't have a tattoo."

"Right. So, come on. Join the parade!"

"That's not my intention. This tattoo that I've been planning for so long is not about showing off. I don't care if no one ever sees it. It's just—"

"Kinda like the one on my butt," commented Arlin. "I get it. It's private. Is it something to do with Grandma Patricia? Like a heart or a cupid with a bow and arrow?"

"No. Wherever she is, she knows how much I loved her. She doesn't need a tattoo to remind her."

"Then what is this mysterious tattoo going to be?"

"Well, I guess it's going to be nothing if I don't get off my ass," Chester declared, standing up and turning around to climb the steps.

"Are we finally off to Big T's? Hallelujah! I was turning into a popsicle!"

"But we have to make one quick stop first."

"Wait a minute! Is this another delaying technique?" Arlin asked as they reached the top of the stairs and stepped out onto the boardwalk.

"We didn't have any dessert with our lunch."

"Yeah, so what?"

"Saltwater taffy."

The Tattoo

Because the design was very simple and used no color, just black ink, the procedure took about an hour. The beauteous Audrey, working in one of the private rooms, shaved the area Chester had chosen, applied some lotion to this patch of exposed skin and, using her trusty Cheyenne Hawk electric pen, permanently etched into his flesh that which he had requested. She had offered to show him her portfolio of original designs, but he said it wasn't necessary, as he knew what he wanted.

Arlin wanted to stay with him during the process as moral support (but really because he wanted to be the first to see the mysterious design). However, before they got started, Chester sent him out into the main lobby with a book of Audrey's design samples and the box of saltwater taffy, to keep him occupied until the job was done.

After wiping the finished tattoo with alcohol and then gently massaging the area with a soothing lotion, Audrey covered it with a sheet of Saran Wrap held on with surgical tape. She gave Chester a small tote bag containing a tube of salve and a list of printed instructions.

"It should heal up in a couple of weeks. Until then, be kind to your new friend."

The Reveal

Chester was zipping up his coat when he exited the private chamber where Audrey had done her magic. Arlin leapt up and was about to hug his granddad when he stopped, for fear he'd do damage to the new artwork and maybe cause him pain.

"How'd it go? You okay? Where is it? Can I see?"

"I'm fine. I just need a drink," Chester replied, heading for the double doors leading outside.

"Wait! Wait for me!" Arlin squealed. "Aren't you going to show me the freaking tattoo?"

"Let's go find a bar at Caesars," Chester suggested. "I can get a quick drink and you can get a coffee. We need to hurry. We've got an hour and a half drive back to Trenton. I've got to get you back home so you don't get in trouble."

When they entered Caesars, Chester finally saw where all the people had been during the time he and Arlin were on the boardwalk. The hall of slot machines was packed, with buttons being pushed and lights flashing and bells dinging. Chester asked one of the employees—dressed as a centurion—where the bar was, and the man pointed to a sign. It spelled out "Toga Bar." Chester grabbed Arlin and started dragging him toward the sign, hoping no one would notice that the boy was underage. Nobody stopped them. It was as if no one noticed or cared.

In the dark blue and green lights of the lushly appointed saloon, they found a small table and sat down. Seemingly from out of nowhere, a lovely young maiden, dressed in a short, toga-like costume, stood at attention by their side.

"How may I serve you?"

Arlin had a rude suggestion flash by in his head, but he kept it to himself.

"I'll have a Jameson's on the rocks," Chester said. "He'll have a coffee."

After the vestal virgin had gone, Arlin took a breath and started in on his grandfather.

"What the hell, Grandpa! Why are you rushing around like a madman? And why wouldn't you show me your stupid tattoo? I mean, after all, I got you here, so at least you could be decent enough to share with me whatever you had Audrey draw on you." Chester remained silent, and suddenly Arlin understood.

"It's obscene! That's it. You got a dirty tattoo! Oh, you rascal, you!"

At that moment the handmaiden returned and placed the whiskey and the coffee on the table. Chester checked the bill, reluctantly paid it, and took a sip of his drink.

"I'm right, aren't I?" Arlin continued. "What is it, a nude lady, all boobs and legs?"

"Arlin, I don't like you very much right now," Chester growled, gulping down his whole drink. "Come with me." He grabbed the boy by his shoulder and pushed him toward what appeared to be the entrance to the restrooms. Choosing the door marked "Gladiators," he led him into the seafoam-green tiled bathroom and stopped in the middle of the space.

"I'm sorry, Grandpa. What's happening now? You going to spank me?" he said jokingly.

Checking that no one else was in the restroom, Chester opened his coat and began unbuttoning his shirt.

"I didn't put my undershirt back on. Audrey said it was too tight, so I stuck it in my coat pocket." By this time his shirt was fully unbuttoned, and he was pulling the shirttails out of his pants. Arlin stared as the image, protected by the plastic wrap, began to appear. Centered on his grandfather's chest was a tattoo consisting of two words:

M I A

BOBBY

After a moment of stunned silence, Arlin's voice echoed off the tiled walls. "What the fuck! Who are Mia and Bobby?"

"Arlin," Chester scolded, "your language has really deteriorated." He buttoned up his shirt and began tucking it back into his pants. "Enough with the fucks. Let's find the car and get on the road. It's getting late."

"But what's with this 'Mia Bobby' shit?"

"Language, Arlin! Come on. I'll fill you in in the car."

The Story of Bobby Legions

Robert Legions the Third was from Glenwood, Georgia, one of the poorest towns in the state. He himself, however, was not poor, having been born into the renowned Legions family, owners of the Legions Estate (formerly known as the Camellia Court Plantation) and proud members of the Sons and Daughters of the Confederacy. His father was CEO of Nexatron Electronics, a company located in Atlanta and specializing in helicopter navigational systems. It was a very successful firm, and a thousand times more profitable than raising cotton or rice, which is what Robert Legions the First struggled with during the dark years after the Civil War. Bobby the Third was expected to join his father in the business but secretly wanted to become a country singer. However, along came the Vietnam War, which brings us back to Chester O'Connor and his coming into contact with Robert (Bobby) Legions.

"Bobby arrived as a replacement for one of our squad who had been severely injured," Chester began as they passed Exit 2 on the Atlantic City Expressway. "I mean, the guy had had both his legs blown off, so he wouldn't be coming back anytime soon—"

"Wait a minute, Grandpa!" interrupted Arlin. "You fought in Iraq? No one ever told me anything about that!"

"No, Arlin, you've got the wrong war. It was a much earlier conflict known as the Vietnam War. You probably don't know anything about it. Way before your time," Chester explained as he stared out the window at the bare trees flying along by the side of the highway. "I never told anybody, except your grandmother, and I made her promise not to tell anyone, ever."

"But why?"

"Because I wanted to forget all of it. I didn't want to relive it every time someone would ask me to tell them about it. It was bad enough to have lived through it, to have these nightmares night after night—"

"I'm so sorry."

"See, that's the reaction I knew people would have. I didn't want to be a figure of pity," Chester continued. "Although now that I hear myself saying that, I realize that it must have been pretty egotistical of me to think that anyone would really care."

"So why are you telling me now? I mean, I really care and I want to hear about this, I mean I really do, but why now, and why me?"

Chester didn't reply immediately. It was as though he was deciding whether to continue on or not. After they had passed a mile or so down the highway, he began.

"I've reached the age when I may not wake up tomorrow."

"Aw, Grandpa—"

"Don't interrupt. It's just that I've been feeling lately that I need to share my war experiences with someone before I kick the bucket. There were things that happened to me, things that I did—I don't want to have to drag this fucking ton of pain and horror and guilt, which has been riding shotgun with me all these years, into whatever is waiting for me in the—what do they call it?—'the Great Beyond.' Anyway, when you offered to help me with this tattoo business, it was like a sign saying that the time had arrived and that you, as the messenger, were to be the chosen one." Chester began to chuckle. "Well, that sounds like some fucking creepy New Age nonsense."

"No, it doesn't, Grandpa. I think—"

"Okay. So let me get on with this before I chicken out. This is really more about a short, skinny kid called Bobby Legions, who I mentioned before, but let me start first with how I ended up in the fucking jungles and forests of Vietnam.

"I was drafted. Back in the olden days, every young man, when he reached the age of eighteen, was required to register for the draft. That meant you were assigned a number, and, like in a lottery, if they drew a little piece of paper out of the bottle that had the date of your birthday on it, you were the winner—or loser—depending on how you looked at it. I had just graduated high school, just turned eighteen, and BAM, I'm in the army. Believe me, you are so fucking lucky—"

"Grandpa," Arlin interrupted, "you keep at me about not using the f-word, and yet you say it all the time."

"When you reach my age, you can say it as much as you want. I have earned the right. Anyway, to continue, there I am in the army, against my will. I struggle through boot camp, get my head shaved, lose twenty pounds that I didn't have, learn how to kill people, get inoculated for diseases I never heard of, get shipped off to a country I never heard of and then, when I got there, was ordered to, quote, 'stem the tide of communism.'" Chester snorted a short, sad laugh. "Now, this 'stemming the tide' business consisted of burning, bombing and shooting anything that moved—" He stopped, and Arlin could see he was struggling. After a few minutes, he continued. "If you want to learn more—my god, there are so many movies and books and documentaries. Look it up on Google. That's what you youngsters do, right?"

Arlin nodded.

"Anyway, back to Bobby. This kid arrives, looking like a ten-year-old, but turns out he's my age. I'm only about six months older. But he's the opposite of me in so many ways. He's short, I'm tall, he's blond, I'm dark, his eyes—blue, mine—brown. He could sing like an angel and I couldn't carry a tune—still can't. But the biggest difference," Chester explained, "is that he *wanted* to be there to fight for his country, 'love it or leave it.' He had volunteered, he had enlisted, no waiting around for the draft. He had bought into the whole friggin' package—Better Dead Than Red, My Country Right or Wrong! Me, I'm ready to shoot myself in the foot to get out of this stupid, crazy, unwinnable war, to get out of this hot, wet, diseased swamp of a country. He, on the other hand, was going to win the war single-handed.

"It didn't take too long for Bobby to begin to see that this noble cause he was so willing to die for was not quite what he thought it was. He wasn't dumb, just brainwashed, and things began to bother him. Like the number of what he called 'colored' soldiers. Now remember, he was from Georgia. Evidently, the recruiting officers in the South didn't want to turn away prospective white enlistees by bringing up the race issue. He talked to me about how he was taught from an early age that the Negro was of a lower intelligence, and lazy. So what were they doing in the army?

"After being in Vietnam for about a month, he began to see that the blacks, just like us white folks, had their own hard workers as well as idle slackers, and when wounded they bled red just like he bled when he cut himself on the machete he was using to slash his way through the ever-present bamboo and vines.

"'This jungle is one mean piece of nature! And the effin' heat,' Bobby complained one hot and humid day when we were out on patrol. 'It gets hot back home, but the heat here is so heavy and wet, like a soggy sponge. You can't ever cool off. And the snakes, so many different kinds! You never know which are poisonous and which are not. Then there are the damned leeches sucking away, and don't get me started with the mosquitoes—it's like they're drilling for oil.'

"One evening, while we were trying to cool off, Bobby asked why, at this time of night, he heard so much laughter. 'We just incinerated an entire town and killed a lot of people, and now all these coloreds are singing and laughing like it was New Year's Eve. What's wrong with them?!' It was at that moment that a cloud of reefer smoke breezed by us and Bobby got his answer. 'Is that marijuana? Oh, my lord, they're smoking weed!'"

"Did you smoke pot, Grandpa?" Arlin interrupted, "while you were in Vietnam?"

"You bet your ass I did! There came a time when the insanity of it all was just too much and you had to medicate yourself to get through the day—and the night. And there were hard drugs as well. When the army eventually clamped down on cannabis use by burning up the local marijuana fields, we moved on to the cocaine and LSD that was smuggled in from Cambodia.

"And don't forget, the government was guilty of pushing pills as well. They gave us amphetamines to keep us full of energy and hyper-alert. You took one of those babies and you felt like you were a god. You knew nothing could stop you, that there wasn't a bullet manufactured that could kill you. Then they issued sedatives to bring you down, back to earth, and to help you sleep."

"Wow, but after you guys got back to the States," Arlin declared, "there must have been an epidemic-sized problem with drug addiction."

"You'd think so, but I read somewhere that only one percent of the returning soldiers were addicted to drugs."

"That doesn't sound right."

"I know, but my theory is that we used drugs intermittently for medicinal purposes, to help us survive being trapped in a tropical war zone. Once we got back home we didn't need them, although sometimes I found myself in a situation where I could have used a little chemical help. Anyway, Bobby discovered the magic of marijuana and codeine and medicated himself almost to the point of unconsciousness. If someone brought beer back from Japan, he was first in line—anything to dull the pain."

"Why are we here, Ches?" Bobby asked me one day. "Why are we really here?"

"You mean, like, what is the meaning of life? Why were we born?"

"No, you fucking New Jersey wise guy, I mean the real reason we've invaded this country and are busy shooting its citizens!" He took another toke of a very fat joint and lay back on his cot. "And don't tell me it's to keep these gooks from taking over the world. They're too busy trying to save their own country."

"Somebody was talking about that the other day," I told him, "and they said the reason we're here is about the minerals, like copper and zinc—billions of dollars' worth of natural resources that the U.S. doesn't want to give up access to. I don't know if that's true, but I wouldn't be surprised."

"Well, I know for sure my daddy's getting rich making helicopter intestines," Bobby snarled, "and the old men running the ammo companies must be dancing with joy. This war is making millionaires out of a lot of useless old men. Meanwhile, here we are trying to push the Viet Cong back north and they're busy pushing us south. It's like a tug of war, but without the rope—and nobody's winning."

"As the months ground on, Bobby continued to become more and more disillusioned about his situation. He had thought he was joining a noble cause, a heroic adventure to save the world from the crimson tide of communism. His great-grandfather had fought in the Civil War, his grandfather in World War I, his father in World War II and then in Korea.

And here he was stuck in a cesspool of a war that made no sense to him. I think he was being torn apart with the guilt of failing to be a hero and of fast becoming a pacifist. And then it happened."

"What happened?" Arlin asked as they approached the turnoff to 206 North.

"We were doing some recon just outside of Pleiku, three of us, Bobby, me and José Garcia, a Spanish kid from Texas. We're heading north on this narrow dirt path when we see this skinny kid up ahead of us, maybe nine or ten, and he's holding a puppy skinnier than him. Bobby and I stop, as we've been trained to do, but José, for reasons I will never understand, begins jogging up to the kid. I start shouting at him to stop, but it's too late. There's a flash, a deafening boom and a cloud of smoke, and as it clears, it's like a fucking magic trick—all three of them are gone, the boy, the dog and José. Bobby and I have been thrown to the ground, and as I get up, I see Bobby lying on his back and there is a small thin arm resting, by itself, on his chest, kind of like it was seeking the comfort of a hug. Bobby takes one look and he starts screaming."

"Oh, my god!" Arlin gasped. "Did this Garcia guy step on a mine or something?"

"We found evidence of dynamite among the blood and bones, and we figured there were sticks of the stuff strapped to the kid and wired to go off, if and when someone showed up."

"Shit! They turned him into a bomb!"

"And the puppy he had in front of his chest masked the device."

*

"Now, all of us had seen patrols go out and return minus a couple of their men. Usually, the wounded and the dead were picked up by our helicopters, god bless those guys, so we didn't always see the aftermath of a skirmish. Sometimes a squad would return with a friend all shot up but still alive, and that was enough to make you want to curse God forever. But after a while we grew so numb—at least I know I did—that it became just another day. Now, Bobby, on the other hand, was so sensitive that any loud sound would set him off. He tried to put up a brave front, but more and more he withdrew into a—jeez, I don't know. He just became like a robot. He followed orders, went on missions, ate very little, slept fitfully and no longer sang his favorite Glen Campbell songs."

"So what happened to him?" Arlin asked as they passed one of the few farmhouses that still dotted Route 206.

"I murdered him," Chester replied with a sigh.

"What?!"

"One morning I found him sitting in the bushes behind the latrine. He was quietly weeping, and his nose was running and his cheeks were all wet and shiny.

"What's the matter, Bobby?" I asked, even though I pretty much knew what the problem was. He took a minute or so to pull himself together, and then it all spilled out.

"I can't, Ches, I can't do this anymore."

"I know, Buddy."

"I smell like dog poop. You do too. Our uniforms never dry out. My socks are like two refugees from a septic tank. I've got this nasty fungus growing between my toes, and I haven't stopped sweating since I arrived on the shores of this—this—"

"God-forsaken country?" I said, finishing Bobby's sentence.

"Yes, and my rucksack makes me feel like I'm carrying a hippopotamus on my back, and then there is the occasional missile hitting the camp and the blood and the yelling for a medic and then getting to know and like someone only to have them—have them destroyed before your very eyes. And that little boy—and his dog!"

"Yeah, I know. None of this makes sense. It's all wrong and evil and terrifying, but we are stuck here and we got to find a way to survive without going bonkers."

"I can't, Ches, I'm already going crazy. I just can't do it."

"You can," I assured him as I put my arm around his shoulder. "You've got me, whether you like it or not, and we're going to just take it one day at a time. It'll be fine."

"What if something happens to you?" Bobby asked, with a new round of tears starting to make tracks down his dirty cheeks.

"Nothing is going to happen to me. I stink too much for a bullet to get anywhere near me."

This got a little smile out of Bobby. "Now, listen. We're due for a leave in a couple of weeks, so when we get to Japan we'll paint the town red—eat, drink and be very merry! Right?"

"A bathtub," Bobby whispered, "and a real bed."

"Yeah, and maybe someone pretty in the bed with you." Bobby frowned and shook his head. Right, I thought, good Southern Baptist boy saving himself for marriage. "So what would you like to do special while we're there?"

He thought for a moment and then, wiping his face—which meant just smearing the tear-infused mud around—he spoke. "I want to find a place to sing karaoke and I want to get a tattoo."

"Aha," interjected Arlin. "The tattoo! So did he get a tattoo?"

"Yep. And he wanted me to get one as well."

"But you didn't."

"Right. And I've regretted that decision my entire life."

"Really? Why? What was his tattoo like?"

"It was the universal peace symbol. You know, the anti-war circle with what we jokingly called the chicken foot in the center. And written underneath it was:

PATRIOT FOR PEACE

"It was centered on his chest, and as long as it was hidden underneath his shirt, he was okay. But of course his fatigues had to come off eventually, and when they did, all hell broke loose. The gung-hos were furious. Here they were, sacrificing life and limb for their country, and this Georgia peacenik had infiltrated the troops. I had quite a job just keeping Bobby safe and seeing that he wasn't beaten to a bloody pulp.

"However, that being said, some of the other guys were secretly impressed with this little pipsqueak who was brave enough to permanently imprint on his body how he felt, and to imprint what many of them felt as well. It wasn't just a sneaky little tat on the inside of his arm or on one of his butt cheeks, but emblazoned across his chest like some superhero's logo.

"One person, however, was not impressed. Sergeant Fuller was so infuriated he was ready to have Bobby court-martialed. He sent him off to the brig for a couple of days while he worked out what to do with him. After consulting the higher-ups, he had him released with the strict order that he must never uncover his chest and that a schedule would be worked out for him to shower alone, privately. Of course, that only made it more tantalizing, and many of the soldiers asked to have a look at the famous forbidden tattoo. When Bobby was soaping up, and you could hear him singing 'Make the World Go Away,' you could bet someone was catching a secret peek."

"So then things improved for Bobby," Arlin declared. "He kind of became a hero, right?"

"For a while," Chester explained, "but his stand against the war didn't stop it from continuing. It only accelerated, and the shelling of our camps increased. It was hard to sleep at night wondering if the next missile would have your initials on it. Bobby became a nervous wreck. He was sure the two of us would never survive. He would actually become physically ill when he knew we were going out on a mission where we would be killing someone.

"It got to the point that I was ready to get him out of the war by telling the CO that Bobby was mentally ill. And then we were all ordered to join a big offensive march to the North. Bobby was refusing to go, and I understood, but I knew he'd be shot or beaten to death if he stayed behind, and I wouldn't be around to protect him."

"What did you do?" Arlin asked as they drove under the New Jersey Turnpike overpass.

"I grabbed him by the strap of his rucksack and dragged him out of our tent to join up with our platoon. I figured if he was with me, he'd be moderately safe. What a mistake that was."

"What do you mean?"

"Somehow he and I got separated from our squad, which was not too difficult considering how dense and overgrown the forest was. The canopy of limbs and leaves cut out a lot of the sunlight, and the maze-like walls of bamboo led us in circles. The banyan trees looked like they could reach out and strangle you, and they were a favorite hangout for pythons. We sweated our way slowly through these green tunnels of foliage, listening for any sound coming from the rest of our unit, but of course they were keeping quiet so as not to alert the enemy. We were also listening and looking for signs of the VC.

"About an hour and a half later, we were deep inside this tropical steam bath when a bullet sizzled by my ear. We dropped down into the tall ground cover to avoid the barrage of bullets that followed. The shots were coming from high up in one of the giant mangrove trees. The Charlie could climb the sides of those huge babies in a flash and sit up there in the branches and never be seen until it was too late. I told Bobby not to move, and we waited until it finally became quiet. I was hoping the sniper would think he got us, and when he came down from the tree to check things out, we would let him have it."

"Jesus!" Arlin sputtered. "Did he? How long were you stuck there? How did you get away?"

"We crawled on our bellies toward the wide stump of a dead mangrove and hid behind it, but our shooter never came down, and after a while Bobby took off his helmet and slipped out of his rucksack. I asked him what the hell he was doing, but he just stood up and started singing.

"Now, a week earlier the Armed Forces Network had started playing John Denver's big new hit 'Country Roads,' and Bobby fell madly in love with it. He sang it and hummed it and whistled it day in and day out. You know how the song talks about longing to return—"

"I don't think I've ever heard that song," interrupted Arlin.

"Oh, my god! You've got to be kidding," Chester replied. "Well, when you get home, look it up on Google or whatever. Anyway, to finish the saga of me and Bobby Legions: he stood up, started singing, and I was sure he was going to get his head blown off. I think the sniper must have been so stunned at seeing this towheaded 'Hoa Ky' standing up and starting to sing that he held off shooting him. I tried to shut Bobby up and I grabbed for his legs, but he turned and started running. He's singing at the top of his lungs and the bullets start up again, but he dives into the bushes and darts back and forth. He's pulling vines out of his way and stumbling over logs and weaving in and out between clumps of bamboo. I need to go after him, but if I stand up I'll be a perfect target, so instead I turn and, spotting Charlie's gun spitting fire, I aim at the flame high up in the tree and pull the trigger. It was like in one of those cheesy westerns where the good guy shoots the bad guy and he falls off the balcony (cliff, roof, tower, whatever) and lands, off-camera, on an inflatable mattress. Only in this case, there was no mattress.

"Before he even hit the ground, I was up and sprinting after Bobby. I headed to where I saw him last, but of course he wasn't there. The good thing, however, was that I could hear his singing and I could follow that. I kept battling my way through the tangles of snake-like vines and thorny bushes, stopping only to try and pinpoint the sound of his voice. I prayed that the Viet Cong wouldn't kill us both before I could find Bobby and shut him up.

"It seemed like hours had gone by before I realized that the singing was fading into the distance. I was losing him, and sure enough, the song died away completely. I stopped and stood there, exhausted and miserable, and began to cry. I knew it was over. I would never see him alive again."

Arlin's car was entering the outskirts of Trenton as Chester sat in quiet sadness. "What happened to him, Grandpa? Don't leave me hanging!"

Chester took a moment to run his hand across his face, and then he continued. "We never found him, dead or alive, and I tried—oh, how I tried! I didn't know if he was killed and buried or if he was captured and imprisoned. I even fantasized that he got to the sea and caught a boat and made it to Manila and then to California, but that would have meant that there was a trail to follow.

"The irony of all this is that if Bobby could have lasted just one more year, he, along with the rest of us, would have been sent home, because the U.S. officially pulled out of the war. That was in 1972. One lousy year was all he had needed to endure.

"I stayed on until 1973 in order to keep searching for the Singing Southerner, the silly title I gave him to keep my hopes up. I bugged every agency involved in searching for missing personnel. I wandered around from village to village, even pushed through some of the jungle, even though the battle was still being fought between the North and South.

"After I got back to the States, I still spent many years maintaining a long-distance search, hoping to find a clue as to what happened to Bobby Legions. I know it's stupid, but I've never given up hope—not that he'll come waltzing through the door someday, but maybe that his remains will be finally found."

"Grandpa, you shocked me when you said you murdered him. But you didn't."

"But I did. I—I should have gotten him help, got him out of that—that useless war. He didn't belong there. None of us should have been there, but—he was—too fragile. No, I have to accept the role I played," Chester argued, struggling to finish his sentence, "in the destruction of Bobby." He turned away from Arlin as tears began to blur his vision. Arlin watched his grandfather weep and tried to remember if he had ever seen him cry before. Even at Great-Grandma Irene's funeral he hadn't wept.

"It's okay, Gramps," Arlin said softly as they pulled up in front of Chester's brown and white bungalow. "You were caught in the same trap he was. You did the best you could. So forgive yourself."

"Thanks, kid. I'm working on it. And thanks for helping me today and for listening to this old man's whining," Chester uttered as he wiped his eyes and gave Arlin a hug.

"It was an honor. But there's one thing I don't understand."

"What's that?"

"Who's Mia? That other name tattooed on your chest. Was she a girl Bobby hooked up with in Vietnam?"

"Oh, my boy, you've got a lot of learning to catch up on. MIA is not a girl, it's the initials for the words Missing In Action. When the war was over, there were about two thousand American men, and women, missing. Of that number, only about 750 have ever been identified and their remains returned to their families. Those not found are labeled MIAs. Bobby is one of those. So, to honor him and to make up for not getting a tattoo when I should have—when Bobby wanted me to—I finally got brave enough, thanks to you, to write on my flesh a memory of a someone who got lost and was never found. Jeez, that sounds so fucking dramatic! It's very simple. I liked the little guy a lot, and he deserves not to be forgotten."

"Well, I'll never forget," Arlin said, looking at his iPhone. "Geez, it's getting late. Dad has started texting me. I got to go. Sorry, Grandpa."

"It's okay," Chester replied, climbing out of the car. "You scoot on home. And remember, today was our secret. 'Loose lips sink ships.'"

"Never fear. Silence here," Arlin responded as he mimed zipping his lip.

"Very quick, Mr. O'Connor," Chester said, congratulating his grandson. Arlin waved as he drove away, and Chester turned and climbed slowly up the steps. He could hear Max barking a greeting. He felt heavy, but lighter at the same time.

*

Sean and Arlin finished up dinner and cleared the table. All through the meal, Arlin had to fight the urge to tell his dad about Chester's tattoo and the tragic tale of Bobby Legions. His left hand was sore from having clenched it until his fingernails left four indentations in his palm. As he was drying the plate that his father, who was on dishwashing duty that evening, had handed him, he asked, "Granddad served in the military, right?"

"Yeah."

"Where?"

"In Vietnam, I think. At least that's what your grandmother told me. A long time ago. I asked him about it once, but he just brushed it off. Said it wasn't worth talking about. Why the sudden interest?"

"Eh, nothing. I just was reading about it in history class."

*

Around ten o'clock that evening, Arlin excused himself from the next *NCIS* episode that was about to light up good old CBS. "I have a test tomorrow."

"Wow. Studying for a test. That's a first."

"Thanks for the sarcasm, Dad. Good night."

Arlin turned on his computer and called up Google. He typed in "Bob Denver" and was confused when up came a picture and a bio for an actor from *Gilligan's Island.* "I guess that's the wrong Denver." He then punched in "Denver—Country Roads" and was rewarded with pages of info about— "John Denver, that's the dude's name!" He clicked on the video icon and the music began.

Country roads, take me home
To the place I belong
West Virginia, mountain mama
Take me home, country roads.

Arlin played the song several times and then, feeling tired after such a momentous day, climbed into bed. "I hope you made it home, Bobby," he whispered as he drifted off to sleep.

Alibi

If you are reading this, then I am dead, passed away, crossed over, moved on, bought the farm, kicked the bucket, whatever. I wasn't sure I could live with what I've done, but guess what, I found I could. I knew, however, that I couldn't die without letting the world know what I did. So this here is my confession. However, let it be known that this is not your standard confession. It's not because I feel guilty or because I fear God's judgement. Contrary to popular belief, there is no God, and no heaven or hell, and if after reading this, you still think I'm guilty, well, that's your problem. This is simply a listing of the facts, and I humbly lay them out in order to get the story straight.

*

You want to know hell, then let me tell you this: living with my husband was pure hell. Howard Estes McCabe was a monster straight out of a Stephen King novel.

The Shining could have been his bible. Not that he was crazy or possessed. He was just mean, mean to the very bone. I didn't know this when I married him. He was very handsome, in a rough sort of way, and when he was sober he could be very charming—in a snake-charmer sort of way.

Like most men when they're in the courting stage, he was sweet as sugar, but boy, once we were united in matrimony, the mask was dropped and the true Howie McCabe appeared. He was a lazy, skirt-chasing, narrow-minded son-of-a-bitch who enjoyed beating up on women, primarily me. Being the sad little wimp that I was then (I was seventeen and totally innocent), I thought that his cruel behavior was because I was not a good wife. I truly believed that I needed to be whipped into shape, and whipped I was. He would slap me if his eggs were overdone. He would hit me if his favorite shirt was still in the laundry. He would beat me if, after a long day at my job clerking at Piggly Wiggly, I told him I was too tired for sex. But I stayed with him because he could be loving, in between the beatings.

Okay, I know what you all are thinking: why did I stick it out, why did I put up with the abuse, why didn't I leave him? Well, first of all, I was uneducated. I dropped out of high school at sixteen. Secondly, I came from a household in which physical and verbal abuse was the norm, so, early on, it just seemed natural to me. And after a while I just became numb.

What I had—a husband, a roof over my head, food and clothing—it seemed enough. That the husband drank too much, that the roof was attached to a run-down, single-wide trailer, that the food was paid for with my salary from the supermarket and that my clothes came from the Goodwill was unimportant. I felt safe. I know, crazy, but I didn't think I could survive on my own.

I continued to live this way until my forty-first birthday. Shocking, right? Like I said, I had lost all feelings for everything—for Howie, for the future, for life. However, I did like to read. That was my escape, that and TV, and I began seeing these articles and programs about Women's Lib and about battered women and how they would end up murdered by their husbands. And I began to get really scared.

Now, as I was saying, it was my birthday and, as usual, Howie didn't remember. We never had any kids, which I guess was a mercy, and the rest of my family couldn't have cared less, so my birthday was just another day slipping into another month sliding into another year of the same old shit. On this particular day, however, I decided to bake myself a cake. It was the first time in all those years that I would have birthday cake to celebrate my entrance into this world of misery and woe.

Howie came home from a day at the Alibi Bar and Grill, his favorite hangout, and noticed the slightly lopsided chocolate cake with little green candles sitting on the small fold-down kitchen table.

"What the fuck is that?" he asked, collapsing on the built-in sofa.

"A birthday cake," I replied, stirring the gravy for his chicken-fried steak.

"Whose birthday?" he slurred. "It sure ain't mine."

"Mine," I answered, pouring the gravy over the meat and the mashed potatoes.

"Really? It's today? I thought you was born in October."

"Nope. I am a spring baby." I put his plate on the little Formica table.

"Well, happy birthday. I'll drink to that." And he pulled out the pint of Jim Beam he always kept in his jeans-jacket pocket.

There was too much liquor in my house when I was growing up, so I developed a real dislike for the stuff. I guess I'm lucky that I never turned to booze or drugs to try and escape the life I was stuck in, like so many of the folks that lived around us. I'll puff on a cigarette once in a while, but they are way too expensive to make a habit of. Howie offered me a slug from his bottle, but, as usual, I refused.

"You too good to drink with me, missy?" he taunted. I chose to ignore him.

"I'm going to get me a birthday present," I announced. "I'm getting me a puppy dog."

You would have thought I'd said I was going to buy a jet airplane and fly to Paris. He reached across the table and grabbed my wrist, twisting it till it hurt.

"What the hell you thinking? You know I am allergic to dogs! We've talked about this a hunnert times! No way are you bringing no mangy animal into this here trailer!"

What he was yelling about was the truth. He *was* allergic. He had an allergy to animal dander, the tiny flakes found in the fur of animals, particularly dogs and cats. He would start coughing, his eyes would water, then his face would swell up, his throat would close and it would be ER time. I had seen it happen a couple of times, and it wasn't a pretty sight.

"There are breeds that are hypo-allergenic. Or you can take those antihistamine pills. You'll be fine," I offered.

"I ain't taking no mother-fucking pills for the rest of my life!" And with that he hit me in the face, hard enough to break my nose. Suddenly there was blood everywhere, on my blouse, the table, the salad. There were red dots on Howie's hands. For a brief moment, even Howie looked shocked.

"Sorry, babe, but no dog, no way!"

*

You know how sometimes in your life you have one of those "light bulb" moments. There I sat, in a ramshackle trailer, facing an alcoholic husband, with blood dripping down the front of my blouse. I should have been in great pain, but I felt nothing, nothing but rage, burning—hot— rage. That's when I made the decision that would change my life.

I apologize for spending all this time writing about my life with Howard, but I felt it was important for me to explain how I got to the moment when I decided to kill him. You can't keep twenty-odd years of unrelieved anger bottled up inside. It's only natural that something has gotta give. The bloody broken nose was the straw that broke the camel's back. So from then on, I spent many hours every day making plans on how I would remove Howie from my life, remove him from this world, forever.

There are many abused women in prison who are there because they murdered their husbands. I was determined to never become one of them. I may have been uneducated, but I was not stupid. There had to be a way to kill Howie that didn't involve a gun, a knife or some poison. An accident or a death by natural causes would be the best. It is said that poison is the number one choice of women for committing a murder, but I know that scientists can find evidence of poison in the blood of the victim. Guns leave soot on the hands and clothes of the shooter, and how can a person be knifed by accident? "Oh, yes, Your Honor. The victim fell on his knife by accident. He fell on it ten times." And so I took my time figuring out the perfect way to eliminate Howard without incriminating myself. After two months, I came up with what I believed was the perfect murder. It was so simple.

I began by buying an old cage used for trapping small animals, like raccoons, squirrels or woodchucks. I came across it in the Goodwill when I was looking for some Levi's to replace my old threadbare jeans. It was the kind of trap that didn't kill the animal, just caged it. It was priced dirt cheap, and I felt it was a sign that I was on the right track. I had been thinking of purchasing a similar one at Andy's Hardware Emporium, but I knew that that transaction could then be traced back to me. Not a good idea.

On my day off, a Wednesday in June, while Howie was down at the Alibi, I pulled the cage out from where I had stored it under the trailer. It was folded flat and fit neatly in the back of my Ford Pinto. Most of my near neighbors in the trailer park were at work, so I was pretty sure no one saw me load up the cage and drive away. Old Mr. Stevens was sitting in his lawn chair in front of his faded pink double-wide and waved to me as I passed by. He was used to seeing me drive off to work, so I was sure it would be just like any other day to him.

There is a stretch of woods that runs along the Tar River, which is about five miles outside of town. It is also close to the town garbage dump. I got off the highway and rumbled down a graveled road to the public boat landing on the edge of the river. Checking to make sure no one was around, I unloaded the cage and carried it deep into the woods. I kept walking until I found a small clearing within sight of the town dump, and there I unfolded the cage and set it up. I rigged the door to close when something went inside to eat the bait. To entice the prey to enter the trap, I emptied a small Tupperware container full of tuna fish in the far corner. And the prey?

Several years ago our town was overrun with cats, feral cats. They were everywhere. The mayor was being bombarded with complaints, so he sought the services of Animal Control. At first they laid out poisoned cat food, but that was soon stopped because of the threat to people's pets and little children. Then they used chemicals that would render the tomcats sterile. That began to cut back on the number of kittens being born, but it was a slow process. So someone had the brilliant idea to transport as many cats as they could catch to the area around the town garbage dump. There they would have a source of food and some shelter, and it was more humane than killing them. Hopefully, they would be too far from town to wander back.

So traps were set, nets went flying, and the cats were rounded up and sent north to the dump. It did cut back on the feline population, and everyone began to breathe a sigh of relief. Which brings me back to Howard and his breathing.

My plan, as you have probably already guessed, was to force Howie into an allergic attack by exposing him to cat dander. His reaction to the presence of a cat was even worse than that of a dog. If he sat in a soft chair that a cat had slept in, he would begin to cough, a signal to get up and get out of that room. He used to frequent Sally's Saloon until the proprietor brought in a mouser to keep the rodent population under control. Fifteen minutes after he walked in, he had an attack. This was what I was banking on happening when I set up my trap.

Speaking of that trap, as with all plans, Murphy's Law took effect on my return visit to the cage. I could smell the problem a mile away. Sure enough, there was a very angry polecat thrashing around behind the closed door of the trap. Covering my nose and mouth with a scarf, I slid open the exit door and stood back. The skunk hesitated for a moment and then took off like a rocket (without spraying me, thank heavens) and disappeared into the undergrowth.

Now I had to drag the cage down to the river and give it a wash, in the hopes that the smell wouldn't turn my real prey away. After returning to the clearing, I reset the trap and, having brought more tuna, placed the fresh bait in the cage. I crossed my fingers that next time I would be more successful.

I was underneath our trailer implementing the next phase of the plan when I saw two legs standing near where I was working. I recognized the dirty blue sneakers as those of Mr. Stevens.

"Whatcha doin' under there, Mrs. McCabe? You got yourself a problem?"

"Ah—well—just making some minor repairs. Our poor ol' trailer is falling apart," I replied.

"Kinda like me," he responded with a soft chuckle. "I'd get down there and help ya if my knees would cooperate, but—"

"I know, Mr. Stevens, and I thank you for the thought. But I've got it under control."

"Well, okay then. Just holler if you get stuck." And with that he toddled away.

I began breathing again, and after a minute or two, I resumed my task. I was scraping away at the wooden under-structure of the trailer with one of my kitchen knives. The wood was already soft with rot, so my goal was to break through the bedroom floor with some very narrow grooves that would appear to be just wear and tear on our poor ol' trailer. I had considered drilling holes, but that would be an obvious giveaway. I just hoped that Mr. Stevens was the forgetful type and that he wouldn't remember me lying under our mobile home making scraping noises.

When I checked on the cage the next time, bingo! Not just one cat but two, a scrawny calico and a black beauty that seemed to indicate to me that bad luck was heading either my way or Howie's. Hopefully, just Howie's.

I had brought more tuna (I should have bought stock in Chicken of the Sea) and a dish for water, which I slipped into the cage. It was important that I moved this project along, as I couldn't leave my two co-conspirators there much longer in case some hiker came along and discovered the cage. I decided that the next night was to be the evening of Howard's demise.

As I'm writing this, I'm beginning to see how cold-blooded all this must seem, but then I remind myself of what I'd been through with Howie and his women and his booze and his beatings. I know now it probably would have been better to just leave him. After all, that's what ended up happening; I made him go away and I was alone. But I realize I wanted revenge. I wanted payback, big-time.

Bringing Sally and Alibi (I had named the cats after Howie's favorite watering holes) back to the trailer camp was a bit tricky, but luck was with me. The lights were out in Mr. Stevens's faded pink double-wide and there was a very noisy party going on down by the Lombardis' place, so I got the cage out of the car and squeezed it under our trailer without a problem. With my heart jumping around in my chest, I climbed up the steps into what was to become the exterminating chamber.

*

It is very hard to kill someone. I'm sure you've heard all those stories about how the victim resisted and struggled to survive and what it took to bring him down. Like that Russian guy who was a favorite of the Tsar's wife and they wanted to kill him, so they poisoned him but it didn't work, so they shot him but he still didn't die. They choked him and hit him on the head, but he just wouldn't lie down and die. I think they finally drowned him, and that did the trick.

With Howard, it was a series of unplanned interruptions that almost ruined my perfect crime. First of all, getting him to bed was becoming impossible. For some reason, on this particular evening he was almost sober and wide awake. He was watching a sporting event on the TV, pro wrestling as I remember, and he was really into it. I kept refilling his glass with whiskey in the hopes that it would make him sleepy. It took two full hours and an untold number of shots of his favorite whiskey to finally bring on a yawn or two. The man sure could hold his booze.

Then there were the cats. From under the floor came the unhappy wails of Alibi and Sally. They were not happy about being incarcerated in a metal cage with no way out, and they were letting the world know their feelings.

"What the hell is that there noise?" Howie yelled, getting ready to stand up and investigate. "It sounds like it's comin' from right inside the toilet!"

"No, no, honey," I replied in a panic. "I think the Lombardis are having one of their wild parties. You know how loud they get." I watched as

Howie headed for the door to the toilet. While he was busy looking for the source of the noise, I turned up the volume on the television. When I looked back at him, he was on his knees with his head in the toilet bowl. However, he was not listening for mysterious sounds. Instead, he was vomiting.

After cleaning him up, I steered him into the bedroom, helped him undress and tucked him in. Within minutes he was off in dreamland, either fast asleep or passed out. It didn't matter to me as to which one it was, as long as he kept breathing. It was important that he inhaled the dander-rich air that was wafting up through the cracks in the floor. I pulled the folding door shut that separated the bedroom from the rest of the trailer and sat down. I was rigid with an adrenaline rush and very, very frightened. Five long minutes passed. This was it, the moment when my plan would either work or—

I heard a murmuring sound, but with the TV and the cats, I wasn't sure if it was coming from the bedroom. I turned off the television and listened carefully, and I could tell it was Howard. He was mumbling my name. Then the sound increased, and it turned into a non-verbal gasp and a gurgle. I stood up and faced the door, torn between looking into the room or running for the hills and never coming back. The sounds became louder and louder, and then suddenly the folding door slid open and Howie was there, only inches from my face. His eyes were beginning to swell shut and there were red patches on his neck and face. His mouth was opening and closing like a fish caught on a hook, and he was making these awful choking sounds. At that moment, if I had had an EpiPen, I would have injected him and saved his miserable life, but then he reached out and put his hands around my throat. I felt him begin to squeeze, and it took all my strength to push him backwards until we fell onto the bed. I was on top of him and trying to pull his hands away from my neck when he began to weaken and his arms dropped away. His breathing became a series of hiccups and then it quit. I sat up on the bed and tried to stop shaking. The deed was done.

After making sure Howie was no longer with us, I moved quickly to the next step, the disposal of the cage and the cats, which was a bit tricky. Actually, setting the cats free was easy. I simply opened the cage door and they vanished into the night. However, the cage itself was more of a challenge. There was the time element involved. I had to drive the five miles to the dump and five miles back without being seen, and I needed to be back home to call the EMS or the police before Howie's body got too cold. It was about two-thirty in the morning when I got to the dump, so no one was there. I tossed the cage onto a pile of rusty pipes and broken shelves and hurried back to my car.

The trip back was uneventful until I drove into the trailer park. Just as I rounded the curve leading to our place, a light went on in Mr. Stevens's double-wide. I almost slammed on the brakes, which would have been a big mistake, but I kept on going until I reached our trailer. I leapt out of my Pinto and started to head for the public phone located in front of the manager's cottage in the middle of the camp. This was because we didn't have our own phone, due to monetary difficulties. It was then I had another "light bulb" moment. I stopped, turned around and headed back towards Mr. Stevens's trailer.

"Mr. Stevens! Mr. Stevens!" I shouted as I beat on his screen door. "It's Jo Anne! Please, I need help!" After a few seconds the front door opened, and through the battered screen door I could see Mr. Stevens standing in his boxers and wearing a sleeveless tee shirt.

"Mrs. McCabe, darlin', what's wrong?" he asked, wiping the sleep from his eyes.

"It's Howard! He's in a bad way. I can't wake him!"

"What happened?"

"I don't know, I don't know! He looks awful!"

"Well, just wait a minute while I pull on some pants." And he turned back into his living room.

We hurried across the street towards our trailer, although hurrying for Mr. Stevens was more of a tilted shuffle.

"I had to git up to pee and I thought I heard a car. Was that you?" he asked.

"Yeah. Howie was in one of his moods, you know how he gets when he goes on a bender, so I just had to get away for a while," I said, and it was kind of the truth.

"Yep, I know, I seen him be kinda crazy. It was smart of you to leave him alone. Let him sleep it off."

I stopped at the steps up to our door and let Mr. Stevens climb in ahead of me. He looked around at our shabby furnishings and asked where Howie was.

"He's in there," I replied, pointing to the bedroom door, "on the bed. I don't think he's breathing."

Mr. Stevens's reaction to the condition of Howard's body was immediate and intense. "Holy shit! He's a mess! He looks like he's bin drinkin' turpentine!" He reluctantly touched Howie's neck. "You're right, darlin'. He's not breathing. I'm so sorry."

Since Mr. Stevens had a telephone, I asked him to call the police, which he very kindly did. They came, I cried, they investigated. I wept, they took the body away. I sobbed, and then I was alone. I waited for them to return and haul me off to the sheriff's office as the murderous widow, but it never happened.

*

Anaphylaxis is the technical term for what killed Howard Estes McCabe. His heart gave out from the stress. That's what the coroner and the doctor determined was the cause of death. They figured he must have come across something that set him off, animal dander that transferred to his skin or clothes from something or someone he rubbed up against. I mentioned that he had spent most of the day at the Alibi Bar and that they might have a cat. The police asked a lot of questions, but they didn't seem too concerned about the demise of a trailer-park alcoholic or about the fate of his grieving widow. I cried very effectively, but it was from relief, not despair.

I buried Howie without a tombstone as I couldn't afford one, and even if I could have, I felt that a little metal tag was sufficient. He didn't deserve anything better. Yeah, you're right, I was a bitter, vengeful woman. So live with it. I have.

It's been five years since I got rid of Howard, and there have been a lot of changes in my life, all of them good. I got my GED and enrolled in night school at Foxboro Community College. I'm majoring in economics. Piggly Wiggly promoted me to produce manager for being such a faithful and hard-working employee, at a much better salary. And I got a dog, a Golden Retriever, whom I named Alibi.

So there it is. I'm giving this envelope to Reverend Sharp to put in the church safe, with instructions for it to be opened only upon my death. I apologize again for the length of this document, but I wanted it to be as complete as possible. As the saying goes, "God is in the details." I do *not* apologize, however, for having murdered my husband.

Jo Anne McCabe, nee Barden

*

The Asheville Citizen-Times:

Woman Arrested for Murder

Crime Committed 25 Years Ago;
Signed Confession Discovered

Due to a mix-up at a local church, Foxboro native Josephine Anne McCabe was put under arrest yesterday, accused in the murder of her husband, Howard Estes McCabe.

The crime, which occurred more than two decades ago, was revealed in a confession, signed by Ms. McCabe, that was mistakenly opened by a lawyer for the family of Joan Ann McCabe, 95, recently deceased.

The alleged confession was in an envelope that the accused, Ms. McCabe, had entrusted to the former pastor, John Sharp, deceased, of the Bethel Baptist Church, with instructions that it be opened only upon her death. Pastor Sharp was succeeded by several new preachers who were not acquainted with Ms. McCabe, especially since she no longer attended services. The latest pastor, Howard Brownlee, who had officiated at the funeral of Mrs. Joan Ann McCabe, found an envelope in the church safe marked "Do not open until my death. J. A. McCabe." Believing it to be signed by the recently deceased, and important to the McCabe family, he turned it over to their lawyer.

In an ironic twist, it turns out that the deceased, Joan Ann McCabe, was the paternal grandmother of the murder victim, Howard McCabe, husband of the accused Jo Anne McCabe.

In a press conference today, the court-appointed lawyer for the accused, Chauncy Brown, said that the document containing the confession was illegally obtained and was therefore invalid. "It should not and cannot be used as evidence against my client," Mr. Brown emphasized.

Quarantine

The Centers for Disease Control and Prevention called it the Coxsackie virus. The public called it the Peru Flu, because that's where the first cases were reported. Kevin Singer, a thirteen-year-old who contracted the disease, called it the cocksucking virus, much to the dismay of his parents. The Coxsackie virus usually only attacked children, but this strain seemed to be an equal-opportunity disease. As it spread north, the number of victims of all ages increased.

The symptoms were the usual high fever and joint pain, but with the addition of a nasty rash. Kevin came home after school to the Singer household scratching a red patch on the left side of his neck. A call to the family doctor confirmed that it was probably Coxsackie and that Kevin should just rest and drink lots of fluids. Kevin's mom, Natalie, asked if the doctor could give them a prescription to fight the infection. He explained that antibiotics didn't work on viruses and that Coxsackie was a virus. One had to just let it run its course.

*

The public was accustomed to flu season being in the winter months, so when the Peru Flu began to pop up here and there in late spring, not many people paid attention. This was a big mistake. By June there were over 150,000 cases reported nationwide, and the numbers were growing. While many of the victims suffered only mild symptoms, there were reports of patients developing heart and lung problems and even meningitis. When deaths started happening, the government finally began to wake up. It was a full-blown epidemic, and as cases began to appear in Europe and Asia, it was declared a pandemic. Local communities began to impose curfews and recommended there be no gatherings of more than fifty people. That was reduced to twenty participants, then to only two, and finally to no contact with anyone whatsoever. Schools were closed (Kevin was elated). Bars were closed (much to Kevin's father Ronald's dismay). Movie theaters and malls closed. Museums were shuttered. Hospitals were jammed with sick people. Restaurants were closed, with only supermarkets, gas stations and drugstores remaining open. And then the other shoe dropped.

The president ordered a complete lockdown. Everyone was ordered to remain in their residence, with only qualified emergency workers, performing essential duties, allowed on the streets. The quarantine, enforced by the National Guard, was to take place in forty-eight hours, in order to allow everyone time to load up on supplies and food. Of course this led to hoarding, fistfights in the toilet paper aisle, empty shelves everywhere and long lines at the liquor store.

*

"We're going up to the cabin," announced Ronald to the Singer family, whom he had assembled in the living room. Natalie sat on the chintz-covered couch with her arm around her daughter, Allyson, age fifteen, who was staring at the screen of her iPhone. Kevin, with his long skinny legs draped over the velveteen armchair, was playing with his Nintendo Switch. Little Eric, age six, was on the floor coloring a large pad with magic markers. "We will be leaving in a couple of hours, so you need to pack some warm clothes and whatever else you want to take."

"I'm not going," Allyson said, never taking her eyes off her cell phone.

"Excuse me?" responded Ronald.

"All my friends are here. I'm old enough to take care of myself, and I can look after the apartment while you're gone."

"All of your friends will soon be housebound," Ronald explained. "Besides, it seems to me you spend most of your so-called 'time with friends' on that damned phone."

"She doesn't want to be separated from Jasper," piped up Kevin.

"Shut up, brat!" Allyson hissed.

"Jasper? Jasper who?" inquired Ronald.

"Her boyfriend."

"I hate you!" Allyson said, throwing one of the pink pillows from the couch at her brother.

"You never told us you had a boyfriend, Ally," her mother said, stopping her from throwing another pillow.

"You're too young to have a boyfriend," emphasized her father.

"And that's exactly why I never told you," explained Allyson.

"Well, boyfriend or not, you are going up to the mountain—we're all going up to the cabin, tonight."

"Why can't we stay here?" Allyson asked in a whiny voice. "It's so much more comfortable."

"It's not safe, sweetheart. Once we're quarantined we can't go outside, we can't go anywhere. New York City is like the epicenter of this epidemic, the virus is everywhere. Up at the cabin, we will be alone and safe. We can wander outside, take a swim, jog and hike with little threat of getting sick."

"And we'll be bringing Nanna with us," added Natalie.

"Oh, god, no!" Allyson yelped, jumping up from the sofa. "You know what she's like!"

"Sweetheart, we can't leave her in her apartment by herself," explained her mother. "You know that. Kiara, god bless her, had to get home to her own family, so your grandmother is all alone."

Eric sat up and looked around like he had just joined the group. "Are we bringing Buddy with us?"

"Of course, punkin," Natalie assured him.

"We would have boarded him at the kennels, like we usually do," explained Ronald, "but they're closed due to—well, the situation."

"Mom, Nanna can't come with us—"

"Allyson Rebecca Singer! She is your—"

"No, really. Kevin had the virus. He will give it to her!" Allyson said, with a smile of triumph.

"The doctor said I'm no longer contagious, so give it up, sister," Kevin announced, with a certain amount of glee.

"That's correct, and all the rest of us have tested negative," confirmed Ronald. "So that's why we're getting out of Dodge tonight, before any of us catches something."

"But, Daddy—"

"No arguments! The Singer family is going on early vacation, and we *will* have a good time!"

*

The Singers' white Acura SUV, packed with cartons of groceries, backpacks, sleeping bags, three children, one dog and two adults headed over to West End Avenue to pick up Nanna. Ronald double-parked in front of the Parkhurst apartments and Natalie got out to enter the old prewar building. After more than a half hour had passed, the doorman held open the door to let Natalie exit, dragging a rolling suitcase and a tiny white-haired woman behind her. It was Nanna Esther, dressed in a Chanel pantsuit with a Gucci scarf around her neck.

"Help! Someone! I'm being kidnapped!"

"Mama, stop!" Natalie pleaded as she and Ronald tried to stuff her into the back seat between Allyson and Kevin.

"It's okay, Esther," Ronald said, attempting to calm her down. "We're going on a nice trip up to the cabin."

Buddy, stuck in the back rear-facing seat with Eric and the supplies, thinking something was wrong, began barking.

"What's that?!" shrieked Esther. "Is there a wild animal in here?"

"No, Nanna," Kevin explained, patting his grandmother's gloved hand. "That's Buddy. You remember Buddy, our dog."

"If I get one flea bite—"

"Buddy doesn't have fleas."

"I've heard *that* before."

Ronald got onto the West Side Highway and headed for the George Washington Bridge. Once over the bridge and into New Jersey, he got on the Garden State Parkway and followed it to the Taconic Parkway exit.

Once he got on that, it would be a straight shot to upstate New York, the village of North Creek and the cabin.

"Where are you taking me?" asked Nanna Esther, looking at the trees rushing by the window.

"Up to the cabin, Mama," answered Natalie. "Remember when we took you up to North Creek for your birthday?"

"What cabin? What birthday?" Esther replied. "Oh, you mean that shack of yours." Ronald bristled but kept silent. "And that was your birthday, Natalie, not mine."

Natalie almost started to engage in an argument but, having been in "no can win" land so many times before, thought better of it. The trip ahead was close to four hours long, and she needed to keep her sanity.

Fortunately, at about two hours into the journey, Esther began to fade and was soon snoring softly, with her head resting on Allyson's shoulder. Earlier, in what seemed like the longest two hours of her young life, Allyson had been interrogated by Nanna Esther about her grades ("only straight A's, I hope"), her hair ("Who's your hairdresser these days? Walmart?"), her clothes ("You got a bra on underneath that too-tight tee shirt?"). And then there were all those stories Allyson had heard a hundred times or more. Most of them started with "When I was your age. . ."

Kevin fared a little better. Not being of the masculine persuasion, Nanna Esther didn't really know what topics to cover. After the standard "How's school?" followed by "What sports are you into?" and the ever-enlightening "What do you want to be when you grow up?" Esther left Kevin to his earbuds and his music.

Eric fared best of all: out of sight, out of mind. He snuggled next to Buddy and drew on his pad until it got too dark to tell one marker color from another.

After one quick stop for some food, and several longer stops to allow Esther to visit the ladies' room, they arrived in the town of North Creek. It was ten o'clock, and as they drove through the center of town, they could see that everything was shut down—and not just because it was getting late. The epidemic had forced most of the businesses to close, and it was evident there was a curfew in place. The streets were empty.

Ronald kept driving until they were away from the dark and depressing village. He continued along the highway for about eight miles and then, spotting the hand-painted sign with their last name printed under the image of a bluebird, turned onto the dirt road that wound up and around the mountain. Fir branches brushed the sides of the vehicle as it ascended the narrow lane leading up to the mountaintop and the cabin.

*

The cabin had been constructed by Ronald's father back in the 1960s, during a period when Arthur Singer, then twenty, was experimenting with being a hippie. The experiment didn't last long, but the cabin did. It was a cedar-shingled, mission-style bungalow with a wrap-around porch. The interior consisted of two bedrooms, a bathroom (which had replaced the outhouse in 1972), a large open space that contained the kitchen, dining and living areas, and a ladder leading up to a small sleeping loft. There was a rustic fireplace against one wall with a large pot-bellied stove installed in the opening, which was used to heat the cabin. An electric-power line and telephone line had been added in 1980. There was running water provided by a pump attached to the well, a septic tank and, living in the nearby woodshed, a backup generator in case of a power failure. All in all, it was a more than adequate place to chill out. This was the vacation home Ronald had inherited when Arthur died in 2007, and now it was to become a refuge.

Ronald drove the SUV onto the patch of gravel that served as a parking spot and turned off the motor. Allyson and Kevin were out of the car before the engine finished shutting down. Natalie opened her door and went to help Esther maneuver down from her seat.

"Why do they make these damn machines so hard to get in and out of?" she groused as her Ferragamos reached the gravel. "I need a step-ladder, this thing is so high off the ground!" She and Natalie then slowly wove their way up to the porch, using a flashlight to light the way.

"Great! More steps. At least at the Parkhurst I have an elevator."

Kevin was helping Ronald unload the car while Eric walked Buddy for his much-needed pee break. Allyson was pacing back and forth, staring at the screen on her cell phone.

"I've got no bars. Oh, my god! My phone isn't working!—Daddy!"

"There's no cell service up here, darling," Ronald replied, toting a freezer chest towards the house. "Remember? Anyway, help your brother with the groceries."

"My life is over!" Allyson cried out, falling to her knees. "What am I going to do? I'm totally cut off from my friends! No one will be able to reach me up here!"

"You mean Jasper won't," said Kevin. "You're such a drama queen. Get over it and help me carry this stuff up to the cabin."

"I hate you! I hate this whole stupid place! I hate the whole world!"

"Allyson, it's dark and it's late," Natalie called from the porch. "Help your brother—now."

Getting up from the ground like a wounded soldier rising from a battlefield, Allyson stumbled over to the back of the SUV and picked up the lightest thing she could find—a pillow.

Inside the cabin, Ronald was putting split logs in the stove to start a fire. The room was cold and damp from being closed up all winter. Natalie was unpacking the groceries and putting things away. Esther was in the bathroom.

"There's no toilet paper in here, and the toilet is flushing green water!"

"It's okay, Esther," Ronald said through the closed door. "That's the anti-freeze I put in the tank when we shut down for the season. I've turned the water back on, so that'll clear up soon."

"And what am I supposed to use to wipe my tush? The bathmat?"

"Here, Mama," said Natalie, opening the door a crack and handing Esther a roll of toilet paper.

"About time."

Eric rushed in from outside, followed by Buddy. He was carrying his Star Wars sleeping bag, and he started to head for the ladder leading up to the sleeping loft.

"No way, shrimp!" shouted Kevin, who had just entered lugging the last two grocery bags. "I'm sleeping up there."

"Mama said I could."

"I don't care. That's where I'm beddin' down, pardner!" Kevin said, pulling Eric away from the ladder.

"Mama!"

Natalie put down the can of peaches she had pulled out of one of the bags and assumed her referee stance.

"Kevin, it's time Eric had a turn being in the loft. You've slept there every summer for the last five years. Now that he's old enough to sleep up there safely, be the good older brother I know you are capable of being—"

"But, Mom—"

"No buts. Case closed. Eric is in the loft. Understand?"

"Yeah, the baby always gets what he wants," Kevin complained. "So I suppose I'm going to have to share the bedroom with Allyson."

"Well, actually, Nanna Esther needs the bedroom, so you and Ally will sleep out here in the living room."

It was at this moment that Allyson staggered into the house.

"Oh, nooooo! Not only am I without my cell phone, now I'll have no privacy and I have to share space with nerd-face here," Allyson cried. "It's not fair!"

"Allyson Rebecca Singer," Natalie said, using her "watch it!" voice. "The world is suffering a big crisis, people are dying, there are children who are very sick. There are families stuck in one-room apartments and not allowed to leave, so we are very lucky to have this place. Sacrifices have to be made, and having to share space with not only your brother but all of us is very little to ask. So calm down and help us get ready for bed."

Eric took this as his cue and scrambled up the ladder. He leaned over the edge to receive his sleeping bag from Kevin and saw Buddy standing at the foot of the ladder.

"That's right," Kevin said, smiling. "Your dog won't be able to sleep with you way up there. Wouldn't you rather be down here with him, huh?"

Eric shook his head. "I'm going to teach him to climb the ladder."

Kevin began to laugh. "This I want to see. You know that it's not possible, right?"

"It is. I saw a dog do it on YouTube. They trained him to pull himself up."

"Well, good luck with that."

Ronald brought in the last sleeping bags from the car, closed the front door and collapsed in the leather armchair near the cast-iron stove. The living room was warming up, and Natalie went into Esther's bedroom to see if it was getting to a comfortable temperature as well.

"It'll do," Nanna Esther admitted, "but there is no room in this closet for my clothes." She opened the knotty-pine door to reveal a space full of sporting equipment—volleyballs, fishing rods, waders, yellow slickers, boots, tackle boxes, board games and cartons of comic books.

"Sorry about that, Mama," Natalie replied, closing the door. "I'll take care of that tomorrow. We'll move some of it out into the shed. It's too late to do it tonight. Time for bed. You must be exhausted."

"But I can't get unpacked—"

"Tomorrow, Mama, in the morning."

"Am I supposed to sleep in my clothes? And I have my beauty regimen!"

"Mama, it's for just one night. Get your nightgown out of your suitcase and—"

"And where do I hang my suit?"

"You can drape it over the bureau for now," Natalie responded, trying to remain calm. "Now, you change and then I'll tuck you in, okay?"

"If I must. But I can tell you, this is no way to run a household."

Natalie bit her tongue so hard it hurt.

*

Later that night, after the house grew silent, Natalie and Ronald lay together in the dark of their bedroom.

"I wish they understood that we're doing this to keep everyone healthy," Ronald whispered as he pulled Natalie closer to him.

"To keep everyone alive!" corrected Natalie. "But like all young people, they think they're impervious. However, there is nothing on this earth strong enough to kill Nanna Esther."

"Not true. Her age makes her very vulnerable," Ronald pointed out.

"I know, I know. It's just that sometimes—"

"So what happened back at her apartment? You were in there for quite a while."

"When I got there she was ready to go."

"She was all packed?" asked Ronald.

"Oh, she was packed all right—two suitcases, her jewelry case, a Louis Vuitton tote bag, and she was sitting on a steamer trunk."

Ronald chuckled quietly.

"It wasn't funny, Ron. It took every ounce of energy on my part to force her to narrow everything down to one suitcase. She was screeching like a wounded bird, and I was unpacking and repacking as fast as I could. I tried to explain to her that we were roughing it, that she wouldn't need her collection of Herrera high heels or more than one handbag. 'Abuse!' she started yelling, 'Granny abuse!'—I just hope I can hold it together for the next few days."

"Weeks, sweetheart," Ronald corrected, "weeks. They don't know how long this virus is going to be around."

"Oh, God, give me the strength."

Day One

Ronald tried to be as quiet as he could while hooking up the coffeemaker and starting to brew his early-morning dose of caffeine. Kevin and Allyson were sleeping the deep sleep known only to teenagers and didn't stir. Eric, however, heard the noise in the kitchen and was down the ladder and out the door, with Buddy trailing behind. Back in the bedroom, Natalie had turned over and, covering her head with a pillow, continued to sleep.

Ronald had just seated himself in his leather armchair to enjoy his first mug of coffee when out of the corner of his eye he spied Nanna Esther exiting the bathroom. She was wearing a pair of dark blue flannel pajamas covered all over with little white puppies doing puppyish things.

"Morning, Nanna. How was your night?"

"All things considered, lousy. The bed might as well be made of nails. And is it always this quiet here? I could hear my heart beating." She made her way over to the coffee and poured herself a mugful.

"Sorry about the bed," apologized Ronald.

"You got non-dairy creamer somewhere?"

"There's milk in the fridge."

"Non-dairy creamer, please. I'm lactose intolerant."

"I'm sorry. I never knew that about you."

"Yes, well, I just found that out about myself recently. Last week, actually."

"Oh, you went to the doctor. Good idea."

"No. My neighbor Lillian, she diagnosed me. Her daughter-in-law has the condition and her symptoms are the same as mine."

Ronald nodded that he understood, and, knowing better than to challenge Nanna Esther's neighbor's diagnosis, kept silent.

"So, you got some non-diary creamer?"

"Sorry, Nanna."

"Sweetener?"

"I think there's some Sweet'n Low in the green sugar bowl."

"Oh, for god's sake, are you still using that poison? I've been using monk-fruit extract."

"Monkey fruit?"

"Monk fruit! It's three hundred times sweeter than sugar and calorie-free and natural."

"Well, no monk-fruit extract in our cupboard. Sorry."

"Typical."

<u>Day Seven</u>

Allyson sat in one of the two Kennedy rocking chairs on the cabin porch. Her father was rocking gently in the other chair and reading a book.

"I am going to die, literally, if this doesn't end soon," she stated, obsessively twisting a strand of her long, straight brown hair. "No wi-fi, no television, no cell phone—"

"There's the radio, and we have a landline—"

"Which you insist is only for emergencies!"

"Ally," Ronald said, putting down his book, "this is a great opportunity for you to explore the world outside of social media. Here we are on this beautiful mountain, the pine trees, the pond, the fresh air, the wildlife—"

"The deerflies, the ticks, the mosquitoes—"

"The snakes," announced Kevin, clutching a small garter snake in his hand as he climbed up the porch steps. He waved it in front of Allyson's face.

"Eeow," she shouted, "get it away from me! Daddy, stop him—"

"Kevin!" said Ronald admonishingly, but with a slight smile on his face. "Stop it and let the snake go. Let it go so it can eat those mosquitoes and flies that are annoying your sister."

"It's not funny! I wish the snake would eat my insect of a brother."

*

Kevin and Eric had adapted to their enforced vacation very quickly. They had become avid hikers and had explored the woods all the way down to the highway, and even around the other side of the mountain. When the water in the pond became warm enough, they dived in and spent long afternoons swimming and pretending they were dolphins or submarines. They were getting tanned in spots that usually never saw the light of day. Not so Allyson. She moped around the cabin. When asked to do a chore, she did so reluctantly and with an attitude. She wrote long, sad letters on her computer, which she couldn't send because there was no wi-fi, and cried at the drop of a hat.

"Ally, you really need to snap out of this," Ronald said, picking up the book he had put down. "Why don't you find a book to read? There are so many in the bookcase in the house. I'm sure you could find one that would interest you."

"Right. There's *The Cat in the Hat* and *Goodnight Moon* and a Betty Crocker cookbook."

"Come on, you know there are other, more interesting books than that to choose from. I saw a couple of Stephen King novels, and I believe there's even a Danielle Steel."

"Oh, pleeeeeze! That's old-lady crap."

"Allyson."

"Well, it is," she stated. "I'd rather read anything else, even a chemistry textbook, than one of those books with that long-haired dude on the cover. What's his name—Fido?"

"You mean Fabio?" Ronald answered, suppressing a smile. "I understand, honey, but you know there are other titles in there worth checking out. This one, for instance," he said, holding up the volume he'd been reading. "An anthology of Edgar Allan Poe, his poems and stories. You'd like it, very sad and depressing. Just your cup of tea."

"Don't make fun of me, Daddy," Allyson replied, her chin starting to tremble.

"I'm sorry, sweetheart. It's just that I'm kind of confused. We've been coming up here for two weeks every summer and I thought you had a great time."

"That was different. When I was just a little kid it was okay, and even last year, at least I could go into town and over to a friend's house where there was wi-fi and where my cell phone worked. But here—I'm a prisoner. Yes, I know, we have to stay in isolation so we don't get sick, but if we were back in the apartment we could watch Netflix and I could talk to my friends—"

Ronald watched as the tears started to fall. He patted his knee and, reaching up to take Allyson's arm, pulled her onto his lap. "I'm so sorry, sweetheart. I can see how hard this is for you. Tell you what: how about you go inside and use the landline to call one of your friends."

"Really?"

"Yes. I should have done that earlier. I just didn't want the phone unavailable if the office needed to reach me, but no one is going to call. All we're getting are robocalls, anyway."

"Oh, I won't hog the phone! I promise. Thank you, thank you, thank you, Daddy!" she exclaimed, rushing into the cabin and letting the screen door slam behind her.

"I am so glad I'm not a girl," Kevin announced as he let the garter snake go and watched it slip speedily away through the grass.

Day Thirteen

Natalie was washing the breakfast dishes when Esther came out of her room holding up a pair of granny panties. "Okay, I'm down to my last pair of undies. How does one get their clothes laundered around here, or do I have to take my dirty clothes down to the pond and beat them on the rocks?"

"That I would pay to see, Mom," Natalie replied, "but just put them in the hamper in the bathroom along with our laundry. I planned to collect your stuff this morning, anyway."

"So where do you do the laundry?"

"We have an old top-loader out in the shed. It still works fine, but we only have cold water. There's no hot water piped out there."

"You got a dryer as well?"

"That lucky we're not. There are a couple of clotheslines behind the shed."

"So my intimates are going to be waving in the wind for all to see."

"Along with everybody else's underwear."

"Well, just don't use any bleach, and I only use the kind of Downy with no fragrance."

"Aye, aye, captain," Natalie answered as she struggled with the large pile of laundry she pulled from the bathroom hamper. "Bring your clothes and follow me."

"What? Where?"

"You asked me where we do the laundry and I'm going to show you. Also, it's about time you pitched in and helped out for a change. You can help me do the wash."

"Wait a minute! You dragged me up here. I didn't ask to be invited to this Motel 6. You made me your guest!"

"You are not a guest, Mama, you are a member of this family. And part of being in a family is to help said family. So grab your dirty undies and whatever else needs washing and follow me," said Natalie as she backed out through the door and struggled down the porch stairs.

"Well, someone sure got out on the wrong side of the bed this morning."

The shed was shingled, like the cabin, and had large double doors that opened to a space big enough to house the emergency generator, a lawnmower that converted to a snowblower, a stationary tub and the washing machine. Natalie dumped the dirty laundry on the cement floor and started separating the dark colors and the lights. Esther, trying to find a clean area on the dusty floor, gave up and dropped her clothes next to Natalie's pile.

"I'm dividing everything into darks and lights, so just add your stuff to the appropriate pile," Natalie instructed as she turned on the cold water to fill the machine.

"You plan to wash my clothes with your dirty things?"

"Mama, we don't have cooties. The boys' shorts won't mind spinning around in soapy water with your pajamas."

"But—"

"I'm not wasting detergent and water doing four loads instead of two," Natalie explained. "You want clean underpants? Put them in the correct pile."

"Well, aren't we the bossy one," Esther said, reluctantly dropping her laundry on top of the appropriate mound.

Later, as they stood around waiting to add softener to the last load in the washer, Esther noticed the boxes of comic books that Natalie had moved out of the closet in her room. They were tucked away in a corner behind the lawnmower.

"So what's with all of these comic books of your kid's? Why are you saving them?"

"Well, first of all, they don't belong to the kid. They're Ronald's. He's been collecting them since he was ten. Secondly, some of them are worth a lot of money."

Esther reached into a box resting on top of the others and pulled out one of the comics. "Wait a minute. This one is dated last year. You mean to tell me he's still collecting these babies? He doesn't read them, I hope."

"Yes, he reads them. He says he finds comfort in them after a stressful day at work. And nowadays they're called 'graphic novels.' See how different they are," Natalie explained, showing Esther one of the old comic books, its worn pages and faded cover enclosed in a protective plastic envelope. "The newer ones are printed on better paper, and the art is really quite impressive."

"So I see," replied Esther, holding up an illustration of a very voluptuous Amazonian female. "Very impressive."

"Anyway, they make him happy, and anything that makes anyone happy, especially these days, is okay with me. What makes you happy, Mama?"

"Well, it certainly isn't busty ladies in armor. Listen, darling, you know I am never one to criticize, but it would be remiss of me not to say that I find a man in his forties reading comic books to be a very immature individual. He is not setting a good example for his children."

Once again Natalie found herself full of rage with nowhere to put it. It was time to hang up the laundry, and maybe hang her mother by the neck until dead, but of course that would never do. "Mama, Ronald is a wonderful father and is a great example for Kevin and Eric and even Allyson.

He is certainly a better father than the man who pretended to care about you and me."

"Don't you start!"

"All right, I won't, but from now on, I want you to show some respect for my husband and the father of your grandchildren. Do you understand?"

"My, you *are* in a bad mood today!"

"You have no idea. Now, grab that bag of clothespins and follow me."

Day Twenty-Four

"Xawolf is not a word, Nanna," said Eric, sitting across from her at a folding card table. On the other two sides of the table were Kevin and Allyson.

"That's right, Nanna," agreed Ally, who was growing very tired of this round of Scrabble.

"It most certainly is too a word," Esther insisted. "It's a rare breed of wolf found only in the Ukraine. Look it up!"

"I just did, Nanna," Kevin replied. "It's not in the dictionary."

"That doesn't mean a thing. If you had an encyclopedia up here in this wilderness—"

"If we had wi-fi," said Allyson wistfully, "we could ask Siri."

*

It had been raining heavily the last four days, and the family had been unable to go anywhere outside without getting drenched. The only excitement had been a big, noisy electrical storm that lit up the sky one evening and created a blackout that lasted for five hours. Candles and the generator kept the house cozy, but now, four days later, cabin fever had set in. To pass the time, they had baked cookies, played Canasta, lost millions at Monopoly, discovered who killed Colonel Mustard in the library with a candlestick and even, in a moment of sheer desperation, travelled through Candyland.

Allyson, as could have been predicted, spent several hours a day on the phone. At first she was put off by the size and weight of the landline receiver and the lack of privacy. But then she discovered that the cord to the telephone was long enough for her to drag it from its place on the side table, by her father's leather armchair, into the bathroom. Once there, she could shut the door and, by speaking softly, achieve a modicum of privacy. Of course, leave it to Kevin and his supersonic hearing to decode what Ally was saying through the bathroom door.

"She's talking to Jasper," he whispered.

"Get away from the door, Kevin!" barked Ronald.

Natalie had also used the telephone to call several of her friends back in the city, to find out how they were coping with the lockdown. The news was not good.

"I love my four kids, Natalie, but a month of trying to keep them entertained while stuck in this apartment is going to send me to Bellevue."

"My supermarket is no longer delivering orders to customers. They can't keep up with the demand. What do we do now?"

"Nat, do you remember that I told you that my daughter has five roommates? They're living in a one-bedroom apartment and she said they are no longer speaking to each other."

"Auntie Lois died yesterday. Now we're all terrified that we'll be next."

"Thank heavens for the internet and Netflix! What would we do without them?"

Natalie didn't share this last conversation with Allyson.

*

Ronald sat on the porch and watched the rain pour off the roof and flood the front yard. He could barely hear the voices of the Scrabble players arguing over Nanna's spelling of the word "speech," and that was one reason he was sitting alone in the rocker. He'd reached the point where he couldn't bear listening to the incessant chatter, the sniping and whining and complaining. He missed the office, the challenge of his work, the routine. He longed for happy hour at Bar None, his local watering hole, and the subway ride home. Who could have guessed you would miss the NYC ratrace?

Natalie came out onto the porch, closing the door behind her. She pulled the other rocking chair closer to Ronald and seated herself down beside him.

"Are you all right, darling?"

"Yes, sure."

"I don't believe it for a moment," Natalie said, placing her hand on his. "I know you, Mr. Singer. What's going on?"

After a long pause, Ronald spoke slowly and softly. "I feel guilty."

"Guilty? About what?"

"Actually, I'm guilty twice over. Once, for dragging all of you up here, away from civilization to what I thought would be Eden revisited."

"You got us to somewhere safe," Natalie reminded him. "You were protecting your family."

"Yes, but at the same time, I was thinking that I was going to skip down memory lane and we'd all go back to the good old days. Instead, we're in a sort of prison, a prison in paradise. And the irony of it all is that I also feel guilty that I've deserted the city, that there are all those people jammed together down there, struggling and suffering and dying, while we're sitting up here away from it all."

Natalie reached up and gently touched Ronald's face. "Ronald Singer, you did the right thing. It would have been just plain wicked to put us all in harm's way when we had this alternative option available. You are taking care of five lives—six, when you count Nanna Esther. If you were back in the city and you randomly picked six strangers to help, there wouldn't really be anything you could do, right? And you'd probably get sick yourself and maybe even die, god forbid."

"No, I understand that. I'd probably be pretty useless. No need for a tax lawyer during a pandemic, but I see how miserable Allyson is. And your mom is suffering—"

"Nanna Esther has been suffering since the day she was born. She thrives on suffering. And Allyson is a typical fifteen-year-old teenager who is going through withdrawal from her cell-phone addiction. Believe me, as soon as this crisis has passed, she'll be back in the city glued to her iPhone. But for now, she has to interact with other human beings face to face, not electronically. And that's a good thing, right?"

"I suppose—"

"And as long as Kevin has batteries for his earbuds, he'll be happy. And have you looked at the drawings Eric has been dashing off by the dozens? Great big splashes of color. It's obvious he's thriving up here."

"And you?" Ronald asked. "Are you thriving?"

"You know what?—I have spent more time with you this last month than I have in the last ten years. I've got you 24/7, no phone interruptions, no conferences with clients, no late nights at the office, no off and away on a business trip—just you and me."

"And Ally and Kevin and Eric—and your mom."

"Well, yes, but it's great being with them as well. Admittedly, Mama pushes some of my buttons, but that we're all together and that we're safe is what's most important. Yes, I am thriving, my sweet man."

And like in one of those hokey moments on the Hallmark Channel, the rain stopped, and in the distance a rainbow began to assemble itself.

Day Thirty-Five

"Ronald!" Natalie whispered as she shook his shoulder. "There's someone outside!" It was close to midnight, and she had been awakened by the sound of footsteps outside their bedroom window. It was a very warm night, and the window was open to let in some cool air.

"Wha'?" Ronald asked, still half asleep. "Prob jus' a deer."

"No, no! I heard footsteps."

Ronald threw back the covers and stepped out onto the cold floor. He fumbled in the dark for his robe. "Iss jus' some animal, a raccoon maybe, trampin' round in the bushes." Suddenly, as he approached the window, a scream—a very loud, high-pitched scream—cut through the darkness.

"That's Nanna!" Natalie shouted. "It's coming from her room!" She leapt out of the bed and met Ronald at the door, where they tried to get through the opening at the same time. After a comical routine worthy of Abbott and Costello, they hurried over to Esther's bedroom door, which was closed. Ronald reached for the doorknob.

"Be careful, Ronnie!" Natalie said, handing him her bedroom slipper. "Take this, just in case."

Ronald looked at the terrycloth scuffy. "Well, whatever is in there, I guess I could beat it to death with this." He slowly turned the knob and, raising the slipper, stepped into the room. In the darkness he could see a figure standing next to Nanna's bed. Esther was still in bed but defending herself with something in her hand. It was too dark to make out what was going on.

"Stay right there, whoever you are!" ordered Ronald. "Natalie, turn on the overhead light."

Later on, they would laugh about the scene that was revealed. Standing over Nanna Esther, dressed in denim shorts, a black Nirvana tee shirt and a Yankees baseball cap, a camo backpack over his shoulders, was a young man of teenage years. Nanna was attempting to fend him off with one of her fluffy boudoir slippers.

"Runs in the family, I guess," said Ronald, indicating Esther's pink shoe. "And who are you, young man?"

"JASPER!" Allyson gasped, peeking through the open door. "What are you doing in here?" Kevin and Eric stuck their heads around their sister's back to see what was happening.

"Before we go any further," Ronald said, handing Natalie's slipper back to her, "I'm going to ask you—Jasper, right?—to step away from the bed. You need to keep away from Nanna, from all of us."

"Daddy!"

"Ally, your friend here may be infected with the virus, or at least carrying it. We have to be very careful."

Jasper, who had been standing in silent embarrassment, finally spoke up. "I am so sorry, Mr. Singer. I didn't mean to frighten your mother."

"Mother-in-law," corrected Ronald.

"I thought this was where Ally was sleeping and I saw that the window was open, so I kinda moved the screen away and climbed in. I'm so sorry."

"Call the police, Natalie!" Esther commanded. "He was going to kill me!"

"No, oh no!" Jasper pleaded. "I just wanted to see Ally."

"Let's move this out of Nanna's room," Ronald suggested. "Everyone into the living room, except you, Jasper. You come with me out onto the porch."

With the whole family watching through the windows, Jasper stood on the grass and faced Mr. Singer, who remained standing at the top of the porch steps. The porch light lit a half circle around them.

"How did you get here?"

"I took the train to North Creek."

"The trains are still running?"

"Yes, sir. There weren't many people on it. I caught the eight o'clock express."

"How did you know where we were?"

Jasper looked down at the ground and hesitated. Finally, catching a glimpse of Allyson in the window, he answered.

"Ally sent me the address in a letter. She gave me directions. She said that cell phones didn't work so good up here, so that maybe my GPS wouldn't be any help. I hitched a ride from the station with some dude and then I walked up this mountain, and here I am."

"Yes, you are, and I hope you have a round-trip ticket, because I need you to turn around and head back to wherever you came from."

"Gee, Mr. Singer, there's no train until tomorrow afternoon. I was hoping I could stay here tonight."

Ronald looked at Jasper and tried to remember what it was like to be so gaga over a girl that you would travel to the ends of the earth to be with her.

"Jasper, I'm sure my daughter is very honored that you made this journey. I am sort of impressed myself, but at the same time, you have done a very foolish and dangerous thing. I don't know how you got away from your parents and out of the quarantine and why you weren't stopped at the train station—"

"They weren't stopping people leaving, only people coming into the city."

"Whatever. The important thing is that you could be carrying the virus, in fact you probably are, and I can't have you exposing my family to it. So I'm afraid you'll have to leave."

"But where can I go?" He suddenly looked like the little kid he really was, even though he was wearing a young adult's skin on the outside.

Ronald was about to step down the stairs and lead Jasper off the property when he heard Natalie's voice behind him. He turned and saw her standing in the doorway holding one of the extra sleeping bags in her arms.

"May I make a suggestion?"

Jasper, exhausted from his adventure, slept on the porch in a bright blue sleeping bag. He was turned onto his left side and facing one of the front windows. On the other side of the glass was Allyson, sitting in one of the dining room chairs and gazing lovingly at her sleeping prince.

Back in their bed, Ronald and Natalie quietly discussed the situation.

"He can't stay here." Ronald was adamant.

"I know, I know, but it seems cruel to send him back after he came all this way."

"Natalie, don't go getting all romantic. This is a matter of life and death."

"Yes, and sending him back could mean his death. Last week you told me you were feeling guilty that you weren't helping people down in the city. Well, here's your chance."

"Oh, you're good! Hanging me up by my own words."

"But it's true. We can work something out. We can set some rules. He can continue to sleep on the porch. I'll wash all his clothes and stuff, decontaminate his backpack."

"Natalie, be realistic. He and Allyson? They'd never be able to keep their hands off of each other!"

"Please, Ronnie, just think about it."

"We'll talk about it in the morning. But I'm telling you right now, he's not staying."

Day Thirty-Eight

Esther wouldn't leave her room. "No way!" she exclaimed through her closed door. "As long as that killer is out there, I'm in here where it's safe."

"Mama, he's been with us for two days and he hasn't shown any symptoms," Natalie explained. "Everyone is okay, including you."

"The radio said that the virus loves the elderly and the very young. I'm not taking any chances."

Nanna Esther had been out of her room to go to the bathroom and had raided the kitchen late at night, so this self-isolation was actually rather useless.

Kevin joined his mother at the door. "Nanna, you better come out. We're having bread pudding for lunch today. I know you love your bread pudding."

"With raisins?"

"I believe so."

"Cinnamon?"

"Of course."

"Vanilla sauce?"

Kevin looked at his mother. Natalie shook her head. "We didn't have any vanilla extract, Nanna. Sorry."

The door slowly began to open. Esther peered through the narrow slot.

"Is Typhoid Marty in the house?"

"You mean Jasper?" Natalie asked. "He's still relegated to the porch, so it's safe for you to come out now."

The door opened all the way and Nanna Esther entered the living room wearing her pale pink Lululemon sweats. Her hair was covered with one of her Versace scarves, as she had been complaining all week that she was in desperate need of a visit to her hair salon. "Mr. André is the only one who knows how to cut my hair."

*

Lunch was set out on the dining room table. Allyson sat facing the window so she could watch Jasper, in one of the porch rockers, eating a grilled cheese sandwich. Eric, in the chair across from Ally, was drawing on his pad while pausing to sip a spoonful of tomato soup. Kevin helped Nanna Esther get seated and then sat down next to her. Natalie joined them at the table after serving up more sandwiches and soup.

"Campbell's and Velveeta for lunch, again," sighed Esther.

"I'm afraid the cupboard is a little bare. It's the best I could do until Ronald gets back."

"Oh, is he making a grocery run to Stewart's?"

"Yes, he should be back soon."

"I wish I had known," Esther said. "I have a few things I really need."

"Oh, what do you need?" asked Natalie. "I'll put it on the list for next time."

"Well, I need an avocado for the bags under my eyes, and I've run out of my Russian Amber Imperial shampoo."

"Stewart's will probably have an avocado or two, but I don't think they carry that brand of shampoo."

"Well, I certainly can't use that Dollar Store stuff that you like. I might as well pour motor oil on my hair!"

This conversation would have escalated into a very heated discussion if it hadn't been for Ronald's return from the grocery store at that very moment. Everyone except for Nanna Esther left the table and assembled on the porch to begin the decontamination process. Jasper moved off to the side in order to be out of the way. Ronald, still wearing his face mask and rubber gloves, started emptying the back of the SUV and bringing the plastic bags up to the porch. After setting them all down, he walked back to the shed and began to strip off all of his clothes. He tossed everything in the washer, added detergent and bleach and set the dial at "large." After starting the machine, he walked back to the house and up the steps, passed the members of his family, who had turned away in order to give him some privacy, and strode through the living room on his way to the shower. Esther tsk'd her displeasure. "Show-off!"

Back on the porch, Natalie was cleaning off the tops of the bags with sanitizing wipes while Allyson and Kevin began removing the cans and packages from inside the bags and wiping them down as well. Eric carried the fruits and vegetables into the kitchen and dumped them carefully into the sink, where they would eventually be washed.

This was a routine they had developed when they realized they were going to be sequestered at the cabin for quite a while. At first it seemed like overkill, but as the radio continued to broadcast the number of individuals infected and the percentages of deaths happening, they knew they had to take extraordinary measures.

By the time Ronald had finished his shower and gotten dressed, the pantry and refrigerator were restocked, and Natalie was washing the fruit and vegetables. He joined her at the sink and filled her in on life in the village.

"I wasn't able to get everything on the list. Some of the shelves were pretty bare. Almost all the shops along the street are closed. Joe, the manager at Stewart's, said he had to stop delivery service because Larry, the young kid he usually hired, was sick. The Health Center is overwhelmed—no test kits, they're running out of masks and respirators. Not good. So how was your morning?"

Natalie glanced over her shoulder at Nanna Esther and the kids enjoying their bread pudding. "It was okay. Nanna was her usual acerbic self. As you can see, we finally got her out of her room. Actually, the bread pudding got her out of her room."

"And what about Jasper?"

"He's still staying outside," Natalie answered. "He wandered around the yard and I guess he took a walk in the woods. I gave him lunch."

"One more week outside, just to be safe. Then we'll figure out what to do with Romeo."

*

That evening everyone was gathered in the living room except for Allyson, who was standing at the screen door conversing with Jasper. He was observing the six-foot rule by staying down at the bottom of the porch steps, even though he was aching to be much closer.

Eric was squatting on the floor with his pad and markers. Ronald was seated comfortably in his leather chair and deep into the dark world of Edgar Allan Poe. Kevin was dancing to some tune on his earbuds, and Natalie and Esther were facing off with a game of gin. Natalie had just laid her cards down and issued a triumphal "Gin!"

"No! You cheated!" Esther announced in a rage.

"Mama, I did not cheat. I won fair and square."

"No one wins twice in a row. You had to have cheated."

"Mama, I do not cheat. For heaven's sake, it's only a game."

While things were heating up at the card table, Jasper had slowly climbed the porch stairs. He stood on the other side of the screen door and stared at Allyson with a look that one only sees on the face of someone who is truly in the throes of first love. Ally turned away and walked over to her father.

"Daddy, can I go out on the porch with Jasper? I'll be really careful. We won't touch or anything."

Ronald looked up from his book. He saw all the longing in his daughter's eyes and was very moved and tempted, but—"Honey, it's not a good idea—"

"Please? It must be safe by—" Ally stopped, and a curious look crossed her face. "What are those red spots?"

"Red spots? Where?" asked Natalie, getting up from the table.

"There," answered Allyson, pointing.

*

The drive to the North Creek Health Center took only a few minutes. But after explaining how understaffed and overwhelmed they were, the doctor recommended they head over to the Moses Ludington Hospital in Ticonderoga. "It's about an hour's drive, but they have a better handle on the problem."

Ronald hurried and got Natalie into the car. She sat in the back seat holding on tightly to Eric. He was very pale, which made the rash on his bare legs stand out even more. Natalie could feel the fever radiating in waves off his body.

"It itches, Momma," Eric said, trying to free his arms in order to scratch his legs.

"I know, darling. Try not to touch it. When we get to the hospital I'm sure they'll put something on your skin to stop the itching."

"My head hurts," he said, leaning on her shoulder.

"I bet it does," Ronald added from the front seat. "Just hold on. We'll be there soon."

By the time they pulled into the hospital parking lot, Eric was hallucinating. He kept talking about the wolves that were howling in the windows of the buildings. "They want to be let out. They're friends of Buddy's. Let them out!"

A nurse dressed in protective clothing from head to toe and wearing a respirator picked up Eric and carried him quickly into one of the three white tents set up in the parking lot. Natalie tried to follow but was stopped by a security officer.

"I'm his mother!"

"I'm sorry, ma'am. You can't go in there. They'll take good care of him, and someone will come out to talk to you soon."

That was when Natalie finally fell apart. Ronald pulled her into his arms and she began sobbing against his chest.

*

Nanna Esther stood behind the porch screen door peering out into the dark. She was holding onto a cast-iron frying pan with both hands. Kevin was looking over her shoulder. Allyson sat in her dad's leather chair and wept.

"Nanna, Jasper's gone," Kevin said, hoping to disarm his grandmother. "I don't think he'll be coming back." This elicited a wail of anguish from Ally.

"I'm not taking any chances," Esther replied. "If that little murderer shows up, I'm ready."

"Nanna, the radio says that this virus can take up to two weeks before a person shows any symptoms."

"Listen, that little Nazi brought the germs into this house that infected your brother—"

"We don't know that for sure. Eric could have picked it up from touching something that came from the grocery store. You remember, we weren't as careful with that first visit to Stewart's as we are now."

"Kevin Marshall Singer, may I remind you that the killer entered this house through the window in my room! The virus was probably on his backpack or on his shoes. Oh, lord, I've been standing in his—I'm probably going to be the next victim to be sick. Oh, my god, it's like Agatha Christie's *Ten Little Indians*—and then there were none!"

Without a warning, Allyson leapt up from her chair, headed for the front door and, shoving Kevin and Nanna Esther aside, rushed onto the porch and down the stairs into the night.

"Ally, where are you going?" Kevin shouted after her. "It's pitch black out there!"

"You come back here, young lady!" Esther commanded. "Right now!"

"I'm going to get a flashlight," Kevin said, turning back into the living room, "and follow her. She's going to get lost out there in the woods!"

Coming from far away in the inky black darkness was the faint sound of Allyson's voice: "Jasper! Jasper! Where are you?" Kevin came sailing out of the cabin, wearing a jacket and carrying a sweater and a flashlight. He flew down the steps and ran off into the black void. "Allyson!—Allyson!—Allyson!"

Nanna Esther stood alone on the porch, the overhead light giving her a ghost-like appearance. "Kevin! Allyson!" she shouted. "Don't leave me here by myself! Please! The killer may come back and—touch me!"

Day Forty-One

Ronald had gathered the family in the cabin's living room. Kevin sat on the couch with Nanna Esther. Allyson slumped in a chair at the dining room table. She was scratching a heart with her fingernail in the surface of the old pine tabletop.

"So, your mom will be staying at a motel where she can be near to the hospital."

"How's Eric doing?" Kevin asked, squeezing Nanna's hand.

"He's been in there almost four days. He must be getting better," Esther added hopefully.

"He's in an induced coma and they're using a ventilator to keep him breathing. The maddening thing is that we can't be with him, we can't even see him. We get updates from the hospital staff, but they're so eff'n busy—"

"But he will get better, right?" asked Allyson.

"Of course he will," replied Nanna Esther. "What a silly question!"

"The doctor said his chances are fifty-fifty. Evidently this treatment with the ventilator, which breathes for him, is very invasive. It can sometimes lead to dependence on the machine to the point that they can't come off it. And it can damage the lungs, and—" Ronald stopped to take a quick wipe at his eyes.

"Well, that does it," Esther announced, pulling herself up from the couch. "I'm out of here."

"What? What's going on, Nanna?" asked Kevin, following her into her bedroom.

"I'm going to pack. Tell your dad to warm up the car."

"Why are you leaving? It's not safe for you to leave."

"Well, it sure as hell isn't safe for me to stay here. I need to get to the train station."

Ronald had stepped into the doorway. Kevin moved aside to let him into the room.

"Esther, Kevin's right. It's too dangerous for you to go back to the city."

"Who said anything about going to New York?" Esther replied. "I'm going to catch the first train to Canada." She took some of her clothes out of the closet and threw them on the bed.

Ronald couldn't help but smile. "The virus is in Canada, Nanna; the virus is worldwide."

"I know that! Don't lecture me! I just want to get away from this bucolic backwater. It's boring and stultifying and—and deadly!"

"Do you have a schedule of trains going to Canada? Where are you planning to go—Toronto, Montreal?"

"I'll telephone the station," she answered as she began folding a blouse. "If you had wi-fi, like any normal person, I could go online. I mean, to not even have a TV! This is the twenty-first century, for god's sake."

"I'm sorry, Nanna. You're absolutely right," Ronald said with sincerity. "Please stay. We need you. I need you."

Esther continued to fold her clothes and place them in her suitcase, but Ronald and Kevin could see her face beginning to crumble. She turned away from them so that they wouldn't see the tears starting to appear on her cheeks. "My poor little Eric."

"Please don't go, Nanna," Kevin said softly. "You need to be here when Eric comes home."

"It should have been me," Esther admitted.

"Don't say that, Nanna," Kevin said, putting his arms around her.

"It shouldn't have been Eric, but it could have been any of us," Ronald insisted. "This is nobody's fault. It's a terrible disease over which we have no control."

"Nanna," Allyson called out from the living room. "The trains stopped running several days ago. Jasper caught the last train going into Manhattan—"

"Don't mention that murderer's name again!" Esther yelled back at Ally. "Well, since there are no trains, and I'm not going to endanger my health by boarding a Greyhound bus, it seems I'm here for the duration."

"Yay!" exclaimed Kevin, giving his grandmother a hug.

"Careful! I break easily," she said sharply, but Kevin could tell she enjoyed the affection. "If I stay, however, there are going to have to be some changes made."

"And what may those changes be?" Ronald asked apprehensively.

"Well, first of all, you are getting a big flat-screen television."

Two Years Later

"When things get back to normal" became the catchphrase of the Peru Flu pandemic. It would be wonderful to think that that's what happened, but as we all know, that was not possible. There was no normalcy; the economy was in tatters, many small businesses never recovered, and the entertainment industry was struggling to get back on its feet. The infrastructure of whole communities was damaged, often beyond repair; married couples filed for divorce, having discovered their incompatibility while being trapped in their apartment during the lockdown; and unemployment was at an all-time high.

On the plus side, however, was the way the internet kept people connected and how schools and businesses quickly moved into the virtual world. There were online classes and grocery shopping by computer. You could tour a museum or watch a dance concert without leaving your bedroom. But at the same time, there were millions of poverty-level families who didn't have access to wi-fi and computers.

And then there were the deaths and the effect this had on families in the aftermath of the pandemic. Over 300,000 deaths occurred in the United States during the twenty-four-month run of the virus. This meant that hundreds of thousands of families lost someone to the flu. Almost everyone knew a friend or relative who had perished. The country was still in mourning.

*

It was summer on the Singers' mountain when the family returned for their postponed annual vacation. Ronald had made sure that over the two winters, cable and wi-fi were installed. One needed to be connected to the rest of the world. Nanna Esther had opted to remain in the comfort of her apartment at the Parkhurst: "I'm too old to rough it." Natalie was relieved, but kept that to herself. Allyson had found a new love, Aaron, a sweet young man who played the guitar and wrote songs about her. He was invited to join them at the cabin when he finished summer school. Kevin had a crush on his science teacher, which, of course, was unrequited, so he had started writing sci-fi stories about aliens in love with humans.

After dinner on their first night back in the cabin, Ronald gathered everyone in the living room. A fire was crackling in the pot-bellied stove, and in a tree close to the house, an owl warned his prey that he was on the hunt.

"I wish I could think of something to say that would make the pain go away, but words are useless. Driving up here, I kept thinking of him in the back-back with Buddy, and him drawing up a storm." Upon hearing his name, Buddy lifted his head, looked around and, not finding what he was looking for, lowered it onto his paws.

"Anyway, your mom and I kept trying to come up with something—" he said, his voice trembling a bit, "so we decided to do this." He picked up a flat package wrapped in brown paper and began to unwrap it. "If you'd help me, Natalie, please."

The two of them lifted the framed drawing and set it on the mantle above the fireplace.

Everyone looked on in silence. Finally, Ronald spoke.

"Thank you, Eric."

The Smell

It was very faint at first, hardly noticeable. It started in the bedroom. My cousin and her boyfriend had come to visit and meet the new baby and I had given them our bed, my husband Jack being away at his job on the oil rig, and I had gone and slept on the futon in the baby's room. In the morning, after they left, I walked into the bedroom and noticed a slightly unpleasant smell. I thought that it might just be body odor in the bedding, and as I was planning on stripping the bed, I was pretty sure the laundry would take care of the problem. When I pulled the sheets out of the dryer, they smelled fine—fresh and lilac-scented from the fabric softener, just as advertised.

After feeding Sara her bottle and changing her, I put her down for a nap. She's turned out to be a night owl, which means she naps off and on during the day, as I do if I want to get through a long night of walking her. It seems that pacing back and forth the length of the apartment is the only thing that keeps her calm. I remade our bed and thought no more about the smell until I went into the bathroom. I was staring at my weary face in the mirror when I caught another whiff of the smell. It seemed to be the same odor, but stronger—a combination of sour milk, rotten eggs and overused kitty litter. Okay, so now I had pinpointed the possible location, or at least I thought I had. Two options: the diaper pail or the drain in the shower. The pail for Sara's dirty disposable diapers contains a scented plastic trash bag for easy removal, and the lid has a compartment that holds one of those deodorizing thingies. That seemed to mask any bad odor.

When I was growing up in the country, we lived in a house that had a septic tank. We were not connected to the town's sewer system, so every so often the raw sewage from our tank would back up and ooze up and out the drains in the house. I remember how gross it was and how it made me want to throw up when I helped my mother take care of the mess. I didn't know if the same problem could happen in an apartment in the city, but I leaned over the shower drain and took a tentative whiff. Nothing. Same for the toilet bowl and the drain in the sink.

The rest of the day was spent doing what I do every day—feeding Sara, changing her diapers, bathing her, soothing her when she cries and longing to get back to work. My maternity leave will be up eventually, and I can't wait to get back to the office, to the daily grind. Who knew that nine to five could be so appealing?! Maybe sitting at my old desk editing advertising copy will make me feel less tired.

I love Sara, I love Jack, I really do, but there is only so much cooking, cleaning and baby-tending that one person can do before they start coming apart at the seams. I've tried to work on a short story I started writing just before the baby arrived, to keep my creative juices flowing, but it's impossible. There is no time, and I'm too exhausted to write anyway.

As the day melted into night, the smell appeared again, but this time it seemed to be in the kitchen. I had just begun cooking some dinner for myself when a stronger version of the original odor wafted up from around the stove. The kitchen is a perfect location for smells, good aromas as well as some not-so-nice ones. Was this scent emanating from the refrigerator—an overripe cantaloupe, a forgotten container of tuna salad? Was the garbage disposal in the sink harboring a glop of dying organic waste? I checked every shelf in the fridge and then reluctantly put my nose close to the drain in the sink. I detected a slightly sweet and sour scent, but not the obnoxious smell that I had encountered earlier. I took my little plate of chicken breast and rice into the living room to get away from the kitchen, but the odor followed me like an evil cloud. I've had no real appetite for weeks, so being surrounded by this toxic smell only stopped me from taking even a little bite.

For the next two days the smell came and went, sometimes quite strong and sometimes hardly detectable. Sara had gotten colicky, so between trying to soothe her and stop her crying and worrying that she wasn't getting enough nourishment, I didn't have time to pay attention to the mystery smell.

*

Sara is my first baby, and I guess I'm extra nervous about doing a good job mothering her. She didn't come with an instruction book, and since my mother is no longer with us, I haven't had a certified mom around to give me motherly advice. Her sister, my Aunt Janice, stayed with me for a week after the birth, and I am eternally grateful to her for all her help. But she's back in Seattle, and I can't keep calling her about every little thing. Jack is hundreds of miles out in the ocean, off the Louisiana coast, and not due back for another two weeks, so I'm really on my own here. He and I email and FaceTime (when it works), but it's not the same as having him here beside me. He wants me to move down to New Orleans so he doesn't have to keep flying back and forth to New York, but that means I'd have to give up my job. He keeps saying that he's making enough money that I don't have to work, but for me, it's not just about the money. I love my job. Clichéd as it may sound, it fulfills me, defines me.

Last Monday I pulled myself together, which is getting harder to do these days, and headed off to the supermarket. I was running out of Pampers and I needed more formula. I had been breast-feeding Sara, but I was afraid she wasn't getting enough milk, so I've been augmenting the breast milk with formula. In all honesty, it's just easier to give her a bottle, and my nipples are feeling greatly relieved. I had placed Sara carefully in the sling carrier, making sure her face was exposed. Aunt Janice scared me half to death with stories of babies suffocating, so I'm always extra careful with Sara.

Gristedes was busy as usual, but I found everything I needed and we checked out fairly quickly. Walking home, with Sara dozing on my chest and my little shopping cart bouncing along behind me, was a pleasure because we were away from that persistent smell. Even the exhaust from the cars and trucks smelled better than whatever it was that was living in our apartment.

A woman was at the entrance to the apartment house as we arrived, and she held the doors for us as I clumsily wheeled the cart into the lobby. I realized that it was the lady who lived down the hall from us, an older woman whom I had seen once or twice. I thanked her and she introduced herself, very formally, as Mrs. O'Brien. I introduced myself as well, and she asked me what Sara's name was. By the time we were all in the elevator, the conversation had faded away into an awkward silence. Reaching our floor, Mrs. O'Brien held the elevator doors open and we both started to head off to our apartments. I thanked her once more for her kindness and turned to put my key in the door.

You know how once in a while you can get a feeling something's not quite right—the hair on the back of your neck stands up or your heart beats faster? All of a sudden, I didn't want to enter the apartment. It was as if someone or something was standing behind the door. I just knew it—I could feel it. Only after I heard the sound of Mrs. O'Brien's door closing did I break out of my paralysis and force myself to unlock the door. As I turned the knob, I told myself I was just being foolish.

The smell was so overpowering that my eyes watered. I could almost see it, feel it, taste it. It was thick and hot like a poisonous soup. I stumbled my way into the baby's room, covering my mouth and nose with my hand, and slammed the door shut. Mercifully, Sara was still napping next to me in her sling and oblivious to the ghastly fumes that surrounded us. The smell had evolved into a noxious mix of feces, rotting fruit, vomit and carrion. What the hell was going on?

I didn't know what to do. We couldn't stay in the apartment. It wasn't safe. It was unhealthy. It was beyond unhealthy. This was dangerous—deadly! Where should I go with Sara? Where could I go? I found myself turning around and around in a circle like some trapped animal.

Finally, I grabbed one of the small bath towels I use to dry Sara and tied it around my lower face. I rushed out of the room and through our front door into the hall. In a panic, I found myself heading down the corridor towards Mrs. O'Brien's apartment. When I reached her door, I began beating on it. The loud racket and the movement of my body as I pounded on the metal door woke up Sara, and she began to cry. I stopped knocking and pressed the buzzer instead. After what seemed an eternity, the door opened and I saw a narrow slice of Mrs. O'Brien's face staring at me from behind the safety chain.

When I think back on it now, what a scene she must have faced looking out into the hall—a masked crazy lady holding a screaming baby and yelling about something or someone lurking in her apartment. It was a miracle she didn't slam the door in my face and call the police. But she undid the chain, opened her door and, putting her arm around my shoulders, gently walked me into her apartment. It was probably just to get me out of the hall before some of our other neighbors opened their doors to see what was going on. Whatever her reason, I didn't care; her apartment was a sanctuary away from that awful smell.

After I calmed down and got Sara to stop crying, I apologized to Mrs. O'Brien and began to try and explain my dilemma. I asked her if she had been experiencing a strange smell in her apartment as well. She said she hadn't, and asked what kind of smell it was. Was it a gas leak? Because if it was, we needed to call the gas company and get people out of the building. I assured her it wasn't that kind of an odor, but more like rotting garbage. She then said that she would go back with me to my apartment and help me find the source of the problem. I didn't want to ever enter that place again, but I reluctantly agreed, as I really had no choice. The baby's milk was there, her clothes, my phone, my purse—damn it—my keys! I had left my keys on the kitchen counter. I was locked out.

Mrs. O'Brien received the news with a nod of her head and then calmly picked up her phone and called the manager, who lives in the basement of our apartment building. Five minutes later he was putting his passkey in the door. I now had two people who could witness what was going on in my apartment—Mrs. O'Brien and Mr. Cruz, the manager. He pushed the door open, and Mrs. O'Brien stepped cautiously into my entry hall. Mr. Cruz followed behind her. I stayed in the corridor, waiting. I knew the two of them would come rushing out with their hands over their mouths. After what seemed like hours, I heard Mrs. O'Brien call out my name, and with my stomach threatening to embarrass me, I slowly entered my apartment.

To my relief, the smell was much less potent, but it was still there. I followed Mrs. O'Brien's voice into the kitchen and found her standing next to Mr. Cruz, who was kneeling next to the sink. I asked him what he had found. He glanced up at me, and the conversation, as I remember it, went something like this:

Mrs. O'Brien: "Nothing, my dear. In fact, I can't really smell anything like what you described."

Mr. Cruz: "I can't smell nothing. I just check your drain and the one in the bathroom. There's nothing there. Maybe it go away already."

Me: "But it was so strong before. It's not as overwhelming now, but it's still pretty awful."

Mrs. O'Brien: "Well, whatever it was, it seems to have dissipated. I truly can't smell anything. Neither can Mr. Cruz."

Me: "But it's still here. Surely you can notice how it seems to come in waves."

Both she and Mr. Cruz, who had gotten himself up from in front of the sink, exchanged a glance. It was that look that people give each other when they know it's time to excuse themselves and get away from an unpleasant situation. Mrs. O'Brien said she had soup boiling on the stove, and Mr. Cruz had to replace a light bulb up on the sixth floor, but he said I should call him if the smell comes back. And so they left, assuring me everything would be all right. But of course it wasn't all right, as was to be proven later on.

*

A few days went by, and although the odor was still there, it was weak and not as disruptive as before. I talked on the phone with Aunt Janice and told her about the smell. She recommended I pour Clorox bleach down the drain and maybe get some air fresheners for each room. She also talked about postpartum depression and how it can sometimes make you a little paranoid, but I assured her it was not that. It was real. She suggested I call my doctor, but I knew that wasn't necessary. When I talked to Jack, he told me to contact the management office and insist they send someone over to check it out. He reminded me that he'd be home soon and to just hold on.

Hold on to what? I really was feeling like I didn't have anything or anyone to hold on to. It was just the baby and me and that fucking smell.

It was when I bundled up Sara and set off for a trip to Walgreens to pick up the air fresheners Aunt Janice had recommended that I noticed I was being stalked by the smell. That's what it felt like—some phantom figure ready to pounce. I'm walking down the street, and instead of the odor fading as we got further away from the apartment house, it seemed to get stronger. By the time we were standing in the middle of the drugstore, it was almost as overpowering as it had been two days ago. I started to gag, and a nice man who I guess worked there asked me if I was okay. I shook my head and headed for the exit. I thought that the air outside would chase the smell away, but it didn't.

I'm stumbling along, trying not to fall down and hurt the baby, batting at this invisible monster that's spraying us with this ghastly perfume. And then I got it. *I* was the source of the smell! That had to be it. All this time, it was me emitting this noxious odor.

It finally made sense why no one else seemed to smell what I could. That was because *I* was the smell. I felt both horrified and relieved about what I had finally figured out. I put Sara in her crib, turned on the music-box mobile with the pretty butterflies to help her fall asleep, and then hurried into the bathroom, where I stripped off all my clothing, checking each item for evidence of the hellish scent. I would wash everything, my blouse, my jeans, my panties and bra, not only with laundry detergent but with bleach, maybe throw in some cologne as well.

Stepping into the shower, I turned the water on as hot as I could stand it and began scrubbing away with the brush I use to clean the tiles. It hurt like hell, but I knew it was the only way I could get rid of the odor. I washed my hair three times and used my favorite conditioner with the citrus scent to hopefully dispel any remaining odor. When I got out of the shower, I felt faint from being under that hot water for so long, so I put on my terrycloth robe and went straight into the bedroom. I stretched out on my back, on top of the bedcovers, and closed my eyes. And waited. For the smell. To return. The minutes passed by, and the only odor I could detect was the sweet, acidic scent of my citrus conditioner. After a while I looked at the digital clock on the bureau and saw that half an hour had passed. I took a deep breath—no bad smell. Tears of relief filled my eyes. It was over.

I must have fallen asleep, because the next thing I knew it was dark and I could hear Sara crying. I usually keep her in our room at night in a bassinet and only in the crib during the day. I got up quickly, knowing she needed a change of diaper and that she must be very hungry. When I entered her room I could smell the usual baby smells—talcum, baby oil and wet diaper—but no dead animals, sulfur fumes or cow manure. I changed her diaper and even found her poop, with its usually pungent smell, not unpleasant. After sitting for a while in the rocking chair and giving Sara her bottle, I got up and carried her sweet little body into our room and lay down with her on the bed. It felt so wonderful to be free of that mysterious, god-awful vapor.

The Note

It is so important, Jack, that you understand what happened next. I'll try to explain it as simply and clearly as possible. I only did what had to be done.

Sara fell asleep, and I, being so exhausted from all that had happened, did as well. It must have been around midnight when I awoke with a start. The smell was back! It was worse than ever—rotting flesh, sewage, decaying fruit, vomit! I struggled up from the bed, leaving Sara tangled in the covers, and ran into the bathroom to throw up in the toilet. When I got up and went to the sink to rinse out my mouth, I saw this image in the mirror: a woman with bloody scratch marks all over her face and neck. Was that me? And the smell? Was that me? Had my attempt at washing away this nightmare failed? I began sniffing all over my body like some demonic bloodhound. But the smell wasn't as strong in the bathroom as it was in the bedroom, and it was almost undetectable on my body. I stepped back into the bedroom and was immediately hit with a nauseating tsunami of that horrendous smell. It seemed to swirl up from the bed like a living being. It was radiating off the covers where the baby was lying.

I couldn't believe it. I didn't want to believe it, but somehow I knew, down deep, it was true. It was Sara. All along it had been my baby, our beautiful baby girl. Something was terribly wrong with our little Sara. I don't believe she was possessed or anything stupid like that. This was not the work of the devil, or a curse or a divine judgement. This was an illness, a birth defect, some horrible, incurable disease. I remember thinking right after she was born that something was wrong, but I had blocked it out until now.

I knew what had to be done. I couldn't let Sara suffer. Imagine her life with this terrible affliction, the isolation, the humiliation, the madness that would surely follow. I couldn't bear it. You wouldn't be able to bear it either, Jack.

It was over very quickly. I filled the kitchen sink with nice warm water, removed Sara's diaper and lowered her in like when I bathe her. The smell almost overcame me, but once she was in the water it subsided a bit, and I wiped her little body softly with her pink washcloth. I hummed that song I always sing to her—"Go to Sleep, Little Baby"—and then I let go of her. She floated for a moment and then sank down to the bottom of the sink. That was the hardest part. She jerked her arms and legs and thrashed about for a few seconds, and then she went still. I'm pretty sure she didn't suffer. At least I hope she didn't. After a little while, I pulled her out of the water and wrapped her in a towel. She'll be in her crib waiting to say good-bye to you, Jack, when you get home next week. And the smell is gone.

The Land of the Three Willows

It is a beautiful place. It is green, so very green, and it seems to go on forever. Even if I walked all day, I could never reach the end. Maybe that is because I don't want it to end. Most of the time I feel very safe when I am there, alone. It is my secret place, and I never let anyone else follow me when I enter this magical land. But sometimes there are shadows that don't belong there, and that scares me.

My name is Ostara. That is not my given name. It is the name I wear when I visit my secret place. I am twelve years old, and I am able to do many magical things. Not magic tricks, like pulling a rabbit out of a hat or making a coin disappear, but real magic. When I am "Ostara the Great," I can turn a stone into a turtle or make it snow in July.

There are mountains far to the north. Sometimes they are blue, like the back of a dolphin, and then they turn Crayola purple. There is always snow on their giant shoulders. However, I have never tried to travel to them, as they appear to be many days away. Besides, I have a bad feeling about what might be behind those beautiful rainbow peaks.

Sometimes my friend Diamond appears along the path. He is a handsome white wolf with silver-like blue eyes that sparkle and give him his name. He is magical too, like me, and his favorite trick is to disappear and then reappear when you least expect it.

The first time I entered this beautiful place, I followed a path through trees so tall they disappeared up among the clouds in the sky. With a flash of white, Diamond arrived in front of me and, after greeting me with a welcoming nod, led me deeper into the woods. As dark and mysterious as it was, I still felt safe with Diamond trotting ahead of me, like the welcoming beam of a lighthouse.

Eventually, the trees began to grow shorter and farther apart, and a large clearing appeared. It was covered with a soft layer of moss and a dark green carpet of plants with tiny blue blossoms. A narrow stream of clear water whispered its way across this magical meadow, and, reflected in its rippling surface, stood three weeping willow trees.

Diamond had seated himself like a white Buddha in front of the middle tree, which was the largest. Its drooping branches rained down around his head almost as if it were caressing him. The other two trees were smaller and seemed to lean in slightly towards the center tree. "This is Darax," said Diamond of the center tree. "She is the mother of Strom and

Stablo." He turned his head first to the left tree and then to the tree on the right. "They are brothers," he explained.

Diamond doesn't actually speak like you or I do. It's just that when he looks at me a certain way, I understand what he's saying. "Darax welcomes you to her queendom and invites you to sit beside her and her two Princes," Diamond said, stretching himself out in a sphinx-like position. I was a little nervous about joining him under the umbrella of branches, but once I sat down, it was as if I had returned to a place I knew well.

Darax and her sons live at the center of what I've come to call the Land of the Three Willows. Their gentle energy radiates out into the fields, the hills and the woods, like the ripples on a pond. Whenever I go exploring, no matter how far I wander, I can feel them watching over me.

Someday I will draw a map of this special place with all the wonderful things I have discovered. Like the Upside-Down Falls, where the water runs up the cliff. I know you think I'm lying, but it's true. The stream, which I have named the Wanderer, continues into the woods until it meets a hill made of stone the color of the deer that I often see drinking from the stream. Here the water climbs up the steep side of the hill and then continues gurgling along its flat, green top. It does, it really does.

Then there is the Cave of Voices. The first time I entered it I was scared, because I started to hear someone talking, but then it changed into singing, and the sound was so beautiful that I was no longer afraid. Diamond had led me to this cave, but for some reason he wouldn't follow me inside. In fact, in all the times that I've visited the cave, he has always waited for me outside.

I have never been in other caves, but I have always imagined them to be dark and scary. The Cave of Voices, however, has walls that glow with a soft, blue-white radiance, so that you feel like you are standing in moonlight. The songs that emanate from the voices echo off the walls and wrap around me like a warm shawl. I don't really know where the singing comes from, even though I have searched every inch of the cave. It's as though the music lives in the air itself.

There are several very old ruins in the Land of the Three Willows: a castle, a cottage, a bridge and a tower. The castle is hollow inside; just the outside walls are still standing, but it's a great place for climbing. It is covered with vines and moss, and I often imagine what it must have been like to live there.

The cottage is very small, as if it belongs to the seven dwarfs or to some magical woodchuck. It has holes in the roof, but sometimes I rest in the room with no openings in the ceiling. I cuddle with Diamond, and he keeps me warm. There is an old wooden shelf on one wall that has a single book resting there, like a lonely visitor. The book is very dusty, and the leather cover creaks when you open it. When I first tried to read its yellowing pages, I saw that it was a volume of poems, but the next time I opened it, it had turned into a book of riddles. "What goes up and never down, makes no sound and is not round?" I'm still trying to figure that one out.

When I need to cross the Wanderer at its widest point, I can use the Turquoise Bridge. Although it is made of big stone blocks, the color of the rock is this pale blue-green, like a mermaid's tail. The bridge is crumbling in places, mostly the side walls, but it seems safe. One day I was looking at the reflection of the bridge in the water and I noticed that there was writing on its underside. I tried to read what it said, but it was just a bunch of words in a language I didn't understand. I hope someday to be able to translate what it's saying.

The tower is on the mesa above the Upside-Down Falls. Although it tilts a little bit, it's still solid, and the stone stairs inside take you up to a room at the top. Here it is brightly lit, with daylight from the four openings that face in four directions. You can see the way the land is laid out, north, south, east and west. There are faded letters painted above each window to tell you in which direction you are facing.

There is so much more to write about, but I must stop for now, as it is getting dark and my candle is burning low. Until next time, yours truly, Ostara.

*

Martin,
This is truly an original and fantastic essay. I'm very impressed with your use of language, and your vocabulary is way beyond what is expected from a seventh grader.

While I really enjoyed reading what you composed and wish I could grade it according to its merit, I'm afraid you misunderstood the assignment.

I always like to start the school year by getting to know something about my students. That's why I asked you to write about yourself, your <u>family</u> and your <u>home life</u>.

I'll be glad to accept another essay in which you use your exceptional writing skills to tell us something about your <u>real</u> life.

C+

*

My Garden

The Land of the Three Willows *is* real! I know how hard it is for outsiders to believe it when I tell them about Darax and her sons and Diamond and the tower and all the other magical things I have seen. But it doesn't matter. I know they are real. I have seen and heard and touched and tasted everything I am writing about.

For example, there is a garden near the castle that was very overgrown with weeds and brambles, some as tall as me. By using my magic, I cleared and restored it to what I imagine was its previous life. Anything and everything can grow there: purple carrots, red potatoes, blueberries, blackberries and green lettuces and herbs. And flowers! Yellow sunflowers (my favorite, because they are always smiling), pink hollyhocks like tiny ballerinas, bluebells, orange nasturtiums, red poppies and chartreuse hydrangea. Color is everywhere!

But best of all, there is a corner of the garden where a special treat for Diamond pops up every so often—a bone. I cast a spell so that bones push their way up through the rich black soil, and Diamond is right there to partake of a gift created just for him. We sit on the mossy banks of the Wanderer and munch on the gifts from my garden.

I am very happy and contented when I am here with my true family—the Willows, Diamond and Jubbie. I realize I haven't told you about Jubbie yet. That will have to wait till next time. I have to sleep now so I can explore some more tomorrow.

*

Martin,
I'm afraid this paper is unacceptable. The assignment was a book report on <u>The Golden Compass</u>, not an essay about your garden.
Please try and use your overactive imagination to write about your reaction to the book assigned.
I know you can do it.
D+

*

Jubbie

Jubbie is so much more interesting than that girl Lyra, the one in *The Golden Compass*. He appeared by the tower on my third visit to the three willows. At first I didn't see him because he blended into the gooseberry bushes that grow around the base of the tower. He does that a lot. He's kind of like a chameleon. I think he's what you call a sprite, also known as an elf or fairy or pixie or leprechaun. Whatever he is, he makes me laugh—a lot. Diamond says his whole name is Jubilee, but I prefer to call him Jubbie. Unlike Diamond, he can talk out loud, but I can't understand what he says. To me, when he talks in his high, tinkly voice, it's gibberish, Jubbie gibberish. He also doesn't seem to grasp what I'm saying in my human language. So to communicate, we have devised ways to act out what we have to say. For example, if Jubbie wants us to climb the tower, he will use his fingers to create a little man walking up steps. And if I want him to show me where he sleeps at night, I close my eyes and rest my head on my folded hands. I found out he sleeps up high in a giant pine tree.

Sometimes there are storms that blow in from the mountains. Diamond, Jubbie and I retreat to the room in the cottage and watch the rain and lightning from the small window opening. It is so exciting, like fireworks on Independence Day. One time a big, bright bolt of lightning struck Jubbie's tall pine tree and I heard it scream. I got very upset, but Diamond let me know that it was just a scream of surprise and that the tree was going to be all right. Jubbie nodded in agreement.

Jubbie can be very mysterious, and I know he has many secrets. He is often away for days, and when he returns I can't get him to act out where he has been. Maybe I'll follow him sometime and see where he goes.

*

Unacceptable. F

*

The Well of Mystery

Yesterday I tried to follow Jubbie, but it wasn't easy. He kept fading into the bushes and the trees. He even blended into the Upside-Down Falls. One minute he was in front of the water, and then he *was* the water. The only thing that gave him away were his green eyes. There they were, two bright emeralds, floating across the front of the falls. Now I know to always look for his eyes when he starts blending into the background.

Hoping that he wouldn't notice me, I kept several yards behind him, and we traveled pretty far. We came to a small clearing with what seemed to be a stone well in the center. Jubbie stopped and took a look around, checking that he was alone (he didn't see me hiding behind a large oak tree), and then, with one quick leap, he jumped into the well. I was astounded and alarmed. I ran over to the well and peered carefully over the edge, afraid of what I might see. There seemed to be no water in the well, and there was no Jubbie, either. I could tell it was quite deep, but instead of being dark at the bottom, there was a faint glow of orange light. It allowed me to see hand- and foot-holds running up and down the rocky sides of the well.

I sat on the edge of the well and swung my legs over the lip. I was torn between my desire to see where Jubbie had gone and my fear of falling down into what seemed to be an endless vertical tunnel. My decision was made easy by the arrival of Diamond from out of nowhere and his insistence that I not climb down into the well. "It's not safe, and Jubbie will be very upset if he finds out you followed him."

Diamond tugged on my sleeve and began pulling me off the top of the well. "We must go now, before Jubbie hears you. I have been sent here to summon you to attend Queen Darax. She has a mission for you," he said to me with his eyes. I really wanted to find out what was at the bottom of this mysterious well, but a royal command was—a command. And so, reluctantly, I joined Diamond for the long walk back to the meadow and the three willows.

*

F. Martin, please give this note to one of your parents.

```
Dear parents or guardians,

     I'm writing you concerning your child, Martin. I am
quite worried about what I observe to be very irra-
tional behavior. Either from some learning disability
we have not been informed about or from just plain
stubbornness, Martin refuses to complete any of the
given assignments. Attention in class is non-existent,
with a lot of staring out the window and drawing in
his notebooks.
     I have tried to elicit information about his family
and his home life in order to better understand what's
going on, but to no avail. I know he is very smart,
and his writing shows an amazing vocabulary, far above
his grade level. From the essays he's been turning in,
I believe his imagination is boundless, but I think
it's running away with him. He needs to put all that
energy into his regular schoolwork.
     As Martin is a new student, having transferred here
from out of state, I don't have access to his earlier
teachers and to anything they could share with me
about his behavior in the classroom.
     Teacher/Parent Conference Night is next month, and
I look forward to meeting with you and learning more
about Martin. Until then, please emphasize to him the
importance of his doing his homework and his paying
attention in class.
     If you wish to meet with me before Conference
Night, please feel free to make an appointment.

     Yours truly,

     Sarah Brownell
     7th Grade English
```

*

The Mission

Today I started to fulfill Queen Darax's wishes by climbing to the top of the tower. She had requested that I position myself there as a lookout because she felt the presence of an intruder. And so I find myself moving from window to window, gazing out onto the beautiful vistas of forest and meadow and mountain, trying to discover evidence of someone who doesn't belong here. It is very tiring to stare at miles of landscape and to try and not be fooled into seeing an enemy behind every tree or under every bush.

Diamond tells me that the Queen fears only two things, fire and the axe. This is understandable, since she and the two Princes are rooted to the ground. He told me about a close call that happened a long time ago. Lightning, like we saw that other time, struck an oak tree that was very old and very dry, and it exploded into flame. The fire jumped from its branches to the limbs of the surrounding trees and then leapt onto the meadow. The Queen watched as the flames raced toward her and her sons, who were much younger and smaller at the time, and she tried to protect them with her weeping branches. Diamond says that's when the two little Princes bent in towards their mother, and they have remained that way ever since.

"But what happened?" I asked. "What stopped the fire from burning them all up?"

"It started to rain," Diamond eyed to me, "so heavily that there was a flash flood that pushed water over the banks of the Wanderer and sent it into the meadow. Thankfully, they were all saved, but the Queen has been very wary ever since." "And with good reason," I thought.

I'm embarrassed to confess that I sort of dozed off while I was in the tower. It was warm and quiet and, in truth, kind of boring. When I awoke, I was upset to see that the sun had moved from the eastern sky to just above the most northwesterly edge of the mountains. Had I failed Queen Darax? Had someone snuck into her domain while I was off in dreamland?

Jubbie came rushing up the stairs as I hurried from window to window, trying in vain to spot an intruder. He grabbed my hand and started pulling me towards the stairwell.

"What is it, Jubbie?" I asked, dreading the answer. "Is it the Queen?" I mimed putting an invisible crown on my head. He replied by nodding and swinging his arm back and forth like he was a baseball player.

"What's wrong?" I asked, foolishly forgetting that Jubbie couldn't understand my language. He squeaked some kind of response and, letting go of my hand, grabbed with both fists what I imagined was an invisible bat and slammed out several invisible home runs.

"I don't understand, Jubbie. What—" And then I got it. It wasn't a baseball bat, it was an axe!

*

Parent-Teacher Conference
Transcript of Taped Conversation

Teacher: Sarah Brownell
Guardian: Mrs. Joseph Davis
Student: Martin Garcia

Brownell: Thank you so much for being here this evening. I'm—

Davis: Will this take very long? My husband is waitin' in the car.

Brownell: Well—we're supposed to limit each meeting to only 15 minutes in order to be able to talk to all the parents, so it shouldn't take any longer than that. Let me start by saying that Martin is very special.

Davis: You know Martin is not our son. We're just fostering him.

Brownell: Yes, I was aware of that. Well—as I was saying, Martin is special. But I am very concerned that he is failing my class. As I said in the note I sent you, he seems—

Davis: What note? We didn't get no note.

Brownell: Oh, dear. I guess Martin forgot to give it to you. Anyway, he seems to be living in this imaginary world, and—

Davis: Oh, yeah, he lives in his own world. He never talks, we never know what the hell is going on in that head of his. He doesn't always do his chores, and he never plays with the other kids.

Brownell: You have children of your own?

Davis: Nah. Joe and me couldn't have kids. That's probably why we sorta started taking in fosters.

Brownell: How many children are you fostering?

Davis: Wow! Over the years we musta parented at least fifteen or more. Right now we only got five.

Brownell: I see. Let me ask you, does Martin seem to be doing his homework? Does he—

Davis: Well, he's always writing. I don't know if that's his homework, but he has these pages full of writing. When he's not daydreaming, he's scribbling away. You know, with five kids, it's kinda hard to stay on top of each one of them about their school-work.

Brownell: Yes, it must be quite a challenge. Getting back to Martin, I was hoping you could fill me in on his history, where he—

Davis: Well, to be honest, he's had a bit of a rough time. I think we're like the fourth foster home he's been in. We don't know nothin' about his mama except that she was young and gave him up for adoption when he was a baby. The family that adopted him, the Garcias, had to give him up when he was about five 'cause the husband was killed in some sort of acci-dent, something about a fire—I'm not sure. Anyway, that was when he was put into his first foster home. The social worker told us that Martin had a lotta trouble with the first family that took him in, and I guess it didn't get much better with the next two homes. She thinks we'll be a better match. I sure hope she's right.

Brownell: How long has Martin been with you?

Davis: A couple of months. He came to us in late June.

Brownell: Well, I'm sure you'll do a good job with Martin. Just see that he completes his assignments—that he does his homework. It's very important.

Davis: You got it. My Joe is very good about settin' rules and disciplinin' the kids. Spare the rod and spoil the child is his motto. He'll see that Martin toes the line.

Brownell: Well, Mrs. Davis, I don't mean that—

Davis: I'm sorry, but I really gotta go. Joe will be havin' a fit if I don't hurry up.

End of Transcript

*

Capture

By the time we had made our way to the meadow, I could hear Diamond howling. As the willows came into sight, I could see him, the white fur on his back standing straight up. He was staring at a figure frozen in place a few feet from the Queen, and he was snarling, his lips pulled back to reveal his sharp ivory fangs.

As we got closer, Jubbie began to fade away—I guess because he was scared—and I found myself approaching the intruder by myself.

It was a man, a large, bearded man, dressed in deerskins and fur pelts. He looked like a mountain made up of bear, fox, coyote, beaver and wolf hides. I was especially unhappy about the beautiful silver-gray wolf's tail that he had wrapped around his neck. Diamond was not too pleased about it, either. He continued to growl and assumed a crouch that I feared was his preparation for an attack.

I cautiously stepped closer to the hairy mountain man and stopped when I saw the axe he held with both hands. He looked at me and then returned his gaze to Diamond.

"Who—who are you?" I stammered, trying to keep my legs from shaking.

"Who the Hades are thou, my little worm?" he replied.

"I'm Ostara," I answered, straightening up so as to appear taller. The hairy mountain man took a step closer to the Queen but stopped when Diamond snarled and looked like he was about to leap.

"Does this beast belong to thee? If so, call him off or I shall remove his head from his mangy body," he threatened, raising his axe in the air.

I hurriedly replied, "Yes sir, I will, but only if you promise to not harm him or the Queen and her sons."

"What Queen? I see not a royal personage," he responded, looking all around. I stepped between him and Diamond and the Queen.

"Please sir, lower your axe. These three trees are the royal family of which I speak."

The hairy mountain man snorted a laugh but lowered his weapon. "The only thing I see before me are three willow trees, and I am in need of their branches for weaving and their wood for burning. So stand aside, thou worthless turd of a boy, or I shall remove your branches, one by one."

I was at a loss as to what I should do. I needed my arms and legs, but I couldn't let him kill the Queen. I looked at Diamond, and he eyed me with a message from Her Majesty. "Darax says this is a man from beyond the mountains and he is violating a treaty that exists between his people and the creatures of her realm."

"Good sir," I spoke quickly, taking a cue from what Diamond had just told me, "I believe you are not observing the rules of the—the treaty."

"What rules?!" he shouted back at me.

"Er—well—" I hadn't a clue.

"You mean the rule about not setting foot in this land of worthless misshapen beings? The treaty that says we may not cross the border unless given permission by some holy muckamuck? Well, I am not letting a faded piece of parchment keep me from earning my livelihood!" He raised his axe. "Out of my way, thou insignificant maggot!"

Out of the corner of my eye I suddenly saw two glowing emeralds floating at the left side of the hairy mountain man. Jubbie! The axe was about to divide my head in two when the mountain man suddenly pitched backward and fell on his side. The axe went flying out of his hands and landed near my feet.

"What in the name of Hades is—" he yelled, and then he started batting at his arms and up and down his legs. Jubbie seemed to be sticking him with something sharp, but then I saw what it really was. A round gray wasp nest was bouncing around in the air above the mountain man. I picked up the axe, which was very heavy, and stepped away from him in order to avoid being stung.

Diamond and I formed a shield in front of Darax and her sons. We would make the mountain man our captive and protect Her Majesty no matter what.

*

Spelling Test
Name: Martin Garcia
1. agitate
2. potential
3. hilarious
4. maternal
5. catastrophe
6. stodgy
7. quench
8. ~~epademic~~ epidemic
9. reprimand
10. insinuate

100 A+
Wow! Great job, Martin. Keep up the good work.

*

Decision

The mountain man was covered in big red welts and seemed to be unconscious. Jubbie had taken the wasp nest back to the tree where he had found it, and now he stood, fully visible, by my side. The concern at this time was what to do with the captive. Jubbie mimed dying by falling to the ground, but I wasn't up to killing the mountain man. "I think Jubbie is saying," Diamond eyed to me, "that the wasp stings might dispatch the intruder if we just let nature take its course." I had heard of victims dying of a wasp attack, but this might not be the case with our captive.

"He's still breathing," I pointed out, "and when he awakens, he will be in great pain. I'm going to use some magic to help heal the welts." I squatted down next to the intruder and skimmed my hands over his body, making sure to not actually touch his skin. My magic works because I believe it works. I simply see in my head what I want to happen and it happens. Why it works is a mystery to me, but this has been true my whole life, so I just go with it. Thinking equals doing.

Our next mission was to figure out where to put the mountain man. He had to be locked up somehow until we could find a way to return him back to the mountains. "Jubbie," I shouted, getting his attention. "We need vines," I said, as I mimed pulling down strands of the vines that climb many of the trees here in the Queen's domain. "We'll use them to tie him up and then we'll take him up to the top of the tower." Jubbie raced off in search of vines while Diamond and I stood watch over the still unconscious mountain man.

Getting the big hairy body of the mountain man up the sixty-five steps to the top of the tower proved impossible. Diamond, using his teeth, tried pulling him by tugging on the vines that were wrapped around his feet, while Jubbie and I pushed on his shoulders, but it was a no go.

"We'll drag him to the Cave of Voices instead," I said, panting from the exertion. "Jubbie, you will stand guard in front of the cave while Diamond and I speak with the Queen about this situation."

Leaving an unhappy Jubbie, we walked back to the Queen and her sons. The two Princes seemed to have moved closer to their mother, which was, of course, impossible, but that's what it looked like to me. Diamond and I bowed to Her Majesty, and I inquired if they were all right.

"The Willow Queen thanks you for your concern," Diamond eyed to me. "She has not been harmed, nor have her sons, thanks to you."

"Well, it was Diamond and Jubbie who really prevented the mountain man from hurting you," I replied to the noble tree.

"Ah, but you bravely stood up to the intruder," Diamond responded, continuing to interpret, "and did not back down even when he made to chop you in half."

I reluctantly accepted the compliment. "Your Majesty, we need your guidance as to what we should do now with the intruder. How do we get him to go back to the mountains?"

Diamond smiled his wolfish smile and answered for the Queen. "Leave him in the cave tonight, and in the morning he will return to his homeland on his own." So that's what we did.

*

```
Memo
To: Vice Principal Adams
From: Sarah Brownell

Would it be possible to speak with you at the end
of this school day? I am very concerned about one of
my seventh graders, Martin Garcia. He is failing my
English class and I don't know what to do to help him.
He is obviously very bright but does not do any of the
work assigned in class.
     I have met with his foster mother, who has assured
me that they are working on the problem, but I haven't
seen any improvement. In fact, the situation seems
worse. He is silent and withdrawn in the classroom.
The only evidence of his intelligence are the essays
he turns in in place of the assignments he is given.
They are stories about magic trees, wolves and giants,
and while the subject matter is typical adolescent
fantasy, personally, they read to me like the writings
of an adult. I find myself wondering if some grownup
is helping him, and if so, why.
     Anyway, I'm attaching a few examples of his compo-
sitions for your perusal. Let me know what you think.
```

*

Different Sounds

Diamond and I returned to the Cave of Voices early the next day. We found Jubbie asleep at the entrance to the cave, with his scarf tied under his chin and up over his ears, as if he had a toothache. When we shook him awake, he clapped his hands over his cloth-covered ears and pointed angrily at the cave opening. It was then that I heard a loud whimpering echoing from out of the glowing mouth of the cave. "Jubbie seems to be indicating that the mountain man made a lot of noise last night," Diamond said, in his usual eyeing way of communication.

I took a cautious step into the cave's soft blue entrance and saw the hairy intruder struggling against the vines wrapped tightly around his mountainous body. His face was wet with tears, and when he caught sight of me, he called out in terror. "Oh, by all the gods, please, please help me! Stop them, please!"

"Stop whom?" I asked, looking about for who or what was frightening him.

"Those banshees, those—those screaming voices from hell!"

I listened for a moment but heard only the usual sweet sounds of heavenly music.

"Please, make them stop or I shall go insane! All night—the shrieks, the curses—the threats! I have not closed my eyes!"

He arched his back and twisted his head from side to side, as if to shake the voices out of his head. I can't imagine what the long night must have been like for him.

"If I release you from your bonds, will you promise not to harm me or my friends?"

"Oh, yes, my young squire! Bless you, bless you! I will not harm thee or thy companions—just get me out of here! Please!"

"And will you make your way back to wherever you belong and swear never to return?" I asked as I began untangling the vines that were knotted around his struggling torso.

"Gladly, my kind lad. Just free these legs of mine and I will use them to run away as fast as I can."

As soon as his arms were no longer pinned to his sides, he began tearing at the vines that imprisoned his legs. Together, he and I had him loose of his bonds and up and standing. With his hands over his ears, he didn't waste a moment but bolted out of the cave and headed north towards the mountains. I remained inside for a few moments, listening to the gentle chorus and their sweet songs.

"It seems that not everyone," Diamond eyed to me, "is attuned to the more pleasant voices of the cave."

I smiled as I rejoined him in the fresh morning air. The Willow Queen had taken care of the problem. We were all safe again, for now. I looked around for Jubbie.

"Jubbie? Where are you? You can become visible now—it's okay."

"He headed off into the woods," Diamond informed me, "dragging the intruder's axe."

"Where is he going with it?" I asked, with some concern.

"I believe he is taking it to his well."

*

Martin: Please see me after class today.

*

Jubbie's Secret Lair

I followed the trail Jubbie had left as he dragged the axe behind him. It led, as Diamond predicted, to the old stone well. This time I was going to be brave and find out where Jubbie had gone, so I slipped over the edge and began a careful and slow descent down the rough sides of the well. As Jubbie is smaller than me, I found the footholds spaced closer together, and it was rather difficult to estimate the distance between them. But after a few minutes, I touched the stone floor.

A warm yellow light radiated out of an arched opening in the rocky wall of the well. It seemed to welcome me in, even though I knew Jubbie might be very upset when I showed up uninvited. I stepped through the archway and moved, as quietly as I could, down a narrow passage towards the pulsating glow of golden light. I became aware of a soft, repetitive scraping sound coming from the end of the tunnel. As I got closer to the opening, the light got brighter, and suddenly I stepped into a very large, domed cave. The source of the glimmering radiance was hundreds of bright spheres hanging from the rocky ceiling like miniature suns. Their luminescence revealed a most amazing scene.

Jubbie was standing at a workbench made of stone and chipping away at what appeared to be the handle of the mountain man's axe. The iron head had been removed and lay at his feet. He stopped when he heard me step into the cave. As he turned around, he began to fade away.

"No, don't, Jubbie! It's all right," I pleaded. "It's only me. I'm sorry I surprised you," I said as I watched his glittering green eyes blink rapidly. "I know I shouldn't have followed you down here without your permission."

As Jubbie began to shimmer back into existence, I took a long look at his surroundings. All around the cave floor were these wooden sculptures placed on stone plinths—animals, flowers, strange creatures I couldn't identify. There was even a statue of Queen Darax. She, like the other carvings, seemed to be made from wood Jubbie must have scavenged from the woods and fields.

I spotted a bear made from what looked like a fence post. Where in the world had he found a fence post?

"These are so beautiful," I said. "Did you carve all these?" I asked, pointing first to the carving of a lizard and then to him. He nodded and then picked up the axe handle that he had been working on. I thought for a moment that he meant to give me a good whack, but instead he held it up in front of me. Climbing up the side of the shaft was the beginning of a carving of a vine. I recognized it as a representation of the kind of vine we used to tie up the mountain man. Jubbie put down the handle and, using both his arms and hands, mimed twisting and wrapping the vine around the wasp-stung intruder. We both laughed and enjoyed the echoing giggles. It seemed I had been forgiven my intrusion.

Jubbie took my big hand in his small one and led me around the cave like a tour guide in a museum. I marveled at how realistic his sculptures were. The feathers of the birds, especially those on a hawk, seemed to flutter as if brushed by the wind. And a bobcat carved out of an oak stump appeared ready to pounce. There was a wolf, looking very much like Diamond, that was all teeth and claws. A porcupine with its quills standing at attention and a skunk with its tail lifted as a warning were facing each other like boxers in a ring.

"This is amazing, Jubbie," I said, stopping to look at a butterfly resting on a mushroom, both whittled out of one pine bough. "But how did you get these big pieces of wood down here in—in your workshop?" He smiled with a grin that hinted at the pride he was feeling. I guess he understood from my gestures what I was asking, because he began to mime pushing large objects along what would have been a trail through the woods. He demonstrated tossing them down the well and then rolling them over and over until they reached his cave.

"Queen Darax should see your work," I suggested excitedly. "She would be very pleased to see that you only used wood discarded by the trees—dead limbs, stumps and the like—and not lumber cut from a living tree." I touched one of the statues, a sunflower like the ones in my garden back by the castle. "How about we take this flower to show Her Majesty what a fine artist you are?" Jubbie did not look happy. I realized he didn't understand what I was suggesting, so I mimed introducing the sunflower sculpture to the Queen sculpture. The look on his face went from confused to happy, and he nodded in agreement. Together we lifted the tall, smiling sunflower and walked it down the long corridor. After struggling to get it up out of the well, we marched off in the direction of the meadow, proudly carrying Jubbie's wooden blossom like a flag of victory.

*

```
Mr. and Mrs. Joseph Davis
2200 NE 71st Street

    Dear Mr. and Mrs. Davis,

    It is with regret that I must inform you that
Martin Garcia, whom I believe you are foster parent-
ing, is failing all his classes. We have given him
every opportunity to improve, but he stubbornly
refuses to do any of his assignments or to participate
in any of his classes.
    Martin is exceedingly bright, and it may be that
our curriculum is just not stimulating enough for him.
Therefore, it is our recommendation that he be placed
in a school more attuned to his needs.
```

Whatever your decision, please understand that by
the end of the fall term, we will, reluctantly, have
to expel Martin.

Yours truly,

Jason Adams
Vice-Principal
Oakleaf Middle School

*

The Bridge

The Queen, after praising Jubbie for his creative endeavors, asked that the sunflower be placed somewhere where she and her sons could gaze upon it whenever they liked. After trying a few different spots, we settled on placing it near the foot of the old bridge that arched over the Wanderer. There the wooden sunflower stood, like a smiling palace guard protecting the royal family. Although it was a little bit away from the three willows, it was still visible to them.

A few days later, when I made my way back from the outside world to the Land of the Three Willows, I checked to see how the sunflower was holding up. To my surprise, I found two more sculptures resting beside the tall flower. It was the porcupine and his friend the skunk. Evidently Jubbie, pleased by the reception his first statue received, had decided to share more of his work with Her Majesty. The new additions, their lifelike features glistening in the sun, reminded me of a visit I had once made to the zoo, and I sat down close to them on the banks of the Wanderer, in order to get a better look. It was while I was admiring the details Jubbie had carved into the wooden statues that I became aware again of the writing on the underside of the bridge.

Who had placed these faded words across the bottom of the bridge? What did they say? What was their meaning?

"Trolls," eyed Diamond, who, like he often did, appeared beside me from seemingly out of nowhere. "Many, many years ago a Troll family lived in the water underneath the bridge."

"Trolls? Like in the fairy tales?" I asked.

"And they were much feared," Diamond continued, "for grabbing anyone or anything that attempted to cross what they believed was their bridge."

"What did they do to the—the trespassers?"

"You do not want to know, my young friend. It is said that what remained of any traveler unfortunate enough to be caught by the Trolls would fit in a bread basket."

I visualized a small basket containing bits and pieces of some poor creature and quickly changed the subject. "What do those words mean?"

I asked, pointing to the faint lettering scattered from one end of the bridge to the other.

"They are said to be, in the language of the Trolls, various curses and also descriptions of their vile acts of beastly atrocity," Diamond answered. "I do not read Troll, so I cannot verify the truth of the legend." He turned away from the stream and began trotting off towards the cottage, giving me a quick glance over his shoulder. I sensed that he wished me to follow, and so, standing up and brushing off twigs and leaves, I headed down the path after him.

The inside of the cottage was a bit chilly, having not yet been warmed up by the morning sun. Diamond had entered the one room covered by the roof and stood looking up at the dusty shelf with the magic book. For some reason, I felt nervous as I approached the shelf. Something inside me whispered that I shouldn't open the tattered cover of the old book. But, as if it had a mind of its own, my hand reached out and slowly lifted the stained leather cover.

At first I thought I was looking at an old comic book, like the ones I had read back in the other world. But then I realized that here were illustrations, colored drawings, with descriptions written in the language I had just seen on the underside of the bridge. These were pictures of Troll families—huge, wart-covered adults with skin the color of green olives and Troll children with bow legs and ears like pig snouts. But as I turned the pages, the scenes became so horrific I could no longer keep looking. Severed heads, limbs ripped off a victim's torso, wide Troll mouths with needle-sharp teeth munching on unidentifiable body parts, and blood spattered everywhere. I slammed the book shut.

"Why did you do that, Diamond? Why did you lead me here?" I asked, shaking with revulsion and anger.

"It seemed a better way to explain about the Trolls. It was important that you understand that the Troll was not a creature from a fairy tale, but a real living being."

"Well, you could have warned me ahead of time."

"My apologies, young sir."

"Okay," I replied. "But are there any Trolls still around? Like, hiding away in caves or somewhere?" I asked, with more than a little anxiety.

"Not for hundreds of years," he responded with his eyes, "and they did not live in caves. They were Water Trolls, and the Wanderer was their home."

I took a deep breath and tried to calm down. I looked out the window at the castle and the tower, all resting peacefully near the meadow, and at the stream flowing towards the Upside-Down Falls. And for the first time, I noticed the large round moss-covered rock sitting in the middle of the

Wanderer. Was that the bald head of a giant Troll? "Don't be ridiculous!"
I thought to myself. But—

*

Social Services Report

```
     We were asked by the Principal of Oakleaf Middle
School to look into a possible case of physical abuse
of one of their students. The school reported that the
student, Martin Garcia, arrived in class on Tuesday,
10/15, with a bruised eye and scratches on his cheek.
When asked how he had gotten these injuries, he
remained silent. It was determined that an interview
with his family was necessary, and an appointment was
set up.

     Date: 10/17
     Present:
        Officers: Karen Arias and Kenneth Otis
        Guardian: Mrs. Joseph Davis
        Client: Martin Garcia
     Starting Time: 4:15 pm

     We met with Mrs. Davis, Martin Garcia's foster
mother, at the Davis residence, 2200 NE 71st Street.
She apologized for her husband's absence, as he was
still at work. She was pleasant but seemed a little
nervous. There were four other children, of various
ages, in the house when we arrived with Martin. They
appeared to be healthy with no obvious physical
injuries. We asked her if she would please excuse them
so that we could speak privately, and she sent them
out into the back yard. We noticed that there was a
swing set and various other examples of playground
equipment in the yard.
     The living room was neat and clean, as was the
adjacent kitchen. We asked to see the rest of the
house, and Mrs. Davis took us on a quick tour. There
were three bedrooms; Martin shared one with another
boy, and the three girls were in the second one.
We were surprised at how neat and organized the
children's rooms were, since kids can be pretty messy,
and were informed that one of the house rules was to
keep their spaces clean and neat. Mr. and Mrs. Davis
slept in the third bedroom. The bathroom was a bit
small, and Mrs. Davis joked about how in the morning
the lineup was like Grand Central Station.
     We returned to the front room, and after being
seated and offered coffee, which we refused, we
```

explained why we were there. Mrs. Davis said that she
completely understood, as they were used to visits
from Social Services and that the caseworkers had
always found everything okay.

We went on to talk about Martin and his injuries,
and how two days ago he had refused to tell us what
happened, and how when we picked him up at school
today he continued to remain silent. Mrs. Davis then
put her arm around Martin, a gesture that seemed to
make Martin cringe. She asked him why he hadn't told
us what happened, but he stayed quiet.

She then told us he had been roughhousing with the
other children on the playset in the back yard and had
bumped into one of the metal supports, which banged
his eye and scratched his face. We then asked Martin
if this is what happened, and after a squeeze from
Mrs. Davis he slowly nodded yes.

We then asked if we could speak to the other children, and after some hesitation, Mrs. Davis agreed
and walked us out the back door into the yard. She
introduced us to each child, and their responses were
unanimous: Martin had fallen against a pipe and hurt
himself.

After thanking the children and Mrs. Davis, we
excused ourselves and returned to the office.

Interview terminated: 4:57 pm

Conclusion: Since there was no obvious evidence of
abuse, we had no other choice than to declare this was
an accidental injury.

Signed: Karen Arias
         Kenneth Otis

*

The Battle

After my introduction to the truth about Trolls, I found myself a bit
wary around the waters of the Wanderer. But as the days went by and
spring led to summer and then to fall, my concerns faded, and I enjoyed
the peace and beauty of this magical land—a place that was so much better
than the outside world. Jubbie continued to carve his bestiary, and instead
of lugging wood down to his cave, he worked on his sculptures in the
bright sunlight. The path leading to the bridge was lined with eagles and
wildcats, horses and foxes, and even an alligator. It was beginning to look
like a revisiting of Noah's Ark.

Diamond came and went in his usual manner, and Queen Darax and her boys let the breeze comb through their branches as their leaves turned from green to gold. I would climb the tower and gaze out upon the woods and meadow and watch the seasons change. The faraway mountains grew whiter with new snow, and I'm ashamed to admit that I never once thought about the mountain man. I should have.

It was midnight and I was fast asleep in the cottage, Diamond warming my feet as he rested at the foot of my bed of pine boughs, when Jubbie pulled on my ear to awaken me.

"Wha—what—Jubbie, what is it?" I grumbled. "Why did you—"

Jubbie was jumping up and down and swinging his arms back and forth. I suddenly recognized what he was saying: the mountain man was back!

"Oh, no! No way! Well, we'll send him right home," I shouted, getting up quickly and heading out the door. "Come on, Diamond. We have to consult with the Queen." But Jubbie was shaking his head violently and pointing to the tower.

"He wants us to go to the top of the tower," Diamond eyed. "He wants to show us something."

I was feeling torn because I knew Darax was in danger, but Jubbie was halfway to the tower, and there was something about his agitation that told me I'd better follow him.

The moon was full-blown and the sky so cloudless I could see the stars. The stairwell was bright enough with the light from the night sky to allow us to rush up to the top room with the four arched openings. Jubbie stood looking out of the north arch and pointing. I stepped up next to him and, following the line of his finger, I saw what he was pointing at: hundreds of tiny yellow lights in the far distance.

"He did not come alone," Diamond announced as he joined us at the arch.

"What are those lights?" I asked, not really wanting to know.

"I believe those are torches," Diamond replied. "He has brought fire."

When we got down to the meadow, I could see Her Majesty shimmering in the moonlight. Her sons had grown taller over the summer and stood next to her like golden gladiators. My heart sank at the thought of what lay ahead for them, for all of us. I realized that each torch that we saw flickering in the night was being carried by one of the mountain man's army of invaders. Diamond estimated that there were two hundred of them and that they would arrive by dawn of the next day. What could we do to stop them—a boy, a wolf, a sprite and three trees?

The Queen, speaking through Diamond, recommended that we escape while we could, that we should not put ourselves in harm's way for their sake. I adamantly disagreed.

"We will not desert you, Your Majesty," I proclaimed. "This is your land, which you have so generously shared with us. It must not be destroyed by these unwelcome invaders. Besides, the only place we could flee to is the outside world, and Diamond and Jubbie would never survive there." I almost added that I probably wouldn't survive, either.

Darax tried to turn her recommendation into a command, but we were having none of it. "We are staying by your side, Your Majesty, no matter what. What we have to do now is figure out a way to stop this invasion."

Diamond continued to interpret for the Queen. "She says there is a big storm blowing in from the west that she can use to slow the mountain men down."

"Great! That'll give us a little more time to set up some defenses," I said. Unfortunately, what those would be was yet to be determined.

Around three in the morning the storm moved in, and it was a wild one. The woods screamed with a thousand voices as the wind tore through the tree limbs. The rain that followed felt like tiny daggers as it fell on our bare skin. The Queen pushed the storm slowly to the north, and from our viewpoint in the tower, we watched the rain pummel the approaching army. We could also see the wind extinguishing some of the torches, like a child blowing out their birthday candles.

Diamond, Jubbie, Queen Darax and I used the delay to work out a battle plan, as it was obvious that there was going to be a battle, a big one—three against two hundred.

Just before dawn, we came up with a strategy. Hopefully, it would work. We didn't even want to contemplate its not working.

The sky did not get much lighter at dawn, due to the storm, which was following the invaders as they tramped onwards through the woods. They were getting closer. We had taken up our positions—Diamond at the north end of the bridge, Jubbie up in his tree and I next to Darax on the berm at the edge of the Wanderer. The stream was boiling with all the rainwater that was falling on its surface. The Queen's branches offered me some protection from the painful drops, but it was difficult to see through the curtain of rain. And then I saw them—hundreds of fur-covered bodies, their images distorted by the rippling, wind-blown sheets of rain.

A few of the torches were still lit, but they were sputtering as they fought with the rain to remain lit. Eventually I could hear, over the howling of the wind, the voices of the invaders. They were chanting some kind of war cry, and with each shout, I saw a flash of steel as they raised their mud-spattered arms. Axes!

As they marched closer to the bridge, I saw some of them hesitate. I figured they had seen Diamond doing his "I'm going to rip open your throat" routine. Eventually the whole crowd came to a halt, and then he stepped forward—the same mountain man who had threatened the Queen before.

"We have come to claim this territory as part of the mountain nation," he bellowed. "Surrender and we will not harm thee. Resist and we will kill thee and feed your pretty parts to the buzzards."

It was tempting to consider surrendering, but I knew that even if we did, he and his army would lay waste to the kingdom and probably murder all of us.

"Her Majesty Queen Darax respectfully declines to surrender," I shouted, trying to keep my voice free from quavering with fear, "and requests that you and your men return to the mountains."

This pronouncement brought a roar of laughter from the hairy mountain man and was echoed by his muddy band of followers.

"We take no orders from a tree, my skinny friend. One last chance. Surrender, NOW!" he shouted, raising his shiny new axe, a replacement for the one Jubbie had turned into ivy. There was a moment of silence when all one could hear was the wind and the rain, and then he screamed, "ATTACK!"

The crowd of men from the mountains surged forward and started to cross the bridge. I heard Diamond snarl, and then he let out a howl that was so ear-splitting that I had to cover my ears. That was the signal. It was now or never. I lowered my left hand and used it to grab hold of one of Darax's limbs. "Now, Your Majesty!"

I felt her energy begin to flow into me and radiate out through my arms and legs. It was like nothing I had ever experienced before. I felt strong and wise and—invincible! I truly became Ostara the Great, the magician who could accomplish anything!

The mountain men were pushing and shoving their way across the bridge. I couldn't see or hear Diamond, but I saw a pair of emerald eyes moving among the legs of the intruders as, one by one, they seemed to be tripping and falling. A second wave of men were over the bridge and heading straight for Darax, her sons and me. I extended my right hand and closed my eyes. I saw an image of Noah's Ark and the animals marching two by two. My inner voice began to pray, "Protect us, O kind friends. Flap your wings, let your claws extend, jaws snap, paws scratch, fangs pierce!" I slowly opened my eyes to a miraculous scene. The mountain men were batting away at hawks and eagles that were swooping around their heads. There were men pinned to the ground by wolves and bears. One man was running around in circles trying to escape his rear end, which was bristling with porcupine quills. A horse was rearing up and stomping on any man who came near it. A snake coiled around the leg of another man and he tried to remove it with his axe, only to remove his leg.

The magic had worked! What I had visualized came to be! Jubbie's carvings, so lifelike in their execution, were now truly alive and vanquishing our enemies. Those formerly brave warriors were now screaming like little children as they fled back into the woods. In a matter of minutes the meadow was empty, except for the injured, who were unable to get up and run. I figured that after a night in the Cave of Voices, they would be able to run just fine.

Jubbie began to fade back into his visible self. He looked around and saw all his statues scattered here and there, some of them damaged but most of them still in one piece. Just minutes ago they had appeared to be alive, but now they were once again his beautiful wooden carvings. He picked each one up carefully and started placing them back on their stone bases.

"Thank you, Jubbie," I said, ignoring the fact that he couldn't understand my language. He knew what I was sending his way. Then I mimed, "Have you seen Diamond?" to which he only shook his head. "Diamond? Where are you?" I called out towards the bridge. "Diamond?"

"Is this what you're looking for, young master?" came a deep, scratchy voice from behind me. I turned around quickly to see the hairy mountain man standing near the stream, holding Diamond in his arms. There was blood on my sweet wolf's white fur, and his bright blue eyes were half closed.

"What have you done to him?!" I shouted, ready to pick up one of Jubbie's statues and smash it over the mountain man's head.

"I've done nothing," he replied. "He did it himself, attacking my men. But I will do something to him now, my little maggot, because thou has caused me great distress. A wolf is only good for skinning and then for wearing to keep out the cold, and your wolf has a particularly handsome pelt that will bring a fine price at the market. Too bad there is some damage to his leg, but I can disguise that easily enough. And the blood will wash off."

I could see Diamond's chest rising and falling with little breaths, so I knew he was still alive. The mountain man had a knife strapped to his waist, and to get to it he was going to have to put Diamond down on the grass. As he started to lower the wolf to the ground, I stepped closer.

"Ah, ah, ah, my little toadstool, no tricks," he said, putting his hand on the hilt of the knife. "You owe me this for all the trouble thou has caused."

I looked at this evil man, this hairy creature covered in the wet skins and pelts of so many unfortunate animals, and a rage began to climb up my body and take residence in my head. I closed my eyes and an image started to take shape: at first just a hulking shadow, but then it grew into a huge, olive-green monster covered in warts, with a very wide mouth and eyes like tiny black stones. He was wet and slimy and I knew what he was—a Water Troll. For a moment I was afraid to open my eyes, because I knew what I would see. But I had to accept the responsibility for what I had called up from the depths of the stream, so I slowly lifted my eyelids.

Standing behind the hairy mountain man was a figure twice his height and twice his width. His green hands were as big as snow shovels, and as he lifted them up and began to place them on the mountain man's shoulders, I saw his long sharp fingernails. The mountain man started to turn around, but the Troll grabbed him by the neck and in one swift move bit off his head. Just like that! It happened so fast that I thought I might be seeing things. He then put the body over his shoulder and, walking to the edge of the stream, dove into the swirling waters.

*

Local Man Killed

Allegedly Shot By 12-Year-Old

In what has been deemed an accidental shooting, Joseph R. Davis, 46, a Portland resident, was pronounced dead yesterday evening by the medical staff at Providence St. Vincent Hospital.

Police, who were called to Mr. Davis's home by his wife, found the victim shot in the head. He was still alive but died on the way to the hospital. Mrs. Davis explained that her husband had opened his gun locker in order to remove a pistol he was planning to sell at next week's gun show. When the alleged shooter, a 12-year-old boy they were fostering, showed interest in Mr. Davis's gun collection, the victim handed the weapon to the boy. "He was sure the pistol wasn't loaded, he kept all his guns unloaded," Mrs. Davis said, "but then I heard this loud bang, and when I ran into our bedroom I saw Joe lying on the floor. It was horrible."

The boy's name is being withheld by the police.

*

Ever After

For many days after the last invader had left and the Land of the Three Willows was peaceful once again, I kept having a recurring nightmare of the Troll biting off the mountain man's head and taking his body into the water. I was afraid he would reappear and take me or Jubbie or Diamond to wherever he went under the water. However, Queen Darax assured me that it would not happen again.

"It was only because you were desperate to save me," eyed Diamond as he licked at the cut on his leg, "and for that I am very grateful." He was back to his old self, and the leg wound was healing nicely. But I knew, down deep in my heart, that what I had conjured up was the result of the anger I was feeling, and that if I wasn't careful, it could happen again. Because of me, a man had died, and it could be said that what I did was in self-defense—but in all honesty, I wanted him dead.

What this last terrible event has taught me is that life is not a fairy tale and that there are no happy endings. I thought this land was safer than the outside world, but evil exists everywhere, even here. And so, I have decided to stay in the Land of the Three Willows, because my friends here need protection. I will not return to the so-called real world. There is nothing and no one there that I care for as much as I care for the Queen, her sons, and Diamond and Jubbie. And while we may not live happily ever after, we will live fully, and with an honest love for each other.

Yours truly, Ostara the Great

*

St. Agnes Home for Boys

Patient: Martin Garcia
Age: 12

History:
The patient was admitted on 12/2 after an unsuccessful suicide attempt. As this had been one of several attempts, juvenile detention authorities determined that he needed medical help with constant supervision. Social Services sent him to St. Agnes.

The subject is tall for his age and underweight. Whether this is from malnourishment or from the beginnings of puberty is yet to be determined. There is evidence of several physical injuries, but the subject refuses to discuss the causes. In fact, Martin seems unwilling to answer most of the questions put to him.

Evaluation:
After administering a Stanford-Binet IQ test, it was determined that the subject is borderline genius. We will be testing him with a CHC test at a later date.

I have now had the opportunity of interviewing Martin three times, and by our last meeting he began to relax and to talk a bit about his situation.

I believe there was some physical abuse involved in the home environment, maybe even sexual abuse.

Among the subject's possessions that were sent along with him to the home were several pages of stories he had written. After getting permission from Martin to read them, I was amazed at their maturity and imagination. They have also become a way to get the patient to open up a bit more. When asked about the genesis of these stories, the subject became somewhat uncomfortable. He insisted they were real but admitted that the land he wrote about might have been inspired by the public golf course he crossed every day on his way to school. It was there that he passed a weeping willow tree that he claimed talked to him. When asked what it talked to him about, he admitted he did most of the talking. I then asked him about the bridge and the other buildings that I read about in his stories.

It seems there was a Japanese-style bridge that crossed a small pond, which I imagine was a water trap at the golf course. He said the underside was sprayed with graffiti which had a lot of bad words that upset him.

The tower in his stories was a water tower that supplied the golf course's watering system. The cottage, as he described it, must have been the clubhouse. The ruined castle was a jungle gym in a children's playground at the edge of the golf course. A kid's sandbox next to the playground became for him an abandoned well.

It seems that Martin spent a lot of time in this public place. My thought is that this was a refuge from what might have been an untenable home life. Martin will still not talk about his time in his foster home or in any of the other foster facilities.

Most telling was the friendship he developed with the golf course groundskeeper, a man named Julian, and the man's dog, Ruby.

<u>Diagnosis</u>:
In my opinion, the patient is somewhere on the autism spectrum, perhaps measurably in the Asperger's scale.

<u>Recommendation</u>:
One-on-one therapy sessions should be continued.
Due to his talent and passion for writing, this should be part of his occupational therapy.
Group therapy, at this point, may not be helpful, as the subject is very introverted and frightened. Perhaps later, when he has acclimated to his environment.

Administer low dosage of Sertraline once a day.

Signed: 12/15
Dr. David Levin

Happy Holidays

Christmas is a really big deal here in our small town. Come late September, some of the merchants start decorating their stores in red and green, much to the annual displeasure of our older residents. But the big push comes the day after Halloween, when witches and skeletons are replaced with Santa and his elves. Forget about Thanksgiving. That is just a quick stop for a meal before heading off to Christmas land.

Elmsville is located southwest of Buffalo, New York, with a population of about 8,000 outstanding citizens. It's been around since 1857, and don't you forget it. Some of the families here never let you forget that their ancestors were here even earlier, as early as 1657. I try and remind them that there was a group of peoples here long before that, but they're not interested.

The story I'm going to tell you is about one of those families who are descendants of the brave white settlers that fought and killed the Indians (Native Americans, to be politically correct), took their land and turned it into farms. Up came the crops as the soil was ripped and torn by the plows. Down came the mighty pines and oaks as up went the picturesque red barns you see on those Christmas cards at holiday time.

*

Actually, of the couple I'm going to talk about, only one of them had the blood of those early pioneers flowing through her veins: Martha Abigail Shepard, married to Anthony Morris, the owner of the Morris Mercedes-Benz dealership. He was Jewish, she was not, and she made sure everyone understood the difference. In fact, Martha Morris made sure that the town understood a lot of things. Firstly, that she was a very important person who would not tolerate bad behavior of any kind. No skateboards on her sidewalk. No loud music while driving down her street. No gas-powered lawnmowers were used to manicure her grass. She even insisted that the garbage collectors not bang the trash cans against their truck. Her list of possible offenses was very, very long. Secondly, she let it be known that even though she was tiny physically, she was a strong woman who wore the pants in the family and that Anthony was merely the breadwinner. All important decisions were hers to make, and woe be unto him who stood in her way.

We had the dubious honor of living next door to the Morris's mansion. Their house was a Victorian Painted Lady with feudal aspirations. There

111

was a crenellated tower that glared out into the street, and I'm sure Her Majesty, Martha, would have installed a moat and a drawbridge if the local zoning laws had allowed her to do so.

In all the years we spent living beside the Morrises, I never once entered their house. Neighborly is not a word I would use to describe the two of them. We would see Mr. Morris leave for work in the morning and return home in the evening. He didn't hang out in the backyard and she didn't gossip over the fence. He was silent and she was a shrieker. Almost every night you could hear her muffled screams coming from the tower or their living room. Once in a while we could even pick out a word or two: "stupid!" "ashamed!" "cheap!" But never a sound from Anthony. I never understood how he could stand it. Maybe he got off on being verbally abused.

Her attacks were not only aimed at Anthony. Anyone in the neighborhood was fair game.

Neighbors walking their dogs were particularly vulnerable. Martha would come flying out of her front door, hands waving like a cop directing traffic, shouting loud enough to be heard in Canada, "Don't let that animal do his business on my lawn! I'll call the police!" and she would chase the culprit and his or her terrified pet back to where they belonged. I had learned early on to walk Waffles, our dog, in the opposite direction, away from the wicked witch of Elmsville.

Children were terrified of her and fascinated at the same time. The bravest of them would sneak up to the front steps, press the doorbell and run away as fast as their little legs could move, in the hopes of seeing her open the door and have a hissy fit when she found no one was there. My own kids knew better than to antagonize Mrs. Morris, but even they would become the enemy if they played ball in the street or squealed too loudly as they ran through the sprinkler in our front yard. Martha would stick notes in our mailbox that listed her latest complaint.

> *To whom it may concern:*
>
> *It has come to my attention that your son set up a stand yesterday in front of your house and was selling some kind of beverage. This is a violation of township rules and it created excess noise and congestion. Please see to it that this doesn't occur again, or I shall be forced to call the police.*
>
> *A concerned neighbor.*

She never signed her own name to these epistles, as if we wouldn't know who the "concerned neighbor" was. Her dislike of children was obvious, but rather sad considering she and Mr. Morris had had a son. Evidently, he left home at sixteen. Rumor has it that he moved to New York

City to be with his lover, but more likely it was to escape his mother. Maybe that's why she was so unkind to young people and her husband.

My wife and I did see the Morrises at certain social events, like the opening of the Elmsville Community Center, which Anthony had funded very generously. Martha was dressed to the nines and, as always, she was wearing several thousand dollars' worth of jewelry. At the annual Fourth of July Fair, Martha manned the Erie County Historical Society's information booth. We stopped by and were greeted rather coldly at first, but then Mrs. Morris warmed up as she began to talk about the Shepard family being the founders of Elmsville. In the winter, Anthony was one of the judges of the Elmsville Ice Sculpture contest, and he congratulated me when I came in second with my winning entry, "King Cobra." I really think the poor fellow wanted to be more friendly and outgoing, but his marriage prevented that from happening. The counterpoint to the ice sculpture event was the Snowman Contest, open to children six to sixteen. My daughter participated in that competition one year, actually the year Martha was at the helm of the judging committee. Lisa was very enraptured by high fashion at the time, so she molded a runway model, in a long sweeping gown, entirely out of snow and topped it off with one of her mother's beach hats. I thought it was pretty spectacular, but evidently Mrs. Morris was not impressed, so my daughter did not walk away with a prize.

The reason we can have these two events every year is due to the predictability of the very cold and snowy weather. Because we are in the path of freezing winds blowing off Lake Erie, we get huge snowfalls, an average of 12 feet of snow per season. The temperature hovers around 19 degrees and zooms up to a balmy 31 degrees. It makes Christmas feel like a real Christmas. Which brings us back to the story I started to tell.

'Twas the night before Christmas—whoops, wrong story. Actually, it was the day after Christmas and the whole town was digging out from several days of the heaviest snowfall in many years. There were drifts so tall you could stand on them to shovel off your roof. If you want to, you can Google some awesome pictures of what I'm talking about. We're used to snow here in Elmsville, but this was ridiculous. I tunneled out from our house to the street and watched as the snowplows continued to pummel the already buried cars with more of the white stuff. I did the best I could with my little snowblower to remove the snow from our sidewalk. The blizzard had been so bad that no one had been able to go anywhere for the previous two days.

As I chugged slowly to the edge of the Morrises' property, I was surprised to see Mr. Morris leaning on a snow shovel and panting like Waffles. The Morrises usually hired a local guy to do their snow removal. I shut off the noisy machine and crunched my way over to him.

"Mr. Morris, are you okay? Why don't you let me help you get rid of this stuff?"

"That would be very nice, thank you. I have a car coming soon to take me to the airport."

"The airport?" I asked, unable to hide my surprise. "Is it even open?"

"Yes, I just got a call that one of the landing strips has been cleared. Martha and I are flying to the Cayman Islands to get away from this weather. We were supposed to leave the day before Christmas, but—"

"Yeah, I think this storm canceled a lot of plans," I replied as I turned on the blower and began removing the snow from his sidewalk. This was the longest conversation Anthony and I had ever had, and to think it took the storm of the century to accomplish that. When I finished, I shut down the machine and, turning around, was surprised to see a black limo slowly edging up our street. Mr. Morris was lugging a suitcase to the only open-ing in the wall of snow that faced the street and waving wildly at the approaching car.

"Thanks so much," Mr. Morris shouted as he stepped in the slush left by the snowplows.

"You're very welcome," I shouted back. "But where is Mrs. Morris? Isn't she coming with you?"

"She went to her mother's before the storm started," he explained, opening the door to the limo. "She's meeting me at the airport. Thanks again!"

I nodded and he closed his door. The car spun its wheels in the snow and then moved slowly down the street. That was the last time I ever saw Anthony Levi Morris.

*

That January, after the storm, the temperature never got above 20 degrees. While it was not much fun for most of us, it was heaven for the kids, with sledding, skating, snow angels, snow forts and snowmen. Because nothing would melt due to the constant cold, the ice sculptures and the snowmen remained in their fixed positions, almost like they were on the day of the contest. It was pleasant to drive by the fairground fields and glance at the art made entirely from frozen H_2O. The ice sculptures sparkled with a faceted crystalline light, and the snowmen (and women) stood like ghosts holding a prayer meeting.

Spring was late that year. It wasn't until the middle of May that tem-peratures began to rise and remain in the 50- to 60-degree range. The snow finally began to melt, and you could see sweet little patches of green peek-ing through the soot-stained white stuff on the ground. In the fairground fields, the icy mermaids, swans and clipper ships dwindled down to mere puddles soaking the grass, and the snowmen began shrinking into minia-ture versions of themselves—all of them, with the exception of one.

As a police buddy of mine tells it, he answered a call early in the morning to hurry out to the fairgrounds to check on some kind of commotion there. When he arrived, he pushed his way through a circle of onlookers and was gobsmacked by what he saw. Sitting on a five-gallon white plastic tub was Martha Abigail Morris, née Shepard. She was wet with melted snow, and my pal determined that she hadn't yet collapsed into a heap because she was still frozen solid. Her eyes were open but glazed over, and her hair hung down in wet strings. She was dressed in a blue flannel nightgown, and her feet were bare. She wore no makeup, and her hands, resting politely in her lap, were void of any rings. There were no bracelets, necklaces or earrings. She, who prided herself on always looking like she had just stepped off the cover of *Vogue*, was just a plain Jane—a very *dead* plain Jane.

One of the fairground security guards said he remembered seeing an extra snowman way back in January but just thought that some kids had been playing in the field and decided to make their own Frosty. He recalled it was rather lumpy and not very sophisticated, unlike the other snowmen surrounding it. "It looked like something a first-grader would build."

An autopsy revealed that Martha had been strangled and was dead before she was encased in a tomb of snow. If she had fought off her attacker, there was no evidence to show that that had occurred. No scratches or bruises, just the imprint of fingers around her throat. Of course, the big question was: who did this terrible thing? And the answer seemed to be: her husband. Where was Anthony Morris, anyway? His employees said that he and his wife usually stayed somewhere warm until winter passed, but now it was late spring.

I told my friend at the police station about seeing Morris leave in a limo back on that snow-removal day in December. Within a week, a big search began to track him down, a search that eventually spread around the world. But he had disappeared over four months earlier, and therefore the trail was very cold. Did he actually go to the Cayman Islands? Or was Canada his choice? Europe? Asia? Antarctica?

The town was fascinated by the whole event. Everyone had a theory about the murder, how it was accomplished, and where Morris was hiding. It was all conjecture, of course. However, through my connection to the police department, I became privy to some of the facts. Let me share them with you:

> Morris had been withdrawing large sums of money from his account every month for eight months prior to his disappearance. Total: $450,000.

> All of Martha's jewelry, from her home and their shared safety deposit box, was gone.

A wheelbarrow was found under a snowdrift in the corner of the fairground field. It contained a torn pocket that matched the blue flannel of Martha's nightgown.

The limo driver who picked Morris up told the police that he dropped him off at the train station, not the airport. The airport was still shut down due to the heavy snowfall.

The Morris home was searched top to bottom and yielded nothing.

*

And so the story of Anthony and Martha grinds on with no true ending. As I see it, this is the tale of a man who was so tired of his marriage to an abusive woman that he became obsessed with killing her. A man who planned and plotted his spouse's murder and his escape for at least eight months. A man who strangled his wife, put her in a wheelbarrow and, in the middle of a roaring blizzard, wheeled her for two miles to a field full of snowmen and covered her in several layers of snow until she was also a roly-poly snowman. Determination, anger! I can't imagine the kind of rage that must have boiled up inside him to give him the super-human strength to carry out such a difficult mission.

*

It's Christmas once more in Elmsville, New York, and the Weather Channel is predicting snow, maybe by Christmas Eve. Somewhere, who knows where, Anthony Levi Morris is living a new life, with a new name and a new look. I try hard not to admire the man who committed such a heinous crime, but sometimes, as I watch the snowflakes begin to fall, I reflect on the irony of it all: Mr. Morris turning Mrs. Morris, the ice queen, into a snowman.

Happy holidays, Tony, wherever you are.

Lower Education

A True Story

By David Michael Massee

I was not a good student. School, to me, was a source of absolute misery. Between being beaten up by bullies and teased and called names ("skinny" and "sissy" being at the top of the list), there was my incapability to understand basic math. Numbers scared the shit out of me, literally. Bathroom breaks were necessary when it was math-test day. I couldn't memorize my times tables beyond my fivesies, and addition and subtraction stopped when I ran out of fingers and toes. Long division? Forget about it.

That miracle, the battery-operated calculator, hadn't been invented yet, and unlike the amazing laptop computer, my brain was not wired to handle arithmetic.

I was a dreamer trapped in a nightmare. Seated at a desk too small for my long legs, inside an overheated room with twenty-nine other restless third-graders, I was being introduced to the joys of the three R's by a terrifying ogre named Miss Fortune. (Her real name, by the way.) My only escape was through one of the large windows that ran parallel to the rows of desks and displayed the glorious blue sky and fluffy white clouds that formed shapes like elephants and a skyscraper and—

"David! Pay attention! Eyes on the blackboard, please! What is the answer to number three?"

This is when my life ends. I find myself sweating in places I shouldn't. My breathing has stopped and the blackboard is doing a wavy dance, with the usually somber Miss Fortune joining right in.

"Number three, please," she repeats, pointing to the offending problem with her all-purpose ruler.

The numerals are doing a square dance, and it takes all of my minimal powers of concentration to stop the hoedown. I squint, bite my lip and clutch my crotch.

$$3. \quad 8 + 12 =$$

Writing about it now, decades later, I want to scream out "Twenty, you revolting old hag!" But I'm sure she was suffering as much as we were. It must have been hell trying to control a room full of antsy eight-year-olds, let alone trying to teach them anything. And just for the record, Miss Alma Fortune, I've learned enough math to get along fine, and there's always my iPhone if I need a little extra help.

The only gold stars I ever got were for acing spelling tests. Every Monday morning, Miss Fortune handed out a mimeographed sheet of the words that would be on Friday's spelling test. So, we had four days to study them. There would be no surprises. What you saw was what you got.

This I could deal with. However, how I dealt with learning the words was not the method Miss Fortune put forward.

"Sound out each syllable," she recommended. "Break the word down into each of its separate sounds." She pointed her all-purpose twelve-inch ruler to a word she had chalked on the blackboard:

responsible re-spon-si-ble

"Listen to the sounds: ree-spawn-seh-bull." Her mouth wrapped around the syllables like she was eating them and then spitting them out.

As for me, I had a much simpler method. I would just memorize each of the ten words typed on the sheet of paper like you would learn a poem or lines in a play script. Sometimes I would attach an image to the word, like for *fatal*—a picture of Miss Fortune lying in a pool of blood.

When Friday came around, I was fully prepared. Miss Fortune would sound out each word, with a definition, and I would end up getting a 100%, an A+ and a gold star on my test. I'd add another tongue-moistened, glue-backed paper star to the chart on the bulletin board. I was a winner!

However, there was a small hitch to my methodology. When we were assigned to write a book report or an essay, such as "What I Did Over Spring Break," I would misspell most of the words I had aced on the spelling tests, because I hadn't really learned them. I had just memorized them long enough to pass the exam. Bummer!

What I Did Over Spring Break

My pairents and I went to Auntlantick City and I swam in the Oshun. It was warm and the sand got into my sanwitch. The seagalls pooped on my dads head.

Now, in my defense, back then there was no spell-check. I honestly never understood why, if we were supposed to spell a word by sounding it out, many of the words didn't actually look the way they sounded. For example, in my essay on spring break, the word *ocean* didn't look like "oshun" to me. *Ocean* looks more like "oh-see-Ann," whoever she is.

Okay, as an adult who has written a few tomes in my rickety life, I have learned a lot about the derivation of words, the influences of other languages, how the insertion of a letter can change the sound of a vowel and all the other cockamamie rules found in proper English. Like double letters when one letter is plenty. For example, *cafeine* will still give you a jolt without that extra F.

But please, you language specialists, here's where I really need some help. *I don't understand the purpose of the silent letter.*

Imagine for a moment an eight-year-old getting his book report back with a big red D⁻ smeared across the top of the page. And all because of too many misspelled words.

wensday

newmoanya

receit

rinkle

biskit

And don't tell me to do what Miss Fortune suggested: "Look it up in the dictionary." How could I look it up if I didn't even know what it started with? I didn't know "rinkle" started with a W or "neumonia" began with a P. Give a guy a break. Remember, this was back in the dark ages, before you could ask a disembodied voice, "Siri, spell 'neumonia.'"

*

I am not alone in observing the absurdity of spelling in the English language. Ben Franklin, Noah Webster, G. B. Shaw and Teddy Roosevelt, men much more intelligent than I, tried to make radical changes to the weird way some words are spelled. They were not successful. So we are still stuck with silent K (*knock* and *knee*) and silent C (*muscle* and *scissors*), as well as the silent versions of the letters H (*anchor*), B (*subtle*), W (*sword*) and G (*gnat* and *gnaw*).

Good old Ben once said that the best spellers were those who couldn't spell. In not knowing the rules, they used their ears and spelled the words the way they sounded. But that didn't work when a silent letter reared its useless head. Okay, enough whining about an eight-year-old's unhappiness with spelling. It's never going to change.

*

For me, happiness in school was three things: lunch, recess and art class. Until the third grade, I felt safe in the room that smelled of tempera paint and white paste. We had art every other day. It alternated with gym, which I hated and feared, in a room in which I didn't feel safe. I couldn't dribble, climb a rope, leap over a hurdle, hit or catch a baseball or pin someone to the mat. I realize as I am writing this that not only could I not accomplish any of those things, but I really didn't want to. But back to art class.

It was heaven to be able to scribble, splash colors, create weird monsters out of clay, and not have to study for a test. I was always drawing funny faces in my math notebook, and my ABCs often morphed into dragons or giraffes or mermaids. Miss Fortune, as you can imagine, was not a fan of such behavior, and whenever she caught me sketching instead of staring blankly at my times tables, my drawing hand received three healthy blows from her handy-dandy wooden ruler.

Therefore, the first two and a half years of art class were paradise: my escape, for an hour and fifteen minutes, from the horrors of math and the unkindness of Miss Alma Fortune. But, like all good things, it didn't last. Miss Baker, our art teacher, whom I adored, left Centerville Grade School to marry a Mister Pettigrew, whom I detested even though I had never met the man. So, starting in the spring of my third grade, we had the pleasure of being taught by a Mrs. Estelle Manders, who approached art the way Miss Fortune taught her subjects. Rules were meant to be followed, certain colors were not to be used with other colors because they clashed, realism was the *only* style of any importance, and we were given specific assignments in that style in every class. None of this "modern art" nonsense for Estelle! No melting watches or purple cows! No spatters or sprinkles or streaks or circles of solid color. Good god, Mrs. Manders, we were eight-year-olds, not graduate students at the Rhode Island School of Design! (I found out years later that Estelle Manders lied about her qualifications as an art teacher and that she was actually a former physical ed instructor desperately looking for a job.)

Anyway, I did my best to follow the "rules," but one day I slipped up, or maybe I had just had it drawing and painting *real* things. The assignment was to paint a tree. Mrs. Manders had brought in some large photographs of big trees, oaks and elms, and rested them on the chalkboard ledge. We all went to work.

At the end of class, in the remaining ten minutes, Mrs. Manders walked around the room and commented on what she saw.

"Very nice, Clarice."

"Ah, Robert, good job."

"Looks very real, Jo Ann."

And then she came upon mine. After a moment of stunned silence, she responded.

"Trees are round, David, not square. And the leaves are never striped like a zebra. The trunks are never pink, and they are never, *ever* shaped like a fish. This is not acceptable!" And with a very dramatic flourish, she picked up my circus-themed tree and tore it into three pieces.

*

I finished out the third grade and was passed into the fourth. To me, the fourth grade was a lost year. I hardly remember it. I know the teacher was a man, and that was good. I stumbled along, and I guess I must have learned something. I took music instead of art to avoid spending time with Mrs. Manders. I did something with a tambourine and listened to a recording of *The Young Person's Guide to the Orchestra*, and then the year was over.

*

All of this has been leading up to the grade that changed my life and the person who made it all happen. I wish to dedicate this last section to Mrs. Josephine Heiner, who really knew what teaching was all about.

Okay, so it's fifth grade and I'm at a very low point in my life. On the first day of class this very tall lady, with a halo of rust-colored hair, enters the classroom and hikes her rear end up on her desk. She adjusts the hem of her skirt, crosses her legs and welcomes us to her world.

"Today is the first day of a journey you and I are going to take, to places you've never been before. I have been told by your former teachers how exceptional you all are, so I know we're going to have an extraordinary time together. It won't all be smooth sailing. Every trip has its rocky moments. How many of you have gone camping with your family and it rained the whole time? Or your car had a flat tire miles away from your grandmother's house on Thanksgiving Day? Well, when we have a bump like that on our journey, we'll work together to get beyond it. How will we do that? We will use each other's strengths and talents. And that's why I want to learn all about what you feel you are good at and what you aren't so good at. I'm going to go around the room and ask each of you to share with us what you do well. But before I do, I need to tell you about my strengths and weaknesses. It's only fair.

"I'm great at listening. All ears," she said, touching her own. "My favorite subject is English, both reading and writing, and I'm very good at teaching it. I'm not so good at science, so I'll need some help. How about we learn about it together?" She then started talking to each of us. At first it was scary and it took some encouragement to get people to talk. But eventually it got to the point where the person talking had to be told their time was up.

I was so ashamed of my lousy math skills I could hardly speak up when it was my turn.

"Okay, David, thanks for that information. Very brave of you to admit it's a problem. But how about what you're good at?"

I told her about my liking to draw. "I guess I'm pretty good at it."

*

And here's what happened as the year progressed and why I'll always be beholden to dear Mrs. Heiner. She called me up to her desk one day and sat me down in her chair while she perched on her desk, which she seemed to prefer to the chair.

"David, I don't know if you've noticed, but our classroom is kind of dull. It could use some brightening up. What do you think?"

I agreed.

"I was wondering if you had any ideas about what we could do to improve the space."

I told her a few paintings placed here and there might help.

"Great! Now, I know you're still struggling a little with your math, so in exchange for some help from Robert (he's really a whiz and said he'd be happy to help you) and a little tutoring from me, would you provide us with some of your art?"

That, dear reader, is what great teaching is all about.

*

While I'm sure that after all these decades my contribution to the décor of the fifth-grade classroom at Centerville Grade School has long since disappeared, it was certainly the talk of the school for quite a while. Using a roll of heavy kraft paper, I painted a mural entitled *The History of the World,* which took me several very happy months of after-school activity time. With the help of several of my fellow fifth-graders, we mounted it above the blackboards and all around the room, even above the bulletin boards and windows. I laugh now when I think of my take on world history. It started with Adam and Eve in fig leaves, and ended with the mushroom cloud of an atom bomb. Somewhere in between I depicted the Rape of the Sabine Women and Washington Crossing the Delaware River. I can't remember what else I inserted.

God bless you, Josephine Heiner!

Meredith's Men
A Novella

We are all prisoners of the age in which we are born. Meredith Olsen was no exception. While she was able to bend some of the links of the chain issued to her by society, for the most part she wore it, as did everyone else (with the exception of a few poets and artists). She followed the rules as laid down by her parents, by her schoolteachers, by her church, by her doctors and by her government.

As a young woman during the Great Depression, she grew up not in abject poverty, but close to it. She was always sure that it was hiding somewhere just around the corner. This fear, coupled with not having any money to waste on the frivolous things a young girl wishes for, colored her perception of life clear up until her death. The memory of only one dress, one coat, one pair of shoes until her feet grew too big, no money for sweet treats or silk hose or that little bottle of Evening in Paris perfume she lusted over at the Five and Dime, haunted her forever.

By the age of seventeen, she was fully indoctrinated with the rules and regulations of being a woman. A wife, a mother and a housekeeper was the number one goal. If, for some unfortunate reason, this was not attainable, then one could try to find employment as a sales clerk, waitress, maid, factory worker, beautician, typist, telephone operator or laundress. Of course, if you could scrape the money together for college tuition, you could begin a career as a teacher or a nurse. But as Meredith's mother pointed out, it was best to find a fine man who would take good care of her. "The husband brings home the bacon, the wife cooks it."

"It was true in my day and it is still true today. A woman's place is in the home," lectured Amelia Olsen, née Johnson. "Your father and I have been married twenty-five years, raised four children, and none of you have starved. Life is hard, as well you know, but it's a lot harder if you're on your own. 'Two by two,' like in the Bible, that's God's plan and it's a good one." Meredith would listen patiently to her mother and then escape to the movies.

Meredith loved the movies. Taking the one quarter she'd saved in her piggy bank, she would go downtown to the Kuhn Movie Theater and buy a ticket to paradise. Sitting in one of the plush red velvet seats, she would enter the black-and-white world of the rich and glamorous. The clothes, the jewels, the food, the nightclubs big enough to accommodate a herd of elephants, the drawing rooms with handsome men and women standing around saying witty things. And some of the women in these films even had careers! They were pretending to be famous authors or singers or artists or dancers or even business owners. They had these wonderfully successful lives. But then, by the end of the movie, they gave it all up to get married. She didn't like it very much when that happened, but she understood. That was the way it was. But she bet the actresses who were hired to play these roles didn't give up their careers for their husbands. No way!

When she got back home, all dreamy-eyed and breathless, it was her ritual to tell her mother the story of the movie and act out the various parts.

"I wish I could be a movie star!" she said one Saturday afternoon after returning from seeing *Roberta* with Irene Dunne. Amelia reacted as if Meredith had decided she wanted to become a prostitute.

"Meredith Olsen, are you out of your mind?! Do you know what kind of life an actress leads? I won't even waste my time discussing such a ridiculous idea. What's more, even though you're pretty enough, in a plain sort of way, you are certainly no beauty, and that seems to be what it takes to be in the movies."

Amelia was wrong. Meredith was very beautiful. True, she wasn't as thin as her favorite actresses, but she was tall and blonde and curvy where it was important. However, she knew her chances of becoming a star were a million to one. She hated it when her mother was right. She was a "plain Jane" from the hick town of Lebanon, Oregon, whose only hope was to marry the right man.

Husband Number One

Whittaker Smallwood was a fellow student at Meredith's high school. She had known him since freshman year, and she had become his official girlfriend in their junior year. At graduation, Whit surprised Meredith by asking her to marry him. Her mother was ecstatic.

"How wonderful!" Amelia gushed. "He's such a nice young man. And the Smallwoods are a very important family. His grandfather was once the mayor, did you know that? And his father owns the largest farm in the county. Oh, my! Aren't you the luckiest girl!"

Meredith nodded and said all the appropriate things, like "I am very happy" and "I feel very lucky"—but underneath it all was a wisp of doubt. Yes, Whit was very handsome and kind and polite, but—

The wedding took place in July. It was a simple ceremony, with only the two families in attendance. Although the Smallwoods were comfortably well off, they were careful with their money (some town folk used the terms "tight" and "Scotch" to describe Walter Smallwood). Therefore, the burden of the cost of the reception fell on the shoulders of the Olsens. The bride wore her mother's wedding dress, which she had altered radically, and Amelia had made a dress for herself using some maroon silk she had been saving for just this occasion. She also cooked all the celebratory food.

The atmosphere at the reception was a bit chilly due to the fact that Whittaker's mother, Lavinia, was not very happy with his choice of a wife. She also made a few acidic remarks about the cuisine.

"It seems the menu is a little heavy on the starches, but I suppose that is the Scandinavian influence." And then she went on to discuss her daughter-in-law's physique: "While she carries her weight well, I'm sure working on Whit's farm will help remove some of that baby fat."

This last comment also brought up an uncomfortable topic. While Whittaker Smallwood was supposed to start a small farm in a corner of his father's many acres, with the expectation of his taking over the old man's estate after Walter passed on, Whit had other plans. He wanted to open a garage, a top-notch, full-service establishment that could do repairs on automobiles, trucks, buses and even tractors. He loved tinkering on his Chevrolet Confederate coupe and kept it in excellent running condition.

"We've got one garage in this town," he said, "and to be brutally honest, Jacob Hessmeyer is a lousy mechanic. You have to drive all the way up to Portland if you want to get any really decent work done."

Walter Smallwood was not impressed. He knew Whit would come to his senses eventually. The young man's great-grandfather had created Smallwood Farms eighty years ago; therefore, the love of the soil must have been passed down through his grandfather and then Walter. Whittaker was meant to be a farmer.

There was no real honeymoon, just a weekend at the beach inside a sleeping bag inside a tent. However, Meredith found herself surprised by what her mother had called "a woman's duty." It was a little uncomfortable at first, but then it felt pretty good. She found—

Hold on there, Buster! I don't know who you are or who gave you permission to write about me, but if you are going to continue to do so, and you probably are, I'm going to need to clarify a few things. Yes, I was pretty naïve, but remember I was only seventeen when I got married. And about the sex, contrary to popular opinion, I liked it a lot. A "good" woman, during my day, was not supposed to enjoy intercourse. I know my mother didn't. Sex was for procreation only. Not me. I found it amazing.

My apologies if I offended you, whoever you are. I'll try and be as accurate as possible, but please remember this is just a story, a work of fiction. I started writing this because of my interest in how women have, over the centuries, been treated as second-class citizens. I created you to represent the many women I have met in my research. In all honesty, I was surprised when you popped up on my computer. I mean, you are more than welcome to join me on this journey, but please believe me when I say I don't know where it's going. Now, let's continue.

Wait a minute, Mr. Author Man. This research you did, was one of your subjects your mother?

I'd rather not disclose anything about the persons I interviewed. Now, back to our story.

Whatever you say. But I bet this is all about your mama.

*

The newlyweds moved into Whit's parents' large farmhouse, and although it was temporary, Meredith found it almost unbearable. They slept in Whit's bedroom with all his school pennants and sports trophies and his twin-sized bed. There was really no room for the few possessions she brought with her. But the hardest thing to endure was her treatment by Lavinia Smallwood. She was used to spending long hard days helping out on her dad's dairy farm, but working on the Smallwood farm was much worse, due to Lavinia's constant criticism of her every step.

"Close the door behind you! Were you born in a barn?"

"Not that way! This way! For heaven's sake, pay attention."

"Hopeless, just hopeless!"

When Whit got home late, after a day of bringing in the last of the harvest, he would find Meredith in their room weeping. He would wrap his arms around her and try to console her with promises.

"It's going to be all right. I'm looking for a place so I can start up the garage. I've seen a couple of possibilities, and any day now we'll be able to move into town. Just hold on, honey."

And she did hold on, all through winter, clear into the next spring. By then there was still no garage, but there was a baby on the way. Whit was busy helping with the spring planting, and his father was starting to design the small farmhouse that was to become his and Meredith's new home. Meredith worked with Lavinia and her hired girl, Greta, in the kitchen preparing the three meals that were needed each day to feed the six hired hands and Walter and Whittaker. That meant cooking and serving up twenty-four plates of food a day—168 plates a week, if you counted Sunday—and then washing all those dishes, including the pots and pans. Meredith would fall into bed at ten o'clock at night only to be awakened by Lavinia at four in the morning to start preparing the breakfast.

I'd be stirring up pancake batter in this big yellow bowl and the smell of it would activate my morning sickness. I'd have to go outside and throw up. Then I'd come back in and stir some more until the next wave of nausea hit. Four solid months of that routine. I wanted to die.

The baby was a boy, a big boy—ten pounds. On the way to the hospital, Lavinia sat with Meredith in the back seat of Whit's Chevy and explained what was happening. When Meredith moaned in agony, Whit's mother talked to her about her own suffering for forty-eight hours before giving birth to her son: "I can assure you it's going to get a lot worse before it gets better." Thanks a lot.

But she was right, as Matthew Smallwood was very reluctant about entering this cold and noisy world. He held on for hours. The doctor finally needed to use forceps to pull him out of the warmth of his mother's womb. As a result, his skull was slightly askew, with a tendency for the top of it to tilt a bit towards the right. It remained that way the rest of his life.

I went into such a deep depression. Today it's called postpartum depression, and it can be treated with drugs. Back then you were just told to get over it, that it would pass. I cried all day and night and fantasized strangling my mother-in-law, shooting my husband and drowning my baby. Fortunately, gazing into Matthew's sweet little face kept me from killing anyone, including myself. And then Whit came to me with the wonderful news.

In June of 1936, Whittaker Smallwood signed a rental agreement on a two-story building on East Elmore Street in Lebanon. It had originally been the shop of a carriage and harness maker but had been sitting empty for many years. While it would need a lot of updating, it was of solid stone construction, and Whit was very happy. "The second floor was used as an office, so with some renovation, it'll make a great apartment for you and me and the baby," he told Meredith.

As was to be expected, Walter Smallwood was furious.

"Why was I not consulted about this foolishness?!"

"Because that was exactly how I knew you would react, Dad."

"And how do you plan to fund this business venture, may I ask?"

"I've been saving most of my work pay for the last few years, and I also used the generous gift you gave me for graduation."

"But that money was to help you get started on your own farm!"

"And it is helping me to get started—in the business I want to create."

"This is nonsense. Times are bad. The economy is a disaster and you want to start a new business! And what about your obligation to Smallwood Farms?"

"I plan on helping you through the season, and then, when everything is in the ground, I'll concentrate on the garage."

When you are young, you feel you can do anything, and in most cases you can. Whit worked on the farm from dawn to dusk and then drove into town to work on his garage, sometimes until one in the morning. On Sundays, he and Meredith and the baby spent many happy hours turning the second floor into their new home. They added a little kitchenette and a small bathroom, and Whit did all the plumbing and wiring himself. Meredith painted and papered and also sewed a coverlet for the new double bed that they had ordered from Montgomery Ward.

When the downstairs garage space was finally clean and cleared of all the detritus of its years as a buggy shop, Whit repaired the concrete floor, filling in the cracks and making sure it was smooth and level. The next step was the ordering of all the modern equipment he would need to make the Smallwood and Son Automotive Garage the most modern facility in Linn County. He had contacted Texaco about the installation of a pump and a tank and the delivery of gasoline. Now all he needed was cash. He hoped to get a loan from his father and was pretty sure that after his dad saw all the progress he had made on the building, Walter would help him out.

It was not to be.

"Very impressive," Walter said, walking around the large open space. "You've done a great job so far. But then, you always were a hard worker."

"Thanks, Dad," Whit replied. "So let's go upstairs and we can talk about the loan."

"I have to get back to the farm. Your mom is bringing the Taylors home from church for one of her luncheons."

"But, Dad—"

"Listen, Whit, your mother and I have been discussing this whole deal, and I'm afraid a loan is out of the question. I can't be lending you money that I know will only be disappearing down the drain."

"Aw, Dad, come on, you know—"

"Now, if this were about money for your farm, there would be no problem."

"That's not fair. I know I can make a go of this—"

"You aren't even twenty years old yet. You don't know how to run a business. Do you realize how hard we have worked to keep the farm profitable? What it takes to run—"

"I'm very aware of what it takes, as I have been working by your side since I was seven. All I'm asking is for you to believe in me enough to lend me the money to buy the equipment—"

"The answer is no. Please understand that I'm doing this for your own good."

I find it interesting that when someone does something hurtful to you, they always claim "it's for your own good." Walter was probably right, but to not help out your own son and support him in his dream was inexcusable. But I'll give Whit credit for sticking to his guns. I mean, we were already in debt, so what the hell—in for a penny, in for a pound! He applied for a loan at the

Umpqua Bank, using as collateral his beloved Chevy and the deed to the land his dad had given him for the farm.

Loans were very rare during the Depression, but because of the importance of the Smallwood name, the loan was ultimately approved. On Saturday, October 3rd, 1936, the Smallwood and Son Automotive Garage officially opened. Business was brisk, although that might have been helped by the free apple cider and donuts being offered to customers.

The next few months were touch and go. It would take time for word of mouth and testimonials to spread through Lebanon and eventually around the county. By January, however, Whit had more business than he could handle by himself, and so he hired another mechanic. He had never intended for the garage to also be a gas station, but out-of-towners kept stopping at the bright shiny new pump to fill up, so he engaged a recent high school dropout to take over that duty.

By spring the garage was bringing in enough money to pay the rent, the salaries and the mortgage payments, and to put food on the table. However, there was nothing left over for anything else, including deposits into a savings account.

Yeah, it was a scary time, truly living month to month. Nothing in the bank. Ever since I was a young girl, I had wanted to go to beauty school, but there was no money for that either. Besides, my mother-in-law made it perfectly clear that my duty was to my husband and that I had a child to take care of. As if I could ever forget. Matthew was a colicky baby, and he didn't sleep that much. A lot of crying on both our parts.

Whit was so proud of what he had accomplished, and rightly so. However, not one word of praise from his father. Son-of-a-bitch!

It was during the fall of '37 that it all began to unravel. Meredith's father was killed when his tractor overturned and crushed him to death. Meredith's three older brothers assumed responsibility for the running of the dairy, but her mother became deeply depressed. For Amelia, this was not the way it was supposed to be. The two of them were supposed to grow old together.

The next event was when Whit was sued by one of his customers for damage to the man's prize Packard. Whit was sure the long, wide scar along the passenger side of the vehicle did not happen in his shop, but he had no way to prove it. It was several hundred dollars he didn't have.

When Meredith developed a cough and a fever that turned into pneumonia, they began to feel that maybe there was some kind of curse involved. It was touch and go for a while, and Whit really feared he would lose his wife of only two years. But after three weeks of driving over to Corvallis every evening to be with her in the hospital, he brought her back home, weak but alive. He figured he would have to pay all the medical bills in installments.

Finally, there was an early frost that hit Lebanon and most of the county and wiped out 90 percent of the crops waiting to be harvested. In an economy already eviscerated by the Depression, this was a disaster on a monumental scale. It affected everyone from the farmers to the owners of the few stores still open, to anyone depending on the income from the harvest. This included the Smallwood and Son Automotive Garage. Business dropped off precipitously, as most folks quit using their cars and trucks and tractors. No money, no gas, no repairs. Whit had to let his mechanic go. He kept the kid on for a while but ended up pumping gas all by himself for the few travelers that came motoring through Lebanon.

Meredith moved in with her mother temporarily to help her mom adjust to widowhood and to help keep the household together. She and baby Matthew slept in her old room, and as she stared at the wallpaper with the pale pink roses, she wept over the loss of her father, and she worried about Whit and how he would work through this mess.

Whit was, at the same time, lying alone in their new double bed from Monkey Ward, staring at the ceiling and worrying about the upcoming mortgage payment and the overdue rent. Looking at all his options, he found he was tempted to approach his father again about that loan, the loan Walter had refused to give him before. Maybe now his dad would relent. But he quickly dismissed the idea, knowing how stubborn Walter could be. The only other answer seemed to be one of complete defeat. He would have to default on the loan and let the bank take everything—his garage, his car and his twenty acres of farmland.

A week later it seemed his luck was improving, when Howard Royer, the person who leased him the property, was willing to forgo his rent until Whit was back on his feet. He said he recognized what a great job the young entrepreneur had done, and besides, he wouldn't be able to rent the place to anyone else due to the disastrous winter frost—"a bird in the hand is better," and so forth.

The next hurdle would be the payment due on his mortgage. He planned to visit the loan officer at the Umpqua Bank and ask if the payment schedule could be adjusted. For instance, could he postpone paying for six months? He knew this wasn't realistic, but you never know.

Let me tell this part, because I want the truth to be known. Whit had nothing to do with what happened next! We never really learned how it started. Whit was with Matthew and me at my mother's place when a phone call came, the worst telephone call you could imagine. It was Fred Benton, the sheriff, and he said the garage was on fire. I couldn't really believe it, but Whit was in his car and on his way into town by the time I hung up the phone.

I told Mama to take care of the baby and I jumped into our old pickup truck and followed after Whit. When I got close to town I could smell the oily smoke, and then, in the distance, I saw the flames shooting high up into the sky. It was like how I imagined a volcano would look.

The fire was so intense that I had to park a block away. When I ran up to where Whit was standing, I could see the tears streaming down his face. It was so unfair. All our hard work, his hard work, turning into smoke and ash. The volunteer firemen were doing the best they could, but they couldn't get any closer for fear of the big underground gas tank exploding. After several hours, all that was left was half of a blackened stone wall.

So there we were—homeless, penniless and deep in debt. Worst of all, there were those who believed that Whit had set the garage on fire in order to collect on the insurance. If they only knew.

"What do you mean, no fire insurance?!" exclaimed Walter, staring in disbelief at his son. They were together in the privacy of Walt's office in the Smallwood farmhouse. Whittaker was seated with his head in his hands. His clothes reeked of the black petroleum smoke. His father stood in front of him like a prosecuting attorney.

"I don't understand! You couldn't have gotten a mortgage without proof that you had an insurance policy on the business!"

"I know, I know. I had fire insurance. It's just that—I—I canceled the policy—"

"What?!"

"Well, I had to reduce expenses somehow, you know, when the frost hit. Business was slowing down, so I thought—"

"But you didn't think! This is what I was talking about, you being too young and inexperienced to run a business. So what are you going to do now?"

"I don't know. I'll still have to pay on the mortgage even though the garage is gone. I hope Howard will just cancel my lease so I won't owe him as well. Then there's the contract with Texaco—"

"I hope you aren't planning on me bailing you out. I hate to say it, but Howard Royer is probably going to sue you for burning down his property, unless, unlike you, he has a good policy on the place. And you'll have to make some arrangement with the bank about a payment plan on the loan that you can afford. I'll talk with Seth Granger and see what he suggests. Once you get back to building your farm, I'm sure they'll see that you're a good risk—"

"Dad."

"Yes, what?'

"I put the deed to the land up as collateral on the loan."

"Jesus Christ!"

Now this is where in the fairy tale, the father is supposed to throw up his hands and give in. He pays all the son's debts, forgives him his youthful stupidity and helps him start over. Together, they build a brand-new garage and the son becomes a very successful and much-sought-after mechanic. He and his wife provide many grandchildren and live long and happy lives.

Okay, smart-ass, cut the sarcasm. It's easy to make fun of a situation you have never lived through. You sit there in your comfortable chair, drinking your coffee and typing away, without a clue of what happened to us. Let me fill you in.

My father-in-law never lifted a finger to help. He wouldn't loan Whit a penny. As he predicted, Howard Royer sued, and then the bank foreclosed. I would have thought Walter would have wanted to protect the Smallwood name, but it seemed it was more important for him to teach his son a lesson.

The morning we got wind of the foreclosure, we were staying at my mother's. Whit knew the bank would take the car and we would be left with nothing. He told me to pack up what few possessions we had, gather the baby's things and any food my mom could spare, and load up the car. By late that afternoon, Whit, Matt and I were on the road heading south, to who knew where.

The journey south led them to the Oregon–California border. Meredith had never been out of the state, and this was a milestone for her. She had expected the scenery to change radically when they crossed over, but for a long time it was just like southern Oregon. As it began to get dark, Whit pulled the car over and they ate some of the provisions. Meredith nursed Matthew and then curled up with him in a sleeping bag in the back seat, and Whit covered them with an extra blanket. He sat up in the front seat with the other sleeping bag tucked around him and kept watch.

This routine was repeated for several nights until they were near San Francisco. It was here that they finally ran out of food. Whit had packed two metal containers of gasoline, so they had enough fuel, but he had no money for meals or lodging. They had taken turns washing up in the service station restrooms, but now they were living in dirty clothes and getting very, very hungry. They felt like the hoboes they had seen passing through Lebanon, begging for food or for a nickel or two.

After a long day of driving, without anything to eat since the night before, Whit knew he had to do something. As the night closed in around them, he saw a light coming from the window of a house sitting in the middle of a vineyard. He turned off the highway and drove up the road leading to the house. When he reached it, he parked and got out of the car.

"Stay here. I'll be right back."

"What are you going to do?"

"See if I can get us something to eat."

"But, Whit—"

He walked away, toward the porch, and had just stepped on the first stair when the front door opened. A tall woman stood silhouetted in the opening.

"Can I help you?" she asked with a slight accent. It sounded like Italian to Whit.

"Ah, yes, ma'am. I'm sorry to intrude like this," he began, feeling awash with shame, "but I've got my wife and our baby in the car and we are in need of something to eat. Anything you can spare." There was a moment of silence. "At least something for my wife. She's nursing my son." After another tense moment, she extended her hand.

"Bring the mother and the bambino in. All we have is oatmeal, but we got a lotta. Please, come in."

Let me tell you, that was the best oatmeal I ever ate!

The woman was Sophia Martinelli, the wife of the owner of the vineyard, and she was living there alone with her six kids while he was away in San Francisco. Things were not good for the wine business. Prohibition had nearly destroyed their livelihood, but with Repeal, they were starting to get back on track. Next fall's harvest would help, but until then her husband was working in the Bay Area.

"He is help build this big bridge now for two years. My sons and I are running the winery while he is away."

After several bowls of oatmeal, she let them wash up, and after a change of clothes, they prepared to continue on their way.

"Thank you so much, Mrs. Martinelli. We will never forget your kindness."

"*Prego.* Now, you take a good care of each other."

"And you stay well," Whit replied, and then added, "Mrs. Martinelli—"

"Sophia."

"Sophia, you said your husband is working on a bridge in San Francisco. Would that be the Golden Gate Bridge?"

"Si, the Golden Bridge. It is going to connect us with the city. No more ferry boats."

"Yes, imagine. Do you think I could get a job on the bridge?"

"Well, it's almost finished. They want opening it this next spring. But they have a lot yet to be done, so maybe."

*

When they reached the Marin County side of the new bridge, Meredith found herself holding her breath as she saw the two red towers thrusting up out of the bay. It was like King Neptune had thrown his tridents high into the sky.

We came around this curve and suddenly, there it was! I couldn't believe how tall the towers were, and all that cable holding up the roadway. As I think about it now, it seemed like it gave me a feeling of hope. It was like a symbol of us feeble little humans being able to create something magnificent even while we were struggling to survive.

Whit talked to some man working there about the possibility of getting a job. The guy said the office that did the hiring was on the San Francisco side of the bridge, so we'd have to take the ferry across the bay. Only there was a slight problem about that. We didn't have the dollar it cost to make the trip.

There was a diner near the ferry depot, and knowing how hungry Meredith must be, Whit ushered them inside. While Meredith took Matt into the ladies' room to change his diaper and to freshen up, Whit approached the woman behind the cash register.

"Excuse me, miss. I'd like to speak to the manager."

"Well, that would be Pete, and he's busy in the kitchen. Can I help you?"

"I really need to talk to somebody in charge."

The cashier must have heard the urgency in his voice. "Just a moment," she said, and headed off to the kitchen. A moment later she returned, trailed by a skinny, middle-aged man in an apron with his bald head covered in a bandanna.

"What's the problem, buddy?" he asked, wiping his hands on his apron, which seemed to be stained in many spots by some unidentified substance.

"I'm sorry to bother you, sir. But I'd like to make you a business proposition."

"Jesus Christ, if you pulled me out here to sell me something, I'll give—"

"Oh, no, sir. It's simply this." And Whit hurriedly told him about being broke and needing money for the ferry. "I have this watch," he said, pulling a shiny pocket watch and chain out of his jacket. "It was my grandfather's, it's sterling silver and it keeps perfect time."

"Listen, my friend, this is not a pawn shop—"

"I know, I know, I'm sorry, but my wife and I and our baby need to get to San Francisco."

By this time, the manager had turned away and was heading back to the kitchen. Whittaker started to follow him but stopped, realizing it was a lost cause.

"Can I see that watch?" came the voice of the cashier. She beckoned him over to the counter. Whit was taken aback, and it took him a moment to finally move toward the woman.

"May I look at it?"

Whit handed her the engraved silver timepiece.

"It's very beautiful. Probably worth a lot. More than I could ever afford."

"I just need enough to get over to the city."

"How about we do this. I'll give you two dollars and I'll hold on to the watch, and when you come by next time you can pay me and get your grandfather's watch back."

Whit was stunned. "I—I—I'm—thank you." Out of the corner of his eye he saw Meredith carrying the baby and coming toward him from the restroom. "Please. I don't want my wife to see the watch."

"Gotcha," said the cashier as she slipped the watch under the counter, "and how about I throw in a couple of free dinners to sweeten the deal?"

*

Whit got a job as a mechanic working on the trucks used on the building of the bridge. He earned four dollars a day. He and Meredith stayed at a local boarding house for the next six months. When the bridge finally opened, his job was over and it was time to start looking for more employment. There was nothing available in San Francisco. Everywhere he looked there were signs: NOT HIRING or NO JOBS. Finally, he packed up the car and, with Meredith and Matthew—who had doubled in weight and seemed very healthy—headed off toward the San Joaquin Valley.

For those of you who don't know, the San Joaquin Valley is the "breadbasket" of California, or was. I don't know about today. Anyway, Whit figured he could find some work on one of the farms, and he was right. He got a job plowing and weeding. It was backbreaking work, and for this he got a dollar a day. Listen, we were lucky he had a job.

The baby and I spent our days in the Gold Rush Hotel in Tinkertown. Now, you have to understand, Tinkertown was one step away from being a ghost town. It was in the middle of nowhere, with the only business still running being the general store. The owner of the general store also managed the hotel, and he rented it to us for two dollars a week. When I say he rented the hotel, I mean we were the only guests. He apologized for the lack of staff, but I was thrilled. We had the run of the whole place, all three floors, with access to the kitchen and the big dining room. We could sleep in any of the twelve bedrooms and bathe in any of the four bathrooms. It was amazing. This was probably one of the happiest times of my life.

Whit continued to pick up jobs at various farms, and things improved minimally. He eventually moved with the family to Sacramento and found work as a mechanic at a service station. Meredith was kept busy raising little Matthew and trying to make a comfortable home for Whit out of the tiny dark basement apartment they had rented. She wrote often to her mother and received letters back full of hometown gossip. At first Amelia wrote a lot about the scandal Whit and Meredith had caused by leaving town like thieves in the night, but as the months passed, she moved on to other subjects.

"The Smallwoods have really shut themselves away. We never see them in town anymore."

"Your brothers are concerned about how milk prices keep dropping."

"I'm making a crazy quilt."

"We miss you so much. I wish you would come back."

*

Nineteen-forty rolled in and Whit took on a second job. He worked days at a service station and then drove off to a creosote factory and stirred the noxious-smelling goo until midnight. Meredith found the odor nauseating and would hang his overalls outside to let them air out. Early one morning her upset stomach led her to wonder if maybe it wasn't the creosote. The doctor at the county hospital confirmed her diagnosis—she was pregnant again.

Marie Amelia Smallwood was born July 28, 1940—seven pounds, eight ounces. Whit got promoted to manager at the service station and things were looking up. He quit working at the creosote factory, and he and the family moved into a two-bedroom apartment on Sutterville Road. Meredith continued her role as housewife and put her creative juices into mothering, cooking and looking after Whit.

December 7th, 1941, everything changed.

You are being so dramatic. Listen, Mister Writer Man, can we move this section along? It was a very painful, lonely time for me, and I hate reliving it. To make a short story shorter, it was like this: the Japanese bomb Pearl Harbor. War is declared by the United States. Whit is drafted. Germany declares war on the United States. Whit is sent to Europe as a mechanic to work on the big M4 Sherman tanks. I'm on my own with two kids for the next three years.

While I understand you wanting to make it simple so we can get through it quickly, there are a few things our readers need to know. For example, the war helps the economy and puts an end to the Great Depression. Your mother moves with you and your children to Los Angeles, where you get work in Burbank at the Lockheed Aircraft factory, helping build P-38 fighter planes.

Yeah. Rosie the Riveter, that was me.

The war years in the United States were years of almost zero unemployment and decent salaries (especially for women), and although there was rationing, very few people were going hungry. The downside was that millions of young men were marching or sailing or flying away from family and friends, many never to return. Over 400,000 Americans lost their lives in Europe and the Pacific.

The frustration of never knowing where your son or father or brother or husband was, except to be told "somewhere in the Pacific" or "somewhere in Italy," and to not hear from them for months, was immense. The worst, however, was the arrival of a telegram from the War Department.

I got one of those. I guess Whit's mom and dad got one as well. Damn, I really didn't want to get into this.

Would you like me to write about it?

As if I could stop you. Oh, go ahead! I'm going to take a break. I hate this part.

The war in Europe ended on Tuesday, May 8th, 1945, V-E Day. On Wednesday, May 9th, Whittaker Smallwood hitched a ride on a Sherman tank heading back to his unit. They were somewhere between Hamburg and Berlin when a German soldier who evidently hadn't heard about the surrender of the Reich fired a bazooka at the tank. It killed everyone, including Whit.

Husband Number Two

It seemed so unfair. To have survived the war and then to die when it was all over. Meredith got the terrible news three weeks after V-E Day. To have celebrated the end of the war in Europe (the battle with Japan would go on until August) and to have waited for the return of your loved one, only to receive that dreaded telegram instead. A very cruel cosmic joke. Meredith mourned for Whit the rest of her life.

Meredith's job at Lockheed ended, and she, her nine-year-old son, her four-year-old daughter and her mother, Amelia, moved back to Oregon, this time to Portland. She got a job as a night operator for the phone company and finally started day classes at the Rose City School of Beauty. Amelia looked after the children.

Upon graduation in 1947, Meredith began to work at Roberto's House of Beauty on Southwest Salmon Street. While she had finally achieved her dream, like all dreams, it wasn't very close to the reality of the job. She hadn't calculated on the tired legs and sore back from standing all day, or the pain in her neck from bending over washing the hair of a dozen clients.

But she liked transforming a tired housewife into a vivacious vixen, or turning a head of gray into one of chestnut brown.

Within a year, the most popular beauty operator at Roberto's was Meredith. It wasn't just because she was very skilled at cutting and coloring, but that she was so outgoing and pleasant. And most importantly, she listened—not pretend listening, but compassionate listening. One could bare their soul to her and Meredith would understand.

In 1950, she received a letter. It was postmarked Seattle, Washington.

Dear Meredith,

I hope this letter finds you and your family healthy and happy. I also hope you still remember me. I was the skinny kid down the road who had a big crush on you. Sometimes we would walk with your brothers to school and you said I looked like the actor Ramon Navarro. Sadly, my family moved up here to Seattle when I was twelve, but I never forgot the beautiful girl who said I looked like a movie star.

After high school I got a job as a garbage collector and eventually I married a nice woman named Irene and we had a son. Unfortunately, Irene got ill and it turned out to be incurable, and so my son and I lost her two years ago. He misses her a lot.

I have my own business now. I install and maintain cigarette vending machines. I have a machine in almost every bar and hotel in town, so I'm doing all right. Keeps me busy and off the streets, ha ha.

I got your address from my cousin Deedee, who's still living down in Lebanon. She keeps up on all the latest news about her high school buddies, of which, I believe, you were one. Dedra Hendricks is her married name.

The reason I'm writing you this is that I will be attending a convention down in Portland next month and I thought maybe we could get together for dinner or something. I hope I haven't offended you by being too forward.

If you feel you would like to write me back, I've included my business card with my current address.

> *Hoping to hear from you,*
> *Yours truly, Clarence Mulligan*

Meredith remembered the cute boy from the farm next door and realized he was probably her first crush as well. Everyone called him C.M. (see 'em) because he hated being called Clarence. "I know I'm in trouble whenever my dad calls me 'CLARENCE!'" He was quiet, not really shy, just quiet. And even at twelve he had acted very grown-up and looked very handsome.

Meredith showed her mother the letter and asked her if she thought she should reply.

"Of course, silly. He seems to be a very polite gentleman, and it sounds like he's got money."

"Mom, it's just us getting together to talk over old times. For heaven's sake, I'm not marrying the man!"

But she did. Five months later she stood with C.M. in front of Justice of the Peace Amos R. Smyth and became Mrs. Clarence Mulligan. She quit her job at Roberto's, much to the dismay of both staff and clients, packed up her kids and her belongings and moved into C.M.'s modest bungalow on Angeline Street up in Seattle. Matthew was very upset about the whole thing, losing all his friends and getting a stepfather, a new brother, and a new high school. His sister Marie was just confused.

I think at this point it's time for you to stop. You're writing like you know my story, but you don't. Have you ever been a single woman, with two kids, who has to work herself down to the bone to provide for her family, who has no time for a social life, who crawls into an empty bed at night and cries herself to sleep? I saw C.M. as a way to improve all our lives, a father for Matthew and Marie, someone to comfort and love me, and, yes, someone who seemed to have a good income. That my children had to make some small sacrifices was unfortunate, but it was necessary. I truly believed that the marriage and the move to Seattle was for the best. Just because it didn't quite work out that way doesn't mean it was wrong.

As I said earlier, this is a fictional story, and it's going wherever it wants. I'm sorry if it doesn't jibe with your version of your life, but I can only let my pen go where it wants to go. However, feel free to jump in at any time, as you have been doing, to clarify or argue a point. Now, moving on.

From the beginning, there were complications. The first was Samuel. Sam was C.M.'s son from his first marriage. Understandably, he, like Matt, was not happy about the changes brought about by the marriage. He now had to share his room with this older guy who treated him like a little kid. Marie had her own room and began to turn it into a girly place with her collection of dolls, enough pink accessories to qualify as an ad for Pepto-Bismol and her photo of the daddy she never really knew. She was not impressed with the pretend father her mom had married.

Meredith hoped that the dynamics of this new family would eventually work out, that the boys would become great pals, that Marie would accept (and finally come to adore) her new father and that C.M. would give his new bride the love and support she needed.

The first crack in this imaginary picture of domestic bliss was Meredith discovering that C.M. was not well off. His cigarette vending machine business made just enough money to cover the mortgage on the house, the payments on his van, insurance on the house and auto, utilities, and, finally, food for the pantry. Anything after that was on an "as needed" basis. There was a small savings account, but that was for emergencies only.

Next was the ongoing feud between Matt and Sam. It came to the point where they were beating up on each other. After Matthew gave Sam a bloody nose, C.M. laid down the law and used a line of masking tape to divide the boys' room in half.

"Sam, you stay on this side," C.M. ordered, "and Matthew, you on this side. You may step over the line only to leave or enter the room. You got it?"

Marie did not take to Clarence Mulligan at first—or even at all, really. It's weird how one can meet someone for the first time and there is an immediate arc of dislike between the two strangers. This was the case between Marie and her stepfather. She found him cold and distant, and he found her spoiled and snobbish. She was ten years old. He was thirty-four.

And then there was the marriage itself. The honeymoon was over very quickly, due to the necessary adaptations that had to be made. There was registering Matt and Marie for school. There was applying for a Washington state driver's license. There was learning about the neighborhood, where the Safeway was located, the pharmacy and the gas station.

Meredith found herself up to her elbows in laundry and dishes. There were floors to be swept and mopped, beds to be made and windows to be washed. Most daunting was the preparation of the meals. Finding a menu that pleased all five members of the newly formed Mulligan family was impossible. No eggs for Sam. No broccoli for C.M. Bread without crusts for Marie. Matthew liked only smooth peanut butter for his sandwiches and hold the jelly, please.

It was obvious that chores needed to be assigned, and that helped a little bit, but sometimes Meredith felt like she was back in Lavinia Smallwood's kitchen. By bedtime she was wiped out.

The bedroom was off limits to the children and was intended to be an oasis from the chaos of daytime activities. Meredith would come—

Hold it, cowboy! How dare you presume to know what went on behind closed doors. I will not allow you to make up some salacious garbage about C.M. and me. Let me set the record straight.

First of all, Clarence was the total opposite of Whittaker. Whit was kind of blond and pale, while C.M. was dark and swarthy. He was handsome in a Tyrone Power sort of way, while Whit was more like Leslie Howard. C.M. was the strong silent type, with no use for idle conversation. "Get to the point!" was his motto. Whit loved to talk about everything, the latest scientific inventions, politics, movies, books. He was so curious—damn, I told myself I wouldn't get all teary. I still miss him so.

Anyway, Whit was almost shy in bed. He treated me very lovingly and took great pains to make me feel good. By the time he shipped off to that terrible war, he had become a wonderful lover.

Clarence, on the other hand, was not a lover. He was a fucker (excuse my French). He was quick and rough—how rough, I was to learn later on. So, Mister Smarty-Pants Writer, bedtime was not a time of relaxation. It was a fast and furious session of in and out. No hugging, no kissing, no talking.

I'm sorry to hear that, but I sort of had an inkling that something like that was going on. Thank you for being so open and honest. May I continue?

Go for it.

Meredith was beginning to wonder what she had gotten herself into. This was not working out to be the beautiful future she had envisioned when C.M. was courting her. It was not that she didn't know that family life was complicated and messy and often painful, but she felt she had been deceived. Most men, when they are wooing a prospective partner, present a very different persona from the one that will appear after the wedding. Clarence had been thoughtful and respectful, quiet but attentive. He had done all the right things—flowers, chocolates, dinner (somewhere other than the local greasy spoon) and an engagement ring.

Now, several months into the marriage, he was a completely different person. Silent, sullen and not interested in anything else going on with the rest of the family. Most of the time, when he was not at work, driving around feeding packs of cigarettes into machines, he was in the basement repairing said machines. On the rare occasions when he came upstairs, it was to eat, sleep or use the bathroom. Once in a while he would lie down on the living room couch and indulge in one of his favorite pastimes.

"Mom," asked Matthew, "what is C.M. doing on the sofa?"

"He's reading the phone book."

"What—?"

"He likes to look up names in the telephone directory."

"Why?"

"I don't know, I really don't know."

C.M.'s hygiene routine left a lot to be desired as well. He didn't believe in deodorant or toothpaste, but he did take a bath once a week whether he needed it or not. However, the thing that upset Meredith the most was the truth about her engagement and wedding rings.

"C.M., Sam said something to me about my rings."

"Yes?"

"He seems to think they were his mother's."

"So?"

"You mean to tell me you gave me your dead wife's wedding rings?!"

"Yeah," C.M. replied, turning a page in the phone book.

"Clarence Mulligan! You actually slipped those rings off Irene's dead finger and saved them to give to the next woman you planned to marry? Why didn't you let them be buried with her?"

"Well, that would have been a waste, now, wouldn't it?"

"Okay, then why couldn't you just have put them away for safekeeping, like for when Sam got married?"

"They fit your finger, right? I had them sized to fit."

Meredith began to realize that C.M. saw the world very differently from the way she did. She also understood why he had married her and that it had nothing to do with love. He needed a mother to handle his son, a housekeeper to clean and cook for him and a woman to satisfy him in bed. She was stuck in Seattle, away from any friends she had in Portland, away from a job she had loved. She felt unable to figure out a way to extricate herself from this disastrous situation.

I'm sure your readers are going "For god's sake, woman, just divorce the s.o.b.!" What they don't understand, especially the younger ones, is that I grew up during a time when "divorce" was a dirty word. In every movie I saw that portrayed an unhappy marriage, the only way out for the long-suffering wife was to shoot either her husband or herself. It gave a whole new meaning to the phrase "till death do us part." When you married someone, it was forever—unlike today, when half of all marriages end in divorce.

I remember talking on the phone to my mother about how miserable I was and how maybe I should get a divorce.

"Good heavens, no! Can you imagine what your cousins would think, and Aunt Flora! No one in our family has ever had a failed marriage. No one ever went through the scandal of a divorce!"

But you were dealing with this in 1953. Surely things had changed enough by then.

Not really. When I look back on those years, the fifties, I realize how much we were still in the dark ages. Only the "Beatniks," in their berets and black clothes, dared to be different. It was such a conservative period. I call it the Last Victorian Age. It wasn't until the sixties that things began to change.

I continued to hold on to my marriage, and this was for several reasons. I didn't want to uproot the kids again; Matt was beginning his senior year in high school. I was thirty-six years old and I was concerned about maybe not being able to get back into the workforce. But by 1958, I had had it.

You mean about the physical abuse.

I mean everything—abuse, lack of money, stifled creativity. You know what was the worst? C.M. had absolutely no sense of humor. Do you know what it's like to live with someone who never laughs? Someone who can't see the humor in everyday life? It's deadly.

So you filed for divorce.

One of the hardest things I ever had to do. But C.M. made it easier for me due to the bruises he left on my arms and the black eye he gave me when I told him it was over. Threatened with being arrested for assault and battery, he agreed to the divorce. Matt had gotten a job and moved out, and Marie was graduating high school, so the timing was perfect.

In the divorce settlement, Meredith was given the house, along with the mortgage, in exchange for not receiving alimony. That was fine with her; it was "a small price to pay" for her freedom. C.M. moved himself, his son Sam and his business equipment into a warehouse in Bothell. There he would live and work for another eight years, until he would grow ill and die from lung cancer. He smoked four packs a day. He certainly stood behind his product.

Everyone smoked in the early years of the twentieth century, or at least it looked like that. Believe it or not, cigarettes were cheap. Before the Second World War, a pack of cigs cost 15 cents. By 1950 they cost 20 cents a pack, and by the time of Meredith's divorce, the price had jumped to an astronomical 25 cents a pack. And they were good for you. Ads with photos of physicians appeared everywhere claiming "More doctors smoke Camels than any other cigarette!"

The rules about women smoking were changing by 1958, but it was still considered not a very ladylike habit. True, the ladies in the movies smoked, but only the ones with a slightly harder edge, like career women, vamps, high-society females, the dame with the heart of gold or the misunderstood artist. Never the girl next door or somebody's mother. And yet 41 percent of the smoking population were women, and that's a lot of mothers and girls next door.

Meredith smoked, and had been smoking since she was sixteen. She would eventually stop, but that was to happen in the future. For now, she was addicted to Kools, feeling that the menthol helped cut down on the sore throats and coughing.

Husband Number Three

With Marie still living at home and the bills starting to pile up, Meredith knew she had to find work. She began contacting beauty salons, either in person or on the phone, and inquiring if they had any positions open.

None of them did, but many said they would contact her if and when that changed. Realizing she couldn't wait around, she started scanning the want ads for anything that she thought she could handle: Dental Hygienist—no, Stenographer—no, Assistant Window Dresser—no. After a week or so, with no viable leads, she almost gave up, until she saw this ad in the *Seattle Times*:

How would you like
to make $500 a week?
Work from home.
No skills required.
Just a pleasant personality.
Call JUniper 5 3804

She figured she was a pleasant person, most of the time, so she called the number. It was answered on the third ring by a female voice, all chipper and excited.

"Grayson Employment Agency! Dot speaking. How may I help you?"

"Uh—I'm calling about your ad."

"Which one, honey?"

"The one about working from home, no skills—"

"Oh, yeah. The *Mortuary Guild* magazine."

"Excuse me?"

"They need someone to sell ads for their bimonthly magazine."

And so Meredith was introduced to that fifties phenomenon (that is with us still), the telephone solicitor. After filling out the appropriate forms, the agency sent her to the offices of the Evergreen State Publishing Company for a brief interview, and, much to her surprise and relief, she was hired on the spot.

For the next three years she called and talked to every undertaker in every county in the state of Washington. Not only did she find she was good at selling advertising space, but she also increased the magazine's number of subscriptions. Something about her voice and the way she really listened to the person on the other end of the line, similar to the way she listened to her clients at Roberto's beauty salon, seemed to inspire trust and helped to loosen the purse strings. She never made $500 a week, but she got by, and she even helped Marie pay for college.

It was around this time that she began attending the local Lutheran church, mainly to revitalize her social life. At Hope Lutheran, she became friends with a couple of young housewives, and this led to some interesting discussions about love and marriage. While Meredith was talking about her recent divorce, one of the young ladies, Maggie Walsh, asked her if she planned on getting married again.

"When hell freezes over! Twice was enough. If I ever get married again, I give you permission to shoot me."

On Sunday, June 16, 1963, Meredith Olsen Smallwood Mulligan wed Curtis Howard Bright at Hope Lutheran Church. At the reception, Maggie Walsh shot Meredith with her son's cap pistol.

*

Curtis Bright had charisma. He looked like a living 8 x 10 glossy publicity photo. He dressed impeccably, his teeth were blazingly white, and not one of his flaming red hairs was ever out of place. To top it all off, his sky-blue eyes sparkled with a wicked sense of humor. That is what first attracted Meredith to him—his sense of humor.

It all began as a simple business relationship. Curtis had heard about Meredith from a friend who knew somebody at the company that published the *Mortuary Guild* magazine. They were talking about this amazing woman who could talk the cheapest Scrooge into buying an ad. Curtis was working at the time as a salesman for an aluminum siding company. This was the era of the door-to-door salesman selling everything from encyclopedias to vacuum cleaners. Curtis didn't like making "cold calls" but preferred working leads given to him by a telephone solicitor who had compiled a list of possible customers from the calls they made.

When he heard about Meredith, he immediately asked for her number, because she sounded like just the sort of telephone solicitor he needed.

So I get this call from a guy who wants to meet with me about a job. I told him I already had a position, but he insisted that he be allowed to come by and talk with me. I don't know why I said yes, but I did, and there he was knocking on my door.

Imagine opening your front door and finding Van Johnson or Kirk Douglas standing there, he was that gorgeous. Now you have to remember that Curtis was a born salesman, and so the next thing I knew I was working for him. It was part-time at first, as I wanted to keep working for the mortuary magazine. It was also not as easy. With the friendships I had built up with all those undertakers, it was not difficult to get them to buy ads. To call a stranger at dinnertime and convince him to let a salesman come by to try and sell him aluminum siding ("lasts a lifetime, never needs painting, is fireproof and insect-proof!") is not a task for the faint of heart. I endured insults ranging from "What the hell are you doing calling me during my supper!" to "Drop dead, bitch!" to silence, followed by the person hanging up the receiver. I don't blame any of those poor souls, either. I would have felt the same. This was before caller ID and today's regulations, feeble as they are.

Before I knew what hit me, I was in a much more intimate relationship with Curtis Bright. He introduced me to my first out-of-wedlock experience.

For those of you youngsters who have had lots of sexual partners since you were in your teens, and for you folks who are in serious long-term relationships without the benefit of marriage, let me fill you in on how it used to be.

Just like divorce was frowned upon, back in the dark ages of my youth, sex outside of marriage was considered immoral and totally unacceptable. In some states it was illegal. Only naughty single bohemian people lived together, like the aforementioned Beatniks. That's why you got married. Look at Elizabeth Taylor, she married eight times (although I'm pretty sure she had some love affairs along the way). Instead of just moving in with the man of the hour, she married him.

Anyway, that's how brainwashed I was. No sex without marriage—until Curtis. There I was, a forty-five-year-old divorcée, and there he was, a thirty-five-year-old single, never-married, dashing, handsome, smart, funny and very sexy man. It was the start of the swinging sixties, times were changing and so was I. I had a test run in bed with Curtis and found I liked what I discovered, and so we got married.

Curtis Bright was not like Meredith's other husbands. Whittaker had been a boy, almost as innocent as she had been. C.M. was a strange, insensitive, abusive lout, but Curtis was the total opposite. He showered Meredith with gifts, with candlelit dinners and trips to Las Vegas and weekends at the beach. Most importantly, however, he flooded her with praise and love, and she blossomed.

She eventually quit her job with the mortuary magazine and worked full-time finding possible leads for Curtis. He was an amazing salesman and convinced a lot of Seattle homeowners to re-side their houses. He and Meredith made a great team. And then the roof caved in.

Meredith got a notice that the bank was repossessing her house, and when she called in a panic, they also informed her that she was overdrawn on their joint account. When Curtis walked into the house after a day of unsuccessful sales calls, Meredith was ready.

"Why did you get a second mortgage on our home?!"

"Ah, I—"

"I don't remember signing any papers, so you must have forged my name."

"Oh, babe, I didn't want to worry you—"

"Well, I'm plenty worried now. What the hell is going on?!"

"Just a little financial setback. I'm on it. I'll have it cleared up in no time."

"Every check I wrote to pay this month's bills bounced. What happened?"

"Well, I had some debts I had to take care of."

"What debts?"

And then it all came out. Curtis had a "slight" gambling problem. Seems some of his afternoons, when he was supposedly following up leads, were spent at the racetrack. Evening visits with prospective clients could turn into a good-ol'-boys' poker game. That aluminum siding convention in Las Vegas was a chance to try his hand at blackjack. And he was adept at playing the numbers, even if that was kind of illegal.

"How much do you owe?"

"Not a lot. It's manageable."

"Curtis, how much?"

"Ah—just a few thousand?"

"JUST A FEW!? How many is a few?"

"Around—$25,000—or so."

"Oh, my god!"

"It's okay, it's okay! I'm taking care of it."

"Who do you owe this money to? These 'few' thousands?"

"Well, that's where it gets a little dicey."

"What do you mean?"

"In order to pay off some of my debts, I consolidated them into one large debt."

"What does that mean?"

"I borrowed enough to pay off most of what I owed, and that way I only had one person I had to reimburse."

"And who was, or is, this generous person?"

"A guy."

"A guy?"

"Yeah, who makes private loans."

"Curtis, please don't tell me you borrowed from a loan shark!" The silence that followed affirmed the situation. "And now we owe the bank and our account is overdrawn and they're threatening to repossess the house!"

"It's not going to happen. I have an appointment tomorrow morning that will take care of everything."

"What kind of appointment? With whom?"

"Don't worry your pretty little head. Let me surprise you."

And surprise her he did. He left the house the next morning and was never seen again. Whether he had just driven off into the sunset or was sent to the bottom of Puget Sound she would never know. When she contacted a different bank, about the joint savings account she and Curtis had opened there, she was told he had closed it out. Her signature—forged, of course, along with his—was on the paperwork.

With the loss of her house, her husband and her job, Meredith returned to Portland to live with her mother. Marie had finished college and was living in a hippie commune somewhere in the wilds of the Cascade Mountains. Matthew was east, in Chicago, working at an ad agency.

For the next six months I cried all day, and it only stopped when I fell asleep. I gained twenty pounds, never left the house and stared at the television from dawn to midnight. Today, they call it clinical depression. My poor mother did her best to try to cheer me up. I'm sure I must have shortened her life.

Then one day I got up, put on the only dress I had that fit, and went for a walk. I climbed up the hill to the Rose Gardens, sat on a bench and talked to God, or whoever was in charge. I made a vow to never allow myself to be controlled by a man ever again and that I would now take good care of myself, by myself.

Her prayers were answered on the day her divorce (her second) was granted. Due to having been abandoned, the decree was issued promptly, with no complications. And at the same time, a job opportunity appeared out of nowhere. A friend of Meredith's mother mentioned that the beautician at Providence Hospital was looking for an assistant. Meredith applied and got the job, and her life began to change for the better.

Providence was one of the first hospitals to dedicate a room to be used as a beauty shop. They realized that when a patient was stuck in a hospital bed for days or even weeks, they would need to at least get their hair washed. What they discovered was that after a person had been wheeled down to the shop, had a shampoo and a comb-out or, as in the case of the male patients, a haircut, they felt better and seemed to heal faster.

Beverly Compton ran the beauty shop and was great in the hair department, but a little behind the times in the makeup area. She was also becoming unable to handle the volume of patients that wanted to avail themselves of her services.

"Honey, I am so glad to have you on board! Now, you say you did makeup out at Roberto's?"

"I did it all, cut, dye, and perm as well as makeup."

"Well, that's great. You know, we get these poor sick women whose skin has turned the color of day-old oatmeal. A little makeup magic, you know—rouge, lipstick, a bright eyeshadow—and they really perk up!"

It was true. As the months went by, Meredith watched many of her patients look in the mirror, after she had styled their hair and carefully worked on their makeup, and smile at what they saw in the reflection. She sometimes felt like she was actually a practicing nurse—of cosmetology.

The years flew by, as they are wont to do, and Meredith became firmly established as the person to go to for a makeover of both body and spirit. Even the hospital nurses made appointments to have their hair done and their makeup improved. Eventually, Beverly retired and turned the business over to Meredith.

One afternoon, a patient was wheeled in and Meredith's path in life changed once again. Margo Francis Stearns was in her seventies and was one of Portland's grande dames. She was a descendent of a lumber baron and was a distant cousin of one of the du Ponts. She was very rich—

But don't hold that against her. She was a lovely woman, very handsome and very generous. We hit it off at once. She was in the hospital for a battery of tests. "I'm feeling very battered at the moment," she joked. I laughed and told her that all she needed was a warm shampoo and a cool drink. She had thick, chestnut-brown hair streaked with gray, which I gently washed and then teased up into a soft bouffant, which was the style at the time. She seemed pleased, so pleased that several weeks later the shop phone rang and it was Margo.

"Meredith, darling, is it possible to make an appointment with you even if I'm not a patient?"

I told her I wouldn't tell if she didn't, and that started a long series of monthly visits. I didn't flatter myself with the thought that I was the best beautician in the state of Oregon, but I did do a decent job. However, I believe it was my listening ability that attracted Margo. I was a great sounding board. She needed someone to hear her, someone who was non-judgmental and had no personal ties to her.

She talked about her recently deceased husband. She told me about her beloved son Lewis and his struggles with depression. I heard about her aborted career as a classical pianist (gave it up to get married; sound familiar?) and how much she had missed her music. She had started playing piano again, in the privacy of her home, just for her own pleasure. I told her how much I would enjoy hearing her play. At first she said she was too rusty to let anyone listen, too nervous.

But that changed as the monthly visits to the beauty shop continued, and one day she invited Meredith to a Sunday brunch.

"Nothing fancy, darling. Just a chance for you to get away from the hospital for a bit. A little girl time for the two of us. I might even give you a sample of my piano playing. Shall we say eleven?"

Meredith was stunned, and when she got home and told her mother, Amelia was astounded as well.

"She invited you up to her house, her mansion?"

"I guess that's what she meant."

"Margo Stearns is the richest woman in the city!"

"I know, I know! What am I going to wear?"

*

On the appointed Sunday, Meredith took a taxi to the Forest Park address of Margo Stearns. Stepping out of the cab, she looked up from the open wrought-iron gate to the French Renaissance–style chateau that sat at the top of the drive. It was like the exterior of a set for a movie version of *The Three Musketeers*.

Adjusting her coat, newly purchased at Meier & Frank's department store, she climbed the slight incline and, reaching the grand entrance, ascended the steps to the large, iron-clad oak front door. There was a door knocker attached, with the head of a bear, and at the side of the door was a white mother-of-pearl doorbell. Door knocker or doorbell? Oh, dear! Which should she use?

The dilemma was solved when the door opened on its own, to reveal a young woman dressed in a simple navy blue dress.

"Good morning, Miss. Mrs. Stearns is waiting for you in the sunroom. May I take your coat?"

Meredith quickly slipped out of her new acquisition, a little disappointed that Margo wouldn't see her in her beautiful camel-hair overcoat. But she was glad she had gone ahead and also invested in a new dress, a pseudo–Yves Saint Laurent sack dress in emerald green.

She was led by the young woman past a massive marble staircase and down a hall lined with paintings of horses and horsey-looking people, until they entered a brightly lit room made entirely of glass. Meredith figured this was what the mystery novels referred to as "the conservatory."

"Meredith, darling! You made it!" said Margo effusively, rising from a round cloth-covered table nestled among large tropical plants and planting a kiss on each of Meredith's cheeks.

"Please sit here, across from me. Oh, and this is Maria," she said, indicating the young lady in blue, "my very own angel. I'd be lost without her."

"Very pleased to meet you, Maria," responded Meredith. "My daughter's name is Marie." The young lady in blue gave her a dutiful smile.

"Maria, if you would bring out the coffee, please," Margo requested as she led Meredith to a seat at the table. On it was a centerpiece of roses surrounded by many different dishes (Flora Danica china, to be precise) holding fruit, pastries, cheeses and cold meats. A far cry from the coffee and oatmeal that Meredith wolfed down every morning before she rushed off to work.

"This looks so beautiful—and tasty!"

"Not very fancy. I could have Cook whip you up some eggs if you'd like."

"Oh, my, no! This is fine—more than fine. It's fabulous."

The brunch proceeded, with Maria pouring coffee and refilling bowls and plates as they emptied. Margo and Meredith spent several hours sharing stories about their early years—Margo growing up in Barton Hills, the richest neighborhood in Michigan, and Meredith surviving in Lebanon, Oregon, whose claim to fame was the annual Strawberry Festival. "Lebanon is the nation's largest producer of strawberries," Meredith explained.

"My word, very impressive. Maybe these berries came from there."

And so started a friendship between two very different women. What united them was their loneliness and—

Listen, Mr. Nosy Parker, it was strictly platonic. Make sure you let your readers know that. I've got nothing against my gay sisters and brothers, but I never leaned in that direction. Maybe I should have, considering my success rate with men.

What I was going to say was that they were united by loneliness and fascination with each other's lifestyle. For Margo, who had grown up in a world of private schools, debutante balls, ski trips to Switzerland, yachts on the Mediterranean and shopping sprees in Paris, Meredith's life seemed pleasantly simple, bucolic, quiet and very down to earth. But of course unless you have actually lived another person's life, which we can never do, you don't really know what it was, and is, like.

"I remember how guilty I felt during the Depression," Margo confessed. "I was married and a mother and living in a twenty-room mansion with a staff of servants and a nanny, and reading the daily newspaper about the bread lines and the soup kitchens and the unemployment rate of 25 percent. I knew I was very lucky. I did see to it that Leo, my husband, donated to various charities, but he did so reluctantly. I think he feared we could end up losing everything. Fear and greed, an evil combination of emotions, and for us totally irrelevant. Between our two families, we had a fortune that would serve us well even if we lost three-quarters of it."

Meredith still had trouble imagining that kind of wealth. "It is good that you appreciated your situation. However, you shouldn't beat yourself up for not being poor. You wouldn't have liked it. Poverty doesn't make you noble or strong. It just makes you hungry and miserable and you feel hopeless, which you are. Growing up poor in the country was an experience I could have done without, and it has permanently colored my outlook on life."

Margo was embarrassed by the way she had fantasized about what she thought was the unpretentious life of a country girl: dirndl skirt, milkmaid braids, running through fields of daisies and square dancing in a barn. Feeling the need to move off such a depressing topic, Margo led Meredith into the music room, where she played a couple of piano pieces for her.

By late afternoon, Meredith was on her way home to the two-room apartment she shared with her mother. Amelia was excitedly waiting for her daughter to share the highlights of her brunch with the richest woman in Portland, Oregon. Amelia had aged a lot in the last few months and was feeling her mortality, but she still looked forward to a juicy bit of gossip.

"What did she serve?"

"What was she wearing?"

"How many servants does she have?"

"What's the house like?"

"What did you talk about?"

Meredith answered as many of the questions as she could and then begged off, with the excuse she was tired and had to go to work the next day. She reminded her mother that, unlike Margo, she had a job.

*

Margo spent the evening thinking about the brunch and how pleasant and informative it had been. After some soul-searching, she determined that she wanted to do something special for Meredith. A party, maybe. Or a trip to Mexico or Hawaii. She was feeling so much stronger physically. This friendship was much better medicine than all those pills the doctors were feeding her.

Margo began sending little tokens of her appreciation to Meredith. Most of her gifts were decorations for the beauty shop: porcelain flowers, original oil paintings of birds and butterflies, decorative mirrors in gold frames. However, during one of her visits to have her hair done, she heard Meredith complaining about one of the hair dryers. "The poor old thing is consumptive, hasn't enough breath left to blow out a candle." A week later, a beautiful hot pink General Electric hooded hair dryer arrived. Meredith was stunned. She phoned Margo immediately.

"Margo, I thank you, but I can't accept this—I understand, but—yes, it's lovely. It's standing here looking like a spaceship—well, if I keep it, I insist on reimbursing you—"

Of course Margo wouldn't hear of it, and Meredith learned she had to keep her equipment-replacement plans to herself. But the generosity and the gifts didn't stop. Margo took her to lunch at Meier & Frank's, with a little clothes shopping thrown in. And then there were visits to Best's Apparel and Nordstrom's, "just to look around" and maybe pick up a few things. Meredith's closet began to fill up.

Margo also began to introduce Meredith to various cultural events like the Oregon Symphony, ballet performances and the road shows that played at the Civic Auditorium. It was at the Civic where Meredith saw her first Broadway musical, *The Music Man.*

Margo guided her through the Portland Art Museum as well as some of the private art galleries. There were dinners at Hillvilla, where the view was as delicious as the meal, and jazz at the Mural Room, where the music was better than the food. There were profiteroles at Lipman's Chocolate Lounge and there was lobster at Canlis, high atop the newly built Hilton

Hotel. Meredith added an inch to her waistline, while Margo never seemed to gain a pound. In fact, she looked like she was losing weight.

"No, no, it's an illusion. I have the most amazing dressmaker who could make Kate Smith look slim. In fact, I'd love to have her make something for you. Wouldn't that be fun?"

"Well, I don't know—"

"Listen, every year I host a charity ball up at the house. It's for Mental Health America, and it's the only time I hobnob with the bores of this town. They may be shallow, but they have deep pockets, so I provide the venue, the food and drink and the dance band. This year it's a musical group called The Fireballs. God knows what they're all about. Anyway, I want you to attend, and since you'll need something formal, dressy—you know, splashy—we'll have Rosella whip something up for you."

You have to understand, it was almost impossible to say no to Margo. I never needed or wanted all the stuff she kept sending my way, but it seemed to give her such joy. And I'd be lying if I said I didn't like all the attention, so I went along with the wining and dining. I agreed to be styled by Madame Rosella, and on the night of the charity ball, I showed up in the turquoise satin gown with the beaded bodice that Madame had made for me. Margo quickly took me up to her dressing room (the size of my apartment) and draped a diamond and azure necklace around my neck. This was not a gift, of course, but a loaner, which she augmented with a pair of diamond stud earrings the size of a couple of olives.

Husband Number Four??

The party was in full swing when Meredith descended the wide marble staircase, feeling like Audrey Hepburn in *My Fair Lady*. However, once on the dance floor, she felt her age as she watched people wildly gyrating to "Wooly Bully" and "Sha La La." She was about to head for the safety of the refreshment table when the music shifted to "What the World Needs Now Is Love." Was that a waltz or a foxtrot? She might be able to maneuver her way through that. As if her thoughts were heard, a distinguished silver-haired gentleman stepped in front of her. "Pardon me, but may I have this dance?"

Lewis Nestor Stearns introduced himself as they moved counterclockwise around the parquet floor.

"Yes, I'm the progeny of Mrs. Margo Stearns, the glamorous hostess of this debacle. And I know who you are, Miss Meredith Smallwood, the makeup magician and hair stylist extraordinaire who works out of Providence Hospital."

Meredith felt somewhat embarrassed by this description and didn't quite know how to respond. She wished Margo had prepared her by first introducing her to her son. In truth, he was proving to be a good dancer, and he certainly was pleasing to the eye. Tall, broad-shouldered, with grey-green eyes and a crooked smile, he spoke with a rich, cultivated baritone voice.

"Mother says you have brightened up her life."

"Well, I don't know about—"

"Don't be modest. I think she feels like you're the daughter she never had."

"Oh, my, no! We're just friends. She's been very nice, and—"

"So that kind of makes me your brother, eh, Sis?"

Meredith was getting more and more uncomfortable with this conversation. She couldn't tell if Lewis Stearns was being sarcastic or sincere. When the music stopped, she told him she was thirsty and was going to go over to the bar. He insisted that he escort her and asked her if she would like some champagne.

"That would be lovely."

As the evening proceeded, with more dancing, dining and appeals from Margo for contributions to MHA, Lewis stuck close to Meredith. Several glasses of champagne had helped her relax, and she even began to enjoy his company. He was wickedly witty and kept her chuckling with his sotto voce comments about various of the evening's guests:

"He's president of the First National Bank and yet has trouble counting to ten."

"What she has paid for plastic surgery over the years would end the National Debt."

"Can you believe he has a twin? One of him is more than enough."

"Yvonne? The blonde? She just celebrated her thirty-fifth birthday. Really. She's been celebrating it for the last twenty years."

While Meredith found his social commentary somewhat humorous, it made her wonder if he said these unflattering things about everyone, including herself.

As the party began winding down, Margo finally took time to join Meredith and her son at one of the small tables she had set up on the patio. She looked tired but elegant in the wine-colored culottes gown she had chosen to wear. An intricate necklace of garnets, set in gold wire filigree, was the only jewelry she wore.

"I'm so sorry to have neglected you, darling, but I had to keep shaming the reluctant guests into making a contribution. I see Lewis has introduced himself. I hope he has taken good care of you."

"Absolutely. I've had a very pleasant evening."

"He's here visiting me," Margo continued, talking almost as if he weren't there sitting in front of her, "all the way from Michigan."

"Hello, Mother. I'm over here, next to Meredith, if you need to reach me for anything."

"Don't be silly, Lewis. But as long as you've offered, why don't you go get us some coffee."

"Aye, aye, mon capitaine," Lewis replied, rising up from the table. "This means she wants to have a little private tête-à-tête with you, Meredith," he whispered as he headed off to the bar.

"He's incorrigible—but under that veneer of sarcasm, he's really just a marshmallow. He's very sensitive, and we've been through a lot together. It's one of the reasons I chose to support Mental Health America. They have helped us so much—a great organization. He's suffered from anxiety most of his life, along with a little paranoia once in a while, but that all seems to have faded away recently."

"Well, he's been very charming. I'm sorry if you had to struggle—"

"Oh, sweetheart, don't concern yourself. Things are fine now. Ah, here comes our coffee."

Lewis arrived with the angel Maria carrying a tray upon which sat a coffeepot and three cups. After he was seated and the coffee had been served, the conversation turned to the success of the evening.

"We did better than we did last year, although the tally isn't finished."

"Did mater tell you about my vacation at the Oregon State Hospital?"

"Lewis, don't start!"

"Actually, it was at the Dammasch branch, out in Wilsonville. We called it the Damn Ass branch. Boy, what a wild party that was!"

Okay, enough already. I'm sure your readers know where this is going, and this is an episode I am particularly ashamed of. If we're going to have to delve into it, let's do it as quickly as possible.

There are several mitigating factors that caused me to make the decision that I did: Mother's decline and eventual death, the closing of the beauty shop at the old Providence Hospital while they built the new hospital, and the foolish promise I made to Margo.

When Mama ended up in the hospital with congestive heart failure, on one of my visits to her room, which she shared with two other women, she told me she had some news.

"One of the nurses mentioned that Mrs. Stearns has been admitted to the hospital. She has a private room on the top floor. No one is supposed to know she's here, but I thought since you're so close to her, you'd want to visit."

I immediately took the elevator up to the tenth floor and found Margo's room. She looked awful, and it was obvious she had lost even more weight. She smiled when she saw me and put on a brave face, but I could tell she was very ill. It was cancer, pancreatic cancer, and she had been struggling with it for some time. We chatted like nothing was the matter, but I knew she was in great pain. Finally, she had had enough of the small talk, and, looking me straight in the eyes, she made a request.

"Meredith, I would like you to look after Lewis. You have been such a help to me, and I've seen how strong you can be. You have so much common sense, and that makes you the perfect fit."

"But he's back in Michigan —"

"Yes, I know. But I've started making arrangements."

"What kind of arrangements?"

"Maria will be sending you a packet with all the information. Just promise me you'll take care of Lewis."

And so I made the stupid promise.

*

A large manila envelope arrived two days before Amelia Olsen passed away and three days before Margo Stearns succumbed to her disease. Occupied with her mother's funeral arrangements and with moving the equipment and supplies from the beauty shop into storage kept Meredith from spending any time perusing the package's contents. It was only after a week of looking at her mother's dishes and nightgowns and photo albums and crying herself to sleep that she finally sat down and had a serious look at the documents sent to her by the late Margo Francis Stearns.

The first page was a personal letter from Margo thanking her for being such a good friend. This was followed with a contract indicating that Meredith was being hired as manager of the household of one Lewis Nestor Stearns, 266 Geddes Ave., Ann Arbor, Michigan. Her salary was to be $250,000 a year (Meredith nearly passed out when she read that). Her duties were to run the household (funds would be provided monthly, up to $10,000), pay all bills (checking account established with renewable balance of $25,000), maintain a budget for Mr. Stearns (his monthly allowance of $5,000) and supervise all medical treatments for Mr. Stearns. She would be responsible for the upkeep of the two automobiles (a Rolls-Royce Phantom V and a Ferrari 250 GTO) and for the maintenance of the Chevrolet Corsair that would be her personal vehicle.

Enclosed in the envelope was a ticket for a roomette on a train to Chicago, where she would be met by a chauffeur and then driven to Ann Arbor. There was also a check for $1,500 for travelling expenses.

"A promise is a promise" was something her father used to say; "never make a promise you can't keep." And so Meredith sublet her apartment, packed up her clothes and mementos and headed east. She also realized that in four years she could become a millionaire, and that was a big incentive as well.

Looking back on all this nonsense, I really think I must have lost my mind. I mean, it was as if I were in this movie, you know, about a small-town girl who makes good and marries this ultra-rich man from a famous high-society family. But I wasn't marrying him (maybe I thought that would happen eventually) and I didn't even love him. I had to keep reminding myself that I was just an employee and that my job was to take care of Lewis and his household.

Managing the house, a twenty-room Prairie Style mansion, was a snap. Supervising Lewis was a nightmare. Even now it's hard for me to talk about it.

Let me. Lewis was prescribed several medications, and it was your job to see that he took them. The most important one was Miltown, a tranquilizer, and unfortunately he would either forget to take it or would take too much. An overdose would lead to drowsiness and confusion. Withdrawal would lead to unsteadiness and depression. Once he even had convulsions, and his heart almost stopped.

His general behavior, even when his meds were being managed correctly, was erratic. One day he would be quiet, polite and introspective. He'd sit listening to one of the hundreds of classical LP's that made up his private collection. The next day he would become this wild man, verbally abusive, throwing things and screaming like a banshee. "Who stole my ID bracelet!!!" "Why are you staring at me?!!"

It began to dawn on Meredith that what Margo had described as "anxiety" was really a serious mental condition. Lewis was very sick. The carrot that had been dangled in front of her face, living in the lap of luxury, was a ruse. She was hired to be nursemaid to a madman.

Things really began to come apart at the seams when Lewis started to appear at her bedroom door in the middle of the night. At first she would let him in, seat him in the overstuffed armchair and let him talk, thinking this would help him exorcise some of his demons. But then he became a bit aggressive, and that scared her enough to start locking her door.

The next upsetting series of events were the love notes slipped under her door. It seemed he had become fixated on the two of them becoming lovers, maybe even man and wife. Meredith was not unaware of the irony. Her dream of marrying a wealthy man, of never having to worry about paying the bills, of being able to buy that bottle of Evening in Paris perfume whenever she wanted, was possible. All she had to do was agree to spend the rest of her life locked in a marriage to a crazy person.

The notes became more vividly obscene, with descriptions of what he wanted to do with her—to her. They were illustrated with anatomical drawings of body parts much larger than those of any human being on earth. Meredith was horrified.

Excuse me. Can I step in here for a moment? I'm sure you don't need to hear from another voice, but I was involved in this part of the event. I could maybe throw some light on what happened.

And you are?

I'm Matthew, Meredith's son. I live and work in Chicago, and in the summer of '69 I was getting ready to drive back to Seattle for my fifteenth high school reunion. I always tried to phone my mom at least once a week, and so I called her to tell her I'd be leaving for the Northwest that next weekend. She said she wondered if I'd have time to stop off in Ann Arbor for a visit. Although it was a little out of my way, I said sure. It'd be great to see her.

So you drove to Michigan, and what happened then?

Well, I got into Ann Arbor in the early afternoon. I found the Stearns estate, which was like driving up to some English lord's manor house, something out of Agatha Christie. I had just shut off the motor when here comes my mom, hurrying down the brick front walk toting two big suitcases and with a carryall hanging over her shoulder. I leaped out of the car to help her, asking her what was going on. She threw one of the suitcases into the back seat and I put the other one in the trunk with my stuff.
"Get in the car! Go! We have to go, now!"
"What the hell is—"
"Just go now, please, before someone stops us!"
So I started the car and we sped down the drive and out into the traffic. When we were a few blocks away, Mom began to explain. Mr. Stearns had gotten so crazy that she feared for her life. She couldn't sleep at night. She was afraid that he would attack her in her bed. She filled me in on his weird behavior, the love notes, his trashing of the rooms, screaming at the help and accusing her of stealing from him.
I remembered her telling me, months earlier, how proud she was of her new position and how excited she was about earning some real money. Now, all she wanted was to get safely away from Ann Arbor and Mr. Stearns. Damn the money!
I had planned to take my time crossing the country, see the sights, taste the local cuisine and enjoy the scenery. Now I'd be spending it with my mother. But having her along was actually a good thing, because we'd have five or more days of meaningful conversation—not the usual "How's work?" and "How's the weather?" nonsense.

By the time they were in Iowa, Matt had gotten most of the painful details. When they stopped for the night in Cedar Rapids, they both collapsed on their motel beds, too tired to continue the conversation. The next morning, after breakfast at Howard Johnson's, they resumed their journey west on Interstate 30, the old Lincoln Highway. They were both very quiet, recovering from the shock of the events of the day before. Matt was the first to break the silence.
"You okay?"
"I guess so. I feel like I'm finally breathing after suffocating for a very long time."

"I'm a little confused about all this. I mean, Marie said you were married to this Stearns guy. So are you going to file for divorce when you get back in Portland?"

"Oh, good lord! I never married that maniac. I don't know where your sister got that idea. I didn't love him, and in fact I never really liked him. It was purely a business arrangement."

"Well, Mom, you have to admit you've often told us how it's just as easy to love a rich man as a poor one, and—"

"Matthew Smallwood, I have never—"

"—and how you'd like to find a millionaire and become a woman of leisure—"

"Well, if I ever said such a stupid thing, and I really doubt I did, then I deserve all that I've been through."

This ended the conversation for the next several miles. After we had lunch in Ames and filled the gas tank, the getaway car continued on its merry way. Meredith seemed more relaxed, so Matt felt brave enough to resume the conversation.

"Mom, I've been wondering if you've ever thought about your history with men—"

"Matthew, don't start!"

"Please, please hear me out. You've been married four times—"

"Three! I did not marry Lewis."

"Right. Three. There was Dad, then C.M. and then Curtis. I was eight when Dad was killed, but he'd already been away for three years. He went off to war when I was five, so I hardly remember him."

"Your father was a wonderful man. I miss him every day."

"The next two gentlemen were something else, you have to admit."

"I did the best I could. I thought it was important for you kids to have a father figure."

"I understand. But let's be honest, they weren't the greatest of choices, right?"

"How old are you now, Matt? Thirty-two?"

"Thirty-three."

"And you've been in and out of love a lot, right?"

"Yeah, I guess. What has that got to do—"

"How many of those encounters turned out the way you expected?"

"Okay, I get your point. However, I have this theory about what keeps happening in your life. Can I share it with you?"

"Can I stop you?"

"Probably not. Now, don't get mad. It's just something I've thought about quite a bit."

And then he shared this idea he had that I unconsciously gravitated toward men who could never measure up to his father. Well, I certainly didn't do that consciously. He may have been right, but that didn't make it any better.

"Okay, Dr. Freud, if that's what's going on, what should I do? What's the cure?"

"I'm just trying to be helpful, Mom. I want to see you happy and not stuck in a situation like you just got in with this Lewis guy."

"That was a business arrangement, not a marriage."

"In a way, that's a shame," Matt said with a chuckle. "You could have divorced him and taken him to the cleaners."

"Matt!"

"Just joking, Ma."

*

As dinnertime approached, they found themselves near North Platte, Nebraska. Feeling hungry and travel-weary, they opted to make this their stop for the night. They found a mom-and-pop motel with a restaurant attached, and after a meal of fried chicken and biscuits, they settled down for a good night's sleep. The plan was to get a really early start.

At seven the next morning, Matt's green Volvo was speeding its way along the sunlit highway. The fields around them were flat all the way to the horizon line, the road ahead as straight as the proverbial arrow.

"Did you sleep okay?" Matt asked his mom.

"Like the dead, thank you."

"Good. Listen, I didn't mean to upset you yesterday."

"That's okay. It gave me something to think about."

"Good, I'm glad."

Matt smiled and looked at Meredith out of the corner of his eye. She was a beautiful woman in the prime of her life, and she deserved better than she was getting.

"Mom, you're fifty now, right?"

"Shame on you. You know a woman never reveals her age. But yes, I've reached that half-century mark. Fifty-one, to be exact."

"You look great."

"Why, thank you, kind sir."

"You know, Mom, the times are changing. The old rules don't apply anymore. You don't have to be subservient to some man. You don't need a man to give you validity."

"Wow, my son the feminist! Look, I've been keeping up with what's going on. I've read Gloria Steinem."

"Mom, you have always been so strong. One of the strongest women I have ever known. You don't need a permanent relationship with some guy—"

"So I don't need a husband, is what you're saying."

"Well, yeah, I guess that's what I mean. You know, you could play the field. Date."

"Are you telling me to be promiscuous?"

"Jesus, Mom! I just don't want you to get into another unhappy marriage."

This discussion went on for two days, all the way into Wyoming and then Idaho. We stayed overnight in Boise and then, after one long push, we landed in Portland. I left Mom off with some friends of hers and headed up to Seattle. Mother said she needed to take care of a few things. She had to work something out with the person who still had a few months left on her sublet. She needed to get her beauty-shop stuff out of storage. Luckily, the new hospital was almost ready for occupancy, so she would be able to move into the new beauty shop if they hadn't found a replacement for her. She also had to find a way to tell her friends and Marie why she had returned to Portland.

Many years later, I was tuned into the national news on TV and I heard the name Lewis Stearns being mentioned. I looked up at the screen and there was a video of this handcuffed, disheveled man being put into the back seat of a police car. His hair was sticking up in all directions and he had this wild, insane look. The announcer said that Lewis had been arrested for the apparent murder of his wife, Lois: "The heir of the Stearns fortune allegedly ran over his young wife in the driveway of the Stearns mansion in Ann Arbor, Michigan. It appears he hit her with his automobile, knocked her down, and then drove over her twice."

I'm ashamed to say that I found myself wondering if he used the Rolls-Royce or the Ferrari. I felt very sorry for his wife, but I was very thankful that it wasn't me.

For the next decade, Meredith concentrated on her work. The new beauty shop was twice as large as her old one, with lots of natural light streaming in through floor-to-ceiling windows. She toyed with the idea of hiring another beautician but decided that she could handle the workload alone if she cut back on the number of appointments per day. She did install a second hydraulic chair and one more hair dryer to stand beside the pink one Margo had given her all those years ago.

Once again, her shop became the place in the hospital to hang out, where nurses and staff could get away from the grind for a little while and where the sound of laughter competed with the snip of the scissors and the whir of the hair dryer. Meredith always had time to hear the latest bit of gossip or listen to someone's tale of woe.

Meredith dated a few times, but there weren't that many men interested in a woman of somewhat advanced years, even if she looked ten years younger than her actual age. Being a cosmetologist of great skill, she played up her good bone structure and flawless skin. Her blonde hair became even more blonde, and increased in volume with the use of falls and extensions. Her figure remained slim but not skinny. She never gained any extra pounds, claiming her work kept her thin. "Being on my feet all day is my exercise. Better than any diet."

*

One of the nurses, Paula Newcross, became a close friend of Meredith's and encouraged her to spend a little more time outside the world of the hospital. "There is a life beyond these walls, you know." They attended the movies, had a drink or two at Huber's Café and shopped at the Lloyd Center mall. Paula was a "joiner," which Meredith certainly was not, and she belonged to a book club and a knitting circle as well.

"Where do you get the time to do all those activities? My god, after a ten-hour day here in the shop, I just want to soak my feet and then go to bed."

"I don't know; just lucky, I guess. I've always had more energy than brains," Paula replied, laughing. "In fact, tonight I'm taking a ballroom dance class."

"Oh, my lord! You are a glutton for punishment!"

Over the next six weeks, Paula exchanged her sensible nurse's flats for her high-heeled dancing shoes and learned the waltz, the tango, the rumba, the cha cha, the samba and even a few of the more modern disco dances. She kept trying to get Meredith to come to one of the classes, but to no avail.

"It's so much fun, and you meet the nicest people. I've partnered with some very interesting men."

"Don't you even start, Miss Newcross. You know my policy about men."

"Boring! You just dance with them, for god's sake! You don't marry them."

After Paula graduated from the GoodTimes Dancing School, she began to look around for places where people could go to dance. Saturday night was a big deal at Earthquake Ethel's disco, out in Beaverton, with drinking, dancing and other, more X-rated activities. It was the sexy seventies, for heaven's sake! Paula made an exploratory trip and was blown away.

"Oh, Merri, you have got to go! It is so much fun. They have this sound system that literally shakes the building like an earthquake!"

"I hate it already."

"No, no! You'll love it. The music is great, the drinks are cheap and the pizza is—well, it's pizza."

I want it known that I resisted as long as I could, but Paula kept chipping away. She was much younger than me, and she finally wore me down. One evening I put on the beaded dress I wore as mother of the bride at Marie's wedding, slipped into a pair of slingback pumps, teased my hair, painted my face and climbed into Paula's little VW. We then set off for our next adventure. It would be quite a ride. Who knew.

Between the level of the music and the noise of the crowd at the bar and on the dance floor, Meredith couldn't hear anything Paula was saying. She had to rely on reading her lips. They wedged their way through the crowd until they were close enough to the bar to order drinks. After a few minutes, a young man (it looked to Meredith like everyone in the place was still in grade school) approached Paula, and she guessed he was asking her for a dance. Paula nodded and mouthed to Meredith, "Are you okay?" and Meredith waved her off to the dance floor.

About an hour later, Paula finished dancing with what was probably her umpteenth partner and rejoined Meredith, who had found a place at a small table. Meredith felt the beginning of a headache and was so ready to leave. Paula grabbed herself another vodka tonic and collapsed in the chair next to Meredith. It was at this moment that the floor began to rumble.

"Oh, good! Here comes one of Ethel's earthquakes! Yeah!" shouted Paula.

Meredith watched, terrified, as the whole room shook, glasses rattled and people cheered and laughed. After a minute or so—a very long minute—the shaking subsided and the music returned.

"Wasn't that amazing?!"

"You know we live in earthquake territory, right? Remember the big quake we had ten years ago?"

"Nope. I was still living in Arizona."

"Well, if you've ever experienced a real quake, you'd know how truly unfun it really is. Now I hate to be a party pooper, but I really would like to leave."

This would have been the end of the evening, much to Paula's disappointment, if not for what happened next. A middle-aged man appeared out of nowhere and stood in front of Meredith.

"Excuse me, but may I have the honor of this next dance?"

First of all, that there had been a gentleman closer to her age lurking somewhere among the youngsters all this time, and second, that he was asking her to dance, left her speechless. Paula had to elbow her to get her to stand up and reply.

"Ah, er—I guess so," and they were off to the dance floor. Roberta Flack was singing "The First Time Ever I Saw Your Face," and, as Meredith recalled years later, this became their song. They danced on into the night, until Paula had to point out that it was almost two in the morning. Meredith made her apologies, and after she and her dance partner exchanged their contact information, she and Paula got into the bug and headed back to Portland.

"You know who that was you were dancing with, right?"

"He said his name was Brad," Meredith replied, trying to read what he had written. "His last name is—Holiday or Halloway, hard to tell in the dark."

"You are so funny. Don't tell me you haven't heard of Halloway's Appliance Stores. They're everywhere. You were dancing with Bradley J. Halloway, the multi-millionaire owner of at least ten appliance stores. You've seen the commercials, right, with the Halloway jingle? 'Make Halloway the only way to never pay too much.' He's got stores in Seattle, Portland, Salem, Spokane, Tacoma, Yakima—I don't know where else."

Meredith was not thrilled with what had just been revealed by Paula. In fact, she was very disappointed that this pleasant, rather ordinary guy, kind of like a shoe salesman or a grocer, was actually a titan of industry. Pass him on the street and you wouldn't give him a second glance. And this millionaire business—"been there, done that." She didn't want to go through all that again. When they say the rich are different than us, boy, are they right!

"He's married—"

(Oh, great!)

"But they're separated."

(So what?! I'll probably never see him again, nor should I.)

However, she did see him again, several times, when he invited her to go dancing. He was an excellent dancer, and she felt very comfortable in his arms. As if by osmosis, she became a better dance partner, and she began to look forward to the weekends and being swept around the floor by Brad. He was always the perfect gentleman—no improper placement of the hands, no innuendos or off-color jokes and no suggestive movements, other than what might be required to make the dance better. It was as if he and Meredith had a business arrangement—partners in dance, nothing more. He wasn't much of a talker, but over the months she learned a few things about him. He came from a poor farming family, left school at twelve to find work, at seventeen joined the army and fought in the Korean conflict. After coming home, he used his army training to get a job repairing appliances, was good at it, eventually opened his own shop, began selling restored washers and stoves and such, moved on to selling new appliances, opened another store, and before you knew it he had a whole chain of stores.

Meredith wanted to ask him about his personal life but didn't want to make him uncomfortable, so she turned to Paula to fill her in.

"All I know is that he and his wife live separately. She has an apartment somewhere near the Columbia River, and he lives out on a farm near Troutdale. They have four grown kids. I don't believe they have any grandchildren yet."

Husband Number Five (Or Was It Four?)

Matthew and Marie did not attend the wedding of Meredith Smallwood to Bradley J. Halloway. Matt had a deadline on an ad campaign that kept him in Chicago. Marie had a—well, to be honest, she just didn't want to be there.

Romance had finally bloomed between Meredith and Brad a couple of years after their first encounter on the dance floor. It happened when Brad was dropping Meredith off after an evening of fox-trotting at the old Organ Grinder restaurant. Besides serving decent pizza, this place served up live music on a giant Wurlitzer pipe organ rescued from an old movie theater. It also had a large dance floor. On this night, instead of the usual peck on the cheek, Meredith gave Brad a full, on-the-lips kiss. She invited him up to her apartment, one thing led to another, and a love affair began that would last up to their marriage seven years later.

Meredith felt very modern being a "kept" woman. Only, of course, she wasn't being "kept," as she still worked at the hospital beauty shop and Brad hadn't installed her in a fancy apartment. While he slept over quite often, he never moved in with her. He never showered her with furs and jewelry. There were no trips to Paris or Honolulu. It was a simple relationship based on dancing, and Meredith was fine with that. At first, his children were not pleased that he had a mistress, but eventually they saw how happy he had become. As one of his daughters admitted later, "Mom was not very loving to us or to Dad. Meredith, on the other hand, had a lot of love to give, and she shared it with Dad and all of us."

Brad's wife, Lorraine, would not grant him a divorce. It was kind of like "if I can't have him, no one else can." However, fate stepped in, as she is wont to do, and Lorraine was unfortunately diagnosed with cancer. After a long and painful battle she succumbed, and Brad was free to marry Meredith.

At first, Meredith was reluctant about getting married again. She found the existing situation perfectly acceptable. With the exception of her first marriage, weddings didn't seem to work out very well for Meredith. She was concerned that they might lose what they had right now—pleasant companionship.

"You stand to lose a lot more if you don't get married," advised Paula as Meredith finished her comb-out. "What if, god forbid, he finds someone else? And what if he dies? You will have no legal right to his fortune!"

"Oh, Paula. I don't want his money."

"Ah, you say that now. But just wait. Come on, girl, don't tell me you haven't thought about those millions sitting in the bank."

"Look, Paula, money isn't everything."

Stop right now! I never said anything like that. It was my goal, from the time I was young, to marry a rich man. There, I said it! I may have lied to myself. I may have pretended I didn't care. I may have picked the wrong man. In fact, I did that several times. But down deep, I believed the only way I would ever feel safe and secure was by having a rich man take care of me. That's the truth. Now, here you go making me sound like an altruistic ninny. "Money isn't everything." Easy to say if you have unlimited funds.

Wow! I'm so sorry. I guess I did get this last part wrong. I think both of us forget that this is just a story, a bit of fictional fluff based on lives of many different women. But thanks for setting me straight.

So Meredith wed Brad on February 14, 1984, Valentine's Day. She was sixty-six and Brad was sixty. It was a simple ceremony, held on Brad's farm out near Troutdale. His four children and a few friends attended. The reception consisted of lots of champagne and barbecued ribs. The honeymoon was spent at the lodge up on Mount Hood.

The divorce took place on August 11, 2004. Meredith was eighty-six and Brad was eighty.

Okay, I'll take it from here. First, it's important to remember that I spent twenty years working very hard to keep this marriage going. But it got too difficult and I got too tired. I had finally learned that you never know a person until you've lived with them 24/7—and not even then.

Bradley was a sweetheart, I'll give him that. However, he was compulsive-obsessive, and that manifested in the manner in which he ate—all the foods on his plate had to never touch each other—and in his hobbies: stamp collecting, coin collecting, bottle-cap collecting, matchbook collecting, rock collecting— you name it, he collected it. He videotaped everything, from changing a tire to me putting on my makeup; from him emptying the dishwasher to his opening and closing the garage door.

We managed to get along with his condition until I discovered that he was incapable of resisting any TV, magazine or mail-order offer and had begun to fill the basement with Franklin Mint commemorative plates, dolls, miniature cars, talking parrots, baseball cards, bobblehead figures, and on and on. All I could see was our money evaporating, and I was worried that we'd end up "in the poorhouse," as my mother used to say.

I was able to start heading off the "free" offers and canceling most of the stuff he was ordering. I made it my job to get to the mailbox first. But then the internet arrived, and collecting ramped up once more. It was almost impossible to stay on top of it, but I kept fighting until—

Again, let me speak to you young folk. It's a myth that once you hit your golden years you are no longer interested in sex. This may be true for some women, but believe you me, it's rarely true for men.

One day, I found out that Brad had discovered chat rooms, and for someone not very talkative, he had become very chatty. He began collecting women from all over like he collected Star Wars action figures. He started sending them gifts and inviting them to visit him. I told him it had to stop or I would leave him, but he just couldn't. The final straw was when I discovered he had scheduled a date with a local woman I knew. I hadn't given up my former life, my beauty shop business, which I still missed, and the respect and love of my children for all this nonsense. So divorce became the only answer.

Meredith got the farm and half of Brad's fortune. She would go on to live another ten years, and spent the time turning the farm into a safe ranch for abused women and their children. When she passed, she willed a quarter of her wealth to each of her two children and the rest to Mental Health America.

So, Mr. Hotshot, do I get the last word? You better believe it. First of all, you left a lot out. I had a good life, I had some great friends and some interesting adventures which you managed to skip over.

Secondly, I have some advice for you. If you want to be a successful writer, be careful what characters you choose. We don't like to be pushed around.

Lastly, like General MacArthur once said: "I shall return."

Watch out!

The Terrarium

Why a terrarium? I don't know. I just remembered the rectangular fish tank we had in third grade that had rocks and moss and small plants and a turtle, and it was like a fairy kingdom to me. Bad things never happened in there, unlike the world I was living in at the time. There were wars going on between countries and one going on between my mom and dad. I was not a happy child.

Anyway, I grew up, married, had kids, and surprise, surprise, I got old. Around the time I turned seventy, my beloved wife Amy died, and, not wanting to be a burden to my children, I sold the house we had lived in for forty years and moved into the Sunny Lakes assisted-living facility. It's a high-end complex of fancy apartments that offer a bit more than your regular retirement village. Amy would have hated it, but I find it to be okay. Three meals a day in a pleasant dining room decorated in peach and maroon. A nurse-practitioner available 24/7. I have a one-bedroom apartment with a tiny kitchenette and a useless balcony, the size of a postage stamp, with a view of the parking lot. If I paid a little more, I could look out over the pond that gives Sunny Lakes its name.

This is a very social place, lots of activities—like bingo, the Sunny Lakes book club, pottery class, guest lecturers, bridge and chess competitions, non-denominational church services on Sunday and movie night on Thursday (with popcorn). There are field trips to museums, concerts and Broadway road-company shows. Unfortunately, both Amy and I were never "joiners" or "member material," so most of these activities don't interest me. I'd rather just hang out in my cozy apartment in my PJs, robe and fuzzy slippers. However, I do take advantage of the once-a-week bus ride to the supermarket. I have a car, but the bus saves on gas. There is a cleaning service that comes by once a week and keeps the place spic-and-span.

Actually, living here is kind of like being back in high school, a high school of teenagers who are in their golden years. There are the cliques, the jocks (golf or tennis, anyone?), the cheerleaders (join us for a sing-along?) and the beauties (sit at my table for lunch?). Need I mention that the ladies outnumber the men here at Sunny Lakes High? I guess when I first arrived here I was looked upon as prime beef, although my feminine classmates have finally come to the realization that I'm really just the dork sitting at the nerds' table. I'm a voracious reader and an avid watcher of historical dramas, but I'm not a conversationalist. I heard someone refer to me as "the silent one."

But back to the terrarium. I don't have much contact with my children these days, as both my son and two daughters live pretty far away. He's all the way across the continent, and one daughter is in Houston and the other is in Minneapolis. We do a lot of phone calling and FaceTiming, and they visit in person whenever they can. My grandchildren send me cards and drawings, but they are growing up and creating lives of their own, which keeps them very busy—much too busy to bother with Grandpa. So I decided I needed something to help me feel less useless and also as a buffer against the news of the outside world, the around-the-clock coverage of disasters both natural and man-made. It's enough to make you suicidal.

There is a no-pets-allowed policy here at Sunny Lakes, although Stacy, the manager, has a rumpled old black Lab named Duke who naps in the lobby and happily greets anyone who comes through the front entrance. The first-floor tenants are encouraged to leave their doors open a crack if they want a visit from Duke, and I would do the same if he would only take the elevator up to the second floor, but he's not fond of the elevator door closing on his tail. Therefore, I started making a list of possible substitutions. Since puppies and kittens are illegal, what would be acceptable to the management? Bird in a cage? Goldfish in a bowl? An ant farm? Was a gerbil or a hamster or a guinea pig in a cage allowable? The image of a rodent racing nowhere fast in a wheel inside a glass cage brought back the memory of the grade school terrarium. A terrarium! That's it! A terrarium with a turtle!

I didn't want a terrarium that took up a lot of room and cost too much, so my visit to the PetSmart website was a disappointment. The terrariums were very big and fancy, with front openings and ramps and other unnecessary doodads. What was also a turnoff was that prices started at almost two hundred dollars. I'm sure if I had driven to the strip mall and spent some time at the actual store, I would have found something more practical, but when I discovered that they didn't have any turtles for sale, I figured I wouldn't waste my time. In fact, they didn't carry any sort of living creature. Wait. I take that back. They had live earthworms and crickets and they stocked frozen mice, but all of this was to feed snakes, which they also didn't have for sale.

After a little more research, I came to the conclusion that I could be creative and just improvise. I reasoned that there were probably a lot of discarded terrariums sitting on shelves at the Goodwill and Salvation Army stores, leftover relics from long-ago science projects or unsuccessful attempts to keep guppies alive. (The mortality rate of home aquariums is heartbreaking.)

However, I was wrong about the imagined abundance of terrariums I thought I'd find at either of the thrift stores. I came across only one at the

Salvation Army, and it had a crack across one end that didn't bode well for a long life. The Goodwill had one the size of a Volkswagen that came with a heat lamp, a bubbler and a scene of the Grand Canyon glued to the back. I guess this was to fool the creatures stuck in there into believing that they were actually living outside in Arizona.

I was about to leave the store when I happened to notice all these shiny glass objects sparkling on a shelf on top of a rack of dead people's clothes. Vases, ashtrays, bowls, water pitchers, shot glasses, candlesticks, punch bowls and candy dishes huddled together like a bunch of unwanted and unloved orphans. It was there that I spied what I at first thought was some sort of cake stand, a plate fused to the top of a pedestal. Only after a second glance did I see that it wasn't a plate, but a glass tub that was resting on this clear glass pillar. It was a trifle dish. Now, unless you're from the U.K., you may not know what trifle is, but it's a decadent dessert made with layers of fruit, boozed-up sponge cake, custard and whipped cream displayed in a bucket-shaped glass vessel. I don't know why it's called trifle, because it certainly isn't one. Anyway, check it out on Google.

For some mysterious reason, this glass refugee from Great Britain called out to me. It was about nine inches wide and ten inches high, which wasn't very roomy for a terrarium, but I began to see the possibility of a tiny Garden of Eden arising in this oversized crystal goblet. Having looked up "terrarium" on the good old internet, I learned that there were two kinds of these gardens-under-glass: the large open terrarium, often with some sort of living creature inside, and the closed vessel with just the vegetation. Some of these had glass covers that could be removed to allow for watering, and some were permanently sealed shut and were self-sustaining, a process I didn't quite understand. I saw photos of terrariums made from Mason jars and brandy snifters, wine jugs and apothecary jars, but no trifle bowls. I realized that the trifle bowl would be a unique example of a semi-closed vessel. All I needed was a piece of glass to cover the top, which would keep the humidity level stable. I could take it off now and then to give it some air. As if the gardening gods had been eavesdropping on my thoughts, right next to the trifle bowl was a stack of clear glass dinner plates. I took one and gently set it on top of the bowl and could see that they were meant for each other. I had my terrarium, and it cost a whole five dollars (plate included)!

I built my trifle garden not with layers of cake, berries, custard and cream, but with a layer of gravel, a layer of charcoal chips, one of potting soil, and finally a layer of moss. I had gone down to the pool behind the Sunny Lakes facility and found two kinds of moss growing around this unswimmable pond of fetid green water. One moss was a bushy green with what looked like tiny dark-green fir trees poking up from the carpet-like moss. The other was grayish-green and was light and airy, as if it had been woven by spiders. They both looked like they'd be a great surface on which to take a nap.

On the muddy edge of this olive-green pond I also spied a small, rough, oval-shaped stone that was the color of cold butter. I added it to my growing collection of flora (but no fauna). I had realized earlier that there could be no turtle in my miniature Eden. There just wasn't room. It was sad, but in a way I was relieved. No dealing with food and health issues, just a few drops of water once in a while to keep the soil and moss moist.

In most terrariums, people add one or two miniature plants, which can be purchased at garden centers. I, however, found a small, broken piece of weathered wood, probably the remnant of a branch that had snapped off one of the swamp maples that dot the edge of the pond, and I chose to let it rise up out of the soil in my terrarium like the trunk of a miniature redwood tree whose top half had been torn off by a terrible hurricane. I have a strong imagination.

When I finished assembling my terrarium, I was surprised, but also very pleased, at how good it looked. With the pale yellow stone in the center, my little redwood tree reaching up from the earth, and the spiky extensions of moss that resembled a grove of tiny pine trees climbing towards the sky, I was a happy camper.

*

It's hard to put into words the effect my little garden had on me. On the surface, there was this pretty glass jardinière containing some moss, a stick and a stone. But to me, it represented so much more. It was an example of my burgeoning creativity. It was a way to bring some much-needed nature into the rather sterile world in which I was housed. It calmed me down by whisking me away from the daily videos of shootings, bombings and evil politicians I was so used to seeing on social media. Sliding the glass plate off the top of the terrarium released the rich, earthy smell of moss and damp soil. It was like walking alone in a forest.

Resting on a small table in front of one of the windows facing the parking lot, that barren field of black tar, white stripes and automobiles, my own private Garden of Eden kept me sane. The windows faced north, so it never got too hot in the miniature woodland. I put a comfortable chair next to the table so that I might sit and gaze into what had become a sort of meditation chamber. I was very happy.

And then I had a visitor.

*

Mrs. Sophie Rosenblatt from 212, down at the other end of the hall, knocked on my door. As I was not used to that sound, I jumped up rather too quickly and almost fell down, but then, pulling myself together, I walked over to the door and opened it. Sophie is quite short and rather round, with large blue eyes partially hidden under eyelids that sag down like half-opened venetian blinds. Her short, curly hair is a shade of rusty iron, and unlike most of the other female residents, she never wore makeup, as far as I could see. She was holding up a medium-sized manila envelope.

"This was in my mailbox by mistake. It's addressed to you."

"Oh—well—thank you," I replied as I took the envelope. "It's from one of my grandkids," I mumbled as I checked the return address.

"Ah—yes. I guess you wouldn't want to have that go missing," she smiled. I noticed that she was breathing rather rapidly, and I didn't think it was from looking at me in my sweats and fuzzy slippers. "I'm sorry," she continued, "but I need to sit down—my emphysema—long walk—my apartment."

I took her arm and guided her into the living room, and she immediately sat herself down in my chair by the window next to my meditation chamber. She was struggling a bit to catch her breath. She reached into a pocket in her housedress and extracted some sort of inhaler, like you see in those annoying medical commercials, and took a zap. I nervously crossed over to the kitchenette to get her a glass of water. I don't know why I thought that was necessary, but that seemed to be what was always done in the movies and TV (except for the shows from the U.K., where tea was the liquid of choice for all emergencies).

"I'm so sorry," she apologized. "I always think I'm stronger than I am."

"That's okay. How're you feeling? Any better?"

"Yes—I'm okay. I usually carry my—oxygen canister—but—like I—said—I'm good—at lying to myself," she admitted, taking a glance at my terrarium. "That's a lovely planter. A gift from your grandkids?"

"Ah—no. Actually, it's my attempt to create a terrarium," I answered, standing there like an idiot with a glass of water in my hand. "Would you like some water?"

"Oh—no thank you. I'm okay, really," she replied. She gestured at the little garden. "So you put this together? It's really nice."

"Well, thank you."

"But isn't it missing something?"

"I'm sorry. Missing? Oh, you mean like a living creature, like a lizard or a turtle."

"Oh, my, no. I think a real animal might be a little crowded in there. I was thinking more on the lines of a figurine—you know, a little China duck or a porcelain dog? Most planters I've seen have one or two of these cute little tchotchkes tucked in and around the foliage."

I shuddered internally at the thought of some pottery puppy romping around in my Garden of Eden, but I smiled and nodded my head.

"Wait a minute!" Sophie exclaimed. "I think I've got just the thing—a nice little friend for your—" She seemed to see what the planter/terrarium was made of for the first time—"that's a trifle bowl, isn't it?"

"Yes, it is."

"Very clever. And I've got a figurine that will look great in there," she announced as she rose carefully from the chair. "Why don't you walk back to my apartment with me? I can give you the rascal right then and there."

"Well—I—sure," I reluctantly agreed. Closing my front door, I took hold of Sophie's elbow. We walked slowly down the hall in what seemed like the longest trek of my life. Sophie unlocked her door, went inside by herself, and returned several minutes later with something enclosed in her hand.

"Here he is," she proclaimed. "He's going to enjoy a change of scenery." And she handed me—

Freddie the Frog. He was a neon shade of chartreuse with hot orange spots, giant googly eyes and a wide, smiley mouth with a lipstick-red tongue hanging out. I was horrified. In no way could I or would I introduce this frog from hell into my peaceful Eden. I mean, he would have taken up two-thirds of the space. "Oh, my! Are you sure you want to give up Freddie? I'm sure he means a lot to you."

"Don't worry about it. I have a huge collection of frogs. He won't even be missed," she explained with a quick laugh. "It's sort of what I do—my thing—collecting frogs. I love frogs. They are so cute. Sometime I'll show you the whole gang, but right now my place is a mess. Another time. Thanks for walking me back to my apartment."

"Oh—no problem. Ah—thanks again for giving me the envelope—oh, and—Freddie." I stood there wiggling Freddie back and forth in an amphibious dance as Sophie closed her door.

*

Freddie was relegated to a box on the top shelf of my closet. I figured I could always pull him out and set him down next to the terrarium if or when Sophie came to visit. I'd say he was getting a breath of fresh air. I certainly couldn't have him inside the glass bowl, hovering over my redwood tree and yellow stone like a dime-store Godzilla.

Several evenings later, I found myself staring at my Eden and starting to have a change of heart. Not that I was about to take Freddie out of retirement. No way! What happened was that I saw a magazine article about this photographer who set up these miniature scenes with tiny figures and then took pictures as if they were real events. I thought that if I were to put anything in my little garden, it should be one of these miniature figures, a little human being to run around in the Garden of Eden.

I started looking on the internet (is there anything you can't buy on Amazon?) and was astonished to find all kinds of little people for sale. It seems these three-quarter-inch-tall humans are popular with model railroad hobbyists and are used to populate those amazing miniature worlds that train lovers create. These plastic Lilliputians wait at train stations, walk to church, deliver the mail, play in schoolyards and go about their lives as if they were living in a miniature Norman Rockwell universe.

The choices offered for sale were phenomenal. They came in sets of up to fifty figures, but I really only needed one for my terrarium. I kept scrolling through the photos of commuters and dancers and farmers (there was even a set of nudists, and for a moment I considered purchasing an Adam and Eve, but that seemed to be a little too cheeky). Finally I found what was called a "sampler" kit, which was a set of six sports figures. This included a woman with a tennis racket, a golfer toting a bag of clubs, a man in racing shorts heading for the finish line, what looked like a swimmer doing the backstroke, a skier of undetermined gender and a referee in a striped shirt. Because the figures were so small, there were no painted facial features, just hair color. But their garments were nicely rendered, so I placed an order.

Two days later, a small package was delivered to the desk in reception. When I picked it up, Stacy quipped that "good things come in small packages" and asked me what was in the itty-bitty box.

"A half dozen itsy-bitsy athletes," I tossed off over my shoulder as I headed for the elevator. "Let her try and figure that one out," I thought, chuckling to myself.

Once locked safely in my apartment, I tore the wrapping off the box and opened it. Inside was a round, fairly flat, gold-colored tin with a clear plastic lid. Think of the shape of a chewing-tobacco tin. I could see the six figures resting inside. I twisted off the top and poured the tiny residents into the palm of my hand.

One by one, I stood them up on my little table and admired the infinite detail each one displayed: the strings on the tennis racket, the shiny skis, the number 13 on the back of the racer's tee shirt and the clubs peeking out of the golf bag. One detail I noticed was on the head of the only reclining figure, and that was a pair of sunglasses. They were painted on the face of what I had thought was a swimmer, but it was really just a man resting on his back. In fact, he had his arms folded behind his head, as if he were sunbathing. He was wearing a pair of dark-blue swim trunks and looked so relaxed and contented that I knew he was the perfect resident for the trifle Garden of Eden.

Not hesitating for a minute, I retrieved a pair of tweezers from my bathroom cabinet and, returning to the table, lifted the reclining gentleman up, removed the glass cover, and placed him gently on the pale yellow rock in the center of my tiny forest. It was perfect. He looked as if he were comfortable and would fall asleep at any moment. Sophie Rosenblatt was correct: my miniature garden had needed a "tchotchke" to finish it off. Just not Freddie the Frog.

*

And so Brent (yes, I gave him a name) took up residence, and in the following weeks, I even found myself chatting with him off and on during the day.

"Good morning, Brent. Looks like another sunny day. How was your night?" Of course he didn't ever respond, because I'm not that crazy. It's just that he looked so happy and contented, and that sort of rubbed off on me. I felt quite relaxed and untroubled as I sat staring into that soft green world. It was so quiet and peaceful that I sometimes nodded off and woke up with a crick in my neck—but with a smile on my face. It was as if Brent was me and I was Brent and I was resting on the rock. Kind of nuts, I know, but I never felt better in my whole life.

As the months flew by, I spent more time gazing into my tiny Eden and less time being out in the big bad world full of anger and violence. I stopped attending movie night and even asked to have my meals brought to my room, and I also didn't go on the bus to the supermarket. I guess my absence was noticed, because the nurse-practitioner stopped by to see if I was all right, and I assured her I was fine. I even introduced her to Brent and my little garden. She thought it was "adorable."

*

It had been about four months since I had put together the soil, moss, tree stump and rock that converted the trifle bowl into a minute forest. That's when things began to go awry. What I'm going to write about now is going to sound crazy, but you have to believe me, it really happened.

I started to have these strange dreams in which I discovered myself standing in a forest and finding it hard to breathe. With each new dream, the temperature seemed to increase, and I started sweating profusely. I would try to walk out of the woods, but no matter which way I turned, I ran into an invisible wall. It seemed the dreams were becoming a never-ending nightmare.

The last dream I remember having was one with me trudging up to a large boulder and seeing, high up on the top, the side of a body stretched out as if dead. I knew I should climb up to where this unfortunate person was to see if I could help, but I was too frightened.

I tossed and turned until I woke myself up and was relieved to see I was safe in my apartment, with no rock and no body. But my relief was short-lived. A real live nightmare awaited me in my living room.

Residing, as usual, on the little table by the window was Brent and my terrarium. Everything seemed the same—the trees and the moss lit softly by the early morning light. All very comforting, like every other day. But something was different. What was it? And then I noticed a bit of white clinging to the top of my wind-blasted redwood tree trunk. I slid the lid off the top of the trifle bowl to get a better look and nearly dropped the glass plate. There was a woman, a tiny plastic figure, perched on the broken crown of the tree, like a white dove. She wore a long, milky-white dress, and her face was hidden under a large white picture hat. Impossible! Where did she come from?

I knew I hadn't added her to my private Eden (even as an Eve for Brent's Adam?), or at least I didn't remember doing such a thing. Could I have done it in my sleep? Sleepwalking, perhaps? But there wasn't a sitting lady in white in my sports sampler when I first opened it, so where would I have found her?

I hurried over to the catch-all drawer in the kitchen, where, among the broken ballpoint pens and expired coupons, I had stashed the gold tin containing the five remaining athletes. They were still there. Maybe I had miscounted and she was hidden under the other figures? No way. Ridiculous. I had laid them all out very carefully. There had only been six, counting Brent.

Somehow, a mysterious lady in white had been positioned on top of my pseudo–redwood tree, and I hadn't a clue how this had happened.

Using my handy-dandy tweezers, I picked her off the tree and put her in my hand in order to examine her more closely. Like Brent, she had no painted facial features, but her hair was painted black—unlike Brent's, which was baby-chick yellow. She was obviously manufactured by the same company as Brent, but how in the hell did she get here? There had to be some rational answer.

I sat staring at this interloper and debating with myself whether to keep her or condemn her to the trash. I finally decided that it would be better to hold on to her until I solved this mystery, so I gently placed her back on the top of the tree. I had the silly thought, as I got her sitting in the same position in which I had found her, that if she were a real live human being, she would never have been able to climb up the side of the tree dressed in a white dress and picture hat. She would have at least needed a rope and crampons.

I spent that whole day trying to come up with an explanation for what was obviously an impossibility. I mean, I knew that I was getting more forgetful as the years went by. That was a given. I used to depend on my dear Amy to keep me on the straight and narrow, reminding me to take my medications or to turn off the gas burner on the stove. However, I'd been doing pretty good on my own. Well, there was the time I put my dirty laundry in the recycling bin, and, I had to admit, famous people's names evaded me quite often. You know what I mean—"what's-his-face in that movie, what's-it-called?"

So it was possible that I added little Miss White Dress to my diorama and that I just didn't remember doing so. Short-term memory, maybe. But where did I find her, and when did I accomplish this acquisition? I hadn't left my apartment in weeks. Could it have been put there by someone who visited me? But the only visitor I had was Rosita, the cleaning lady, and I can't imagine her taking the time to bother sticking a plastic figure in my terrarium. But if she didn't do it, who did?

That was when I started getting really paranoid. Was it Stacy, our manager, sneaking into my living room late at night? After all, she had a master key that opened every door in the facility. Or was it Trevor, the maintenance wizard, climbing up to my pint-sized balcony and jimmying open the French door so he could slip silently into my darkened living room and plant the Lady in White? Oh, come on! This was crazy thinking! It had to stop.

That night at bedtime, I took my melatonin and tried to go to sleep. Useless. I don't know when I finally sailed off to the land of Nod, but it was not a restful sleep. I just recall pulling myself up through a jumble of shadowy figures as the light of an early dawn penetrated my dreams. I awoke to the thought that, hopefully, when I got up and walked into my living room, the mysterious woman in white would be gone.

It was not to be.

*

Not only was the uninvited guest still clinging to the top of the tree, but two of her friends were sunning themselves on what looked like a little beach. I was stunned. I couldn't believe what I was seeing. A man and a woman, both in swimming attire, were sitting close together on what seemed to be a thin, flat piece of tree bark. It resembled a sandy beach. They were gazing out through the curved glass wall of the bowl as if they were looking off at the distant horizon of a vast ocean. What in the name of god was going on?

I sat staring back at this tiny couple, and for the first time I was truly frightened. This could only mean that I was going insane, that I was hallucinating and that maybe I needed some medical help. I thought about calling my son or one of my daughters—that was probably the best thing to do—but I was reluctant to disrupt their lives. And in all honesty, I didn't want to end up having to leave Sunny Lakes for some mental institution. I was embarrassed and ashamed, but I wasn't going to let this destroy my life.

I told myself I could handle this. I would prove to myself that what I was seeing was not madness, that these figures were real, three-dimensional pieces of plastic and somehow they were being placed in my Eden by someone. Who that was was yet to be discovered. Why was totally irrelevant. I was just going to make it all go away.

I nervously removed the glass lid and, using my tweezers again, picked up the two sea-gazers and the Lady in White. I dropped them on the table, got an envelope out of the drawer under the table, and after inserting them in said envelope, sealed it and stowed it away in the drawer.

"Okay, Brent, the garden is all yours once more. No more visitors," I said as I slid the lid back over the bowl, feeling sure that that was that. Or at least I hoped it was.

Of course, it wasn't.

*

The next morning, on my way to the kitchen to make my morning coffee, I avoided checking the terrarium. I dawdled next to the sink for a while, performing unnecessary tasks like wiping down the counter, which was perfectly clean, and moving dishes from one place to another and back again, until I could stand it no longer. I had to see if I had succeeded. Holding my mug of coffee, I sauntered casually over to the table and took a quick peek at the terrarium. Brent was relaxing on his boulder as usual, and—the Lady in White was back on top of the redwood, and the sea-gazing couple were on the beach!

Starting to shake, I immediately put down my mug before I spilled it, and threw open the table drawer. The envelope was gone. The uninvited invaders were back, and their paper prison was gone! Who was doing this? I was pondering this question when I suddenly noticed that the interlopers weren't alone.

Standing up to his knees in the moss was a commuter, fully equipped with fedora, trench coat and briefcase, as if waiting for the 7:45 a.m. express, a train that was never going to arrive. And leaning next to the pseudo–redwood tree was a construction worker wearing a yellow hard-hat and holding what looked like a chainsaw. Was he planning on cutting down my precious tree? I was freaking out.

I went back to my bedroom, crawled under the covers and put a pillow over my face. This couldn't be happening—but it was. What do I do now? One thing I decided was to leave everything the way it was. I wouldn't try to make it go away. It was obvious that that was a losing battle. And then I had what I thought was a brilliant idea. I would get one of those "nanny cams" like you see on TV, where a married couple wanted to see if the governess they hired was up to no good with their kid. I could set it up and secretly record what was going on and who was responsible.

Once again Amazon came through. I purchased a Reolink E1 Pro Home Security Indoor Camera, which was motion-activated. I also signed up for an app that would let my computer keep a record of what the camera was picking up. I was informed the camera would arrive in two days. Those two days were a couple of the worst days of my life.

The evening of the first day saw me struggling to go to sleep. I was too nervous and excited about the possibility of finally solving this mystery. By dawn I awoke, exhausted from my night of sporadic catnaps. I was ill-prepared for what greeted me as I stumbled into the living room. Not only was the commuter still waiting for the train and the construction worker still leaning against the tree along with the other uninvited visitors, but new figures were standing in the moss. An older woman, dressed in a red raincoat and holding an open red umbrella, hunched over as if she were hurrying to find shelter. A young boy stood stiff and formal on the sea-gazers' beach, dressed in his Sunday-go-to-church clothes.

There were now a total of eight plastic people, if you counted Brent, inhabiting my Garden of Eden. The terrarium was no longer a peaceful place for meditating, but more like Central Park on a weekend.

The next night, I stayed up until three in the morning, hoping to apprehend the culprit who was placing these unwanted figures in my trifle terrarium. I ended up asleep with my head on the hard surface of the table. When I awoke, drooling on my folded arm, I was too out of it to continue my surveillance, so I got up and lugged my groggy self off to bed. I don't know what happened the rest of that night, but when I woke up, I was very unhappy to find two more invaders in the garden, a young woman in an apron holding a mixing bowl full of something yellow (pancake batter, perhaps?) and a toddler in a blue snowsuit with his hands encased in green mittens.

Later, around ten that morning, Stacy called from the front desk to say a package had arrived for me. I hurried down to pick it up, ignoring the fact that I was still in my sweat pants, terrycloth robe and fuzzy slippers. I hadn't been out of my apartment in weeks, so I must have startled the folks in the lobby. Stacy looked a little alarmed as she handed me the box with the smiley Amazon Prime logo on the side.

"Are you okay? We haven't had the pleasure of your company lately."

"I'm doing just fine," I lied.

"What's in the box?" Stacy asked, as nosy as ever.

"A mousetrap," I replied haughtily. "Actually, I'm trying to catch a rat—a large rat!" I added as I raced down the hall towards the elevator.

"Wait a minute!" Stacy hollered. "If you've got a problem with vermin, I need to call the exterminator!"

"Just a figure of speech. Don't concern yourself!" I yelled as the elevator door closed.

Setting up the camera was much more complicated than was advertised. The technical language in the user's manual was, for me, like reading instructions written in ancient Sumerian. However, by sundown, I had the system up and working. The camera was hidden among my collection of James Patterson mysteries on the middle shelf of the bookcase directly across from the terrarium table. I was sure no one would notice my little electric spy.

That night I actually slept soundly. I believe it was because I was totally wiped out from two nights without adequate sleep and from my feeling that this surveillance was going to finally provide a solution to the mystery.

How wrong can one person be? Just ask me.

*

I was not surprised by the first thing I noticed as I stepped into the living room, which was bathed in soft morning light. There were shadowy outlines of more little figures standing in the moss of the terrarium. I counted at least four more, which brought the final count up to fourteen. I told myself I would take care of them later. Right now I had other business to attend to.

I opened my laptop and called up what the hidden cam had recorded. With fingers crossed, I stared at the screen, hoping to see the person who was trying to drive me insane. For a very long minute nothing happened, and then a black rectangle popped up on the screen. The date and time appeared in glowing white numbers along the bottom. The hour read 3:24 a.m., with the seconds flashing by in their position at the right of the time numerals. Someone had come into my apartment and activated the motion sensor early this morning. The image that finally appeared was quite dark, almost black. I hadn't left a light on for fear the culprit would be discouraged from entering the room, but now I regretted my decision.

I stared at the poorly lit screen, looking for any movement, and after a while I saw what looked like shadows rising up from the inside of the trifle bowl. Even though the camera recorded in color, everything was cast in shades of grey. Eventually I could make out the pseudo–redwood tree and the shadowy figure leaning against it. And one by one, I could make out most of the other thirteen little people. Wait a minute! Fifteen little people—sixteen! As I watched, figures began to rise up through the soil and the moss like zombies. Eighteen! Twenty! I lost count due to the dimness of the picture, but I estimated that the total number of tiny troublemakers was close to two dozen.

Okay, I had my answer. There was no evil full-scale human being trying to make me loony tunes. Oh, no, it was just a group of evil plastic Lilliputians, each about the size of my thumbnail, coming from god knows where (the depths of hell?) to populate my little garden of Eden. That sounds perfectly reasonable, doesn't it? Nobody would think me wacko if I shared my story with them, right? I could show them the video, but we all know how easy it is to manipulate images these days.

I stepped over to the terrarium and checked out the new arrivals: a butcher, a mailman, a stevedore, a pretty ballerina, a hunter, a doctor or dentist, even a lion tamer (without his lion). I should have been charmed by all these adorable little figurines, but they only filled me with dread.

I mean, how was all of this done? How could these inanimate things, these tiny statues made of molded, painted plastic appear out of nowhere? Could they suddenly come alive when I wasn't looking and climb up and out of the terrarium and—?

I had to put a stop to this invasion, which was obviously going to continue until the trifle bowl was filled to the brim with tiny everyday plastic people. I hurriedly removed all the unwanted figures, leaving only Brent on his rock, and jammed them into a leftover pickle jar I used for storing pocket change. I then walked out of my apartment and down the fire-exit stairs to the back of the building. I crossed the narrow band of grass, and when I reached the edge of the pond, I screwed open the lid to the bottle. Squatting down, I scooped up from the ground a handful of pebbles and stones and dumped them in on top of the figures in the bottle. Fearing some of them might escape, I quickly screwed the lid back on and, with a mighty heave, threw the jar as far out over the pond as I could. It sank almost instantly in the ugly pea-green water, which I knew would certainly hide it from prying eyes. I didn't know if someone saw me, but I didn't care. If a person was curious enough to want to muck around in that cesspool, let them try.

That night I moved my beloved terrarium, restored to its former serenity, to the nightstand in my bedroom. I did that in the hopes that the little fuckers, excuse my French, wouldn't be able to find it. After all, there was no one to guide them—unless—Brent? Was he inviting them, sending them directions like a GPS on how to—no, no, that was just my paranoia rearing its ugly head.

I covered the bowl with a cloth napkin as an additional deterrent, like one would cover a parrot's cage to keep it quiet, and then I turned out the light. I hoped sleep would come soon, but of course it didn't. It arrived close to dawn.

*

Okay, so all that I have told you in the last fifteen or so pages has led up to this morning. I'm about to pull the napkin off of my terrarium, and I'm scared. I mean, all this old man wanted was a peaceful little place, a bit of the beautiful outdoors, to keep him calm and happy, and what did he get? A miniature garden overrun with escapees from a "Leave it to Beaver" world. Well, let's see if I got rid of them for good. Here goes—

"I'm so glad you're back, Daddy. You were gone so long, I missed you."

"I missed you too, honey. But it was only a couple of weeks."

"It was too long."

"Well, I had to clean out Grandpa's apartment, all his stuff, and he had a lot."

"Is he going to come live with us?"

"Well, it seems he has other plans."

"What do you mean?"

"Ah—I—okay, your mother said that you're a very grown-up seven-year-old and that you'll be all right with what I'm going to tell you. Okay?"

"I'm going to be eight in two months."

"Correct. So here's what happened. It seems that Gramps just walked away."

"Walked away—from what?"

"His apartment, his life—us."

"Where did he go?"

"Well, that's just it. We don't know. He just disappeared. The police are looking for him, and we've hired a detective to help in the search."

"Like those guys on the TV shows."

"Yes. Like that. We'll find him and bring him back here to be with us. He probably just wandered off and got lost. That often happens with older people."

"Like little kids do, sometimes."

"Yeah, but don't you worry about it. It's all going to work out. I promise you. So, what do you think about all those little toy people I brought back for you? I found them in a big glass bowl in Grandpa's bedroom. They're so tiny, right?"

"Yeah, they're much smaller than my Pocket Princess dolls."

"Which one of the little figures is your favorite?"

"Well, there are so many. I like the pink ballerina a lot, and the little boy in the snowsuit is so cute, but I think my favorite is the man in the saggy pajama bottoms and bathrobe and fuzzy slippers. He makes me giggle."

The Sciopod Solution
A Novella

It started on New Year's Eve. Dukie Robinson was standing in the Happy Time liquor store on 125th Street in Harlem. His gun was aimed at the chest of the clerk behind the counter. When the clerk reached for the baseball bat that he kept for occasions such as this, Dukie pulled the trigger. What happened next astounded both Dukie and the clerk. Instead of sending a bullet into the clerk's heart, the gun began to come apart and fall in pieces onto the tile floor. Within seconds, what had been Dukie Robinson's prize possession, a Phoenix semi-automatic compact .22 pistol, lay on the floor, a smoking pile of rust. Needless to say, the clerk's Louisville Slugger worked just fine.

Meanwhile, out west in L.A., Officer David Spencer, a rookie policeman facing a hostage situation at a local nightclub, was told to hold his fire. He was one of ten other cops aiming their guns at the front door of Los Globos on Sunset Boulevard. When the hostage negotiator alerted the officers that the suspect had agreed to surrender and was going to come out, the tension level increased. The door slowly opened, and a figure holding a gun appeared. Spencer, sweating profusely, sure that the suspect was going to kill someone, fired his weapon. But nothing happened. The Glock 19 simply disintegrated in his hands, as did the rest of the officers' rifles and handguns. Smoking piles of rust dotted the parking lot, like little towers of metallic dog shit. Fortunately for Spencer, the destruction of his Glock prevented the death of the hostage that the suspect had held in front of himself as a shield. The gun Spencer thought he saw was actually the hostage's cell phone.

Out in the middle of the Pacific Ocean, at the Waikiki Gun Club in Honolulu, Hawaii, every one of the people practicing at the target range experienced the destruction of their favorite weapon. After the shock of this strange event passed, the cursing could be heard a mile away.

In Afghanistan, the Taliban could no longer fire their Kalashnikov assault rifles and submachine guns or their rocket launchers. Even the bombs they strapped to their bodies were useless. All their weapons, many manufactured in Great Britain and the United States as well as Russia, sat in smoldering heaps of rusting metal. Many wondered if this was a message from Allah.

All across the United States, from Maine to Oregon, from Texas to Montana, gun owners awoke on the first day of the New Year to find a handful of rusted metal pieces resting where their weapons used to be. In gun cases, backpacks, handbags and locked safes—in closets, in attics and basements—in glove compartments and car trunks—in the drawers of desks and bedside tables—even in the freezer compartment of the kitchen refrigerator—all destroyed.

Perhaps the most alarming aspect of this sudden destruction of every firearm on earth, and unarguably the most spectacular, were the explosions that began to happen on every continent. In Kansas, the Hodgdon Plant, the largest manufacturer of gunpowder in the United States, blew up in a fireball that was seen all the way to Wichita. At the same time, its facility in Louisiana went up like a supernova of Fourth of July fireworks. And speaking of fireworks, every company that fabricated those cherry bombs, firecrackers and Roman candles, enjoyed by millions during the Independence Day celebrations, disappeared in a blaze of glory. Also adding to the firestorm was the cousin of gunpowder—ammonium nitrate, which was an additive in fertilizer used worldwide. Suddenly, fields, farmyards, compost piles and warehouses became rivers of flame.

Every depository of gunpowder and ammonium nitrate in the world, in all the continents westward from Asia to Australia, erupted into smoke and flames. It was a night and a day that truly rocked the world. Fortunately, as it was the New Year, there weren't too many workers on factory duty, so the injuries were kept to a minimum. Unfortunately, there *were* some deaths, and that was one of the many unpleasant side effects of this bizarre event.

Managers at the fifty or so military-arms manufacturing plants around the world, including Lockheed Martin, Northrop Grumman and Boeing in the U.S., all were baffled to find that their weapons, large and small, in storage and in the factory, had turned into nothing more than a carpet of rust.

Announcements from domestic gun manufacturers in Europe and the U.S. echoed the same news as that from the military-weapons companies. Their inventory had turned into red dust. Smith and Wesson in the States and Heckler & Koch in Germany reported opening shipping crates only to find them empty except for rust-colored metal filings. Gun dealers, upon seeing and hearing the bad news, rushed to their businesses and found their shelves stocked with boxes of rusty air. Even the guns with plastic bodies had turned into ugly, shapeless globs of melted goo. The walls of their stores, usually hung with eye-catching examples of rifles and pistols, were empty except for the display hooks and the faded shadows of what had once been there. Pawnbrokers found nothing but metal residue in their satin-lined display cases where they had kept the many firearms that customers, in need of some quick cash, had left with them.

And then there were the bullet makers. Of the hundreds of companies that manufacture ammo, such as Red Bear and Liberty Ammunition in America and Delta Mike in New Zealand, all found their workplaces burnt to the ground due to the exploding gunpowder, or their inventory of bullets reduced to empty, corroded casings.

*

On the morning of New Year's Day, Billy Joe Burk, proud owner of a Bushmaster AR-15 semi-automatic rifle, entered the side door of the synagogue Congregation Rodeph Sholom on Bayshore Boulevard in Tampa, Florida. His mission was to take out as many Jews as he could, even if it meant losing his own life. When he reached the inside of the temple, he yelled "Make America Great Again!" and began to shoot. However, when he pulled the trigger, nothing happened. Surprised and very confused, he began cursing and tried shaking the rifle. As he explained to the police later, "All of a sudden the fuckin' thing started to get hot, and I dropped it on the floor. I looked down and it was like melting, and then it was just this crusty puddle of broken pieces. I bet that piece of shit was made by some stupid chink in China!" When the security guards saw that his gun was useless, they wrestled Mr. Burk to the ground and someone called 911.

*

At the very same time that Mr. Burk was entering the synagogue in Florida, Lyle Ferris walked into the Starbucks at 1500 Broadway in the Big Apple. In his backpack he carried a homemade pipe bomb. Lyle had been fired as a barista from Starbucks (not the one he was standing in, however) for being rude to a customer and antagonistic to his fellow workers. He felt that he had been treated unfairly. After all, the asshole who ordered the venti—half-decaf, dash of hazelnut, one Splenda and almond milk—had complained that it wasn't almond milk (it wasn't) and that the coffee was too hot. "I mean, come on! So what if I called him 'a flaming faggot!' and Shelia and Toby, the other baristas, treated me like shit from then on!"

Lyle had decided that Starbucks needed to learn a lesson. He had researched how to make a pipe bomb online and even ordered a book entitled *Bomb Making Made EZ.* And it *was* easy. He actually made two, one that he tested in an empty clearing in the New Jersey Pine Barrens and one for planting in Starbucks. He had nearly blown himself up with the test bomb, but he was pleased with the results.

After putting his backpack on a chair and sitting at one of the small tables, he looked around at the hungover New Year's Eve revelers nursing their grandes and at the rest of the crowd that had watched the ball drop in Times Square the night before. If he had any second thoughts about doing the deed, they vanished when he saw the fake smiles on all of the baristas behind the counter. Opening his backpack, he gently removed his beautiful creation, disguised as a holiday gift in a silver box. He slowly placed it on the edge of the chair opposite him and carefully flicked a hidden toggle switch that activated the bomb. It was now alive and ready to explode when any curious person, spying the nicely wrapped box with the big red bow, picked it up.

Lyle got up from his seat, put on his backpack and started to exit when he was stopped by a woman's voice. "Excuse me, sir," she said, handing him the gaily wrapped package, "you almost forgot your gift." Lyle fainted.

When he came to, he was surrounded by the Starbucks staff. "You okay, man?" asked the manager. "We called 911, but they said they're so busy with all these weird emergencies it may be some time before they get anyone here." Lyle sat up quickly and looked around for his package. "Take it easy, man. You looking for your present? It's right here. Clara's got it." A sweet, middle-aged woman stood in front of Lyle, smiling a wide grin as she held out the box he had disguised as a gift. "I'm sorry, sir, but it seems to have melted, whatever it is. Maybe it was a cheesecake or a bottle of something that broke, because stuff is oozing out of the bottom."

*

By the third day of what the media had labeled "Gunmelt," World War Three was about to begin. Russia accused the United States of sabotage, the U.S. blamed North Korea. Great Britain looked to Ireland as the culprit, and Australia was sure it was China. Switzerland maintained its neutrality. Every other nation was busy investigating every other nation, trying to find out how and why this weapon and gunpowder annihilation was happening. Since there wasn't a gun left in the entire world that worked, and any other device that depended on gunpowder was inoperable, what could a country do to protect itself? There were still plastique explosives like Semtex and C-4 that were now worth their weight in gold, but they often needed a gunpowder-filled blasting cap to set them off. That was when the specter of the infamous "weapon of mass destruction" reared its deadly head. Shaky index fingers hovered over the dreaded red button.

The United Nations called an emergency meeting on January 4. The members had to scramble to get there from the far corners of the world. It was very strange to see representatives from many different countries arriving at the various airports surrounded by their security guards armed with machetes and clubs.

James P. Dickerson, current president of the NRA, issued a statement:

> As we struggle to survive unarmed during these disastrous times, I am reminded of the demands made by the various gun-control groups. Well, your goal has been achieved. How's that working for you?

Riots had broken out in the streets as looters, seizing the opportunity to work unencumbered by the possibility of being shot, smashed store windows and broke down doors. The police still had tear gas and tasers at their disposal, but the public fired back with pepper spray, bottles and rocks. In New York, the NYPD Mounted Unit of twenty-two horses and riders was called into action and began trying to control the crowds. It was the true definition of chaos.

The President of the United States declared a state of emergency and ordered the scientific community to begin research into the cause of this catastrophe and to find a solution ASAP. Leaders of the other First World nations followed suit and drafted the best of their forensic scientists to come up with answers. While the rest of the world continued to spin out of control, scientific investigators began examining the millions of corroded and melted pieces of what had once been firearms and bombs. Any gunpowder that was found immediately burst into flame when exposed to the air. For many of the scientists, this only emphasized the apparent futility of their mission.

*

The Danakil Desert is located in northeastern Ethiopia. It is one of the lowest and hottest places on earth, with a daytime temperature of up to 122 degrees Fahrenheit. It gets only about an inch of rain a year, and the few lakes that exist are all crusted with salt. The Afar tribe are the only people who are hardy enough to work in this hell on earth. They survive by mining the salt, which they transport out of the desert on the backs of camels for sale to the rest of the world. There is a range of mountains to the north called the Danakil Alps, and resting among them is a volcano known as Mount Ayalu.

About twenty years ago the Afar, unloading the salt bricks they had mined, told the buyers about the strange thing they had seen near Mount Ayalu. During the night, a blinding white light had flashed on and off at the base of the volcano. At first they thought the mountain was erupting, but as the light was at the bottom of the volcano and was a pulsating white, they realized that this was something else.

A few of the more superstitious among them thought it was an angry angel sent by Allah. When they made an exploratory visit to the volcano a week after first seeing the phenomenon, the light had stopped, and there was no evidence of anything ever having been there. Two decades later, the event was all but forgotten.

*

While the President kept assuring the public that the government was getting close to correcting the gun problem, the truth was that it was still a complete mystery. Despite all the modern technologies available, from mass spectrometers and electron microscopes to chromatographs and different light sources, nothing helpful was discovered. The ruined weapons were analyzed again and again, but the tests only revealed the makeup of the materials used in their composition.

*

Tommy Garcia and his girlfriend Rosalie were beginning to come down from a weekend of cocaine. Being totally addicted to the stuff, Tommy was starting to freak out. As he found himself rather low on cash, he knew he had to find a willing—or unwilling, it didn't matter—donor who would contribute to the "Keep Tommy Stoned Fund." As he tossed and turned next to Rosalie on the lumpy mattress in her bedroom, he glanced over at her son's toy chest. It was white particle board, with an alligator painted on the side and the boy's name, Kevin, written in black marker across the green, bumpy skin of the gator. Tommy was about to crawl out of his own skin when he saw, lying among the Legos and the stuffed animals, the answer to his prayers.

Later that day, he entered the neighborhood CVS store and walked back towards the pharmacy. There he was greeted by the pharmacist, a balding gentleman wearing horn-rimmed glasses and a nametag which read Ajeet Tendulkar.

"How may I help you?" he asked in a soft baritone voice tinged with a slight Indian accent.

"Give me all of your cash," Tommy muttered, "and throw in a few bottles of Percocet while you're at it."

"I'm very sorry, sir, but I'm afraid I cannot do that," Ajeet responded, with the gentlest of smiles.

"Hey, man," Tommy barked, "don't fool around. Do you see what I'm holding in my hand, what I'm aiming at you?!"

"Yes, indeed I do. It seems to be a water pistol. A fine replica. I'd say a Colt 45, is it not? Very detailed reproduction."

Tommy was devastated. "No—no! It's real—and—it's—it's loaded!"

"I'm so sorry, but surely you're aware of what has been happening. You must have seen it on all the news. They call it 'Gunmelt.' There are no real guns left. They have all been destroyed."

Tommy wasn't about to give up. "Well, this is one that didn't get—it's still good. So ante up, or I'll—I'll shoot you."

He was still arguing with Ajeet when the police arrived and carted him away to the local station house.

*

It was a physicist at Utrecht University in the Netherlands who made a small discovery that hinted at a possible cause of the worldwide disaster. Dr. Eva Van Dijck was working late in her lab and had taken a short break. She had brewed herself a cup of Earl Grey tea and was taking it back to her workbench when she caught her heel on the cord of the high-intensity lamp clamped to her table. The mug of black tea that Dr. Van Dijck was carrying went flying up over the workbench and landed on top of Evidence #2765, the melted, rust-stained remains of a Beretta M9 semi-automatic pistol. The porcelain mug rolled off the table and fell to the floor, where it broke into several pieces. On the table's surface, the tea puddled around and over the carcass of the dead gun, much to Van Dijck's disappointment; but knowing that she still had hundreds of examples waiting in storage, she simply began the cleaning-up process.

After picking up all the shards of the broken mug, being careful not to cut herself, she arose and turned to the mess on her workbench. She was surprised to see the ruined weapon covered in a fine layer of some kind of white powder. All of the tea had evaporated, except for a few drops at the edge of the table. Wasting no time, Dr. Van Dijck took a glass slide and, using a small spoon, sprinkled a tiny amount of the powder on top of the slide and protected it with a cover slip. When she put the slide under the microscope, she discovered that the powder was composed of crystals. However, they didn't look like any crystals she was familiar with. After a quick look online at some photos of other common crystals, she was still confused.

Her next step was to try and determine the chemical and molecular makeup of these mysterious white crystals. As tempting as it was to try and accomplish this on her own (and become known as the person who saved the world and won the Nobel Peace Prize), she realized that she had to let the rest of the scientific community know about her discovery. She needed help.

*

Economically, the world was coming apart at the seams. Since all of the world's most powerful nations based their economies on the military and now there was literally no military, there was nothing left: no factories, no jobs, no incomes, no profits. It affected everyone. A depression was beginning that could make the Great Depression of the 1930s look like a Labor Day picnic.

Bank robberies increased; in fact, all robberies in general increased, because if you found you needed a gallon of milk, you just took it. What was going to stop you? A gun? Store owners were using thugs to try and prevent theft, but after a while they couldn't afford to pay for this protection, so the thugs beat up the owners and took whatever was left in the store as compensation.

Trucks were being hijacked before supplies could reach their destination, and therefore the goods on the shelves of the supermarkets were dwindling. Hospitals were running low on life-saving drugs. Of course, a black market was quickly established where you could, for an obscene fee, purchase medicine, food and other necessities. But this wouldn't last long, because money was beginning to become useless. It had no real value.

The rioting in the cities continued, with more looting and burning. Whole neighborhoods looked like they had been bombed. Anyone who had half a brain carried a knife or a club.

Many city employees had left their jobs. Trash was piling up in the streets, and the police, having lost their firepower, were reluctant to go out on patrol. Public transportation had come to a standstill. The power plants were still grinding out electricity, but for how long was the question.

The rich had fled the metropolitan areas for the safety of their country estates but soon realized that it was only a temporary solution. Trying to create, without weapons, a fortress against the madness that was heading their way was an exercise in futility.

*

When the news of Dr. Van Dijck's discovery of the white crystals that had appeared on the remnants of the ruined guns flashed across the computer screens of every lab working on the crisis, there was a sudden run on Earl Grey tea. Samples of the mysterious white powder were bombarded with X-rays, microwaved in spectroscopes, and spun in nuclear magnetic resonators. The universal result of every test was that this white crystalline powder was composed of molecules never, ever seen before.

*

The town of Unity, Oregon, population 71 and used to the simple life, adapted very quickly to the change. It was, after all, a town inhabited by survivors. They had lived through brush fires, the closing down of the lumber mill and the drop in cattle prices. Their rifles, now made useless, were replaced with bows and arrows. That meant that wild game was still on the table. The lake and the river were still full of fish, and the farmers had cows full of fresh milk.

Hiram Granger, a Native American descendent of the Nez Perce tribe, ran Stratton's General Store and unofficially became the strategic commander. His first order of business was to close off the only road into and out of Unity—Route 26. Using Fred Napier's bulldozer, the townsmen placed boulders on the highway at both ends of town. Patrols were set up to man the barricades, and everyone took turns, including women and children. All the supplies still in the general store and the remaining gasoline at the Burnt River Market would have to be rationed. "We'll be losing electric soon," Hiram announced, "so be prepared to rough it. Let's treat this like we're all going camping, and as long as we stick together, we can get through this."

Unity is located in the middle of Baker County, which is bordered on the east by the state of Idaho. As anyone who is familiar with the history of Idaho knows, it has been, for many years, a testing ground for survivalists. Hiram wondered what would happen when those anti-government anarchists discovered that their cache of weapons had been rendered absolutely useless. "Just so long as they stay in Idaho," he declared to the residents at a town meeting. "But if they decide to attempt an invasion, we'll be ready."

*

The small team of volcanologists studying Mount Ayalu in Ethiopia was headed by Dr. Tamsin Decker. It was her job to monitor the seismic activity, the lava flow and the gas emissions of the volcano, not only as scientific research but also for any signs of a possible eruption. The facility was located near the mountain, to be able to post a warning and therefore prevent, or at least minimize, a disaster.

Dr. Decker did not mind the heat and the isolation. In fact, she preferred it to the madness that was going on in the so-called civilized world, the exploding gunpowder reserves (which had screwed up their seismic readings) and the mysterious "Gunmelt." Fortunately, no phantom enemy seemed to be interested in taking the volcano hostage, so they really didn't need the few weapons they had that had dissolved into dusty detritus while they were asleep on New Year's Eve. As long as their generators had enough fuel and the sun kept beating down on the solar panels, they would be fine.

Dr. Decker was studying the tilt level of the lava field on one of the many monitors in her office when she was interrupted by Negasi, her assistant. The tall young man, who had recently graduated from Addis Ababa University and become an invaluable member of the staff, cleared his throat. "Pardon me, Dr. Decker."

"Yes, Negasi, what is it?" Tamsin replied, not taking her eyes off the screen.

"The ultrasound readings." He hesitated. "There seems to be an anomaly."

"Oh? Interesting. What's going on inside dear old Ayalu?"

"I do not quite know. I think you should look at it. I mean, please check the monitor. What I am seeing is a negative space located in the western face of the mountain."

"A negative space?"

"A void, if you will. It just appeared out of nowhere on the computer. I have never seen it before today."

Tamsin switched her attention over to another monitor. It displayed a cross-section of the interior of the mountain. There was a simulated image of the volcanic core, a red-orange tube surrounded by a blue-gray mass that represented the rocky composition of the mountain. Down to the left at the base of the mountain was a medium-sized circle. It was inky black.

"Have you checked the probes? Is there a possible glitch in the equipment?" Tamsin asked.

"We have checked everything four times. All the systems, the software, the cables, everything. It is all working fine."

"So what do you think is going on?"

"Well, if we analyze what the ultrasound is telling us, and it is its job to show us what is going on inside Ayalu—I would say that it is showing us—a cavern, an open space inside the mountain."

*

The scientific community now had a substance to work with. They agreed to label it the Van Dijck crystal, in honor of its discoverer. Hoping to find out how it worked, how it had destroyed billions of weapons, laboratories from around the world began attempting a myriad of tests. They had no intact guns or bombs to use in their experiments, so they continued to examine the existing damaged firearms. It seemed that the crystals had eaten away at the metal like a high-powered acid. It was also determined that when the chemical came upon any amount of gunpowder, it ignited it. In order to test this hypothesis, several labs tried to make gunpowder. Modern gunpowder, known as a smokeless propellant, is composed of many different chemicals, including nitrocellulose and paraffin. Unfortunately, the moment all the ingredients were combined to create a small sample of gunpowder, it exploded in a bright flash of fire. There wasn't even time to spread some of the mysterious Van Dijck crystal powder on the sample in order to study the effects. Every attempt ended in the same way—bang, whoosh!

*

When the lights went out all along the East Coast, the National Guard was ordered to head to all the power stations. When they arrived at some of the sites, they found the generators shut down and no one in the buildings. An officer located a note stuck on the unlocked door of one of the larger facilities. "We need to be with our families. Gotta keep 'em safe. Sorry." The soldiers immediately began bringing the power plants back on line, and electricity was restored. However, brownouts continued to happen through the next few days, and would do so for months.

*

The scientists at Mount Ayalu, trying to discover what might be going on inside, had rebooted their computers to see if the strange black hole on the image of the interior of the mountain was an error. It wasn't. It stubbornly kept reappearing, no matter what changes they made in the color of the image on the monitors.

Negasi, Dr. Decker's assistant, spent several hours determining what he believed to be the size of the black void. "I rotated the image 360 degrees so I could estimate its actual shape. It is a circular cavity approximately 40 feet wide and 50 feet high."

"Can you detect if there is any volcanic activity inside this hollow?" asked Dr. Decker. "You know, like escaping emissions, lava—"

"Not really. You will notice," Negasi said, pointing to the monitor, "that the image remains totally black. It is almost like there is something preventing the ultrasound from penetrating this—this bubble. Like there is a shield or something."

"Weird," Dr. Decker uttered softly. "We really need to know what this is, if it is a precursor to an eruption or the beginning of a new fissure that will be spilling fresh magma out the side of the mountain. This is not good."

*

With angry and frightened citizens on almost every continent marching in the streets, and many world leaders being deposed and in some cases assassinated, the pressure to find a solution was beyond intense. Nobel Prize–winning scientists were working day and night, alongside their less famous colleagues. Up to now, the only thing they knew was that the Van Dijck crystals caused a reaction that melted metal (curiously, only the metal and plastic that was used in the manufacture of guns and bombs) and that they ignited gunpowder. How they actually accomplished this, where they came from and how they were dispersed was still a mystery. Here was a compound composed of molecules never before seen that, within two days, had destroyed all the weapons on earth that depended on gunpowder. Unfortunately, this meant that governments and even some private citizens were considering using alternatives, such as nerve gas, plastique putty, high-power lasers ("death rays") and, most alarming, atomic devices. The infamous red button loomed larger than ever.

*

There are 1,500 potentially active volcanoes in the world. The country with the highest number is, surprisingly, the United States, with 169 active volcanoes. Most of these are located in Alaska, with the rest spread among the western states, Mount St. Helens being one of the more famous. Kilauea and Mauna Loa are the two most active volcanoes found among several others on the islands of Hawaii. In fact, the islands themselves were created by eons of volcanic activity.

Dr. Decker had worked in Hawaii for a couple of years with Kaleo Tiller, a respected volcanologist and author of several definitive books on the mystery and majesty of volcanoes. Hoping that Dr. Tiller might have an insight into the enigmatic black smear on the computerized image of Mount Ayalu, Tamsin decided to give him a call. After finally getting access to a working phone line, she made contact.

"Dr. Tiller? Hi. This is Tamsin Decker—"

"Tamsin! What a pleasant surprise. I was just about to email you. In fact, I was just going to send out an email to several of our other colleagues as well, but the internet is so iffy."

"Yes, well, here I am. I don't know for how long. Like the internet, phone service is dicey these days. So how are things? Have you been okay with this Gunmelt madness?"

"Yes, we're all right. No terrorists at our doorstep yet. But there is something going on here that I wanted to run by you and Peterson, also Tanaka and maybe Statzberger."

"Would it happen to be a problem with your ultrasound equipment?"

There was a short silence before Tiller responded.

"Are you having problems as well?" he asked.

"There is a sort of a—black void on the images coming in from the sensors. I was going to send you a picture—"

"Is the sonar indicating that this—void is located at the baseline of your mountain?"

"Yes. Is that what's happening with you?"

"The ultrasound is showing that both my ladies have these black patches on their lower sides—the sides facing west."

"Wow! It's the same here. What do you think they are?"

"I wish I knew. It could be a bulge indicating a possible eruption building up, which is not something we want to happen. But as both of these black smudges are in the exact same position on the west side of both the mountains, I believe they have to be something else."

"Do you have any idea how large they are?"

"We calculate they're about 30 to 40 feet wide by 50 feet high."

Tamsin looked at her monitor and felt a cold tremor climb up her spine.

*

Mitzi Brownhart stared at the face in the bathroom mirror. It had been a pretty face once. Now it was just the pale, wrinkled, saggy-jowled image of her grandmother. Mitzi was only forty-two years old, but she felt ninety. Well, what did you expect? Between being deserted by her husband and left with two ungrateful teenagers to feed and clothe, and having lost her job due to all the layoffs at the weapons plant, her world was rapidly falling apart. All around her was chaos: electric brownouts, gasoline shortages, food shortages, crazy people running around with knives and baseball bats, no heat in the apartment, water the color of piss when you turned on the tap, nothing but really bad news on the TV and the internet (if and when they were even working), and cell phone service gone forever. Alcohol and marijuana no longer helped dull the pain.

Mitzi had toyed with the idea of ending it all. She had a few Ambien left, and some codeine left over from that carpal tunnel operation two years ago. Plastic bag over the head and goodbye, cruel world. She would have used the pistol her husband Eddie had given her for protection, but this "Gunmelt" stupidity had taken care of *that*. However, as the long days and longer nights passed, she found herself feeling more angry than depressed. In fact, she found herself so enraged that all she could think about was getting even, revenge for what had been done to her. But how? She had thought briefly about doing in Karen and Brian, but that wouldn't make much of a statement, and murdering her kids would just be murder.

It was when she ran into her friend Barbara on the garbage-strewn streets of downtown Baltimore and heard her talk about the President's upcoming visit that an idea began to blossom in her enraged brain.

"Yeah, the son-of-a-bitch is making a tour of some of the messed-up cities to reassure the public that everything is under control," croaked Barbara. "Ha! Just look around. This is 'under control'? Things will never get back to normal."

Mitzi shook her head in disgust and pulled her coat tighter around her shivering body. It was going to be a very hard winter. A lot of folks weren't going to make it through to spring, maybe not even herself. So why not go out in a blaze of glory? And so she stood on that dirty sidewalk, in front of that burnt-out shell of what was once a Starbucks, and made a silent pledge.

"I'm going to kill the President of the United States of America."

*

After many conferences among volcanologists from around the world, it was determined that an exploratory examination of one of these strange black voids was necessary. Almost every active volcano in every country had experienced the same phenomenon: a black, oval-shaped blob about 40 by 50 feet located on the inside of the lower west side of the mountain.

The plan under consideration was to drill a small hole deep into the side of the mountain at approximately the location shown on the monitor. If magma began to spew out, they would have an answer—not one they particularly wanted, but it would mean they could alert the area of a possible eruption.

Since Dr. Decker and her staff were the first to report the anomaly, it was decided that the initial drilling attempt would be into Mount Ayalu. That the volcano was in such a remote area was also a determining factor. The next experiment after that would be performed on Mauna Loa in Hawaii by Dr. Tiller. Fortunately, new equipment had arrived at the Ayalu site around Christmastime (Tamsin jokingly said it came from St. Nicholas), including a much-improved heavy-duty diamond drill and several state-of-the-art fire proximity suits to replace the outdated and tired ones that had been around for the last twenty years.

Dr. Decker's assistant, Negasi, along with a crew of four other volunteers, suited up in the aluminized, insulated fire proximity suits, which also had self-contained breathing apparatuses. Hopefully, the suits would protect them from heat reaching up to 2,000 degrees Fahrenheit. Tamsin was in contact with the team by radiocom and would be watching the drilling process through the videos sent back to her lab by the cameras built into their helmets.

The last eruption of Ayalu was recorded in the year 2000, so Dr. Decker felt that the only real danger to Negasi and his crew would be from fresh magma that could come spilling out of the newly drilled hole, along with toxic fumes. Hopefully, the hazmat suits would be protection enough.

On the morning of February 26, the drilling began.

*

Mitzi glanced at her face in the rearview mirror. "Looking pretty good for a dead person," she chuckled. "A little blush and lipstick makes me look almost human." Her hair was curled and sat on her head like a misplaced puppy. "Too bad I gotta cover it up with my knit cap." She was dressed in the dark blue suit that she had found at the Salvation Army and had planned on wearing when she went out on job interviews, for jobs that didn't exist. "Makes me look thinner. That's good."

The President was supposed to arrive in Baltimore at 1:00 p.m. EST. His motorcade was driving up from Washington, and he was scheduled to give a speech in front of the War Memorial Building. Mitzi had it all worked out, thanks to her friend Barbara. Barbara's husband was a Baltimore policeman who just happened to have been selected as one of the President's motorcycle escorts, and he would be riding along with the convoy when it entered Baltimore. Therefore, Mitzi figured he would have the skinny on the route, the number of vehicles, the arrival and departure times and what kind of security measures were being taken. Knowing how clever Barbara was at wheedling information out of her husband, and knowing how she loved to share such information with anyone who'd listen, Mitzi was ready.

*

After drilling for four hours and having had to add several extensions on the twelve-inch-long diamond drill, Negasi felt a change in the vibrations—a softening, as if the hardened lava was beginning to crumble. The drill started to spin quietly and faster, which was an indication they had broken through the side of the mountain. As the drill was carefully removed from the tunnel cut in the rock, the sensors picked up a sudden rush of carbon dioxide. However, no magma followed, which was a good sign.

"At least there is less chance of an eruption," Dr. Decker relayed over the radiocom to Negasi and his crew, "but the gas is deadly. Be very careful."

The next step was to insert into the hole a small halogen lamp attached to a minicam in order to see what, if anything, was in the space. The camera, with a cable trailing behind it, was strapped to a miniature trolley, and it quickly travelled through the newly drilled tunnel. When it reached the opening to the mysterious vault, it stopped and sent back an image to Dr. Decker's computer.

"I don't see anything yet," she said. "It is very dark, and—wait! Something just flashed, metallic—and there is something else—glistening—Oh, my god!"

*

So here was the plan. Mitzi would park at the North Gay Street parking facility late at night, before all the barricades were in place. She'd wear a diaper and bring bottled water and some Oreos, her favorite snack, to stave off hunger. At 12:45 p.m. the next day, the President's entourage would be exiting Route 83 and turning onto Fayette Street, then driving west for two blocks and turning right onto Gay Street, where it would stop in front of the Baltimore War Memorial Building. When Mitzi could see the presidential limo turning, she would hurry back to her red 2002 Ford Fiesta and pull out of the parking lot. Instead of turning left on North Gay Street, she would make a right, which would put her going the wrong way, as Gay Street is a one-way street. The street would be closed to traffic by then, so she would have a clear shot to the front of the War Memorial Building. She would blast through the wooden barricade, mow down any motorcycles blocking her way (hopefully not Barbara's husband's), and wipe up the sidewalk with the President as he exited his limousine. There wouldn't be any guns to stop her, and if she was lucky, the killing impact would finish her off as well. Martyrdom! No plan is perfect, but Mitzi was sure this one would work.

*

It was dark when the Better World Brigade from Idaho arrived at the wall of big stones that blocked Route 26 in Unity, Oregon. The blockade prevented these interlopers from driving their SUVs and jeeps into town, so instead, they took a walk around the boulders and pushed through the brush. To their surprise, they were greeted by fifteen citizens of the town, each armed with a bow and arrows. Every kind of bow, from a high-powered Bowtech Realm SR6 to a Genesis bow in hot pink, was aimed at the chests of the uninvited guests.

"Whoa, my friends!" shouted Scott Rawles, leader of Better World. "We come in peace."

"Like hell you do!" responded Fred Napier.

"You're here 'cause you want our gasoline," replied Fred's wife Helen, she of the hot pink bow and arrow.

"Not at all," answered Rawles. "We're on our way to California. Just passing through—well, trying to pass through, but you folks kinda put a crimp in our plans."

"You'll have to find another route, I'm afraid," came a voice from behind the line of archers as Hiram Granger came forward out of the dark. "I recommend you go back the way you came and hook up with Route 84. Drop down to Nevada. Much faster."

"Well, thank you, friend," replied Rawles, "but that means using up a lot of our precious gas—"

"You know, I don't quite understand," Granger interrupted, "why you were coming this direction in the first place. You're heading north, more in the direction of Washington state than towards California."

"Oops, you got me," Rawles said in an "aw, shucks" tone of voice. "The truth is, we're really looking for recruits to join up with us on our way to California. Thought we'd stop off at some of the little communities like yours all across the state. Ask around to see if there are people like us who are really angry with our government and ready to bring it down. There's a movement starting at Camp Pendleton—that's where we're headed—a lot of unhappy soldiers. The revolution is coming, no doubt about it."

"Well, sir, thanks for dropping by, but we are doing just fine. I think I speak for most of the citizens of Unity when I say we aren't interested in joining up with your group."

Rawles took a good look at the line of archers and sighed. "Seems you got a fine-looking army of your own, mister. Ah, well, you can't blame a man for trying."

"We're just working on getting through this crisis together, safely and peacefully," Hiram said in a calm but firm manner.

"I understand completely," Rawles replied. "Speaking of 'getting through,' would it be possible for us to pass on through your town?"

The line of archers took a sudden step forward as Granger answered. "I'm afraid not. Sorry. As you can see, there are several tons of stone that would have to be moved."

"Well, okay then. I guess we'll be on our way. I don't suppose, however, that you could sell us some gasoline? We got some containers—"

"I told you that's what they were looking for all along!" Helen Napier shouted. Hiram put a calming hand on her shoulder.

"It's okay, Helen," he said, turning to Rawles and his men. "I'm sorry, gentlemen, but we can't spare any gas."

"Yeah. I got it. Gas supplies are dwindling all over. Well, I guess we'll just keep on going 'til we can't." Rawles signaled for his men to return to their vehicles and, with a tip of his cap, turned and followed them. The sound of engines revving up was followed by the smell of exhaust as the Better World Brigade turned around and drove away into the night.

"They'll be back," Helen muttered, "mark my words."

*

Negasi and the rest of the crew, having returned to the lab, joined Dr. Decker in front of the monitors. Images of glowing tubular shapes criss-crossed against the black background, while something resembling icicles hung like transparent stalactites from what they presumed to be the ceiling of the cave. It definitely was a cave.

"I saw a globe—an orb—I mean something that looked like—I don't know," Dr. Decker exclaimed. "It was there for a second and then it wasn't. We need to keep an around-the-clock watch. Record every minute."

Negasi was stunned by what he was seeing. "We need to get in there, physically, find out what all of that is!" He pointed to the images. "Nothing in nature could have formed that!"

"Due to the 'Gunmelt' madness, we haven't any explosives to blast an opening big enough to let us in, and even if we did, we couldn't do it for fear it would cause a lethal eruption," Dr. Decker explained.

"Then we will borrow a tunnel-boring machine, one of those TBMs they use in the salt mines. We only need a tunnel about three feet in diameter, wide enough to crawl through. We have got to get inside that cave!" Negasi could hardly contain his excitement.

"I'm not sure—wait! Look—there—" Dr. Decker pointed her hand up to one of the monitor screens. An iridescent orb peered out at them with what looked like several shiny black eyes.

*

About a thousand very angry men, women and children were crowded in the park across from the Baltimore War Museum. Bundled up to keep warm, many held signs that were certainly not pro-President: "WHEN WILL THE NIGHTMARE END!" "GIVE US JOBS, NOT PROMISES!" "EMPTY SHELVES = EMPTY STOMACHS," and, perhaps the banner most representative of the mood of the crowd, "DO SOMETHING, ASSHOLE!"

The police were trying their best to keep the irate herd of demonstrators behind the barricades. The cops stood shoulder to shoulder holding protective shields and wearing helmets equipped with bullet-resistant acrylic visors, although no bullets would be coming their way. There might be rocks or bottles, maybe even a Molotov cocktail or two, but no bullets.

When the presidential convoy turned the corner and started down Gay Street, a roar arose from the park that could be heard ten blocks away.

The President, riding in the second car, wanted to believe the shouting was cheers of approval, but he knew better. He squeezed the First Lady's hand and steeled himself for what was going to be another unpleasant experience.

What happened next, as reported on TV and the internet, was like something out of a bad action film. The demonstrators were the first to see the flash of red zooming the wrong way down the street, heading straight for the presidential entourage. It smashed through the wooden sawhorses, sending splintered planks flying in all directions, and headed for the four vehicles just beginning to stop in front of the memorial. The driver of the red car swerved to try and avoid running down a couple of the motorcycle cops but sent one of them flying anyway. The door of the President's limo had just been opened by one of the Secret Service agents when the red Ford Fiesta made contact with the first automobile. This was the one in front of the President's car that was carrying more Secret Service agents. The impact was as if a gnat had run into a rhinoceros—no contest. The little red car was not a match for the steel-reinforced, bullet-proofed Lincoln limousine. The lightweight Fiesta simply pushed the heavy limo backwards into the President's vehicle, flipped into the air and landed upside down on the street next to the third limo. From a tinted window in the third automobile, a very startled mayor of Baltimore saw the driver, a woman in a woolen knit cap, hanging upside down in the car.

*

Tamsin had alerted Dr. Tiller about their success in opening a hole in the side of Mount Ayalu. She withheld what they had seen in the cave except to say that she would share that information with Dr. Tiller once he had tunneled into one of his own volcanoes. She didn't want to influence his initial reaction to what he might uncover, plus she felt it was imperative to keep the Ayalu discovery secret for a while, so as not to alarm the public.

In the meantime, Negasi had negotiated with the managers of the salt mines about renting their TBM. Since the machine was very large, cumbersome and heavy, it would take a day or so for it to be driven up the winding dirt road to the mountainside. Negasi was impatiently counting the hours.

A review of the images of the interior of the cavern recorded during the last twenty-four hours didn't reveal anything new. Since the camera was stationary and the lab technicians were not able to move its focus, the picture remained the same. The orb with the black dots did not reappear, but there was a moment when a blur of something rushed across the screen. They slowed the image down in an attempt to get a clearer view, but it remained a blur.

*

The President had called an emergency meeting of his cabinet members, as well as some of the scientists working on the "Gunmelt" situation. To say he was in a foul mood was an understatement—he was furious.

"What the hell is going on?! Two months into this insanity and still no progress?! Gentlemen, and lady, please tell me you have something positive to share with us today!"

After an uncomfortable moment of silence, one of the visitors spoke up. It was a professor from the U.K., a Dr. Alexander Higgs. He was part of a team of international scientists working out of a lab in Falls Church, Virginia.

"Mr. President, it may appear we are not making much progress, but in fact we have made some important discoveries. As has been reported to you, we now know the composition of the powder that has caused the disintegration of the weapons. We know how it works, and—"

"Okay, okay! But where did it come from? How do we rectify the situation? How are we going to get back to normal, get our weaponry back, our guns?"

"We believe the powder is airborne, and—"

"But there's no white dust blowing around. No one reported ever seeing the stuff flying around in the air before all this happened!"

"That's because the microscopic crystals are actually invisible. They can only be seen when they are exposed to tannic acid. That's when they turn into the white powder that we see on the weapons."

"Tannic acid? What the hell is that?"

"Tea, Mr. President, it's a chemical in tea."

"Great! How very British! This is ridiculous! Answer me this: If this shit was, or is, blowing in the wind, why hasn't it affected us? I mean, we must have inhaled it. It would have gotten in our mouths, our ears—"

"We are working on that, Mr. President. I'll try and explain. Because the Van Dijck crystals are so small, they can't be seen, felt, smelt or tasted. They are like the bacteria we find already in the air around us. So far, we have found no evidence that they affect human beings or animals negatively. They seem to have one mission and one mission only, and that—"

"—is to destroy our ability to protect ourselves. I thank you guys, and lady, for all the work you've done so far, but now it's time to step up to the plate and find a solution. When next we meet, I want some real answers. Solve this fucker!"

The President shook hands with the departing scientists and turned back to face his cabinet.

"Okay. You heard the Brit. Doesn't sound very hopeful to me. Things are falling apart around us and they haven't found diddly-squat. At the rate they're going, it'll be the next century before they come up with a way to stop this nightmare and put us back in business."

Pointing to the head of Homeland Security, the President added, "Ted, I want you to stay on their asses, see that they remain focused, whatever it takes!"

"Yes, Mr. President," he answered, trying to sound positive. "About that other situation you asked me to update you on."

"What other situation?"

"That attempt on your life, sir, in Baltimore last week."

"Oh, yeah, right. What have you found out? Was it a terrorist attack?"

"Doesn't seem to be. It looks like she was acting on her own."

"Crazy bitch. What's her name? What's her status?"

"Still in a coma. The car was registered to an Edward Brownhart. We believe she's his wife, Mitzi Irene Brownhart."

*

Hiram Granger was awakened by a loud banging on his front door. He glanced at the wind-up alarm clock ticking away on his bureau as he pulled on his overalls. It was 2:30 in the morning. By the time he got to the door, the knocking was accompanied with shouts.

"Hiram! Hiram! We need your help! Matthew's barn's on fire!"

Hiram opened the door to find Fred Napier stamping his feet and pointing to the bright orange flames that were climbing up the weathered boards of his neighbor's barn.

"I couldn't reach you by phone since the service went down," Fred yelled, "and I couldn't get hold of the volunteers. Helen's driving down to the firehouse now."

Hiram pulled on his muck boots, and he and Fred started running towards the fire. A couple of other men were helping Matt get his terrified cows out of the barn, and Frida, Matthew's wife, was spraying the flames with a garden hose. It wasn't doing much to help stop the fire.

Just then a wail began as the siren on the firehouse roof started spinning.

"That'll wake 'em up!" Fred shouted. "Hopefully they'll get the truck here soon."

"May not be soon enough. You see any buckets around?" Hiram yelled as he ran over to the horse trough.

"There's a couple of old milk cans!"

"They'll have to do. Bring them over."

He and Fred dunked the ten-gallon metal cans in the big trough just long enough to get an amount of water that they could physically carry to the blaze. They splashed the water on the burning planks, but it just turned into steam. The flames increased.

"Might as well just piss on it," Fred shouted. "It'd work just as well!" But he and Hiram kept returning to the trough and back to the fire until the Unity Volunteer Fire Department arrived.

By five a.m. the fire was out, but the barn was just smoke and ash. Matt and Frida poked at the edges of what had been their 150-year-old barn in the hopes of finding something worth saving. Hiram and Fred sat on the steps of the Granger farmhouse and watched the couple moving slowly around the cooling remains.

"Are you thinking what I'm thinking?" Fred asked, wiping the soot off his face.

"That this wasn't an accidental fire?" Hiram replied. "Maybe. I smelled some gasoline—"

"Me too! And you wanna make a bet on who wasted their precious gasoline in order to do this?" Fred continued. "Our military friends from Idaho?"

"Could be. I just hope this visit is a one-time event."

But it wasn't.

*

Negasi was the first one to crawl through the newly drilled tunnel, in front of his co-worker Douglas. Wearing his hazmat suit and oxygen helmet with the built-in light and camera, he felt like a little kid on his first day of nursery school. The suit was big and puffy, like something a toddler would wear, and being on his hands and knees only emphasized the image. Even the excitement that he was experiencing was like that of a child. Inch by inch, he was crawling closer to the adventure of a lifetime.

Dr. Decker and her staff were watching the flashes of light hitting the tunnel walls from Negasi's lamp as he approached the opening of the cave. "About ten feet more," he whispered, breathing heavily from the exertion of snaking his way along. "I can see the tubes. Can you see them?"

"Yes!" Tamsin responded. "Yes! They look like they're vibrating—or is that just the shaking of the camera?"

"They are vibrating, and—and there is—humming—a soft humming." Negasi crept to the edge of the opening. He swung his legs over the edge and dropped down to the pile of rubble left by the TBM. "Oh, my lord, Dr. Decker, do you see this?"

"Yes, Negasi."

The camera revealed a vast, dark cavern with a smooth floor and walls and, high above, hundreds of sparkling crystal stalactites. The vibrating tubes that rose up to reach the crystals were of different dimensions, some the size of a man's arm and one as large as a redwood tree.

"My lamp cannot illuminate all that is here, but Douglas has just entered the space with more light. We will set up the floods and you will be able to see what I am seeing. It is—it's—incredible."

"How are the carbon dioxide levels? Check your sensors, please."

"They are very high. We will not be taking our helmets off anytime soon, I am afraid."

At that moment the monitor screens lit up brightly as the floodlights were turned on. The smooth walls seemed to be iridescent and shimmered with metallic shades of blue, magenta and green. The opalescent tubes were imbedded in the stone floor, as if they descended down to a lower level, and high above they appeared to be attached to some of the stalactites.

"It is so—beautiful," Negasi whispered softly. "What do you think this is? Who is capable of creating this—this whatever it is? How could someone carve a cave this big and fill it with—with—I guess you would call it an apparatus?"

"I don't know, but we're going to try and find out!" exclaimed Dr. Decker as she stared at the rainbow-colored image on the screen in front of her.

*

The room in the Johns Hopkins Hospital was painted a very pale pink. This color was thought to have a calming effect on patients. When Mitzi finally awoke, she thought at first that she was in Bev's Best Beauty Salon. That's where she usually went to have her hair cut and curled. After a few fuzzy minutes, objects that didn't belong in a beauty shop began to come into focus: an IV pole with a couple of bags of liquid dripping down into a plastic tube, a TV up high on a wall and, sitting in a chair by the door, a policewoman. When Mitzi tried to turn her head to the right, to see what else was there, the sudden blast of pain was so bad she almost vomited. Her moan brought the policewoman to her feet, and she immediately radioed the news to her superiors.

At the same time, through the door came a nurse followed by a doctor. They moved to each side of the bed, where the nurse checked the IV catheter in Mitzi's left hand while the doctor checked her vitals on the monitor that was wired to her body. An oxygen cannula was clipped to her nose, and a neck brace held her head in a rigid, no-nonsense position.

"Good morning, Ms. Brownhart," the doctor said softly. "Do you know where you are?"

Mitzi moved her jaw up and down slowly, trying to find her voice. Nothing came out of her mouth but an "Ahhhhhh."

"That's okay. Don't try to talk," the doctor cautioned. "Not all of your systems are up and ready to go yet. I'm Doctor Davis, and this is Nurse Aaron. You're in the hospital because you had a bad automobile accident. You have a broken leg and a broken rib which bruised your lung. Fortunately, you have no other internal injuries, but unfortunately, you have had a very severe head concussion. That's what has us worried the most. You've been in a coma, but it looks like you're back with us, and that's a good sign."

Then the doctor, using his little penlight, lifted Mitzi's eyelids and checked her pupils, which were still somewhat dilated.

"I'm afraid it's going to be a pretty long recovery period. Your brain has been knocked around in your skull, and it's going to need time to get over that trauma. But we're here to take good care of you, so don't you worry." He wrote some instructions on his iPad, handed it to Nurse Aaron and turned to leave the room, but Mitzi made a soft, guttural noise.

"What? Do you need something?"

"Izzy dad?"

"What?"

"Izzy dad?"

"You want your father?"

"NUH! Dad! Diddy—"

"I'm sorry, I don't understand."

"Dad?" Mitzi pleaded.

Nurse Aaron spoke up. "I think she's trying to say 'dead.'"

"Is that right, Ms. Brownhart?" Mitzi lifted her right hand. "Are you asking if someone is dead?"

"Ta pressssitdent."

"Oh! Oh, no, it's okay. You didn't hurt him. Don't worry. He's just fine."

"Shit!"

*

One of the Unity volunteer firemen had found an empty red plastic two-gallon gas container in the field behind what used to be Matt Simpson's cow barn. Now Unity had proof that this fire had been started on purpose, that it was a case of arson. Hiram put out an alert that everyone should be vigilant and never go anywhere alone, and that all households should set up a rotation of family members to stand guard over their property at night. Since there was no phone service, either landline or cell, and no internet, communication was very difficult. Hiram found a few sets of walkie-talkies in the stockroom at Stratton's General Store and, keeping one for himself, saw to it that when a person was on blockade duty, they were always equipped with one. A unit was also kept at the firehouse. The remaining unit went to the lookout station he had created in a deer blind up in the tallest tree in town. Hopefully, whoever was manning it would be able, using binoculars, to see trouble if it were heading their way and let the others know. The firehouse siren would then be set off to alert the town.

Hiram hadn't slept much since the fire at the barn. Living alone, his wife a victim of cancer seven years ago and both of his sons having moved far away, he had to stay up most of the night to keep an eye on his property. He took a couple of catnaps during the day, but they were often interrupted by someone in town having an emergency. Like looking for Georgina Halverson's four-year-old grandson, who had wandered off and was eventually found asleep in the basement of the Burnt River Community Church. Or when Lester O'Brien's dog, Patsy, got her head stuck in the bicycle rack in front of the school. Vaseline and a hacksaw did the job.

Around 1:00 a.m. one night, Hiram had just dozed off when the siren began wailing. He awoke immediately, grabbed his flashlight and headed outside to his jeep. Once he was on Main Street, he contacted the lookout station with his walkie-talkie. He reached Fred Napier, who was on duty up in the deer blind.

"There are two sets of headlights coming up from the south on 26," Fred reported.

"Good job. Are the wires in place?"

"Yeah, Lester and Matt are doing that right now."

The two men were tightening the cables that had been strung across the highway about half a mile south of the boulder barricade. One wire was hung at about three feet high, the other at eighteen inches. They were secured to a very large oak tree on one side and a telephone pole on the opposite side. The cables were being pulled tight with hand winches— tight enough to begin cutting into the wood, almost like a garrote around some poor victim's neck. In the dark of the night, the inch-thick braided wires, which were sprayed a flat black, virtually disappeared.

"How far away are the vehicles?" Hiram asked as he drove towards the southern barricade.

"About five or six miles, I think," responded Fred.

"Okay. I should be at the barricade in a minute or two. I'll park and continue on foot."

Matt and Lester, having finished the rigging of the cables, jogged several yards away to some tall bushes where they had hidden their bows. The dense foliage and the lack of moonlight provided perfect camouflage. They hunkered down to await the arrival of the visitors from the Better World Brigade.

When Hiram got to the barricade and started his walk around the boulders and down the highway, he got on his walkie-talkie and told everyone to go silent.

"We don't want the uninvited visitors to hear our voices, or even a beep or a squeak."

Matt Simpson told Frida what happened next.

"We heard the sound of the two jeeps first, and then we saw their lights coming over the hill. I think their plan was to abandon their vehicles at the barricade and sneak into town. Anyway, Hiram had just arrived near where Fred and I were hiding and he took up a position away from us in a gully across the highway. It was good that the night was darker than a nun's habit.

"So here they come barreling along like they were trying to win the Indy 500. They must have been doing at least 85 miles an hour, maybe more. When the lead car hit the cables, it was like a scene from *Fast & Furious*. It flipped up and over and flew through the air, landed upside down and then skidded—I don't know—a hundred feet or so. I wish my cell phone worked. I could've taken pictures."

"What about the second car?" Frida asked as she poured more coffee into Matt's mug.

"Well, I guess he must have tried to hit the brakes, but it was too late. The top cable had snapped, but the bottom one was still working, so it caught the jeep under the front bumper, which caused it to spin as it flipped into the air. It then did a cartwheel down the road and landed on top of the first car."

"Dear Jesus! What happened to the driver in the first car?"

"Oh, he never stood a chance. Twisted all up like a pretzel and pressed flat as a pancake. But the two guys in the second jeep survived. One's got a broken leg, some cuts and bruises and maybe a concussion. The other has a dislocated shoulder, but they both survived. Hiram and Fred trussed them up and drove them over to Doc Maslen's."

"What happens now? What are you going to do with them?"

"That's the only good thing about this. The guy with the injured leg is Richard Rawles," Matthew said, grinning.

"Why is that good? Who is he?"

"Little Dicky Rawles is the son of the leader of the Better World gang, Scott Rawles."

"So? This is good why?" Frida asked, sounding confused.

"So, now we have a hostage!"

*

Inside the cavern in Mount Ayalu, Negasi and his crew were busy collecting samples. They were taking scrapings from the sides of the tubes and scooping up bits of the ceiling crystals that had fallen to the ground. While inspecting the walls, they discovered the faint imprint of the outline of what had once been an opening. It was completely sealed off.

"It is almost as if it was fused shut, that the stone was melted and then cooled," observed Negasi. "I think this was the opening used to bring in all this 'equipment.'"

"It could also have been the way the cavern was created," opined Dr. Decker. "Maybe a tunnel was burnt into the mountain and when it reached a certain depth, the carving or melting was continued until a large cave was formed."

"But what kind of apparatus could accomplish such a feat?"

"I don't know. A very powerful laser, maybe?"

"To my knowledge, there is no laser on earth powerful enough to do what has happened here," Negasi countered, "unless it is some secret weapon developed by the U.S. or China or Russia." He turned the camera towards the crystal ceiling and panned down one of the pearlized tubes. "Maybe all this came from outer space," he said half-jokingly.

"Let's not get carried away," Tamsin advised. "Your oxygen is getting close to running out, so pack up your samples and get out of there. We'll continue tomorrow."

The team began placing their findings in leak-proof plastic boxes and sealing them with tape. With Negasi in front, they started crawling back through the tunnel. The camera on the trolley was left behind to keep a twenty-four-hour watch on the mysterious crystal cave.

Something else was also keeping a vigil.

*

The police detective was tall and handsome, in a rough sort of way. Mitzi thought he kind of reminded her of Eddie, her husband, when he was younger. The officer stood by her hospital bed and smiled down at her.

"Allow me to introduce myself, Mrs. Brownhart. I'm Detective Bowers, and we've been waiting quite a while to ask you some questions. The doctors say it's okay to talk to you now, so—if you feel up to it."

Mitzi felt like shit, but he was being so nice. "Yeah, okay. But I really don't remember much—anything, really, except waking up in this stupid bed with my leg in a cast and my head hurting like hell."

"It was quite an accident. You are lucky to be alive."

"I guess so."

"We've been wondering if it really was an accident," the detective added, switching gears. He didn't seem so nice all of a sudden. "I mean, witnesses saw you speeding down the street going the wrong way in a restricted area."

"Yeah, they keep telling me that. What the hell was I doing? The doctor says I'll start remembering—or maybe not. I'm honestly in the dark. It's like at one moment I'm having coffee at my kitchen table and the next thing I know I'm waking up here."

"So you don't remember driving head on into a limousine?"

"Jesus, no! Did I do that?"

"Mitzi—may I call you Mitzi?" Bowers asked.

"That's my name."

"Mitzi, there are some men from Homeland Security standing outside in the hall. They'll be asking you even more questions, and they won't be quite as gentle as I am being. So why don't you tell me what was really going on. That'll cut down on the pressure, and then you can get back to healing. Now, to start, the doctor told me that when you first awoke, you asked if someone was dead."

"I don't remember that. I'm telling you the truth. It's so confusing. I wish I knew what I was—"

"Were you hired to kill the President?"

"What! Kill what president?"

"The President of the United States."

"You're kidding!"

"Was this your own plan, or did you have help?"

By this time, all the bells and whistles were going off on her monitor, showing a very rapid heartbeat and increased blood pressure. Nurse Aaron was by her side in a flash. "I'm sorry, sir, but you'll have to stop. The patient is having an episode and you need to leave, please, right now."

"I'm sorry, Mrs. Brownhart, if I'm upsetting you, but we have to get to the bottom of this. I'll be back when you're feeling better." And with that he left the room.

Mitzi was totally bewildered. Kill the President? Is that what she tried to do? "He's a number-one asshole and he isn't doing a damn thing about the mess we're in, but that doesn't mean I would try to murder him. I do remember wanting to kill myself. Yes, I was so depressed, and—" Nurse Aaron had replenished her morphine drip and she felt herself beginning to float away. Her eyelids were wanting to close, and she knew that sleep was just around the corner. "I can't remember, I want to remember, I need to remember—remem—" and she was gone.

*

Dr. Alexander Higgs was working on Experiment No. 35. He was trying to develop a coating that could be sprayed on a weapon to keep it from being destroyed by the Van Dijck crystals. So far, he and his staff had created thirty or more varnishes, and each one of them had failed. Since there were no undamaged weapons left to use for their tests, they had decided to clean up the remains of destroyed guns and use them. The trick was to wipe off as much of the white powder as possible and quickly apply the selected varnish before the invisible crystals, still floating around, could attack the exposed weapon. If the glaze worked, no new white powder would appear on the gun. So far, none of the coatings had worked. The varnishes, created with many different chemicals, ranged from a spray that didn't stick, to a slime that was so slippery one couldn't hold on to the weapon. There was one that was as sticky as honey and one that turned to ice the moment it touched metal.

Other labs around the world were also trying to find solutions. One in Germany was working on developing a new metal that would resist an attack of Van Dijck crystals. Another in France was attempting to develop a virus that would eat up the crystals. Back in the U.S.A., a company specializing in air-filtration devices was trying to create a filter that would keep the crystals out of the air in an enclosed environment. But even with all this research and feverish experimentation, a true solution to the Van Dijck plague was a long way off.

*

Using an electron microscope, Dr. Decker examined some of the crystal shards that Negasi and his team had swept up from the cavern floor. What she found was that they matched the molecular profile of the Van Dijck crystals. She had received a World Science Association bulletin that had been sent to scientists around the world concerning the crystal composition. She immediately contacted Dr. Tiller in Hawaii.

"I'm sending you a video of what we have discovered inside the cave."

"Thank you, Tamsin. We have just broken through Kilauea. A camera is sliding down the tunnel as we speak. I imagine we might find something similar to what you have uncovered. I've been notified that they are drilling into Katla in Iceland and Vesuvius in Italy as well."

"I'm totally baffled by all this—this—whatever it is," Tamsin confessed. "I've been analyzing the crystal substance and I'm sending my results to you and to the WSA. It matches the molecular makeup of the Van Dijck crystals, which are evidently the cause of this 'Gunmelt' crisis."

"To quote Lewis Carroll, 'curiouser and curiouser.' I'll keep you posted, Tamsin, about what we discover in our chamber," Dr. Tiller said as he signed off.

*

The morning after the car wreck in Unity, Richard Rawles, Scott Rawles's son, lay on a cot in Hiram Granger's living room. His companion was locked in the basement, nursing his bum shoulder. Little Dicky had a cast on his right leg and was in great pain.

"Sorry about not being able to give you a stronger painkiller than aspirin," Hiram said apologetically, "but Doc Maslen said he's running low on the hard stuff." Richard moaned softly and then cursed.

"I'd give you a whiskey, but the doc says it's not a good idea. Also, Matt Simpson has a stash of weed which he uses for his arthritis, but since you burned down his barn, I don't think he's feeling too generous."

"I didn't burn down his fucking barn," Richie declared.

"Well, someone from your gang did."

"It wasn't me!"

"So who was it?"

"I don't know," he answered, and then moaned again. "It hurts so bad. Shit!"

"I really am sorry, Richard. I wish we hadn't had to resort to violence. But we have to protect ourselves, and I'm guessing you and your friends weren't just dropping by for tea last night."

"What happened to my guys?"

"I believe Bobby Joe is going to be all right. He's got a banged-up shoulder, but we got him comfortable down in the cellar. I think his name is Bobby Joe, although he won't tell us if that's right. Won't speak at all, actually. As for Samuel, we got his name off of his driver's license. Unfortunately, he didn't survive. You fellas were going so fast."

"Shit! Wait till my dad hears about this," Richard muttered, obviously in great pain. "You guys are toast! He'll be coming soon, and—"

"We're looking forward to that. We want to have a chat with him, maybe convince him to cool it down a bit."

"He'll be here and he'll be bringing reinforcements, you can count on that."

*

Mitzi was in a dreamy fog caused by the morphine flowing through her veins. The doctors had her hooked up to an infusion pump, which allowed her to push a button whenever she felt she needed more painkiller. However, being Mitzi, she found the doses of morphine didn't get her quite high enough, so she kept pressing the magic button nonstop until the safety lock kicked in.

"It's not working!" she would complain, and Nurse Aaron would patiently explain that she had reached the limit of the dosage prescribed by her doctor. "You have to wait until some time has passed before you can get your next dose from the machine," he said.

Mitzi would grumble and whine for a few minutes, but eventually she would drift away. It was during one of these somnolent sessions that Mitzi had the first of what would become a very strange recurring dream.

It always started the same way: she would be lying in her hospital bed with her broken leg elevated and through the bathroom door would float three milky-white globes. They wobbled around the room, leaving a faint trail of bluish vapor, and then ended up floating along the foot and sides of her bed. At first she was scared. Had these weird apparitions come to harm her? Were they emissaries of Death come to whisk her away? Each one had a row of small beads that looked kind of like black olives spaced evenly, like on a necklace, around the middle of what she thought of as their equator. She eventually determined that they were probably eyes, eyes that went all the way around the—orb—the head. That was it! They were heads, and the olives were eyes.

With every recurrence of the dream, she began to relax. The globes didn't seem to be dangerous. In fact, they seemed to be—what was the right word?—friendly? Yes, that was it, friendly. When they hung around her bed she felt better, her pain was less. She almost felt normal.

By the fourth dream, she found herself looking forward to the visit of the floating heads. Their presence seemed to make her feel more than just better, she felt great! And then the most amazing thing happened. They spoke to her.

*

Negasi was back in the cavern, using ground-penetrating radar to try and discover what was below the floor in the cave. He could tell that the humming tubes penetrated the surface and seemed to empty into another open space below where he was standing.

"The radar is showing that there is a smaller cave underneath this one. All the tubes seem to originate from there."

"Is there any way to get access to that level?" asked Dr. Decker over Negasi's radiocom.

"We are checking every inch of the floor and walls. One interesting detail: when I touch the smaller tubes with my glove, I can feel which direction whatever it is inside is flowing, either up or down. And in the one large tube there is no movement in either direction, or at least I can't detect any."

"So maybe the tubes are extracting something from the crystals and sending it down to the cave below."

"That could be a possibility. And a few of them could be sending something up to the layer of crystals," Negasi replied as he moved the radar across the floor. "I wish I could see deeper into—wait! I think I have found something."

"What is it?"

"It is a slightly raised area here on the floor. It looks like a circle, a perfect circle. There is almost no delineation between it and the rest of the floor. You could not even fit an ID card into the space around it. It is like a manhole cover. I think this might be the way down."

"Is there some way to move it— slide it away or open it?"

"I cannot see anything like a handle or a hand hole. It is just a circle, almost like someone drew a circle on the floor," he replied. "I am looking around for a possible lever or button. Yes, I know, it sounds like something out of a cheesy movie, but you never know."

"Well, whatever you do, please be careful."

"I may have to resort to a pry bar or a—oh, wait, there is one crystal chip here that did not get swept up with the other samples," Negasi announced. "It is rigid, as if it is stuck in the ground. I cannot move it. I will try and twist it—what the—"

"Negasi, are you all right?" Dr. Decker called out. "Negasi?"

"Yes, yes, I am fine. It is just that this crystal has started to glow—and now—the circle is starting to lift—and—it is sliding to the side," Negasi explained as he moved away from the circle. "It is open! I can see inside! Can you see?"

"Sort of. It's not that clear on the monitor, but I can see light coming out of the opening."

Negasi stepped cautiously to the edge of the open circle and peered down the hole. "The tunnel curves down to the right. It is kind of like a chute—like a slide at a children's playground."

"Can you send a camera down to see what's there?"

"I can do better than that. I am attaching a tether to my suit so I can lower myself into the opening."

"No! It's too dangerous. We don't know what's down there," Dr. Decker insisted.

"Only one way to find out. I will be careful," Negasi replied. "Here I go!" he shouted as he slid onto the chute and disappeared.

*

It was around noon when the siren on top of the Unity Firehouse began to yowl. The lookout had spotted a large convoy of SUVs, pickups and jeeps driving towards town, in rows of three across, and kicking up dust from the shoulders of the highway. The townspeople, having been alerted, rushed to the barricade with their bows and arrows and anything else that could serve as a weapon. They stood side by side like some medieval army, until the line of people stretched across the road and onto the sidewalks. Fifty neighbors determined to protect their town.

Hiram Granger stood in the center of the line and waited for the arrival of Scott Rawles and his followers. As the caravan got closer, he stepped forward and climbed up on one of the boulders. He was weaponless and held one single eagle feather in his left hand. The first row of cars pulled up to the barricade and, after a few seconds of silence, the driver's door of the truck in the center, a Silverado 1500, opened. Scott Rawles, dressed in camo and wearing a red trucker's cap with "Better World" embroidered across the front, jumped out.

"Good afternoon, Mr. Rawles," Hiram said, gently smiling.

"Where's my boy?"

"He's okay. We've made him comfortable. He's doing just fine."

"Cut the shit!" Rawles shouted. "I want to see my son. Take me to my son!"

"In due time," Hiram replied. "First we need to set some rules."

"Fuck your rules! Lead me to my son, now!" Rawles spit out as he attempted to climb up and over the boulders.

"Mr. Rawles, I'm going to ask you to remain where you are until we have come to an agreement."

"You can take your agreement and shove it! You are holding my son against his will. The message you sent said you have injured him and killed one of my best men—"

"Mr. Rawles, your men injured themselves. We're sorry about the unfortunate death of Samuel—that was his name, correct? But your men were driving way beyond the legal speed limit."

"Stop with the shit, you half-breed! Don't play macho games with me! Do you see how many trucks I have behind me? All I have to do is give the signal and they are spreading out and coming around your stupid barricade and driving over every field and through every fence until we have your hick town surrounded!"

"Sounds like a plan," Hiram replied politely. "But that would mean you wouldn't get to see your son, ever."

"Is that a threat?"

"You mean a threat for a threat? Now, wouldn't that be childish on my part? No, I'm just stating a fact. So, rule number one: You will come with me to see your son, alone—by yourself. Number two: You will send all of your troops back to wherever they are encamped, except for one vehicle and a driver. Number three: After visiting with your boy, you will take Bobby Joe and your driver back to your camp and remain there until contacted."

Scott Rawles was beyond irate. "Are you crazy?! What about Richie?"

"Young Richard will remain here so that Dr. Maslen can continue to look after him."

"No—no—NO! He's coming back with me!"

"I'm sorry, Scott; may I call you Scott? Your son is not up to travelling yet."

Rawles was thinking that if he had a gun, this son-of-a-bitch Granger would be one dead Indian. But as there wasn't a working weapon available at the moment anywhere on earth, he had to come up with a different battle plan.

"All right. We'll follow your rules—for now. But I want my 'driver'—jeez, you make it sound like I've got one of those prissy chauffeur guys—I want Ralph to come with me. I'm not entering a possible trap alone without some backup."

"I don't blame you. I think we can live with that request," Granger replied, extending his hand in order to help Rawles climb up over the barricade. However, before Scott joined Hiram on top of the boulder, he shouted to his men to turn around and drive back to their campsite, which they did, but only after much grousing. Ralph, the "driver," then linked up with Rawles and Granger, and the three men set off to walk to the farmhouse that was serving as both a hospital and a jail.

Ralph, the "driver," never felt the eagle feather as it brushed across his shoulder.

*

Several psychiatrists spent time with Mitzi Brownhart, trying to determine her mental status. Was she insane, or was she some sort of religious zealot? Was she fully aware of her actions, or totally out to lunch? She still claimed she had no recollection of the event, even though her doctor testified to her lawyer that when she first awoke, she mumbled something about the president being dead.

Dr. Donald Fanon was the most recent shrink to visit Mitzi. He was hired by the Department of Justice to evaluate whether she was sane enough to stand trial for the attempted assassination of the President of the United States.

"I've already told a million people I would never, ever have even thought of murdering that asshole," Mitzi explained, "but if everyone says what happened happened, then it must have happened, and I musta been out of my mind."

"And you never experienced what we call a fugue state before?"

"A what state?"

"You know, a period where you don't remember where you were or what you were doing."

"How would I know if I had one of those if I don't remember it? Jeez."

"Okay, let's move on. It says here that you've been having a recurring dream. Can you tell me about it?"

"Oh, yeah. But I'm beginning to think that these visits at night are not dreams."

"What do you mean?" Dr. Fanon asked, looking up from his notes.

"Well, the first few happened while I was still doped up, but now that I'm using less of the drippy stuff, they seem to be much more real than dreams."

"Interesting. Tell me what these dreams—these visits, if you will—are about."

Mitzi sat up in her bed and began regaling the doctor with the saga of the three floating orbs with the black-olive eyes. She became more and more excited as she described the feelings of elation she experienced when they appeared.

"And lately they have begun to talk to me!" she announced with a big smile.

"Talk to you? Okay, and what do they say?"

"Well, at the moment I can't understand what they're saying, but it's definitely a language. It's kinda like they're trying to communicate. I'm hoping I'll be able to figure out what they're talking about soon."

"Very interesting. And what does this language sound like?" the doctor asked, a bit bemused by what he determined was Mitzi's happy hallucination.

"Oh, it's very nice, very beautiful. It's kind of like a combination of tinkly bells and soft beeps, very heaven-like."

When Dr. Fanon got ready to file his report, he was still up in the air about his findings. Mitzi Brownhart was either a formidable actor or she was truly suffering from a mental illness, perhaps aggravated by her concussion. "Tinkly bells and soft beeps," indeed!

*

The humming sound Negasi had heard in the upper chamber was two times louder in the cave where he was standing. The vibrating tubes from above pierced the ten-foot-high ceiling of this smaller cave and terminated in what appeared to be many translucent vats. These cauldrons ranged in size from that of a beer keg to one that looked as large as a hot tub. All of these tanks were interconnected by hoses that eventually fed into the one very large tube in the center of the room. Negasi was awestruck.

"Negasi!" Dr. Decker called out loudly. "Are you all right? We're not getting an image. We can't see anything. Negasi?"

"Oh—my—I—Sorry, it is just so incredible! I am okay. It is difficult to—I am trying to take it all in. I am guessing this is some sort of manufacturing facility. It looks like a factory, but one designed by Elton John. You can look through the sides of these tanks, these boilers, and see a shadow of what's inside—different colors, some pink or coral, some more bluish. The substance in the vats near the large tube in the middle seems to be white."

"White?" Tamsin asked. "Does it look powdery, or more of a liquid?"

"Hard to tell, but—it seems to evaporate as it enters the large middle tube. And I just noticed that there is a ring of shiny white spheres spinning around outside the top of the central tube. I'm guessing they are there to create some kind of suction or air flow to help push what's in the tube up into the upper chamber. It is funny, but these globes kind of look like the one we got on the video, you know, the one with the black dots around the middle."

"Is there an instrument panel around, or some kind of controls that you can see?"

"Not from where I am standing," Negasi replied. "I am going to start walking to my left, past the slide I used to get down here. This room is not very big. It is probably no more than twenty feet wide." He began moving around the tubes and skirting along the outer edge of the cave. "Amazing!" he exclaimed. Tamsin and her team could hear his breathing mixed with the humming of the vibrating hoses. The monitor showed that his heart rate had increased since his descent into this second chamber. The meter on his oxygen helmet also indicated he was down to one-quarter capacity.

"Negasi," Dr. Decker warned, "you're getting low on air. It's time to start thinking about getting back to the outside."

"Right. I will just finish circling the cave and then I—what?—wow!" Negasi said excitedly. "One of those spheres just dropped down in front of me, and now it is spinning around my helmet and—and zipping up and down and around my suit!"

*

Mitzi was out of bed and sitting in a wheelchair when Dr. Fanon entered her room. He pulled the only other available chair over to where she was seated and placed it directly in front of her.

"Good morning, Mitzi," he said as he sat down. "I understand you asked to see me."

"Yes, sir!" she replied enthusiastically. "Have I got news for you!"

"You seem to be feeling much better."

"Yeah, I do. I'm completely off the hard stuff. They got me on pills. Much better. No more juice machine. I thought I'd miss it, but it's nice to not be so fuzzy anymore. Anyway, that's not what I asked you here for."

"I imagine it's because you're beginning to remember some things. Let's talk about what—"

"Oh, no, it's not that! I still don't remember doing what they said I did. It's still a total blank, but—"

"Mitzi, you seem very—hyper. Tell me what's going on?"

"I've done it!"

"Done what? What have you done?" Dr. Fanon asked, beginning to be concerned.

"I broke the code!"

"What code?"

"The language barrier! Remember when I said I couldn't understand what they were trying to say?"

"Who are 'they'?"

"The floating heads! You remember, the three white glowing balls that visit me at night. Last evening, all of a sudden I could understand what they were trying to tell me! It's like a miracle!"

"You can decipher what the 'bells' and 'beeps' mean?" the doctor asked, deciding to go along with her fantasy for a while.

"You got it! At first I didn't know what was going on, but then it was like they were whispering in my head, and it all made sense!"

"I see. You heard voices—in your head."

"Well, no. It was more like they were whispering in my ear. Yeah, that's what it was like."

"And what did they whisper?"

"Wow! All kinds of stuff—how I was to help them—how they have this mission and that I am chosen to get their message out into the world!"

"Well, that sounds like some pretty serious stuff," the doctor said, believing that Mitzi was in the middle of a full-blown psychotic episode.

"Let me ask you, Mitzi, have any of the night nurses, or maybe the police officer outside your door, met your floating friends?"

"Oh, no. The heads don't trust what they call the 'Ordinaries.' They're afraid of them. They said the 'Ordinaries' would either harm them or imprison them."

"But they trust you?"

"Seems so. They call me a 'Chosen One.' How about that!"

Dr. Ronan arose from his chair and smiled at Mitzi. "Well, you continue to feel better and I'll be back to see you tomorrow."

"Okay, and Doctor, I've started to write down what they are telling me. Kinda like a diary. I'll show it to you next time when you come."

In Dr. Ronan's estimation, Mitzi was not competent enough to go to trial. "Floating heads," "Ordinaries" and being the "Chosen One" were not very indicative of a sane mind.

*

Scott Rawles stood at the foot of the four-poster bed on which his son, Richard, lay, his leg resting on several pillows. Hiram had transferred him to his own bed in his bedroom in order to make him more comfortable.

"Hi, Dad," the boy said nervously.

"Hi, yourself!" Scott responded angrily. "Looks like you got a little banged up, thanks to these local yokels. You okay, I mean except for your rib and your leg?"

"Yeah, I'm all right. I'm sorry about the jeep and—"

"Let's get you up and out of here," the senior Rawles barked as he came around to the side of the bed and began to try and lift Richie off the mattress. Hiram intervened.

"I don't think that's such a good idea, Mr. Rawles. Your son is not in any shape to travel. I would prefer you stick to our agreement."

"Fuck your agreement! He's coming back with me right now!" Rawles roared at Hiram. "Ralph, stop standing there like an idiot and help me. You get on that side of the—"

"Don't, Dad," Richard pleaded, pushing Scott's hands away. "Hiram, I mean Mr. Granger, is right. I got bruises on my bruises, and my head is kinda wonky."

"He's got a concussion," Hiram explained.

"Yeah, thanks to you!" Scott answered, ready to take a swing at Granger.

"Please, Dad, it'll be better if I stay. Mr. Granger has been very kind, and the doctor is taking good care of me. The neighbors have been feeding me, and—"

"Been feeding you a lot more than food, it sounds like to me. You been here, what, two days? and now you're all lovey-dovey." Rawles turned toward Granger. "You've brainwashed my boy."

"Dad, please, listen," Richard continued. "These people here are good folk, and Mr. Granger here has been telling me the history of the town. This is a kind of sacred place. I—I—I think we should just leave them alone and move on south—"

"These so-called good people killed one of my men, and look what they did to you!"

"That was our fault—my fault," Richard explained. "I'm sorry about Sam, but Bobby Joe is okay. They've got him set up all comfortable in the basement, and the doctor reset his shoulder."

"You're making this sound like the Mayo Clinic," Scott said angrily, and then he pointed at Hiram. "And this guy ain't Mother Teresa."

Hiram stepped next to Scott and put his hand with the eagle feather on the man's shoulder. Scott started to pull away and then stopped.

"Mr. Rawles, you should listen to your son. He is much smarter than you give him credit for."

Scott Rawles found himself unable to move. No, that wasn't true. He was fully capable of moving. It was just that suddenly he didn't *want* to move. He just wanted to sit down quietly on the edge of the bed and put his arms around his son. No more arguing. No more battle plans. No more leading his men on a quest for a "better world." He was weary, too old and tired for this nonsense.

Hiram walked over to the driver, Ralph, and whispered something in his ear and at the same time brushed the eagle feather across his back. The man smiled and nodded and then headed toward the door to the cellar.

"Your driver is going to check on Bobby Joe, and then you and he can return to your camp."

"I'd rather stay here with my son, if that wouldn't be too much trouble?"

"No trouble at all," Hiram smiled, carefully placing the eagle feather next to the photo of his wife that sat on the bureau across from the bed.

*

The holes drilled in the volcanoes in Hawaii, Iceland and Italy revealed the same mysterious setup of tubes and crystals. However, no attempts were made to carve tunnels into them like the one at Mount Ayalu in Ethiopia.

"We haven't got the equipment on hand to get inside there safely," Dr. Tiller explained to Tamsin over the phone. "Plus, we don't want to take a chance on causing an eruption. My ladies are very active, as are the other ones being investigated."

"Probably a wise decision," Tamsin replied. "And since I have your ear, I wanted to share with you the information I forwarded to the World Science Association. I tried calling you yesterday, but the phone was down. Anyway, let me update you. We found a smaller cavern underneath the bigger one—"

"Amazing!" Dr. Tiller exclaimed. "Did it contain tubing similar to the main cavern?"

"Actually, the tubing from above extended through the ceiling of the lower cave and terminated in these tanks."

"Tanks?"

"Yes, vats of various sizes. What we have determined so far is that the tubes are taking pieces of the large crystal stalactites—"

"The ones hanging in the upper chamber?"

"Right, and flushing them down into these cauldrons, where they are seemingly being transformed into a liquid or a gas. We haven't been able to access a sample of it yet, so I don't know which one it is. However, I have a theory."

"And that is?" Dr. Tiller asked.

"Well, we know from the pieces of crystal stalactite I analyzed that they are the same as the Van Dijck crystals found on the remnants of destroyed weapons."

"And?"

"I think that what we have discovered is a factory, a manufacturing plant, where the crystals are being refined into a microscopic dust which is then somehow being sent out into the atmosphere."

"Any ideas how this is done? And who is running this—whatever it is?"

"Not at the moment. But I haven't told you the most interesting part of our visit into the small chamber."

"And that is?"

"My assistant, Negasi, has been the main explorer in the caves. I haven't been inside them yet, so I've been depending on his observations. When he discovered the opening to the smaller chamber, he entered it by way of a chute—"

"A chute?"

"A slide, if you will, and when he got into the space we lost all visual contact with him, but fortunately his audio was still working. While he was walking through the environment, describing what he could see, we suddenly hear him getting very excited. He said he had discovered a group of spheres spinning around the top of the large central tube."

"Spheres?"

"Orbs, globes. He took photographs of them, along with the tanks and the tubes, which I will send to you. But the most amazing thing is that one of the spheres split off from the others and dropped down in front of him. He said it spun around him and then returned to the ring and continued spinning with them. You'll see in the photos what I'm talking about."

"A spinning sphere—how big?"

"Well, each one seems to be about the size of a soccer ball. You will see a row of black bead-like protrusions running horizontally around their middle sections."

"Very intriguing. So what do you make of this sphere's action, of its descending and spinning around your assistant?"

Tamsin thought for a long moment. Her first reaction was that it was a security device that was programmed to automatically react to an intruder. But why didn't it take an aggressive action? Shouldn't it have tried to disable, or even destroy, Negasi?

"I think—it was curious about Negasi. I really think it was just checking him out."

*

The President was having his lunch in the Oval Office in order to meet with the head of Homeland Security, Ted Reinhurst. He was picking at what looked like a lettuce salad.

"Naomi has me on this fucking diet," he explained. "Says I'm eating too much and that it's all wrong, too much sugar and salt. She's certain that my overeating is caused by all the stress I'm under, all this crazy shit, the riots, the economy hitting rock bottom, the weapons crisis."

"Yes, sir, it's pretty bleak out there," Reinhurst agreed.

"Then, Teddy, my boy, I'm hoping you've got some better news for me, some good news."

"Well, sir, I have some updates. I think some of them could be labeled good."

"But not all of it, am I correct?"

Reinhurst took a deep breath and looked down at his iPad. "There's been a breakthrough in the search for the source of the Van Dijck crystals."

"Good, that's good! So, who's been manufacturing those little motherfuckers—Iran? Russia?"

"Actually," Reinhurst replied, with a little hesitation, "the information comes from Ethiopia."

"Africa? What the— Are you trying to tell me some poor little third-world country has the resources and the brain power to create this—this nightmare?!"

"No, sir. The report I received this morning, and it's been verified by other sources, states that a laboratory has been discovered inside a mountain in Ethiopia. We don't know, at the moment, who is responsible—"

"On a mountain?"

"Well, no, sir, *inside* the mountain, actually, and it's a volcano. It's called Mount Ayalu."

The President looked totally bewildered, but after a moment or two a smile began to sneak across his face. "You had me going there, Ted. Thanks for inserting some much-needed humor into your report. However, let's get back to the issues at hand."

"It's not a joke, Mr. President," Reinhurst explained. "The lab was found inside the lower slope of an active volcano. I don't have all the details, but we have a report that an Ethiopian government team is on their way to the volcano to investigate. And there seems to be the possibility that there are more of these facilities located inside other mountains."

"Jesus Christ! And where are these other labs located?"

"Well, we're told one of them may be in a volcano in Hawaii."

"Oh, come on now! This has to be a giant pile of bullshit! First of all, no laboratory could survive inside a volcano, all the equipment would melt or burn up, right? And the guys working there, making this crystal shit, they'd be dropping dead left and right. I mean, there's all that lava stuff and smoke."

"We'll know more soon, Mr. President."

"It'll all be some ridiculous hoax, you can bet on it! More fake news," the President declared, pushing his unfinished salad across his desk. "You want some salad, Teddy? I can't finish it. I'll call and get you a clean fork," he said, reaching for the intercom.

"Ah, no thanks, sir. I had my lunch already."

"You sure? Okay. Well then, what's next on your report? Something a little more realistic, I hope. No flaming laboratories."

"We've had some success with crowd control using high-pressure hoses and tear gas. Cattle prods work pretty effectively as well."

"Okay, and any more info about that terrorist attack on me last month in Maryland?"

"You mean the Brownhart woman?" he asked, to which the President nodded a yes. "No affiliation with any terrorist organization, sir. It seems she's just a deranged person who we think had some sort of grudge against—the government. And what's more, it looks like we won't be prosecuting her, due to a diagnosis of diminished capacity by the psychiatrist in charge of her case. The staff at the hospital say she keeps claiming she's the 'Chosen One' and that she's getting orders from aliens on how to solve the Gunmelt crisis," he said, with a slight smile.

"Well, send her over here," the President said jokingly. "I'll take any help I can get!" He reached into one of his desk drawers and pulled out a Snickers candy bar. "Don't tell Naomi."

*

Mitzi sat in her wheelchair near a window that looked out at the Baltimore harbor. Her friend Barbara had sent her a note to let her know she was taking good care of the kids and not to worry. Mitzi had started writing in a small notebook that Nurse Aaron had purchased for her in the hospital gift shop.

<u>March 10</u>

I'm not allowed any visitors, even my kids, but that's OK. I have more important things to do. Last night my three angels gave me my first set of instructions. I call them "my angels" 'cause that's what they are. They told me that I needed to listen carefully and to let the "Ordinaries" know these four things:

They mean no harm to anyone.
They want to create a pathway to peace. (Whatever that means.)
They have put into motion a plan to eliminate the use of weapons.
They want me to be their spokesperson.

<u>March 11</u>

I really don't understand what's going on here, but I do know that when they enter my room, I feel wonderful. I can have had a rotten day, with my headaches, the police harassing me, my leg itching and then here they come and, whoosh, it all falls away. Last night I told them that it was weird but that I thought I loved them more than my own family. I also said that I wanted to know more about them, but only if that would be all right. This is what they told me:

They are a race of beings that have been on earth much longer than us guys.
They are called S C I O P O D S. I made them spell it twice so that I would get it right.
They eat insects, flies and gnats and mosquitoes. Yuck.
They live in tunnels underground, abandoned mines, places like that.
They use the melted rock deep down inside the earth as a source of energy, which is something I don't really get.
They talked about volcanoes and workshops, but that went way over my head as well.

<u>March 12</u>

My lawyer told me today that they're moving me out of the hospital and putting me into another facility. Probably tomorrow. He said it was a place for people who might harm themselves or others. I knew right away that he was talking about a prison for the criminally insane. The looney bin. I may not be too bright, but I'm not stupid. I got real upset, 'cause this could mean I'd never be visited by my angels ever again. I really lost it, started crying and cursing until Nurse Aaron had to give me a shot.

When I woke up it was very late at night. I thought I was all alone, but imagine my joy when I saw my three friends hovering around me. I told them about having to leave and they were just great. They assured me that they would be with me wherever I went. Then they gave me another message. They said it was very important, that I should copy it down word for word and give it to someone I trusted. This is what they dictated:

The secret you seek rests in the heart of the earth.
Climb to the top of the mountain and we will show you
the way inside. Leave your hate and fear out in the snow
and join us around the warm fire of peace.

(I don't know what the hell this means. I guess it's supposed to be a poem. Poetry was never my forte.) Anyway, I was supposed to show it to someone I trusted. I thought about good old Dr. Fanon or my lawyer, but then I finally decided to give it to Nurse Aaron.

*

Negasi stood in the open doorway to Tamsin's office. He rapped gently on the door frame.

"Excuse me, Dr. Decker?"

"Oh, good morning, Negasi."

"May I speak with you for a moment?"

"Of course, of course. Come in, please."

Negasi entered and went to a chair opposite Tamsin's desk. "May I sit?"

"Oh, don't be silly. Sit down, for heaven's sake. You're so formal this morning. What's up?"

Negasi laid some papers on Tamsin's desk and took a deep breath. He hesitated for a brief moment and then began to speak.

"Last night I was so excited and wound up that I could not sleep."

"Very understandable," Dr. Decker said in agreement. "We are in the midst of an extraordinary event."

"Indeed, and a very confusing one for me. I am seeing and experiencing things that defy all the rules, things that go against every scientific principle I have ever learned."

"Right. I understand. What's happening down in Ayalu's belly is, in so many ways, upsetting and scary for all of us. It's hard to try and keep an even keel when you're living through what we are seeing. What I've been trying to do to maintain my sanity is to remind myself that so-called scientific truths are being overturned all the time. What was absolute a hundred years ago is often made obsolete by the new discoveries in the next century."

"Yes, this is very true. However, there is something going on here that is beyond just scientific anomalies. When I'm hobbling around in my hazmat suit in that—that factory from another world, I feel a—a presence."

"A presence?"

"I feel like there is an entity observing me. Last night, after dinner, when I got back to my room, I was just sitting there and I had this memory. May I share it with you?"

"Please do," Tamsin replied, sitting back in her chair.

Negasi began to talk about his great-grandfather, who had lived to be 103. Negasi remembered him fondly and recalled that he was a great teller of stories.

"The one that popped up in my memory last night was a tale he told about an ancient race of creatures called the Sciopods. He said they had lived in Ethiopia millions of years before humans even existed. Unlike us, they were pale beings with large round heads, and to protect themselves from the intensity of the sun, they lived underground in caves and tunnels. When they ventured out into the daylight, to keep from being burnt by the sun they extended this—this limb or leg, I didn't quite understand this part, with this umbrella-like appendage over their head for shade."

Tamsin smiled. "Sounds like a very interesting mythological creature."

"That is what I thought as well. So I did some research and I found all this," he responded, picking up the sheaf of papers he had put on the desk. "I discovered that Pliny the Elder wrote about the Sciopods way back in A.D. 77. He claimed they were real and that they were seen roaming in the mountains of Ethiopia by reputable witnesses. These sightings appear in other writings as well, again and again, until the beginning of the Renaissance."

"And you think this might have something to do with what we are finding in Ayalu?" Dr. Decker said, trying not to smile.

"I know, I know," replied Negasi with a flush of embarrassment. "I am sounding like one of those people who believe in things like UFOs and Yetis. But yesterday, when that one spinning globe came down and started whirling around me, it was like—"

"Like it was checking you out?"

"Yes."

"I concur."

"Really?"

"Yes. That's what it sounded like to me. Now we just have to see if this orb has that limb your great-grandfather was talking about that serves as a sunshade."

Negasi was taken aback. "Oh, I see. You are having me on. Well, I deserve it. It was a ridiculous idea."

"No, no. Just the opposite. I think you've keyed into something. We just have to do now what we scientists do best."

"What is that?"

"Run some tests."

*

Hiram Granger, Matthew Simpson, Fred and Helen Napier, Lester O'Brien and Dr. Maslen sat around Hiram's dining room table. Each one of them had a mug of tea in front of them. It was late and everyone was tired.

"So what's the next step, Hy?" Matt asked. "We got four hostages and dwindling supplies and the threat of those 'Better World' bozos coming here to rescue their leader."

"I'm running out of medical supplies," added the doctor.

"And the whole town is getting low on coffee," said Helen, "which makes for some very depressed individuals. This orange pekoe swill does not do the job," she added, indicating her mug, "and we'll soon be out of that as well."

"I made contact with someone over in Prairie City. They're still getting some supplies delivered, so I proposed an exchange of goods," Hiram explained.

"What kind of exchange?" Lester asked, scratching his dog Patsy's ears. Patsy was sitting on the floor next to him with her head in his lap.

"Our milk for their medicine, fresh venison for some canned goods and coffee," answered Hiram, smiling at Helen. "They'll meet us at the barricade next Monday. I'll need a list of what you need, Doc."

"Great. I'll have it for you in the morning," replied the doctor.

"Good. Thanks. So, now, about the hostages. Richard's dad and his driver are up in my sons' old room."

"Are they locked up, at least?" asked Helen.

"I have a key, but right now it's not necessary. They're asleep. They seemed a bit tired out after they arrived," Hiram added, smiling. "Lester and Patsy here have volunteered to keep an eye on them. Bobby Joe is still in the basement and Richard is recuperating up in my room."

"Where are you sleeping?"

"I'm on the couch in the living room, which is just fine, because it keeps me alert to any action going on outside."

"Okay. What about this Rawles guy's followers?" inquired Fred. "You know they will be coming back, right?"

Hiram leaned forward and put his arms on the table. "I think we all need to sleep on that one for now. I'm tired and I'm sure you are as well. Let's get together tomorrow. A fresh morning for some fresh ideas." And the meeting adjourned.

After everyone had left and Lester and Patsy had gone upstairs to take up their positions by the hostages' door, Hiram slipped out of his boots and jeans but kept his flannel shirt on, as it was cold in the living room. He lit a candle and, sitting in his big leather armchair, opened a drawer in the side table next to him. He removed a tooled leather pouch, pulled the drawstrings open and shook out into his hand a small, brownish "liberty cap" mushroom. Closing his eyes and humming softly, he lifted his hand up toward the ceiling and then, lowering it, dropped the mushroom into his mouth. He pulled a plaid afghan up over his knees, sat back and waited.

*

While Mitzi was being wheeled out of Johns Hopkins and placed in a police van heading for the Clifton T. Perkins Hospital Center, the cleaning woman, Rosalie, found a notebook on the floor under Mitzi's bed. Her first instinct was to toss it in the trash. It was hospital policy to dispose of anything found on the floor, as it could be carrying infectious germs like staphylococcus. But instead, she picked it up with her gloved hands and slipped it into a plastic bag. On her coffee break, she stopped off at the lost and found and left it there with the attendant. She then headed to the cafeteria, and while standing in line at the cashier's station, she spotted Nurse Aaron.

"Hey, Mr. Aaron, how you doin'. You was in charge of that crazy lady in 511, right?"

"You mean Mrs. Brownhart?"

"Yeah, the one who tried to off the President."

"Actually, we don't know what she was trying to do. But yes, I was her day nurse."

"Well, I found a notebook under her bed. I think it was hers—it had her name inside."

"Really? What did you do with it?"

"I shoulda trashed it, I know, but I thought she might be missin' it, so I took it over to lost and found."

Nurse Aaron remembered Mitzi showing him a page from what she called her journal and a message on it that said she should share it with someone she trusted. Some sort of poem about mountains and snow.

"Thanks, Rosalie. I'll look into trying to get it back to her."

After his shift, Aaron changed into his street clothes and took the elevator down to the first floor. On his way out, he stopped at the lost and found and retrieved Mitzi's diary. Once he was on the bus heading home, he took the notebook out of the plastic bag, wiped it with a sanitizer sheet and opened it up. By the time he reached his apartment on East Fillmore Avenue, he realized that this journal was an important piece of evidence. In his eyes, this was very vivid proof of Mitzi Brownhart's unstable mental state. He would contact the authorities tomorrow and turn it over to them.

*

Dr. Decker had called an emergency staff meeting. When everyone was in the room, she began to speak.

"As you know, we have shared our findings with the WSA and with other volcanologists, as well as the Ethiopian government. What we have uncovered is now public knowledge, pretty much, worldwide. As I feared, panic has set in, and we can expect a visit from government officials any day—"

"No!" exclaimed Negasi. "We cannot let that happen!"

"Please, let me finish—"

"You know what they will do! They will take over, they will keep us away—"

"Negasi, stop! Let me finish. The United States government has already sent inspectors to Hawaii and they've closed down the Kilauea project. I talked to Dr. Tiller and he said the army is guarding the mountain while government officials are starting to inspect the site."

"And that means," Negasi interjected, "the same thing will be happening here!"

"Yes, it probably will, so in the time remaining, we must copy all our data and store it away safely. I can't imagine the government wanting to destroy what we have discovered, but we have to be open to all possibilities."

"Dr. Decker," Negasi interrupted again, "may I continue to work in the caves? At least until—"

Tamsin looked at the young scientist standing beside his chair, his whole body shaking with anger and longing.

"We really need your coding skills, Negasi—but if you can give us a couple of hours of data analysis, you can use the rest of the time to keep exploring the cavern. Lord knows, there is so much we still don't understand."

"I know, I know! Thank you, Dr. Decker!" he replied, starting to head for the doorway.

"Where are you going?" Tamsin asked, reaching for his arm.

"I want to get started on the analysis so I can suit up as soon as possible," he explained. "We haven't got much time before the invasion of the politicians!"

*

The early morning sun woke up Hiram as it peeked through his living room windows. He sat in his lounge chair, feeling a little spaced out, as he remembered his midnight journey to the "other place." He recalled watching the candle begin to dance and the flame change its color from yellow to a rainbow of hues, blues and greens and purples. The living room ceiling had opened up to reveal a night sky glimmering with a million stars and flaunting a giant pearl of a moon. He had felt a cool breeze skip across his face and weave through his hair. He then remembered taking a deliciously deep breath and calling out softly to his Wyakin, his spiritual guide. "I am in great need of counsel," Hiram asked in the language of the Nez Perce.

Out of the darkest corner of his living room, a large shape began to appear. It moved slowly across the pine floor and into the moonlight, and then Hiram saw that it was his shadow spirit, the bear, which had been with him since his thirteenth birthday.

"I honor you, my great companion," Hiram said, "and call on you now for guidance, because we are about to be attacked by a tribe of unhappy and confused warriors. In your wisdom, I ask this and will abide by your recommendation."

The bear lifted his huge paw, with yellow claws sharp as arrows, and placed it on top of Hiram's head. A bright, clear vision floated in front of his closed eyes. He had his answer.

*

Ted Reinhurst sat in his office at the Department of Homeland Security on Martin Luther King Jr. Avenue in D.C. On his desk lay the journal of Mitzi Irene Brownhart. He was skimming through the pages, stopping when certain words caught his eye: "volcano," "Sciopod," "workshop." Earlier, he had been reading the reports coming in about both Mount Ayalu and Kilauea when an assistant brought him an envelope dropped off by the police. It had been scanned and x-rayed and deemed safe to open. In it was the pink fake-leather notebook belonging to Mitzi that the nurse Aaron had turned over to the police.

How could she have known about the volcanoes? What's she going on about with these imaginary globes that are giving her all this so-called information? And that sappy, flowery message:

> The secret you seek rests in the heart of the earth.
> Climb to the top of the mountain and we will show you
> the way inside. Leave your hate and fear out in the snow
> and join us around the warm fire of peace.

What the hell does that mean? It's like something off a Hallmark greeting card! But a lot of what she wrote jibed with the information coming in from the inspectors at the volcanoes.

Reinhurst hit his intercom and asked his assistant to call the superintendent at the Perkins Hospital. Yes, it was a hospital for the criminally insane, but it was also a prison for those defendants still undergoing evaluation to determine their mental status. Mitzi would be held there while the doctors decided if she was sane enough to go on trial. Maybe she wasn't so crazy after all.

*

When Negasi and his crew reentered the crystal cavern, he immediately slid down into the smaller cave. While his team continued to measure and photograph the tubes and other apparatus up above, he concentrated on the spinning white globes in the lower chamber. He watched them as they circled around the top of the large central tube in a clockwise direction. Trying to remain objective, he observed that they didn't move together like some mechanical device, but rather more like a group of living entities. At times their speed increased and then decreased, causing one or more of the orbs to bump into one another. Also, their journey around the central tube was not as though they were always traveling on a level track. It was more like a kiddies' roller coaster, up and down.

Moving right up against the side of the big tube, feeling its vibration and hearing the soft hum, Negasi looked directly up at the spinning globes. As they whirled around high above his head, he noticed that once in a while one of the orbs turned its central ring of black beads downward toward where he was standing. At first he feared it was going to spray him with something lethal, but each time it came around, nothing seemed to happen.

He was getting dizzy staring at the globes as they raced around the tube, and Douglas had just radioed him from the upper chamber. He was needed to help move a piece of their heavy equipment. He wobbled over to the slide in preparation for being pulled back up through the opening. It was then that he felt a slight pressure on his suit around the area of the calf of his left leg. He turned quickly and looked down. One of the globes was attached to the fabric of his hazmat suit. His primal instinct was to try and shake it off, but it stuck to him as if it were magnetized. His heart rate began to increase as his adrenaline kicked in and he moved into "fight or flight" mode. He was about to grab anything he could find to try and smash to pieces the glowing white object that was clinging to his leg when—

"No harm," came a voice over Negasi's radiocom. It wasn't Dr. Decker's voice or Doug's. It almost sounded like his own voice, only more musical, like wind chimes or a distant bell. He began to feel his fear melt away, and it was replaced with an intense sense of joy. *"No harm, friend."*

*

Mitzi sat at a table in a room labeled "Visitors' Lounge," which she knew was a euphemism for "Interrogation Room." Across from her sat Dr. Ronan and two persons she didn't recognize. A nurse (think "prison guard") stood at attention by the door.

"It's good to see you again, Mitzi," Dr. Ronan said. "You're looking well."

"Thanks. I'm up and walking—well, walking with a cane, and my headaches are gone."

"That's good," Dr. Ronan replied. "So, we're here to catch up on how your treatment is progressing—"

"Who are these two?" Mitzi interrupted, pointing to the other two people—an uptight middle-aged man in a navy blue suit and a heavyset woman in a white lab jacket.

"Oh, I'm sorry," Ronan apologized. "This is Ted Reinhurst from the Department of Homeland Security and Dr. Leonora Finch. Dr. Finch is the superintendent of this facility. I thought you two had met before when you—you were brought here."

"Never had the pleasure," Mitzi said. "Kinda got thrown in here and locked up without so much as an explanation. Let me tell you, there are a lot of very scary people running around here. And where is my lawyer? Shouldn't my lawyer be here?"

"This is just a visit, Mitzi," Dr. Ronan explained, "to see how you're doing."

"Mrs. Brownhart," Dr. Finch said, getting directly to the point, "do you know where you are and why you are here?"

"Well, it sure as hell ain't no beauty spa," Mitzi retorted. "Of course I know why I'm here and what this place is. It's a place where you stick crazy people who've done bad things. And you folks believe I'm one of those persons."

"Actually, we try and help people who have, as you say, done bad things."

"And from what I've been told, again and again, I tried to do one of those bad things, right?" Mitzi replied. "But I'm doing a good thing now, a really good thing."

"And what is that, Mrs. Brownhart?" Reinhurst inquired, breaking his silence.

"I'm glad you asked, Mr. Bratwurst, because it concerns your Homeland Security Department. In fact, it concerns the whole world's security."

"It's Reinhurst, Mitzi," corrected Dr. Ronan.

"Rheingold, Rainburst, whatever! I've been chosen to be the voice of the Sciopods."

"And who are these Sciopods, exactly?" asked Reinhurst.

"They're the 'angels' who are going to save all our asses!" Mitzi replied excitedly.

Reinhurst looked at both Dr. Ronan and Dr. Finch and shook his head. He reached into his briefcase and pulled out a notebook covered in fake pink leather. Mitzi reacted immediately.

"You found my notebook! I've been asking everyone around here if they'd seen it. Where did you find it? I haven't been able to write down the latest messages."

"It was under your bed at Hopkins," answered Dr. Ronan as Mitzi extended her hand toward the book. Reinhurst pulled the pink volume away.

"Let me get to the reason I'm here, Mitzi. May I call you Mitzi?"

"No. Give me my notebook."

"I'm sorry, but at the moment, it's federal property, Mrs. Brownhart."

"I want my notebook! It's mine!"

"You'll get it back, in time. But first I need to ask you some questions. There is information in this book that only our intelligence bureau has access to. How did you get hold of it?"

"I told you, my Sciopod angels dictate these messages, most of which I don't understand, but they seem to be leaning towards stopping people from killing each other."

"Why have they chosen you to be their spokesperson?" asked Dr. Finch.

"Why not? Am I not just as useful as anyone else—like you, for instance? But oh, that's right, I'm crazy. I'm seeing things and hearing things that aren't there. But you know what, Doc? When you give me those meds that are supposed to make those things go away, my angels just become brighter and louder."

"Mitzi, as I understand it," Dr. Ronan interceded, "you have nightly visits of these—"

"Angels—almost every night. Sometimes they don't show up, but that's because they're very busy guys."

"Right. Now, you say these 'angels,' in the shape of glowing white orbs, come into your room and dictate messages to you."

"Correct. And I write them down in my little pink book. I'm supposed to pass these messages on, but every time I try to show them to somebody, they just look at me like I'm a crazy woman with delusions of grandeur. Right, Doc?" Mitzi directed this last statement toward Dr. Finch.

"Mrs. Brownhart," asked Reinhurst, "let us say that we believe you. Would it be possible to meet your 'angels' one of these evenings—tonight, perhaps?"

"Listen. I'd be thrilled to introduce you. It'd be proof I'm not nuts. But they won't show up as long as there are 'Ordinaries' in the room. I mean, it's fortunate I'm still in solitary, so that—"

"You're in a private room until we can find you an appropriate room-mate," Dr. Finch explained.

"Whatever. But I can guarantee you that if you lock me in a room with some madwoman who is ready to drink my blood, my little guys won't ever show up. Right now they still come to me, they give me messages, I write them down, that's it. Well, I *would* write them down if I had a pen and something other than toilet paper."

"Mrs. Brownhart, I have an idea," Reinhurst offered. "What if I give you some questions to ask your—friends? Questions about events the public knows nothing about."

"Wow. You're smarter than syou look," Mitzi answered. "I'm up for giving it a try. But before I do, you need to agree to two things."

"And those are?"

"That I'm to ask my 'angels' only one of your questions, and that I get my notebook back."

Reinhurst hesitated, looked again at the two doctors for affirmation. They both nodded in agreement. He took a sheet of Homeland Security stationery out of his briefcase and wrote down the one question he wanted Mitzi to ask. He then handed the paper over to her, along with her pink notebook.

"Great. And I'll need that pen, if you don't mind," she said, checking it out. "Expensive pen, nice. Government issue?"

*

While survival was getting harder everywhere, it was particularly difficult in the urban areas. Sky-high apartment buildings with frequent electrical brownouts meant limited elevator service. Climbing forty stories to get to your apartment may make you healthier, or it might kill you. Getting stuck in an elevator when the power went out was no barrel of laughs either. Travelling to work, if you still had a job, became a marathon. Bicycles, scooters and skateboards were everywhere.

One of the unexpected statistics was the increase in the percentage of suicides due to the inability to cope with the hardships of living without social media.

Dear Mom and Dad,

I can't get through one more day like this. I'm crying all the time. Without my cell phone and my iPad and my computer, I'm without my friends. I can't even reach you. My classes keep getting canceled due to lack of heat, lights and, most importantly, wi-fi. I don't see things getting any better ever. Please forgive me.

Your loving daughter, Tiffany

P. S.: Please take care of Boodles. His leash is hanging in the closet.

Since guns were no longer available, the most common form of suicide was by hanging. The next most popular method was jumping from heights, and the third-most-used technique was poison, particularly pesticide. It got to the point that when walking down the street, you had to keep looking skyward just in case someone was leaping out of a window. And you hoped you would never enter your apartment house's lobby one day and find the super hanging from an overhead light fixture or the doorman lying dead in a pool of vomit.

*

Scott Rawles woke up to the smell of coffee and bacon. He hadn't slept as peacefully as this for months, even with Ralph in the next bed snoring like an angry rhinoceros. He stretched his arms, swung his legs over the edge of the mattress and stood up. It was a sunny morning, and as he walked out of the bedroom and headed down the hall to the john, it almost felt like the good old days, before it had all gone to hell. He took a quick glance into the room where his son Richie was recovering on the big four-poster. He was sleeping like a baby.

When he came downstairs, he saw Granger standing at the stove cracking an egg into a frying pan.

"Good morning, Mr. Rawles. I hope you slept well. How do you like your eggs?"

It was getting harder to dislike this hombre, what with his calm demeanor and seemingly honest generosity.

"I could do with some of that coffee I'm smelling."

"Grab a mug off the shelf. If you need milk, it's in the refrigerator."

With his coffee and eventually his plate full of bacon and eggs, Scott sat down at the kitchen table. Hiram joined him, and they dug in.

"I'm really sorry about what happened," Hiram said between bites. "We never meant to hurt anyone. I thought the cables would just slow your men down, stop them, you know."

"I sent them to do some reconnaissance," Rawles explained. "I don't know why they were going so fast."

"Forgive me, Scott, but I can't believe they were just coming to check us out again. After that little bit of arson last time—"

"Listen, Mr. Granger, I gave orders to my son to see how many vehicles you had and then do a census on how many people live here. Nothing more."

"Okay. And what was the reasoning behind that?" Hiram asked, fingering the eagle feather that peeked out of his shirt pocket.

"I just wanted to make sure—" Rawles began, and then stopped.

"I think it's time to be honest, Mr. Rawles," Hiram said as he reached under the table and brushed Scott's knee with the eagle feather. Rawles stiffened and then relaxed.

"Yeah, well, truth be known, I was planning to sort of take over your little town—just for a while—until we got back on our feet. Things are getting a bit tough back at our camp. Running out of supplies, water."

"I understand."

"And I may have told Richie and the boys that they could retrieve any provisions they saw just laying around."

"You mean steal," Hiram said—as a statement, not a question.

"Whatever. Look, you got a good thing going here. I guess I was sort of hoping we—we could—"

"Be part of it?" Hiram asked, smiling. "Funny thing, but I woke up this morning thinking the same thing. You want to talk about it?"

*

Dr. Decker and Negasi stared at the white globe sitting on the doctor's desk. Actually, it was floating about an inch above the surface instead of sitting. It continued to hum and vibrate as the two watched in an almost trance-like state. The doctor was the first to speak.

"And you say it spoke to you?"

"Yes! Well, I mean, I heard something. I mean, it was like a voice in my head," Negasi admitted. "I know, it sounds like I am crazy, but it was as if I were hearing my own voice filtered through a synthesizer. 'No harm, friend'—that's what I heard."

"I believe you," Tamsin replied. "At this moment, I'm ready to believe anything."

"What is the next step? It has not shown any aggressive behavior. It let me pluck it off my suit and carry it out of the cave."

"Well, I for one would like to see what's going on inside. If it's mechanical, we could see how it works."

"And if it is not? If it is—something else?"

"The only way to find out is to get inside."

"You do not mean to open it up, not like an autopsy?" The voice in his head whispered in its musical tones, *"No harm, friend."*

"No. We don't want to destroy it. Let's just x-ray it."

It was difficult to get a clear photograph of the interior of the orb due to its constant spinning and vibrating. After trying to stabilize it with various restraints, Negasi, about to give up, had an idea.

"What is your name?"

"What do you mean?" Dr. Decker asked in confusion.

"I am sorry. I was addressing the object," Negasi explained.

"Oh, I see. Did you get a reply?" Tamsin asked, half in jest.

"Not yet. I will try again. What—is—your—name?"

After a long pause Negasi heard in his head a bell-like response: *"Leahcin."*

"L-e-a-h-c-i-n, is that correct?"

The globe began to glow brighter and change color.

"I will take that as a yes. Pleased to make your acquaintance. My name is Negasi, and this is Dr. Tamsin Decker." The orb turned a bright orange and then returned to its original white.

"My friend Leahcin, we wish to take an x-ray of you. Therefore, we need for you to stop spinning and to remain absolutely still. Can you do that for us? We mean you no harm, friend."

The globe began to slow down until the whirling became minimal. When it had stopped completely, the orb dropped to the surface of the floor and tilted to one side.

"The spinning seems to be integral to its mobility," Dr. Decker observed. "It needs to whirl to move around."

"I think it cannot remain still for long, so let us get it x-rayed. I will place it in front of the x-ray machine."

With the globe in place, they stepped into the observation booth, pressed the x-ray button and turned to the computer screen. When the image came up, Tamsin gasped. "I don't believe it!"

*

Reinhurst was on the phone with the President.

"We have her in a safe house in Virginia. Our best interviewers are with her. They'll be able to get to the bottom of this. But I have to tell you that when she came back with the answer to the question I had written down, I was blown away."

"What was that question again? Something about mountains, right?"

"I asked for the names of the volcanoes involved in this weird situation and where they were located."

"And she came back with a list?"

"A very long list, sir. Seems these crystal volcanoes are peppered all over the world."

"But wait a minute," the President interrupted. "She could have gotten that information off the internet."

"Yes, she could have, if she had had a computer at the hospital. But she didn't. She was locked up in solitary—bed and toilet, period."

"Okay, so what's next?"

"Well, sir, we've installed a concealed camera in her room in the hopes of getting some video coverage of these floating balls she claims are giving her messages."

"Good idea," the President continued. "This woman, this Mitzi, does she seem sort of normal? I mean, in your estimation, is she sane or totally bonkers?"

"I think she's—she's very neurotic, but she's not psychotic. I can see that she's enjoying all the attention she's getting, but she also seems very serious about her mission, as she calls it."

"Well, keep her working on her mission and keep her happy. No extreme measures, water-boarding, that sort of nonsense."

"Of course not, sir," Reinhurst replied, amazed again at how out of touch the leader of the free world was. "She's in pleasant surroundings, homey atmosphere, nothing to worry about."

"Thanks, Ted. Hopefully, when next we speak we'll have some answers to this fucking situation." "Don't hold your breath, old man," thought Reinhurst as he said goodbye and hung up.

*

The day all the museums in the large, and even small, cities closed down and locked up their treasures was a very sad one. This action had become necessary, as there was no way to guard against theft. When a gang walked into the Louvre and removed the Mona Lisa from the wall and, ignoring the sound of alarms going off all around them, simply carried the painting out of the building, that was the last straw.

Malls and movie multiplexes had been dying off anyway, and now they were completely empty except for homeless people who had set up camp in their dark, cold environs. The homeless population was increasing daily due to massive unemployment, and even middle-class families found themselves struggling to find food and shelter.

Almost all schools and libraries were closed, including universities and colleges. One of the exceptions was in Unity, Oregon. The Burnt River High and Elementary School remained open, thanks to teacher and librarian Georgina Halverson.

"Our kids need to keep learning, no matter what. School helps them handle the tough stuff that's happening around them. Makes them feel a little bit more secure and in control."

Georgina had joined Hiram and most of the other town folk in a meeting at the Burnt River Community Church. She had just finished speaking about her plans for the school's fall term and was being thanked by Hiram when Scott Rawles appeared in the doorway. A wave of whispers rippled up from the seated families.

"Folks," Hiram announced, raising his voice, "I'd like you to welcome someone who wishes to become a new member of our community, Mr. Scott Rawles."

The effect on the crowd was like they had been zapped with a cattle prod.

"What the hell are you talking about!" shouted Fred Napier.

"That's the man that burned down the Simpsons' barn!" added his wife, Helen. The church erupted with the sounds of shouting and cursing. It took Hiram several minutes to get things under control. When it was finally semi-quiet, he began to explain the reasoning for this new development.

"Scott and I have come to an agreement. His actions toward us were based on good old-fashioned fear. He and his men have lost their homes due to fires both natural and manmade. They have—"

"Is that the reason he set my barn on fire?" Matt Simpson asked angrily. The crowd joined in with catcalls and threats. Scott turned to Hiram and mouthed a request, at which time Hiram raised both his hands. In his left hand he held the eagle feather.

"Mr. Rawles would like to address you. I'm going to give him the feather to hold. You know the rule: whoever holds the feather has the floor until the feather is passed to another speaker. Let's be courteous," Hiram requested as he handed Scott the black-tipped feather. The leader of the Better World Brigade took the eagle feather and, with a look of slight embarrassment, began to speak.

"First of all, my apologies to you, Mr. Simpson, for what happened to your barn. I'm afraid one of my men got a little carried away."

Matt Simpson leaped up from his seat in the pew. "Carried away?! You—"

"Matt!" Hiram barked, indicating for him to sit down.

"My orders were only for them to retrieve some gasoline, since we were running—" An angry rumble indicated the crowd's dissatisfaction with his explanation. "Right. You're right. I guess it was more like stealing—but setting a fire was entirely the idea of one of my more gung-ho members. I did not ask him to do such a stupid thing. He has been punished, and we will be helping you rebuild your barn." If he had expected cheers and applause, the cold silence that followed let him know that such accolades would not be forthcoming.

"Anyway, let me tell you briefly why we left Idaho and why we would like to join up with you. Yeah, eventually we want to get to Camp Pendleton in California, where the revolution is happening, but with fall upon us and our supplies running out, we need to lie low. When this gun-melting disaster hit, the Feds ordered us to get off our land—yes, public land, but land we'd been on for decades, land that was our home. They'd just been waiting for the opportunity to move us out. Without weapons for protection, we were defenseless. We remembered Ruby Ridge, and maybe you do too. Anyway, when we wouldn't leave, they came in with tanks and flamethrowers and that was that. Now, you have to understand, we're survivalists, so we moved up north to the Owyhee Desert. You ever been there? Flat and dry as cardboard, and that's when we got hit with wildfires. Even the toughest of us couldn't make it work. We sent our women and children to live with relatives in Boise and Twin Falls and set out on our recruiting mission to California."

Fred Napier stood and asked to be given the feather. Scott stepped down from in front of the altar and handed it off to Fred.

"That's quite a story, and I'm sorry for your loss, but we," he said, indicating all the people sitting in the pews, "are trying to survive as well. How many men are in your convoy?"

"Fifty-two, counting my son and me."

"Well, sir, if you join up with us, that will almost double the population of our little town. That'll put a big strain on our resources."

Hiram interrupted by taking the feather from Fred's hand and turning to address the entire gathering.

"Your concern is legitimate, Fred, but there are two things here that are important to remember. Mr. Rawles and his group are survivalists and have many skills that they can teach us. And, man, we need everything we can get our hands on. Secondly, many of you who are sitting here are members of this church, and if you know your church architecture, you know I'm standing on the area called the sanctuary, a word that also stands for giving someone a place that is safe from harm. Unity has always been a welcoming place. It should continue to be just that. What is being proposed here won't be easy, but, as the old saying goes, there is safety in numbers." Hiram looked out over the crowd of his neighbors and friends. "Time to take a vote."

*

Dr. Decker and Negasi stared at the computer image of the x-ray they had taken. The subject of that x-ray was now spinning around the room, earnestly taking a look at everything, like a tourist on a holiday.

"It appears to me to be an insect," Tamsin observed.

"But with some of the characteristics of a human mammal," added Negasi.

"True. I can see legs and arms with human musculature, but the torso is more like the thorax of an insect—a grasshopper or an ant."

"The rest of the interior of the shell seems to be equipped with navigational devices. And those black beads we thought were eyes are openings, windows, as it were, that give these creatures a 360-degree view of our world—their world. Amazing!"

"Correct. But why do they stay locked up in these globes?" Dr. Decker wondered.

"An interesting question. I have a couple of theories, but why don't I ask the creature itself?"

"I'm still having trouble getting my head around how you two communicate, you and—Lincoln. Is that right?"

"Leahcin was what I wrote down," Negasi replied, turning to watch the globe bobbing back and forth from the monitors to the coffeemaker and then to the shortwave radio. "I do not know what the gender situation is here, but I cannot keep referring to this entity as an 'it.' So for now, I am going to use 'him' or 'he,' until proved otherwise." He stood up and walked over to the whiteboard that was used for working out calculations. The globe was moving back and forth across the board's surface in what was apparently an attempt to understand what was written there.

"Leahcin?" The orb stopped its examination and spun its way over to Negasi. "We have many questions to ask you. Is that all right?" A reply didn't come right away, and Negasi had just about given up when suddenly he heard that familiar musical voice playing inside his head.

"*What is it you wish to know, friend Negasi?*"

"Wow! Thank you for letting us look inside. And for letting us see you, as well. We were wondering why you seem to be sealed up in the globe. Do you ever leave? Can you leave?"

"*The sphere is for safety—and for voyaging—travelling—movement. We work in environments that can be toxic. Many gases that could kill us. We live beneath you, out of the way of the killing rays of the Sunstar. But when we surface, we have to stay in our spheres or we shall perish.*"

"I understand," Negasi affirmed. "However, as there are no windows in this room, if I were to dim the lights, would it be safe enough for you to exit your sphere?"

The globe rose quickly up to the ceiling, blinked a flash of orange and then dropped down onto one of the lab tables. It settled onto the surface in a movement similar to a hen roosting on a nest. There was a soft click, and very slowly the top of the globe began to lift up and rise like an umbrella.

"Oh, my god!" Negasi gasped. "It is like my great-grandfather said! The Sciopod and its sunshade!"

Tamsin and Negasi were tempted to move closer for a better look, but stopped when a tiny blue-white head appeared at the edge of the opening. "*No harm,*" tinkled the voice in Negasi's head.

"Yes, Leahcin, no harm. You are safe."

*

It was a pleasant bedroom with her very own bathroom. Much nicer than in her dingy, outdated apartment. And if you ignored the two federal agents, who sat on the couch watching sports on the TV, the living room was quite comfortable. The kitchen was fully stocked. Three square meals a day and no crazies trying to kill you in your sleep was a great deal. All she had to do was keep reporting what the Sciopods were telling her.

October 16

But there's a problem. My angels showed up the first night I arrived and then immediately left. They haven't been back since. I'm really upset. At first I just sorta brushed it off as them being not used to coming to a different place. But then as the days passed, I got worried. I thought I'd get into trouble if I didn't deliver the goods and then I'd get sent back to that awful place. I was almost ready to make up some shit. But that would be sabotaging my mission.

October 19

My alien visitors are back! Hallelujah! It was those stupid government dorks all along, who had installed a hidden camera in my room. The Sciopods got wind of that, and of course they wouldn't come near this so-called "safe house." I found the camera stuck in a figurine of an American eagle resting on the top shelf of the bookcase. I was so mad I almost threw it at one of the couch-potato agents.

The Reinhurt guy apologized, and now we're back on track. He had a list of new questions and asked if I could kinda sneak them into my conversations with my angels. Since a lot of the questions were ones I wanted to ask anyway, it wasn't a problem. Here's some of their answers:

As Sciopods, they've been living around here for millions of years.

Twenty years ago a search party arrived in Africa from their mother planet, which is located in what our astronomers call the Triangulum Galaxy, a.k.a. Messier 33. (I just write down what they tell me to. I had to ask them to spell these last two suckers.)

They travel in these pods, ergo the name Sciopods, I guess.

They are here to save our planet. (When I asked them why, they said for two reasons: to preserve the living environment for the six billion Sciopods who reside underground here on earth, and to stop the human race from annihilating itself. Good luck with that.)

They are oxygen breathers. The pods, those beautiful white globes, manufacture oxygen for them. So I guess there are little aliens inside.

Yes, they are responsible for the gun-melting crystals. The search party that came here recently brought with them this new technology as a solution to stopping the genocide of the human and Sciopod races.

<u>October 20</u>
When I showed Reintwit my notes, he got all excited and demanded that I tell them to "cease and desist" at once. I almost laughed in his face. I told him I'd pass on his message, but not to hold his breath.

I mean, the damage is done, right? The guns and stuff are destroyed. Anyway, I'll see what they have to say about all this when they come by tonight. I so look forward to their visits. It's hard to get thru the day.

*

Although the vote wasn't unanimous, most of the townspeople welcomed Scott Rawles and his crew to Unity. With the generosity that can usually only be found in small towns, the residents opened their homes to these strangers. Storage rooms became bedrooms, living room sofas did double duty, little kids shared their toy-filled rooms with big truckers. Some of the brigade were even put up in a heated cow barn, not the most fragrant of venues, but better than the tents they had been suffering in with the bitter cold.

"If you can't beat 'em, join 'em," joked Matt Simpson.

"Keep your friends close and your enemies closer," quoted Fred Napier, feeling that that was a more appropriate saying. The town was jam-packed with pickups, jeeps and SUVs. There were even two RVs that were allowed to hook up to power and water lines, but with no guarantee that electricity or water would keep flowing on demand.

"Just so they understand that this is temporary," added Lester O'Brien. "First sign of spring and they're outta here."

"Just so Hiram understands that this is temporary!" added Helen Napier, not a champion of Scott Rawles and his Better World buddies.

*

Hiram and Scott sat at the breakfast table. It had been decided that Rawles would continue to stay in the Granger home, since his son was recuperating upstairs in Hiram's bedroom. Ralph, the driver, had helped Bobby Joe get up the stairs and out of the basement, and the two of them had moved into the Halverson house. Georgina was pleased to have some men back in the house. Her husband had been gone for fifteen years.

Hiram poured a dash of milk in his coffee. One cup of java in the morning was all he allowed himself, not for health reasons, but because he was running out of coffee.

"When you were talking yesterday at the meeting," Hiram said, stirring his cup, "you mentioned the Owyhee Desert."

"Yeah, hot as hell and flat as a French crepe."

"I was born up there," Hiram revealed.

"Shit, I'm sorry," apologized Scott.

"It's okay. My folks were part of the Nez Perce nation. It's kind of where the early tribes got their start."

"Again, my apologies," Scott repeated, trying to make amends.

"No, no, you're right. It *is* flat and hot and barren. I hated it. Couldn't wait to get out of there."

"So you moved here, then?"

"After I finished college, yeah. Got married, had kids. It's kind of funny, but it's like Unity just called out to me. Historically, this was said to be a very sacred place where, in the days before you white folk arrived, my people came to communicate with their spirit guides. There are these stories about seeing the spirits rise up out of the earth like circles of white light. I don't know about that, but I know I feel something very special here. Always have."

"Well, I have to say you have a great little town here," Scott admitted.

"Yep, and that's why I'm sort of reluctant to leave it."

"Leave? You thinking of leaving? Why?" questioned Scott. "Oh, I see. You want to join up with us on our spring journey to Camp Pendleton. Great!"

"Not exactly," replied Hiram. "There is a possible journey forming in my mind, but it's not to California. I'm having this recurring dream—"

"A dream?"

"Yeah, of a mountain, a tall mountain covered in snow."

"Well, hell, there are tall mountains in California. Mount Shasta—"

"Yes, true, but this seems to be kind of a mystical place, and it wants me to go there."

"I'm not really into 'mystical,'" affirmed Scott, "but I know I'm wanted in Camp Pendleton, 'cause that's where me and my men can make a difference."

Hiram nodded and got up to put his cup in the sink. At the same time, he withdrew the eagle feather from his jacket pocket and, stepping behind Rawles, brushed it softly across the man's back.

"I'd like to talk to you about an idea I have."

*

When the creature named Leahcin climbed up and out of the white globe and slid down its side to the top of the table, Negasi and Dr. Decker were astounded. It, they or "he," as Negasi preferred, stood about ten inches in height, was pale white with a tinge of blue and had a head that appeared to be larger in proportion to "his" insect-like torso. He resembled one of those illustrations of an elf that Tamsin remembered having seen in the fairy-tale books she had read as a little kid.

"I'm going to take a photo for documentation," Tamsin said, aiming her camera at the dragonfly-like Leahcin, but Negasi grabbed her wrist.

"He just shouted no!" Negasi explained. "I am sorry, but he says they are not yet ready to be exposed to the rest of the world."

"Well, that's going to be happening soon. Your government officials will be here soon, and there will be no hiding away then."

Negasi was well aware of what was ahead for Leahcin and his kind. There was so much to learn about this amazing race of creatures before the authorities stepped in and ruined it all.

"Leahcin," Negasi began, "I have many questions for you, and I hope you will be able to help me. I have the feeling you picked me for a reason. Is that correct?"

Once again there was a period of silence.

"What did it say?" asked Dr. Decker.

"Nothing, he seems to be thinking—wait—he says he came to me—because he knew he could trust me. Thank you, Leahcin."

"Does he trust me?" asked Dr. Decker. "I'm not hearing his voice."

"He is not sure," relayed Negasi, "at least at this moment."

"I understand—I think. Could you ask it—him—why all this is going on? Why they are manufacturing these crystals that are causing such havoc?"

Negasi had so many other questions he wished to ask: Why is it you speak English? Leahcin, seeming to hear Negasi's thoughts, answered: *I don't—my language is translated in your brain as your speech is translated in mine—this is true of all other languages.* How old are you? *I am 115 human years, but to answer your companion's inquiry, we are attempting to stop warfare and killing by destroying weapons.*

"He says they have created these crystals to try and stop wars and shootings, by using the crystals to destroy weapons—I guess he means guns and bombs."

"Well, he has certainly succeeded in doing that, but that has not stopped people, humans, from killing each other."

"Leahcin, I know you just heard what Dr. Decker said. Your mission has accomplished your goal, but it has caused many terrible tragedies. It is as though you have made things worse!"

"We are aware of the reverberations of our actions. This was only step one. I believe you have a term, 'wake-up call.' That is what this was. Now we shall prepare step two."

"And what is that?"
"Nature's revenge."

*

<u>October 24</u>
"Nature's revenge" was what my angel told me to write down. When I showed that to Reinhurst, he said, and I quote, "What the fucking hell does that mean!" I told him he had a potty mouth and that I had no idea what it meant, but that it was in response to the question he had asked me to ask them. I hate being in the middle of whatever is going on here, but I know it's my job, my destiny. So I do what I'm told to do: write down the messages from my angels, share them with Liverwurst and then ask my angels the stupid questions he writes out for me.

The question he wanted an answer to was what was next now that our nation's weapons were destroyed. I personally believe that all my angels are trying to do is what all those Miss America contestants used to say: "I will work toward world peace."

However, maybe they're going at it wrong. I mean, things are pretty bad right now. One of the couch-potato feds said there are these riots in the prisons and all these bad guys are escaping, no way to stop them. I bet that hospital for the crazies I was at will be next, all those nuts running around.

And there is this nasty new flu epidemic killing off a lot of people 'cause there's no shots or medicine available. I think I'll be okay 'cause we're so isolated out here, and as long as I don't kiss one of the feds, ha ha, I will survive. Remember that Donna Summer song? Anyway, my angels have something in the works called "Revenge of Nature," and it doesn't sound good.

*

"Okay, as I understand it, there are these crystal factories in volcanoes all around the world," the President stated to Ted Reinhurst as they sat in the Oval Office, "that have been spewing out this gun-melting shit in order to put an end to terrorism and killing."

"Something like that," replied Reinhurst.

"And the workers in these crystal factories," the President continued, "are little green men—"

"White, pale white—"

"Whatever! These sons-a-bitches are alien beings—"

"Actually, they claim to have been living here long before the human race."

"But they originally came from outer space, right?"

"That's what they told Mrs. Brownhart, and we've heard similar stories from Hawaii and Africa."

"Teddy, do you hear the two of us? We sound like a couple of UFO nuts! This whole scenario is like a bad sci-fi movie. A delusional woman is getting messages from floating soccer balls and we take what she says as gospel truth. I can't go before the American people and talk about the little whatever-color-they-are men from who knows what planet. I've said it before and I'll say it again, this has to be a hoax on a grand scale, and I want to get to the bottom of it and find out who's behind all this—this bullshit!"

"Mr. President, the press has gotten wind of what's been going on, and videos are showing up on the internet. You will have to make some sort of statement soon. Whether any of this is true or not, and personally I believe a lot of it is real, we have to put a positive spin on it while we investigate it further."

"I hate this so much! Our country is falling apart and I have to talk about little green men," the President groused as he unwrapped a Snickers bar. "Okay, I'll work with the press secretary on some sort of response. Meanwhile, what have our investigators discovered over there in Hawaii? How many of these little fuckers have they captured?"

Reinhurst shook his head as he reluctantly responded. "None, sir—"

"WHAT! What do you mean, none!"

"It seems they have disappeared."

"Disappeared?"

"When our team got to the volcano, they saw a few of these globes slipping away into what seemed to be a warren of deep tunnels. By the time the investigators were suited up and into the actual factories, there wasn't a trace of the creatures left."

"See!" the President exclaimed excitedly. "It's just what I was saying! A giant hoax! Now you see them, now you don't, and that's because they don't exist."

"Sir, you've seen the photographs, the videos of the factory in Mauna Loa, the orbs floating around."

"Photoshop. For god's sake, man, you know what these special-effects guys can do these days!"

Reinhurst, feeling it was useless to argue and time to move on, decided to bite the bullet and bring up the unpleasant subject of the latest message from Mitzi's angels: nature's revenge.

"What? These so-called tiny terrorists are talking about mother nature getting back at us? Well, she's been doing a bang-up job on her own for years: tornadoes, floods, wildfires, hurricanes—what's she going to throw at us now?"

"At the moment, we don't know. Supposedly, we will find out within the next few days."

"This is why my hair is turning gray."

*

The Ethiopian officials had had more success in capturing some of the Sciopods. But their success was short-lived, because when they opened the globes, they found none of the inhabitants alive. It appeared that they had died either by suicide or by the sudden exposure to the noxious gases surrounding them. The scientists were disappointed, but at least they had some bodies to examine and on which to perform autopsies.

Negasi and Dr. Decker were horrified by the brutality of the attack on the Sciopods. The authorities had shown up unannounced and had taken over the lab, the tunnel and the caves. Most of the orbs had escaped, but a few stragglers were caught. The investigators had cracked them open like they were chicken eggs. Negasi, fearing the worst, had hidden Leahcin in the footlocker in his room. Although members of the military who were attached to the investigative team inspected all the rooms in the facility, they did so quickly and cursorily, so Leahcin was never discovered.

Later that night, Negasi locked his door and opened his footlocker to let Leahcin out.

"I am so sorry about all this," he said as he set the white globe on top of his desk.

"Do not concern yourself. This was expected. It was known that there would be sacrifices."

"But what happens now? How can I keep you safe?"

"I will remove myself from my vehicle. It will be easier to hide if I am not tethered to it. I realize such an object stands out and is an easy target."

"But won't you need it eventually?"

"Yes, but for now I need you to help me put our next event in motion."

"Of course, whatever you wish," Negasi replied. "What exactly is the next event?"

Leahcin had lifted up the top of his pod and was crawling out. *"You will make contact with representatives from each of the 241 countries and territories that exist on earth."*

"Pardon me?"

"You will tell them that they must stop all aggressive actions and begin to cultivate benevolent behavior."

"Are you talking about the United Nations?"

"No. There are only 196 nations that are members of that organization. We are reaching out to all countries."

"But how would I ever be able to accomplish such a feat? I would not know how to begin."

"You will find a way."

"Leahcin, even if I could reach each and every one of these leaders, why would they listen to me, and even more importantly, why would they obey your directive?"

"Because if they do not, a series of destructive events will occur that will harm many millions of the human species."

"Is that a threat I am hearing?"

"It is a warning."

*

Mitzi Irene Brownhart sat across from the President of the United States in the main lodge at Camp David. Although she was surrounded by Secret Service agents and there were Marines standing guard at all the doors and windows, the atmosphere was one of relaxed civility.

"First of all, sir," Mitzi began, "I want to apologize for what I tried to do to you. I'm beginning to remember a little, you know, some flashes of these images. I don't know what the hell got into me. I hope you can forgive me."

The President smiled the famous grin that had won him the election and waved his hand as if to dismiss the whole event. "It's okay, Mrs. Brownhart. Except for some non-life-threatening injuries to a couple of my Secret Service guys, no real harm was done. However, I don't think your car will ever be the same."

"Thank you, sir. It was my husband's car, so it doesn't matter what happened to it."

"I see. Right. Anyway, a side effect of your—accident seems to have been to open you up to some mysterious abilities."

"Yes, sir."

"You seem to be in contact with—what do you call them?"

"My angels, and actually they contacted me first. That's why I'm here. They insisted that I relay their latest message directly to you and to do it in person."

"That's what Ted—Mr. Reinhurst—said, and so here you are. I insisted we meet here at Camp David in order to give us a little more privacy."

Mitzi opened her pink notebook and started to hand it to the President, but it was intercepted by one of the Secret Service agents. He examined it quickly, flipping through the pages, and after determining that it didn't contain anything dangerous like anthrax or ricin, gave it to the President.

"I thought it would be better for you to read my notes, 'cause sometimes I kinda screw up and misquote what they say to me. It's dated yesterday, October 30. I took it down word for word."

The President turned to that entry and started to read aloud.

<u>October 30</u>

A representative from every country and territory on every continent and on every island is to be chosen to meet and begin discussing ways to settle disputes through means other than warfare and violence. If this meeting does not come about in one month's time, a disaster will be set into motion to prove that we, the Sciopod Nation, are serious about what we are asking of the human race.

"Mrs. Brownhart," said the President in a quiet but angry voice, "this is a threat, and I do not appreciate being threatened. If this is truly a message from your all-powerful aliens, then what they are asking is impossible to accomplish in a month, or a year, or ever! If, however, this is some cockamamie con game, as I suspect it is, then you are about to be arrested for conspiring—"

"Wait! Please, Mr. President, read the rest of the message. But maybe not aloud," Mitzi said in a pleading tone. The President glanced down at the page.

If the President is skeptical about this message and does not believe it has been sent by us, emissaries of the Sciopod Nation, let the following information be proof of our existence:

His mistress's name is Ginger Champagne.
Address: Miramar Apartments, 1301 15th Street NW.
His and her safe's combination is 37-12-2-71.
It contains $500,000, antique jewelry and the remains of a Colt 45.
Her pet name is Reddy.
His pet name is BigBoy.

The Leader of the Free World turned beet-red and handed the notebook back to Mitzi, but not before taking the presidential pen and scratching out this last bit of unwelcome information.

*

The message requesting that representatives be selected to assemble at an as yet unannounced destination was delivered by courier to as many nations as possible. It was a slow and fruitless process. Most embassies and presidential palaces ignored what they determined was simply a prank. "Discuss world peace? Isn't that why we have a membership in the United Nations? Please!"

*

Leahcin sat on Negasi's knee, looking somewhat like a ventriloquist's dummy. They were discussing the campaign to recruit representatives for the world conference on rescuing the earth. Things were not going well.

"You must understand, most of the leaders of these nations do not believe any of this," explained Negasi. "They are too concerned with all the problems they are having to deal with to even consider a fantastic request from creatures of another world."

"*We are not from another world. We are from* this *world!*"

"Yes, yes, I'm sorry—"

"*It is interesting how your scientists always talk about the first woman, Lucy, her fossils being over three million years old, discovered here in Ethiopia, correct?*"

"Yes, right. We call her Dinkinesh."

"*But no mention of the first man. Biologically, there had to be two in order to create a third. Is that not correct?*"

"Well, yes," Negasi replied, beginning to wonder. "What are you trying to say?"

"If you were able to extract DNA from Dinkinesh and compare it to our DNA, what do you think you might find?"

"You mean your Sciopod DNA?" Negasi asked. Leahcin nodded and smiled. It hit Negasi like a zap from a taser. "Your ancestors interbred with the first humans! That would mean—"

"We are brothers under the skin, as it were," Leahcin said, with an even larger smile.

*

Hiram Granger sat in the Simpsons' living room talking with Matt. It had been snowing lightly, and there was a warm orange glow radiating out from the fireplace. Matt put another hunk of split oak on the fire and returned to his seat.

"When are you planning to leave?" he asked Granger.

"As soon as the snow stops, if it doesn't get too deep," Hiram responded.

"And where exactly are you going again?"

"That's just it, I'm not quite sure. I just know my dreams keep telling me it's somewhere on a mountain."

"And you're going with Scott Rawles in his truck?"

"Yep. This voice in my dream said it's important that he come along."

"You do know how crazy you sound, how crazy this whole thing sounds?"

"Yes, I do, but these are crazy times, Matt. And I have to follow my instincts."

"Okay, I understand that part. You've always been the person we've listened to because of your 'instincts.' But to set out on a journey to somewhere, you don't know where, with Scott Rawles, Mr. Barn Burner, of all people. Why not take Fred or Lester—or even me?"

"Rawles is a tough survivalist. He has skills I don't have. More importantly, Matt, is that I need you to take over keeping the town running safely. Can you do that for me—for Unity?"

"Yeah, sure, but I still don't like this whole deal, this whole wild goose chase."

"Matthew, something is going to happen on this mountain and I have to be there."

Matt stood up, took the poker and stabbed at the logs in the fireplace. "I only hope it's something good."

*

By the middle of November, it was obvious that no "save the world" meeting was ever going to take place. Although the internet had kept running, though only in fits and starts, and with electricity a very iffy thing, it was almost useless for communicating. The few messages that showed up on computers were mostly composed of memes about little green men and crystal meth caves. No one took the Sciopod ultimatum seriously. Almost no one.

*

<u>November 15</u>
My angels are not happy. They can't believe people are not listening to them and doing what is required. I have a direct line to the President that they installed in the safe house after our meeting two weeks ago, and I read to him their latest message. Here's what they dictated to me:

On December 30th all five volcanoes located in the Hawaiian Islands will erupt, with earthquakes causing tsunami waves that will hit Japan and the West Coast of the United States.
This can only be prevented if there is evidence that an assembly of representatives is beginning to form on a dormant volcano found at this location:
Latitude 45.3736 degrees N
Longitude 121.6960 degrees W
We share this information with you in the hopes that you will join together in peace on the mountain.

When I repeated this to the President, he just laughed. But he said he'd have his guys look into it, whatever that means. Sounds very scary to me.

*

Human blood can have a bluish tint to it until it is exposed to air, either through an incision or injury or when it is taken as a sample. It then turns bright red. In Leahcin's case, it remained blue even as it dripped into the test tube. Negasi surreptitiously sent samples of his and Leahcin's blood for DNA analysis to a trusted friend of his at Addis Ababa University. While the friend was very curious about the color difference, he went ahead and tested the two samples. The results were sent back by courier to the Ayalu laboratory.

Negasi knew from his study of genetics at school that all living matter shares a certain percentage of the same DNA. For example, humans and cats share 90 percent of their DNA. But for a creature supposedly from another galaxy to have 95 percent of the same genetic makeup as a living organism from earth could mean only one thing: somewhere along the way, a Sciopod had mated with a human. Negasi and Leahcin were related. In fact, all humanity was related to the Sciopods.

When Negasi returned to his room, he found Leahcin pacing back and forth across Negasi's desk. He seemed agitated, and, turning towards the volcanologist, he began to speak in that mysterious cranial way.

"*My friend, I have much to tell you, and it is most unpleasant.*"

"What? Are you all right? Did one of the inspectors see you?"

"*No. I always hide under the bed whenever I hear them in the hall. Their boots are very heavy.*"

"Good. So what is the matter?"

Leahcin stopped pacing and sat down on a dog-eared copy of *Earth on Fire* by Dr. Kaleo Tiller, which Negasi had been reading.

"The humans are ignoring our directive. We will have to follow through with our demonstration."

"Are you talking about this peace conference plan of yours? I told you at the time it was a noble gesture, but not one that would be accepted by the various nations. We humans are hard-wired to dismiss what we do not understand."

"But in two weeks the Sciopod Nation will be releasing energy from the volcanoes in Hawaii as a warning, as an incentive to at least try and assemble a—"

"When you say 'release energy,' are you talking about volcanic eruptions?"

"Yes. We will be allowing the magma that we have kept dammed up to flow up the tubes and burst out of the mountains and pour into the sea. This will involve earthquakes and tsunamis."

"Leahcin, this is ridiculous. Even if you were able to accomplish such a thing, it would be wrong for so many reasons. You would be doing exactly what you are trying to correct—using violence and destruction to force people to do your will."

"Yes, this is true. That is why I am distressed. I would prefer to find another path, but time is running out. If we do not begin to work together, to find solutions for all the madness that is happening here on earth, there will be no earth left. We had thought—somewhat foolishly, it seems—that you humans would understand and would volunteer to join us on this mission to save both our races and the earth."

"I do not know what I can do. I have notified as many friends as I could reach about you and the Sciopod Nation and your amazing technology. But I am just a lowly research assistant with no political clout, and—"

"You are more than you think you are. We do not want politicians, military leaders, kings or presidents to be representatives of the countries of the world. We only want one wise human being from each nation to join us who has no other ambition than to help establish a safer and more benevolent world. Therefore, instead of waiting for volunteers to show up, we have decided to make our own selections. I have nominated you to represent Ethiopia."

Negasi sat himself down on the edge of the bed and stared in shock at Leahcin. "Me? I do not understand."

"In every country, we are searching for the best candidate. Once the world realizes that we are serious, those who are chosen will assemble on Wy'east Mountain to begin the healing process."

"Wy'east Mountain. Where is that?"

"It is a dormant volcano in the United States."

*

It was late December before Granger and Rawles were able to leave Unity. The snow that had started as a light dusting had turned into a series of blizzards that left a record amount of the white stuff everywhere. A single warm afternoon caused the eight-foot drifts to thaw a little, only to have them turn into landlocked icebergs when the temperature dropped to 10 below. The town had never seen a winter storm of such power.

"Mother nature is letting us know who's really in charge," said Lester O'Brien as he helped Scott chip away at the wall of frozen snow that encased his truck. Fred Napier, using his bulldozer, removed the wall of boulders and continued to plow his way along Route 26. Hiram finished collecting the supplies necessary for this trip into the unknown, and by the early morning of the 27th, he and Scott were on their way—heading west, on a hunch of Hiram's.

It was not an easy journey. With no state highway maintenance workers riding their snowplows and spreading salt along Route 26, there were stretches of highway that were like skating rinks. Toward the evening of their first day out, they had to stop and spend an hour moving a large fir tree that had fallen across the road. By the time they had pushed and pulled it far enough out of the way to drive around it, they were exhausted.

"Let's find a place to stop and bed down," Scott suggested. "I'm beat, and hungry enough to eat a horse."

"Fine with me," agreed Hiram.

They drove on for a few miles until Hiram spotted an old barn off to their right. Its roof was covered with about two feet of snow, and it seemed to be tilting slightly to the east.

"Let's check it out," he said. "At least we'll be inside, out of the elements."

After pulling over to the side of the highway, they carried their backpacks and sleeping bags through the knee-deep snow and entered the barn through partially open doors.

"Well, it ain't the Ritz, but it'll do," Scott said, dropping his gear on the cracked concrete floor. "Cold as a nun's tits in here. We need to build a fire."

"In here?" queried Hiram. "Isn't that sort of dangerous?"

"Naw. We can build a fire pit out here in the middle of the floor with those," Scott said, pointing to a pile of broken cement blocks stuck in one of the corners of the barn. "There are enough holes in the sides and roof of this old barn to let out the smoke."

Using some dry hay and pieces of old wood that had been part of the stalls for either the horses or the cows who used to be the barn's residents, the men started a fire. After a meal of venison jerky and canned tomato soup, they bedded down for the night.

"Well, we made it this far," Scott said with a big yawn. "Not very far, actually, but since we don't know where the hell we're going, I guess it doesn't much matter."

"I will know soon, Scott," Hiram replied as he turned over in his sleeping bag and faced the fire. He pressed the eagle feather close to his heart.

By midnight the fire had died down a bit, but it still painted shadows on the weathered walls of the barn. Hiram opened his eyes and looked over at Scott, who had scrunched down so far into his sleeping bag that only his "Better Nation" hat was visible. Hiram had been dreaming, dreams about green tree-covered mountains and one very tall white mountain with circles of bright white light spinning around its summit.

Hiram struggled to reach the leather pouch tied to the belt of his pants. He pulled it up out of his sleeping bag and, opening it, took out another "liberty cap." "Sorry to bother you again, Wyakin," he whispered as he swallowed the little mushroom, "but I know you understand." He closed his eyes and waited.

*

Ted Reinhurst stood at one side of the safe house's all-purpose card table while Mitzi sat on the other side. On top of the table was a map, and Reinhurst was pointing to something in the middle.

"This is the location our research department came up with following the coordinates you gave us."

"I'm not so good with maps," explained Mitzi. "What is that white spot?"

"It's a mountain. Mount Hood, in the state of Oregon, to be exact."

"But they said it was a dormant volcano."

"It is. The last time there was a minor eruption was around 1805," said Reinhurst. "What we want to know is why the hell your 'angels' want half the world to show up there."

"Well, like they dictated, to hold some kind of peace conference."

"And now they're threatening to blow up Hawaii if all these countries, including the U.S.A., don't get their asses up to the side of this mountain in the next three days!"

"They gave you guys a month's warning," Mitzi reminded him.

"Look, even if we wanted to do what they're asking, it would take at least six months to pull this off. International conferences take years of planning. With the world's infrastructure shot to hell—by the gun-melting escapade of your 'angels,' I might add—getting these so-called representatives there," he said, tapping angrily at the center of the map, "is an impossibility!"

"Okay, I understand. But what can we do?"

"Not we, *you*! You have to tell them to call it off."

"Now wait one damn minute! I'm just the interpreter here. I can't order them to do anything," Mitzi replied. "The eruption is to take place one minute after midnight on the 29th. I guess that's early morning on the 30th, right? What plan does the President have?"

"He's convinced it's a hoax. He wants to wait and see."

"Oh, my god! And what about you? Do you think it's a hoax?"

Reinhurst sat down with a heavy sigh. He looked at Mitzi, and she saw a weariness in his eyes that indicated many sleepless nights.

"I believe it's going to happen."

*

It did happen. On Thursday, December 30, at 12:01 a.m. HAST, 6:01 a.m. EST, the volcanos Kilauea, Mauna Loa, Hualalai, Mauna Kea and Haleakala exploded with a roar that shook seismographs around the world and sent tsunamis racing across the Pacific Ocean towards Japan and the United States.

Dr. Tiller, heeding the warning Tamsin and Negasi had sent him weeks before, had left his facility the day before the eruptions. He stood on the deck of a friend's yacht and watched as the sky boiled with ash and black clouds. Steam, from the lava flowing into the sea, rose like giant white chrysanthemums. The glowing red rivers of lava were reflected in the doctor's glasses and in the tears running down his cheeks. The eruption of one volcano was an acceptable danger; the explosion of five across the islands was a catastrophe from which there would be no recovery.

All around him, other small craft were gathering as the island residents fled the holocaust by any means possible. Bobbing in the water were what Dr. Tiller thought at first were glass floats for fishnets, but he eventually figured out that they were the Sciopods. "Of course," he realized, "they're fleeing as well. They've just sacrificed their own homes." At that moment a giant swell lifted all the boats and the floating white globes and pushed them further out to sea.

*

The President was awakened at 6:05 a.m. by his chief of staff. Throwing on a robe, he was quickly escorted to a briefing room. Among all the military staff and the few faithful members of his cabinet still on board stood Ted Reinhurst like a beacon of shame.

"Don't say it, Teddy. Let's just get down to work. Fill me in." The Secretary of Defense began by showing him some footage of the destruction. "We got this just now. Communications, as you know, are touch and go. This was sent by one of our subs that surfaced near the main island. That's where the majority of the volcanoes are."

"And the tidal waves?" the President asked, picking up his coffee mug.

"The tsunamis have started across the Pacific in two directions," answered Ted. "West to Japan and east to the West Coast."

"And when is this tsunami supposed to make landfall?"

"Well, sir, it's not just one wave, it's many—one right after the other, and they're moving at 600 miles an hour. Right now, the first wave is expected to hit Northern California and the rest of the Northwest coast in approximately three hours."

"Jesus Christ!" the President exclaimed. "Have they been alerted? Have they started evacuations?"

"We're doing our best to reach as many authorities as possible," the defense secretary explained. "We're asking amateur shortwave radio operators along the coast to spread the word. Without the television and internet satellites working properly, it's difficult—"

"Fuck the satellites! Use Morse code or smoke signals, whatever! We've got to get the people to higher ground!"

"The Japanese ambassador has been notified and is working to alert his superiors in Japan. They have a little more time before the waves start hitting—about six hours. Alaska, Southern California and the west coast of South America will be getting battered by giant surf later in the day."

"What time is it now on our West Coast?" asked the President.

"A little after three a.m.," Ted answered.

"Shit! Everybody's asleep," the President continued. "What about Hawaii? Was everybody asleep there as well?"

"I'm afraid there are going to be massive casualties. We think some people got off the islands in boats, but we don't know how many yet."

"Okay, everybody, let's get to work. Rally your staff and do whatever you can to prepare for this—this disaster," ordered the President. "GO! Don't just stand there like zombies!"

The heads of the various departments began to shuffle out of the room, many of them looking as if they were in shock.

"Ted, you stay here, please," said the President. "We have to talk."

*

Hiram woke up to a violent shaking of his bed. At first he thought it was Scott letting him know it was time to get back on the road, but it was still dark outside. After another day of travel, he and Rawles had stopped at a motel that seemed to still be in business, although the woman running it explained that there was no electricity or hot water. Hiram said that it didn't matter, they just needed to get out of the cold. She told them to take any room they wanted, as they were the only travelers that had come by in the last five days. There would be no charge, as she was leaving the place by the end of the week.

Hiram sat up and put his feet on the floor as the rumbling began to diminish. Scott had awakened and was staring at the chair by the desk as it rocked back and forth.

"What the hell?!" he exclaimed.

"Seems to me we've just had an earthquake," replied Hiram.

"Great. What's next? A tornado? It's just one goddamned thing after another. Blizzards, wildfires—"

"I think this is connected to our journey to Wy'east mountain."

"Hiram, you find everything connected to everything. And why do you keep calling Mount Hood Wy'east? We're heading to Mount Hood, aren't we?" Scott asked as he started pulling on his boots. "You said you saw a sign in your dreams that spelled out 'Mount Hood'."

"I prefer to call it by its Native American name. Wy'east is what the Multnomah tribe called it for centuries before you folks got here."

"All right, all right, don't start. It's just that it's such a confusing-sounding name. I keep thinking you're asking, 'why east?' Like I've taken a wrong turn or something."

"Are you okay?" Hiram asked, noticing that Scott's hands were shaking.

"What do you think? It's not every day you get woke up by an earthquake instead of an alarm clock! Do you think it's done doing its thing?"

"There will probably be some aftershocks, but I think the worst is over."

"Well, I don't know about you, but I'm wide awake. We might as well hit the highway. What do you say?"

"Okay by me, if you're all right driving in the dark."

"Man, I've got eyes like a cat."

Twelve miles down the road, Scott slammed on the brakes as they came around a curve and faced a wall of snow.

"What the fuck!"

He and Hiram climbed out of the truck and stood in front of a two-story-high pile of snow.

"Avalanche," said Hiram, "caused by the quake, I would imagine."

"Great! What now, O mighty warrior?"

"We find another route."

"But we got no GPS!"

"Have you got any kind of a map?"

"You mean one of those old paper things that's folded like an accordion? And after you open it up you can never get it folded back together properly?"

"You've got a lot of old junk in the back of your truck."

"True. Most of it is stuff I was getting ready to dump," Scott said as he and Hiram began walking around to the back of the pickup. "If there *is* a map in here, I will truly believe in miracles." They both began trawling through the crate of broken tools, oil-stained rags and old newspapers when Hiram stopped and held up a beat-up copy of a Rand McNally 1995 Road Atlas.

"I guess you better start believing."

*

Negasi looked at the readout from the Ayalu seismograph and was stunned by the power of the earthquake caused by the eruptions in Hawaii. Although he was an entire continent and ocean away from the event, it registered 5.1 on the Richter scale. He couldn't imagine what the number was at the epicenter.

He went to his room and, without saying a word, picked up Leahcin and put him carefully into his canvas backpack. He then stepped out into the hall.

"Where are we going, my friend?"

"We are having a meeting with Dr. Decker. Stay down in my bag so the soldiers will not see you."

They proceeded up the stairs to Tamsin's office, and after shutting and locking the door, Negasi pulled the little Sciopod out of his backpack and set him down on Dr. Decker's desk. Dr. Decker did not look at all happy to see one of the perpetrators of this newest catastrophe.

"What you have done is monstrous, and completely at odds with what you claim is your mission to promote peace in the world!" Tamsin said, finding it difficult not to grab Leahcin by the neck in order to strangle him.

"I know it appears counterproductive, and if there were any other way—"

"What is he saying?" Dr. Decker asked, since she wasn't able to hear his voice in her brain, as Negasi could.

"He agrees and wishes there were another way."

"The death toll in Hawaii is in the tens of thousands, and the shores of Japan are being bombarded with forty-foot waves. Nagasaki is completely under water. Seawater has flooded the beaches of Oregon and Northern California. Seattle has ten feet of water rushing through the downtown area. And it's not over yet."

"This event was determined to be the least destructive of the many choices we considered over the many years we spent trying to find ways to stop the madness."

When Negasi repeated this statement to Tamsin, her jaw dropped, and it took her a moment to recover.

"If this was the 'least destructive,' what in God's name was the most destructive?"

"He says it was between a hydrogen bomb and the pneumonic plague," relayed Negasi.

"Oh, my lord! This is unbelievable. And what happens now?"

"Hopefully, the world will listen to what we are trying to say and begin to assemble a peace conference per our instructions."

"And if we do not?" asked Negasi.

After a long pause, during which what Leahcin said was translated for Dr. Decker, the answer came.

"We will be forced to set off more eruptions in Europe and Asia."

*

<u>January 2</u>
I can't believe my angels would do such a terrible thing. But it looks like they did. Last night they showed up and I read them the riot act. They said they understood my anger, but how else could they get the world to wake up and pay attention?

The President talked to me on our private line, and when I told him that if there was no evidence of progress in instrumenting the conference (what a mouthful) the Sciopods said they planned more eruptions, he told me to tell them to hold off, that he was working on their request. He was in contact with the leaders of many of the nations, and they seemed to be willing to discuss the problem and to find possible solutions.

When I relayed his message to my Sciopod friends, they said I should let the President know that political leaders were not invited to participate in this convocation. The representatives must be humans with no ties to their own government other than being honorable citizens. Furthermore (these guys sure like to use long words), the Sciopods in each country would choose the delegate. I nearly fainted when one of my angels said they had picked me to represent the United States.

Then the President asked, and I quote: "Okay, so what the hell do they want from us?"

I just now passed this question on to my angels, and here is their response:

Transportation for delegates to the mountain (I guess they mean Mount Hood in Oregon)
Housing at the site
Food service—accommodating dietary needs (insects for the Sciopods? Yuck)
Transportation of delegates back to their country of origin

So I'll pass this on to the President and we'll see what happens.

*

Granger and Rawles found a county service road on the map, and by backtracking a few miles, they got off Route 26 and onto 97. From there it was better driving, but still a rather slow go, due to the cars and trucks abandoned along the highway for lack of gas. By late afternoon they reached the banks of the Columbia River and I-84. They continued on this federal highway into the town of The Dalles, where Scott stopped to refill the fuel tank with some of the precious gasoline he had stored in containers before leaving Unity.

"Hey, Granger, it looks like Momma Jane's Pancake House is still open for business. You up for some flapjacks?"

"Sounds good. I hope they still have coffee. I am in need of a big cup of java."

Although it turned out the menu was pretty limited, due to shortages, there was indeed coffee, and after a meal of chicken-fried steak and mashed potatoes, Hiram and Scott pushed on to Mount Hood. They exited 84, got onto Route 35, and after skirting several boulders that had tumbled down on the highway because of the earthquake, they entered Mount Hood National Forest. Ahead of them, rising up in the evening sky, was the 11,249-foot snow-covered mountain.

"You know, Scott, it's usually a six-hour ride to get here from Unity—"

"Yeah? Well, it took us two and a half days, but we're here. And I hope you know what you're doing."

*

Bad news travels fast. Even with limited television, radio and internet service, the reports coming from those countries devastated by the eruptions, earthquakes and tsunamis reached every continent, nation, city and village. The world now knew about the Sciopods, this underground race that had been secretly watching over humankind since its first ancestors crawled up out of the mud. Most of the inhabitants of the 241 countries, nations and territories that make up Planet Earth became aware of the demands of the Sciopods.

Of course, many factions developed: the believers, the doubters, the ignorers and the let's-kill-'em-allers, who, if they could have resurrected some of the now defunct guns, would have mowed everyone down, women and children included. Fortunately, the plan of only one participant per country, who would be selected by a Sciopod, made the process a little more simple. But there would always be those poor souls with inflated egos who couldn't understand why they weren't chosen to represent their nation. Even a few generals and a president or two tried unsuccessfully to get their names on the list.

The choosing of the delegates was pretty much a secret process. What the Sciopods were looking for was a human being, of any gender and any age, who was naturally generous, honest, hardworking, skilled in any category, open to change and, most importantly, kind. Not many of the current so-called world leaders would be able to fill the bill.

After a delegate was selected, a Sciopod would visit this person, usually at night, to let them know—using their gift of brain translation—that they would be going to the Sacred Mountain. So far no one had refused the honor, which only reinforced the wisdom of the choices. There had been requests that family members be able to accompany the delegate, but when informed that this could not happen, the candidates accepted the ruling. Some of the more religious delegates compared their being chosen to the annunciation. You know, angels and pronouncements and white glowing orbs.

The next step was a difficult one: transportation. Getting the delegate to the closest airport was achieved by whatever means available—car, bus, train, horse, donkey, even elephant. Once the delegate was at the airport, the Sciopods had to depend on the United States to send some sort of aircraft to pick the person up. All commercial airlines had been grounded due to fuel shortages. The President had promised to provide transportation, per the demands of the Sciopods, for all 241 representatives, be it by helicopter, jet or even Air Force One. He contacted wealthy friends and, promising them free jet fuel, coerced them into using their private jets and their flying skills to bring these visitors to Oregon. Some of the larger jets were used for the long flights from China, Australia and New Zealand. Whenever possible, several delegates were brought to one airfield in order to fly them as a group to their destination, thus saving time and jet fuel.

*

<u>January 5</u>
I am so excited. This coming Saturday I am being flown across the country to Portland, Oregon! The only other time I've ever flown in a jet airplane was when we took the kids to Disney World in Orlando.

At first, the President told me I might be going on Air Force One, but instead a nice man who's some big mucky-muck in the Apple organization is flying me in his private jet. Imagine, little Mitzi Irene Kovacs, born in Silver Springs, Maryland, is flying across the country to be a representative for the United States of America. Put that in your pipe and smoke it, Mr. Eddie Brownhart! I'd love to bring Brian and Karen along, but that's not allowed, so Barbara will continue to look out for them, bless her soul.

One of my angels branded me last night. I know, it sounds like I was lassoed, tied up and had a red-hot Lazy H burnt onto my rear. But this was different, and so amazing. It seems that in order to identify the selected representatives and prevent any imposters from crashing the party, we're all getting an image printed on top of our left hand. It's kind of like when they stamp your hand at a club or a carnival, only it's more permanent. It's an invisible blue BK that only appears under ultraviolet light. I asked my angel what the BK stands for, and she said it means "Be Kind." Sounds like a good idea, but not always easy to do.

I've started packing. We're limited to one suitcase and one carry-on, kind of like the restrictions the airlines used to impose. However, I guess this is about our accommodations when we get to the mountain. I imagine they don't want a lot of luggage to get in the way.

I'm tired and I'm going to go to bed for now. I hope I can sleep.

*

Negasi was sitting on one of the very uncomfortable seats in the military transport airplane that was his ride to the conference on the mountain in Oregon. They had just taken off from the Royal Air Force Base in Oxfordshire, England, after refueling. They were on the last leg of the twenty-two-hour flight from Addis Ababa, and Negasi's posterior was numb from having to sit on the thinly upholstered metal seat that folded down from the side wall of the plane. Obviously, no first-class treatment for the soldiers who usually rode in this army-issued tin bucket. Negasi had walked back and forth among the crates of equipment and supplies that were strapped to the floor of the plane in order to get some relief. The only thing that made this long journey bearable was knowing that he was going to be part of an important historical event. He rubbed the top of his hand where Leahcin had lasered on an invisible BK and sat back down.

He had invited Leahcin to join him, but the Sciopod assured him he could get there on his own. Before leaving, Negasi retrieved Leahcin's sphere from his gym bag, where he had put it to keep it away from the eyes of the security guards. Fortunately, at first glance it looked like a soccer ball, so there was really no problem. Leahcin was visibly happy to have his protective bubble back and would be using it to make the long journey to the Sacred Mountain.

"I will see you soon, my friend."

*

One could imagine renaming Mount Hood Ghost Mountain. The ski lifts were not working, there were no hikers or climbers, the various camps were empty, and Timberline Lodge was uninhabited, except for a few members of the staff. Since 1938, this hotel had been the place to go for a winter retreat, and it was open all year round as well. But now, as Hiram and Scott entered the huge, log-beamed lobby, all was as quiet as a cemetery.

"You ever see the movie *The Shining*?" Scott asked as they approached the registration counter. "They based that scary hotel on this place. Shot some of the exterior scenes out in front."

An attractive young woman behind the desk greeted them. "Good evening, gentlemen. May I help you?"

"Er, yes, thanks," Hiram replied, not used to being in the middle of such impressive surroundings. "Do you have a room available? A double—I mean, with two beds?"

"Sir, we have seventy-seven rooms available for you to choose from, as you are the first visitors we've had the pleasure to see in the last two weeks."

"Wow!" Scott exclaimed. "Business that bad, huh?"

"With the electricity going on and off, we don't dare run the ski lifts, since there's the possibility someone will get stuck up in the air. We can't heat the swimming pool or the sauna. With the gas shortage raging on, very few trucks are bringing us supplies, so our kitchen is serving a very limited menu. We can't hold on to staff. Our internet is down, so taking reservations is impossible." The desk clerk took a breath. "So have I sold you on staying here with us yet?"

"Well, it actually sounds like my kind of place, Miss Tracy," replied Hiram, reading her nametag. "Peace and quiet. So—how much is one of your famous seventy-seven rooms?"

"Well, the off-season rate is $150, and it's been off-season even during the on-season. So, gentlemen, I guess it'll be $150."

"Do you take cash?"

"That's all we take. No internet service equals no credit cards. Personal checks—same story."

Hiram reached into his denim jacket pocket and pulled out a money clip holding a thick slab of bills.

"Hey there, Mr. Moneybags!" Scott commented. "You been holding out on me."

"It's my rainy-day fund," Hiram explained as he handed the clerk three fifty-dollar bills. "There you go, Miss Tracy."

"Thank you very much," the clerk replied as she put the cash into an ordinary metal box. "So what brings you here to Mount Hood, Mr.—er?"

"Granger, Hiram."

"He doesn't know," answered Scott. "Just following a dream. I'm Scott, Scott Rawles."

"Well, Mr. Rawles and Mr. Granger, welcome to Timberline Lodge. Here are your keycards. Your room is number one, just down the hall to your left."

As Scott reached for the keycards, the phone behind the counter rang suddenly, causing Tracy to make a little jump.

"Oh, jeez!" she gasped. "That's weird. The phone has been silent for days." She picked up the receiver, handling it as if it were a snake. "Good evening, Timberline Lodge, Tracy speaking. How may I help you?" She nodded and, using a pen and notepaper, wrote down two words. Even though the writing was upside down, Hiram could read what it said: National Guard.

*

The Portland International Airport landing field resembled a crowded parking lot, like one you would find at a Wal-Mart. There were airplanes with passengers from all over the world resting in every corner of the airfield. Every jetway had a large airplane parked at its gate and a long line of aircraft waiting behind it for their turn. Some of the passengers had gotten out of the planes and onto the airfield, rather than sit any longer on board in discomfort. The airport officials, working at a frantic pace trying to get everyone off the aircraft and safely inside the terminal, were confused by often finding only one passenger on many of the planes. The order to turn the airport over to the National Guard came directly from the President of the United States, so they didn't question what was going on, but it was a daunting operation.

The smaller private jets that had been pressed into service were landing at either the Troutdale or Hillsboro airports, which specialized in noncommercial air traffic. At all three of the airports were yellow school buses lined up, ready to transport the new arrivals to their destination. These buses would eventually join a convoy of khaki-colored trucks and jeeps, manned by members of the National Guard, that would accompany them on their journey.

*

The President was implementing the requests of the Sciopods in order to prevent further disasters. He had called up the National Guard and was ready to add a platoon of active-duty soldiers if necessary. He had dipped into the nation's reserve of emergency rations and was sending truckloads of food to the mountain resort. While he could do this legally, because he had declared a state of emergency for the entire nation, both the Senate and the House were screaming bloody murder:

"People are starving all over this country and you are feeding foreigners from countries we've never even heard of!" *Senator Howard Lomax, Texas*

"Why are we helping support this hippie, Communist, leftist, anti-American rally, shamefully being held in one of our beloved National Historic Landmarks?!" *Rep. Robert W. Smithfield, Arizona*

"Rumor has it that the President is funding a meeting between world leaders and Martians on top of a mountain up in Oregon. Whatever." *Senator Leslie Anne Baker, California*

*

Hiram woke up to the sound of trucks, many trucks, rumbling into the parking lot just below the windows of his and Scott's room. Getting out of bed, he hobbled over to the blackout drapes and pulled them open. There were about a dozen various military vehicles, from Humvees to canvas-covered six-wheelers, pulling up in front of the lodge. Scott joined him at the window.

"Wow! The cavalry has arrived! What do you think's going on?"

"I believe this is part of the preparation for the event that is going to happen here," Hiram replied, beginning to get dressed.

"So I don't have to worry about the army coming to take you and me off to some island prison, never to be seen again? Need I remind you that I've been through this before, back in Idaho?" Scott asked, pulling up his pants.

Outside, men in uniform started spilling out of the trucks to begin unloading crates and boxes. Some soldiers lifted canvas bags onto their shoulders and carried them towards the empty area at the far end of the parking lot. There was a lot of shouting and pointing.

Hiram and Scott headed down the hall toward the registration counter. Miss Tracy was talking to a pudgy, red-headed man dressed in fatigues. She handed him a keycard and he headed down the hall to the right.

"Who is that guy?" Scott asked. "What's going on?"

"That's the adjutant general," Tracy answered, looking like she had been up all night (which she probably had), "of the National Guard. Seems the President has ordered the appropriation of the lodge for some important gathering, a summit of some sort."

"That's interesting," Scott said, smiling. "A summit on a summit."

"He requested a room to use as a command center, so I gave him a key to the manager's office. I was going to recommend one of our conference rooms, but he said they would be needing every available space for the arrivals."

"Arrivals?" asked Scott.

"I guess he means the dignitaries, the delegates who are attending whatever this is. I'm afraid that's all I was told. Oh, and I'm sorry if you were planning to stay on, but the general said all guests would have to leave. Evidently, this is a very hush-hush meeting, or whatever. I'm so sorry."

"What did I tell you! The army shows up and we've got to leave!"

"What's the name of the general?" asked Hiram.

"Oh, let me see, I have it here on this copy of the President's order. Adjutant General Donald Byrne."

"Thank you, Miss Tracy," Hiram replied as he reached in his jacket pocket for the eagle feather.

*

Mitzi sat back against the rigid seat in the school bus. It was certainly a far cry from the soft leather lounge chair she had relaxed in as she was whisked across the country in the Apple mucky-muck's private jet. She was one of twelve passengers on a school "short bus." When they left the Hillsboro airport and headed to the Columbia Gorge and she saw the river and all the lush evergreen foliage, Mitzi was blown away. She had heard the Pacific Northwest being referred to as "God's country," and now she knew why.

*

On the same highway, and two buses behind Mitzi, was Negasi. He was also in awe of what he was seeing outside the school-bus window, but he was not prepared for the cold. To leave the arid heat of the desert and within twenty-four hours be riding through the cool, damp air of Oregon was definitely a shock. When they got closer to the mountain and the temperature began to drop, he wondered if he would be able to function.

*

"General Byrne?" Hiram inquired, rapping on the door frame. The officer was hanging up his parka and spun around quickly.

"Yes?" the general replied. "Who are you?"

"My name is Hiram Granger," he answered, "and this is Scott Rawles."

The general gave them a quick looking-over. "Are you the two guests who signed in last night?"

"Yes, sir."

"Well, I'm sorry, but I'm going to have to escort you off the mountain."

"I understand completely, General Byrne, you have a job to do," Hiram said, extending his right hand as if meaning to give the officer a friendly handshake. Byrne reacted automatically, and as he gripped Hiram's hand, Granger put his left hand on the general's shoulder. Scott noticed that it was holding an eagle feather.

"However, we have a job to do as well," said Hiram. "My friend and I are part of this event, so we will be staying—with your permission, of course."

The general looked a little confused and stepped back. His body was at first rigid with military attitude, but then he seemed to soften a bit, and a smile lit up his face.

"Absolutely," he declared. "You must be the gentleman we were told about. Forgive me for not recognizing you. And your companion—what is his importance to this event—his title?"

"He's my—bodyguard."

"Bodyguard?!" Scott exclaimed as he and Hiram walked down the front steps of the lodge and into the parking lot. "How am I supposed to be your bodyguard and protect you without a weapon? Spit on the attacker?"

"I had to think of something."

"I kinda thought I was your navigator or your survivalist specialist."

"That you are," Hiram assured him.

"And what did he mean when he said he was told about you?" Scott asked.

"I have no idea. Mistaken identity or something."

"You know, all this madness began when our guns were disabled. That event has caused more confusion, disasters, poverty and death than probably—the Black Plague."

"Well, I wouldn't—"

"So now here we are on this mountain, surrounded by soldiers—without weapons, I might add—and you don't even know why we're here."

"I think the answer is arriving right now," Hiram replied, gesturing to the first school bus pulling into the parking lot.

*

By one o'clock in the afternoon, eight school buses and five "short buses" had unloaded all their passengers. The lobby of Timberline Lodge was jam-packed with people of every age, gender and color. There were turbans, fezzes and yarmulkes, muumuus and saris, kente cloth and denim, dreads and buzz cuts.

Miss Tracy and her assistants were overwhelmed in attempting to assign rooms to the 241 delegates. She had been told to first use the ultra-violet light, employed for checking currency, to reveal the BK applied to the left hand of each legitimate guest. Hiram volunteered to help, and his next suggestion was to try and find a linguist to help translate the innumerable languages that were swirling around the lobby. He found someone who spoke four languages; it was a start, but it wasn't enough. That was when a tall young Ethiopian stepped forward. It was Negasi.

"Excuse me. May I make a suggestion?"

"Yes, of course," replied Hiram. "Do you speak any of these dialects?"

"Some, but I am not proficient. However, the Sciopods are capable of translating any language."

"The who?" Hiram asked.

"The Sciabots," Scott explained. "You know, those white round floating things that supposedly started all this. Where have you been? You said you saw them in your dreams."

"The Sciopods are supposed to join us here for the conference," Negasi continued. "They have this way of communicating non-vocally, and they are very good translators."

"Non-vocally?" Hiram said, trying to make sense of all the new information that was coming his way. "What does that mean, and what exactly is the reason for this gathering?"

"It is a peace conference. We are representatives from every country on earth."

Suddenly, Hiram's head became flooded with all the images he had seen in his dreams and in his sessions with his Wyakin, Spirit Bear. This was why he had had to come here to the Sacred Mountain, to Wy'east. He was to be part of this momentous chapter in history. He felt both elated and frightened, and he was about to ask Negasi another question when the noise in the lobby increased and he heard shouts and cheers. He saw that people had turned toward the windows facing Mount Hood and were pointing and jumping up and down.

From the very top of the snow-covered mountain, a cloud had formed that Hiram thought at first was just a mist rising from the peaks due to the warmth of the sun. But as it blew closer to the lodge, it began to break apart, and Hiram could see that it was made up of basketball-sized white orbs.

"Sciopods! Sciopods!" A chant rose up in unison from the conference participants. It seemed that "Sciopod" was pronounced the same in every language.

"Jesus, Mary and Joseph!" exclaimed Scott. "Would you look at that! They're coming this way! I hope they're friendly!"

The cloud had split into two lines and was descending toward the lodge. Several people from the crowd rushed to hold open the front doors. The globes wrapped around the building, as if to hug it, and then one by one they flew into the lobby.

Hiram and Scott stood in total awe of the scene that was unfolding in front of them. High above their heads, the ceiling and the wooden beams were awash with a white light radiating from the spheres as they spun around in concentric circles. After a minute or so, they began to swoop down over the crowd and fly back and forth above the upturned faces.

"I believe they are looking for their human companion," Negasi explained to Granger and Rawles. And at that moment, one of the globes stopped and hovered over Negasi's head. *"Hello, my friend."* "Hello, Leahcin."

Hiram turned in a slow circle and watched as the pods began to hang, like Japanese lanterns, over each one of the hundreds of heads of the people standing in the lobby.

"This can't be real," Scott whispered. The room grew very still as each person began to listen to what their Sciopod was brain-translating. Scott found himself shaking and sat on the edge of one of the big leather couches to calm himself down. That's when he noticed something else.

"Hey, man, look up. You got a visitor."

Even before Scott had said anything, Hiram had felt a presence above his head. Now, as he slowly lifted his eyes upward, he was dazzled by the white light and he heard a voice. *"Hello, my friend."*

*

By that evening, the National Guard had taken over the kitchen and had prepared meals for the representatives. The cooks tried to follow the many dietary restrictions—not always successfully, but they did the best they could.

Tracy had worked out that if she put three guests in each of the seventy-seven rooms and had the National Guard set up ten cots in the Barlow conference room, she could accommodate everyone. Hiram and Scott volunteered to sleep in the lobby. Negasi and Hiram, working with their personal Sciopods, were able to translate for Miss Tracy, and this moved things along very efficiently. By 11:00 p.m. almost everyone was settled in their rooms, General Byrne and his men were bedded down in the tents set up on the slopes of the mountain, and Scott and Hiram were talking softly in the empty lobby.

"I'm a little upset that I didn't get one of these floating gizmos," Scott said, pointing to the Sciopod resting on the side table next to Hiram.

"You can share mine. Its name is Selui, by the way. And I've been telling you everything it's been saying to me, right?"

"Yeah. It's just that I kinda feel I'm not really needed here."

"Oh, my man, you are very much needed. The next few days are going to be quite difficult. I'm going to need all the support I can get."

*

Hiram hadn't shared everything with Scott that Selui had told him. Earlier, after dinner, Hiram had excused himself and taken a long walk among the tall Douglas fir trees that embraced the lower slopes of the mountain. His Sciopod drifted alongside him and they talked in that brain-whispering way.

"Why exactly am I here?"

"You are to be the leader."

"But I'm just an ordinary guy who manages—managed—a general store."

"And that is why we have chosen you. You are honest, generous, you listen more than you talk, you are organized, especially in the way you run your business."

"But I am not a leader."

"That is not true. In the past few months you have led a town through many crises. With the help of your Spirit Bear, you have found solutions to several serious situations. You know what I say is the truth, or you wouldn't be here."

"I only know that the Sacred Mountain called to me. I didn't know why."

"And now you do."

"Yes, but isn't this a conference that will affect lives around the world?"

"That is the reality. We must start repairing the damage done to the earth and find a way to live together peacefully."

"A very noble and difficult goal. In all probability, an unreachable one as well."

"You are forgetting one ingredient that has never been part of past attempts at peace accords."

"And what is that?"

"Us. We Sciopods will be working alongside you humans. You are not alone."

"All right, I understand all that you're saying. But if I'm not mistaken, it'll be only me standing in front of hundreds of people and—and me trying to guide them. I don't even know how to begin."

"Just take a breath, open your mouth and the words will come."

Hiram stopped next to a bench, sat down and stared up at the mountain. The sun was setting behind him, leaving only a dusting of gold on the summit of Wy'east.

"I have one more question, Selui."

"Yes? Does it concern your companion, Mr. Rawles?"

"How did you know I was—"

"Mr. Rawles is to be your biographer. He will return to your village and relay what happens here. He will be a witness to what we accomplish."

"That sounds like I won't be going home."

"Do not try to see into the future. It is a road not yet open to us."

*

At 10:00 a.m. the next day, all of the delegates were seated at long tables in Ullman Hall, the largest meeting room in the lodge. Clipped somewhere on every participant's garment was a tag, provided by Miss Tracy, with the attendee's name and country, nation or territory. A glowing white orb rested on the table in front of each member. Mitzi Brownhart patted the side of her Sciopod and smiled. When she left the safe house in Virginia, she hadn't known then that only one of her angels would accompany her. Fortunately, the pod, humming in front of her like a contented cat, was her favorite angel, Lorak.

While the National Guard had helped set up the tables and chairs and would continue to work in the kitchen and laundry, General Byrne was informed that there could be no military presence at any of the upcoming meetings. At first he bristled and did some huffing and puffing, but a surreptitious brush of an eagle feather ended his resistance. When all of the soldiers were either back up on the slope or on guard duty at the entrance to the lodge, the first meeting began.

Hiram stood on a dais set up at one end of the room so everyone could see him. Selui floated a few inches away, near the left side of his head. Scott sat at a small table to his right, notepad and pen in readiness. "Nothin' but a fuckin' secretary," he thought, but secretly felt rather pleased to be a part of this incredible journey.

"Good morning and welcome," Hiram began, stopping long enough to let the Sciopods start the translation process. "I am not going to take up our valuable time with a long speech. We all know why we are here. It is more important for us to begin actively working toward our goal of trying to identify and rectify the many problems that plague our world.

"I am a Native American. My ancestors arrived here about 15,000 years ago. Many of you have ancestors who populated your homelands thousands of years ago as well. I am sure they would not only not recognize the world we live in now, but they would be horrified by what they would find. I will not waste time listing all the man-made ills that they would see and that have brought us to this crossroads. We will be visiting those ills together as the week progresses.

"Today we will start our journey by working on what is probably the most difficult problem we face: getting along with each other." There was a nervous rustle as people heard the translation and looked around at the faces that surrounded them.

"We will start by each of us choosing a partner. I want those of you who feel there is a person here who is your enemy to partner with that person. The rest of you are free to choose whomever you want."

At first there was no movement at the tables, and then the representative from Palestine arose slowly from his chair and looked around the room. A few seconds later, a woman stood up and then carefully made her way around the tables and chairs to stand beside the Palestinian. She was from Israel. The man who had been sitting across from the Palestinian graciously gave up his chair to the woman, and the two enemies sat down. As if this little drama were a signal, the room erupted with activity as all the rest of the attendees searched for a partner. A few more enemies sought each other out—a Russian sat across from a Ukrainian, a South Korean found someone from North Korea—but for the most part, it was more like a mad rush not to be left without a partner.

"When you have settled down," Hiram continued, "we'll begin. Choose one of you to be the interviewer and the other the interviewee. When that's decided, the person conducting the interview will ask questions of the interviewee in an effort to learn as much about that person as possible. Your Sciopod will help with translations. This interview will continue until lunch. After lunch the reverse will take place, and that interview will terminate at four o'clock. We will then gather here after dinner to discuss what we learned. Please begin."

*

And that's the way it started: getting to know your enemy, getting beyond the surface, turning a stranger into a friend. Hiram partnered up with Scott, and they got beyond the "hippie half-breed" and "macho redneck" nonsense. In a Hollywood-like moment, Mitzi sat down with Negasi and was impressed with his intelligence and his gingerbread skin, and he was fascinated with her honesty and her freckles.

In the next few days, committees were set up to begin dealing with the overwhelming number of critical issues. Water—the lack of, the misuse of, the polluting of. Hunger—the starving of whole nations. Poverty—lack of affordable housing, unemployment, homelessness. Climate change—storms, flooding, drought, Arctic melting. Overpopulation—warring over land rights, crumbling infrastructure. Fortunately, the Sciopods had some very helpful suggestions and offered access to much of their technological wizardry. But everyone knew that nothing was going to be solved overnight. This whole process was going to take many years and many struggles, but at least it had begun—and it had been started by the people, not by governments. And as long as there was proof that this process was continuing, the Sciopods promised they would not institute Armageddon.

*

Hiram realized that he was in for the long haul. His trip to the Sacred Mountain was only the beginning. When Mount Hood was reclaimed, as it would have to be, his Spirit Bear would lead him to his next venue. Already he felt a little tug, and he was having dreams about geysers and hot springs. Scott would be heading back to Unity, to his men and to a new mission: driving to areas that needed affordable housing and renovating existing abandoned structures so everyone had a roof over their head. "I got the men, the tools and the skills. What the hell!"

*

The President sat at his desk and stared at Ted Reinhurst. "Run this by me again, Teddy. This information came from where?"

"The CIA. One of their operatives in Germany was contacted by an employee from the ThyssenKrupp Steel company."

"And this guy just volunteered this information out of the kindness of his heart?"

"Well, not exactly," replied Reinhurst. "Economically, things over there are worse than here, so I guess he thought he could sell what he knew for a little cash."

"And he said—"

"That Krupp has developed a new steel that is impervious to the Van Dijck crystals."

"Do we think this is for real or a scam?"

"The CIA says that ThyssenKrupp's main foundry has been cold for months, but now it's up and running hot 24/7."

"My god, this could mean we're back in business!"

"Well, not yet. It means the Germans are back in business. I'm pretty sure they're not about to share the formula with anybody."

"Then we have to make Krupp an offer they can't refuse. And if that doesn't work, then we appropriate the formula."

"Stealing it will be very difficult, if not impossible."

"Ted, my boy, this is the U.S.A. We can do anything. Let Ryan over at CIA know that we have a 'Mission Impossible' for him."

"Yes, sir."

"We're going to get our guns back," the President said gleefully, unwrapping his first Snickers of the day.

The World Through My Eyes

I was born in Corvallis, Oregon, the son of a farmer. How I ended up on the East Coast, working as a designer in the theatre, is one of the many miracles for which I am eternally grateful. My tenure off-off Broadway led to the joy of designing for off-Broadway, which eventually earned me access to Broadway. Dreams do come true. The greatest miracles, however, are my soulmate, Carol, and our amazing son Jules.

The experience I gained from functioning many years in the world of theatre led to my teaching in the Theatre Department at Fordham University at Lincoln Center. It is said that the teacher learns as much from their students as vice versa, and perhaps even more, and that was certainly true for me. The biggest lessons I learned were tolerance and patience.

After thirty or more years of designing and teaching, I grew tired of collaboration, which is at the heart of every theatrical production, and decided it was time for me to work only for myself. I had been painting huge theatrical canvases that were backdrops for plays, but I had never put paint onto a small framed canvas. It may sound selfish, but I had reached the point where I wanted to be alone with my brushes, my music and my thoughts. What I discovered was how meditative it was to splash paint on a blank white surface. I became a full-time painter in 2003.

When I work, I try not to think too much. I try to let the paint find its own way, unencumbered by my egocentric ideas, especially with my abstractions.

I have been told that I don't have an identifiable style. I suppose that's because I don't like to paint the same thing twice. However, I do love circles.

Often I am asked, "What is it supposed to be?" "What does it mean?" I much prefer to have the viewer tell me what it means to *them*. A mistake I made early on was to title my canvases. This is because I find that it often-times influences what the viewer sees. I understand now why many of my fellow artists number their works or leave them untitled instead of giving them names. Unfortunately, I get a kick out of thinking up titles.

Michael Massee
Waterford Works, NJ
masseeart.com

9 798993 827803